A Chosen Few

OTHER BOOKS BY CAROLYN RAWLS BOOTH

Bandeaux Creek, 2005

Aunt Mag's Recipe Book:
Heritage Cooking from a Carolina Kitchen, 2004

Between the Rivers, 2001

A Chosen Few

BETWEEN THE RIVERS: BOOK III

By Carolyn Rawls Booth

CHAPEL HILL
PRESS, INC.

Library of Congress Catalog Number 2008923297
First Printing

Publisher's Cataloging-In-Publication Data
(Prepared by The Donohue Group, Inc.)

Booth, Carolyn R. (Carolyn Rawls), 1936–
  A chosen few / by Carolyn Rawls Booth.
  p. ; cm. — (Between the rivers ; bk. 3)
  ISBN: 978-1-59715-052-1
  1. Rural families—North Carolina—20th century—Fiction. 2. Collective settlements—
North Carolina—20th century—Fiction. 3. North Carolina—Fiction. 4. Historical
fiction. I. Title. II. Series: Booth, Carolyn R. (Carolyn Rawls), 1936- Between the rivers

PS3602.O66 C46 2008   813/.6   2008923297

For many are called, but few are chosen.

MATTHEW 22:14

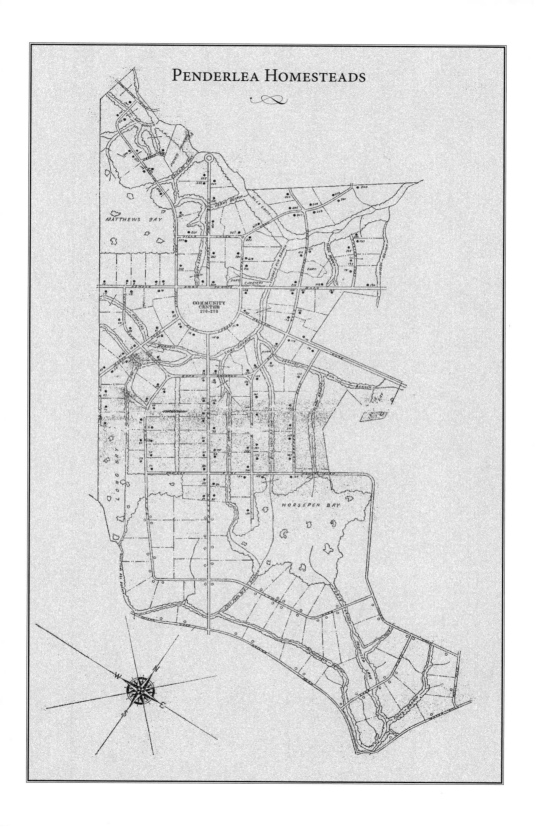

PENDERLEA HOMESTEADS

ONSLOW COUNTY, NORTH CAROLINA

When Jeanne McAllister first came home in the winter of 1932, Darcy McAllister was furious with his mother. "You mustn't let her!" he said. "I simply won't allow it!"

"It's not for you to say, son," Emily replied. She'd come to the general store in Jacksonville to tell him that she'd had a letter from his sister.

"You'll let her come home as if nothing happened?" Darcy had never forgiven Jeanne for deserting him as well as their mother. Raised almost as twins, his sister had been the closest person in the world to him after Emily. The night of Jeanne's automobile accident, she'd been driving to Jacksonville to meet him and his betrothed, Gardenia Croom. After the accident, Jeanne had been pieced back together by Dr. Jon McNamara, who happened to be her mother's fiancé. Jeanne had fallen in love with him, and they'd run off together. Neither had been seen or heard from since.

"Darling, Jeanne is a broken doll, but she is my child and I would give anything to have her back. Anything," she said. "If she has left Jon, it was only a matter of time. Her heart must be broken." She touched his arm. "But promise me one thing, she must never know that I—that you—have suffered because of her. We mustn't give her that satisfaction."

The train had arrived in Jacksonville an hour late. Emily was there with Faulkner's new book, *Light in August*. Jeanne would think it very natural to find her mother, an avid reader, with her nose in a book waiting for the train. On the other hand, Emily was expecting to see a wreck of sorts, a woman who like herself had been disappointed by love. Not so. Jeanne McAllister stepped off the train like a movie star in her long white coat with its thick fur collar turned up against the wind.

Short blonde curls poked out beneath a cloche hat that Jeanne had pulled down across her forehead and over her ears. She handed the porter a coin, glancing only momentarily in the direction of her mother, who stood several feet away under the covered walkway.

Darcy had wanted to come with Emily—thought he should—just in case. "Just *in case* of what, Darcy?" Emily had asked. "Are you expecting a *catfight*?" Darcy looked hurt. She put her hand on his arm. "Nothing is going to *happen*, take my word. I can handle Jeanne."

From the platform, Jeanne raised her head and looked about until her eyes fell on her mother. Emily nodded, lifted her hand. "Hello, Jeanne."

Jeanne walked toward her. "Hello, Mother," she said, touching the brim of her hat, giving it a slight downward tug. The wind shifted suddenly, blowing her coat open. She pulled it together with one hand and held onto her hat with the other.

"Come on, it's warm in the car," Emily said. "Boss is collecting your baggage." Jeanne looked for the old Negro driver who had worked for the family since way before her time. Seeing him with the porter, she followed her mother to the car. Emily opened the door of the back seat for Jeanne and went around the car to get in on the other side. They slipped in simultaneously, their arms touching lightly. For a minute or so, nothing was said by either. Emily removed her hat and shook out her hair, a gesture to cover her uneasiness more than anything.

Jeanne sat perfectly still, looking across and over the front seat. "Mother, I'm sorry," she said.

Emily took a deep breath. "That's all that needs to be said."

"No, there's more..."

"No, not tonight," Emily said. "That's all that needs to be said tonight."

"How're you, Miss Jeanne?" Boss said, hefting himself into the driver's seat. "It's good to see you back in Onslow County." He started the engine of the gray Packard.

"It's good to see you, Boss," she said, without a trace of emotion.

"Mind if I turn the radio on, Miss Emily?"

"As long as there's some music, Boss. You know I don't like the fights." Loud noise from an arena came on over the radio before the driver began to turn the dial. She knew the fights were what he'd had in mind. Boss settled on a station, and they listened to the last few bars of *Georgia on my Mind* before the news came on. "Just turn it off, please," Emily said.

The drive home seemed longer than usual to Emily. On either side of the road, the eyes of deer and other wildlife stared at the ominous machine, their eyes reflecting the headlights of the Packard bouncing along the sandy road. Jeanne held onto the strap that hung over the rear door. Emily could smell her perfume, something familiar blended with the light smell of tobacco. What was it that she'd planned to say to her only daughter after all these years? The words escaped her.

When they pulled into the lane leading to the house, Jeanne said, "Home again, home again, jiggety jig." They turned and looked at one another. Emily couldn't suppress her smile. "What?" Jeanne asked, smiling now. "That's what you always said when we'd been away and we turned into the lane."

"I know," Emily said, reaching for her daughter's hand. She squeezed it tightly. "I'm glad you remembered. Welcome home, Jeanne."

⌒

The next few months were not easy for Emily or her daughter. During the day, they stayed out of each other's way. As the weather warmed, they took to meeting on the porch at four o'clock for a glass of wine. What Jeanne did in her room the rest of the day was a mystery to Emily. Once, her daughter had left her door open, and Emily saw books and papers on the large semicircular desk in the center of the room. The desk and the room had once belonged to her brother Reece. The books, the papers, a few clothes scattered about the bedroom reminded Emily of a typical scene when brother and sister had lived there as children. It was but one of the ways in which Jeanne reminded Emily of her brother, who had also traveled to the beat of his own drum.

Dinner followed the drinks at six o'clock, only the two of them at the large dining room table with the delicate chandelier tinkling above them. On Sundays, Darcy and Gardenia, together with their children, joined them after church. Jeanne revealed little about the four years she was away. Emily never asked direct questions, but gradually some things came out.

Jeanne and Jon had parted ways about a year after they'd left Wilmington. In the year that they were together, Jeanne had several skin grafts that had taken months to heal. The jagged scar across her forehead was barely visible, but there was very little expression around her eyes. Jeanne was past thirty now; she should have little crow's-feet, but none existed. Concealed by her heavy makeup, as was the scar? What Emily wanted to know most of all—Jon's whereabouts—was never disclosed.

Later, in the spring, Jeanne loosened up a little. When Darcy and Gardenia were about, she showered her attention on the children, but became interested when the conversation turned to politics. Some of her views surprised Emily, who had only recently left her sanctuary to attend a rally in Wilmington for presidential hopeful Franklin D. Roosevelt.

"When I was in New York last year, I met some of Eleanor Roosevelt's friends," Jeanne said, out of the blue. "She's the one who should be running for president, don't you agree, Mother?" They were on the veranda in the rear of the house overlooking Lake Catherine, where hundreds of snowy white cranes fished along the shallow edges. All around them blossoms of wild azalea and yellow jasmine scented the air. Darcy had taken the children out to play on the long rope swing that hung from one of the giant oak trees.

"That's not likely, is it?" Emily said, thinking it seemed odd when Jeanne spoke of people and places she'd known or been while they were estranged.

"She's an amazing woman, but I doubt I'll see a woman president in my lifetime."

"Mine, either," Gardenia said, sleepily. She was stretched out on the glider while Jeanne and Emily sat at a small wicker table playing pinochle. "I'm not so sure about that," Jeanne said. "The vote has empowered women in the last twenty years. They're much more involved in politics. Look at me, for instance."

Gardenia sat up and looked at Jeanne. Emily stacked her cards and lay them down on the table, giving Jeanne her full attention. "You are?" she said.

Jeanne laughed and threw her head back, revealing a pale neck that did not match the bronze glow of her makeup. "Oh, just a little. Don't worry, I'm not thinking of running for anything."

Gardenia lay back on the divan. "I hope not. Darcy would have a fit. You know how he feels about a woman's place being in the home."

"Darcy is like his uncle Reece," Jeanne said. "He wants his toys waiting for him in his toy box when he comes home."

"I think you will find that true of most men, Jeanne," Emily said.

"I disagree, Mother. There are one or two out there who recognize that the world is changing," Jeanne said. But she stopped short, and got up from her chair. "I'm ready for a glass of wine," she said. "How about you, Mother? Gardenia?"

That was the way most conversations had ended when the subject came near Jon. Had Jeanne been hurt by Jon? Had he left her for another woman? Or had she left him when she found that his attention was no longer entirely on her? That would be like Jeanne. But her refusal to bring up the subject made Emily feel that heartbreak was behind it. Jeanne had never been able to open up to Emily—to anyone really. Friends from school had called her aloof. When they'd come home with Jeanne from school, it was Emily they'd talked with around the kitchen table. Yet Jeanne had friends, many of them. She wrote letters daily, and received them as often. None were from Jon—that Emily knew of.

Jeanne had left again in late August, saying she'd been asked by the Women's Committee of the Democratic Party to help with Roosevelt's campaign. There were a few letters between then and November when Roosevelt was overwhelmingly elected president of the United States. Jeanne called from a celebration somewhere in New York, announcing that she would not get home for Christmas. "There is so much to be done. Eleanor has asked for my help, for everyone's help," she said. "You wouldn't believe the things she plans to do, Mother. I love her so much!"

Emily had been taken aback by the statement. She'd never heard Jeanne say she loved anyone *so much*.

Gradually, Emily became accustomed to the idea that Jeanne's new life really didn't include her, but she was thankful that now at least there was an address where Jeanne could be reached. Emily wrote long letters to her daughter, letters that never touched on the past, or anything but the most pleasant subjects—Darcy was carrying a new line of shoes, the children were growing like weeds, old Boss was down in his back with rheumatism—trivial, but pleasant.

There were short notes and birthday cards from Jeanne, but only brief remarks about what she was doing. Her most recent address was Hyde Park, where she said she was working as a volunteer ... *with two of Eleanor Roosevelt's personal friends who are involved in the arts and crafts movement. We're putting more and more people to work every day at the Val-Kill Furniture Factory. It's the most exciting thing I've ever done.*

Often a month or more would pass before Jeanne would write again. Emily was surprised by her envy, not so much of Jeanne, but of the women around her daughter who were involved in New Deal politics. For awhile, Emily came close to playing the role of a rejected heroine in a Victorian novel, but her envy propelled her into becoming active again. She decided that moving back to Wilmington was unnecessary. The roads had improved so much in recent years that she could be with her friends in the Democratic Women's Club in a little over half an hour. They welcomed her with open arms.

At the December meeting in 1933, the main topic of discussion was an article in the *Wilmington Star* announcing Hugh MacRae's new project in neighboring Pender County. MacRae was well-known in Emily's circle of friends, whose interests included such public projects as Greenfield Park and gardens. MacRae's focus was even larger. His belief that diversified truck farming would save southern agriculture had first become a reality in Castle Hayne. Emily had visited there on several occasions and witnessed firsthand the success of the Dutch flower growers. St. Helena and Van Eeden were less successful, but the new farm city in Pender County, known as Penderlea Homesteads, was to be the crème de la crème of his diversified farming projects. Hugh MacRae was a hero in Emily's book. He was doing something about the poor farmer whom she and others felt were the real losers in the Great Depression.

PART ONE

Utopia

CHAPTER 1

MAY 1933 — PENDER COUNTY, NORTH CAROLINA

Nathan Hill's truck rattled and clanked through the early morning mist across the flat fields of St. Helena. Dark figures, stooped and bent amid the rows of beans and cucumbers, paused to gape at the well-drilling rig — an oddity in rural eastern North Carolina, where the underground water table was only a few feet below the earth's surface.

Len Ryan, Nathan's nephew, was driving the rusty beat-up truck whose cab top had been removed. "Slow down!" Nathan shouted. "You're liable to run him over. You can't stop this damn thing on a dime!"

Len downshifted into low gear, figuring he still had a ways to go before he reached the gentleman standing at the end of the lane waving them on. "I see him," he said. He was thinking that the dang fool ought to get out of the middle of the road.

Nathan peered over the dirty windshield. "Yes, siree, that's Mr. Hugh MacRae himself. Got more money than you can shake a stick at, but the nicest fellow you'll ever meet," he said, flashing tobacco-stained teeth. Nathan never smoked a cigar anymore, he just gnawed on the end of it like a piece of chewing tobacco. "Yep, I been knowing him since before you were born. Never been there myself, but I hear tell he lives in a damn castle in Wilmington," he said. "Owns the Tide Water Power Company, too, you know."

"I know," Len said.

"I wouldn't be lying when I say he's probably the richest man in North Carolina," Nathan continued. "Got land all over the place. One big spread he calls *Invershield*—not far over yonder near Rocky Point. That's where he plants all these different kinds of grasses—grazes his cows on 'em—to test them out, you know." He sat up straighter, a better position for pontificating. "You see, Mr. Hugh's got it in his mind that pastures could be green all year round if we planted the right grasses." Nathan cleared his throat and spit out over the door to make his final point. "He don't have to do it. No, siree. That's just the kind of person he is."

Len had heard it all before. If Uncle Nathan, who seldom expressed admiration for another man, had a hero, it was Hugh MacRae. Next thing he'd be telling was about MacRae's belief that a farmer could make a living off just a few acres of good land.

"Yessir, he proved it first right here at St. Helena," Nathan said, as if on cue.

"Proved what?" Len asked. He enjoyed egging his uncle on.

"You know, I told you before." But Len knew he'd tell him again. "I know I did, but anyhow, it was thirty years ago when he bought up a bunch of land on either side of the railroad from Burgaw to Wilmington. He put advertisements in all the newspapers across the ocean inviting farmers to come to America and take him up on his offer of a piece of uncleared land in Pender County where they could start a new life." Len slowed the truck to a crawl, easing over a board-covered drainage ditch. Nathan craned his neck out the window and pointed. "That's some of them immigrants out there in the field now." He sat back and smiled.

"Betcha he could've found some takers right here in the United States," Len said.

"No, no. Listen here, this man is smart. He wanted some purebloods—*good stock*, he called it. No telling who would have applied here in America. It wasn't meant to be a handout."

"Oh," Len said, understanding what his uncle was getting at.

"Castle Hayne, just down the road was next, then Van Eeden. Farm colonies, he called 'em." He shook his head from side to side and clucked his tongue. "I'm telling you what's the truth. Mr. Hugh's way ahead of his time. Wa-a-ay ahead of his time."

Len looked out over the truck crops that would be shipped all over the East. He'd seen the wooden crates stamped with *St. Helena, N.C.* on the loading dock at Burgaw and wondered if some day he might see *Colly Farms* stamped on crates filled by him.

"Start turning!" Nathan shouted. "He wants you to pull over there." He grabbed the steering wheel, pulling it to the left. "Over there! This rig won't turn on a dime either!"

Len's ruddy complexion flushed to a deep red. *Here I am almost nineteen years old—been driving this rig since I was fifteen—and he still thinks he has to tell me how!* He pulled the rig into an open area, near Hugh MacRae. Nathan jumped out of the truck and took a few steps toward the white-haired gentleman who was dressed in a black suit, the pants legs tucked into tooled leather cowboy boots.

"Morning, Mr. Hugh," Nathan said, lifting his hat to reveal a pale, balding head. He pumped MacRae's hand. "I thought we might've beat you here."

MacRae stood next to a large white bay horse who nibbled in the lush grass at the edge of the field. Len was reminded of a picture in a magazine he'd seen of an oil tycoon out west. The older gentleman tipped his wide-brimmed hat back on his head. "Morning, Nathan. I see you got my letter," he said, his tone warm and gentlemanly. "I appreciate you coming on such short notice."

"No trouble—no trouble a'tall," Nathan said, a wide grin carving deep crevices into his leathery brown face. "This here's my nephew, Len Ryan. Knows just about as much about pumps and wells as I do."

Len reached out to shake MacRae's hand. Len had grown six inches in the last year and still wasn't quite comfortable with his long limbs. Since he'd been working with Uncle Nathan, he'd taken to wearing army-type pants tucked into boots that laced up to just below his knees, items of clothing that had been handed down to him from a cousin, a World War I veteran. By noon, he'd strip off his shirt and be down to a khaki-colored undershirt. But Len's freckled skin burned easily, and he always had to pay for that.

MacRae lifted his hat and tipped it a little farther back on his head. He studied Len. "Pleased to meet you, my boy," he said, sizing up Len like a hog on the auction block. "If you were a farmer, I'd say you were just the kind of young fellow I'm looking for."

"I *am* a farmer, sir. Just help Uncle Nathan out from time to time." He looked MacRae directly in the eye. "I was raised a farmer."

MacRae's eyes, as deep and gray-blue as the early morning sky, met the young man's. His mouth twitched slightly beneath the stubble of a gray beard, "Oh, I see," he said, studying Len. "You *own* your land?" he asked, his grip still firm about Len's hand.

Len shifted his weight from one foot to the other. He wondered what MacRae was getting at. "Yes, sir, I reckon you could say that. It's my family's land, if that's what you mean," he said. Hadn't he heard the story all his life about how Aunt Mag, one of three daughters of Archibald Moore, had inherited the land and given it to Len's mother, Maggie Lorena? Her brothers had been furious. "It was Moore land," Len added, aware that a man of MacRae's holdings would likely recognize the New Hanover County name that had been on deed books since the early 1700s. "It's Ryan land now," he said.

MacRae appeared to run the words over in his mind, then laughed heartily. "Oh, I see. I was afraid you'd say you were farming another man's land." He dropped Len's hand and looked about for Nathan.

Len resumed his customary position of hanging onto the side mirror of the truck with one foot on the running board. He'd sent his mama a picture of him like that last year from up in Greensboro. She'd pinned it on the kitchen wall, saying he looked so grown up. "I'm not a tenant farmer, if that's what you mean," he said.

"Not much future in working another man's land," MacRae said, his gaze on the fields beyond. "You see, what we're doing here on my farm colonies is making more on ten acres of new land than you could make on a hundred acres of worn-out land like you've got over there in Bladen County." Len followed MacRae's gaze, looking out over the nearby fields. He thought he'd never seen so much green, but he didn't much like the idea of MacRae throwing off on the fields his father, Tate Ryan, had toiled over for twenty years.

"These immigrants here on St. Helena are hard workers, I tell you," MacRae continued, stomping through the muddy ruts in the lane in his high-heeled boots. Len followed along. "They know how to make something off a little bit of land." When he stopped in his tracks, Len almost ran into him. "You ever been to Europe?"

"No, sir."

MacRae started out again toward Nathan. "No, I don't suppose you have. Just a country boy," he said under his breath. "Well, I'll tell you, these boys come from the old country…know how to make crops on less land than this." He pointed across the field. "You see, they don't have these great big farms in Europe. Land is scarce. What they have over there is well used, but they make the most of it, else they would have died out a long time ago."

"I reckon they don't plant the same crops in the same place year after year for one thing," Len said.

"You know about crop rotation?" MacRae asked.

"Yes, sir. Our county agent has been preaching it a right good while."

"Well, now," he said. "You *are* the kind of young farmer I'm looking for on my new project." MacRae turned on his heel and called out, "Say, Nathan, where do you think that well ought to go?"

Uncle Nathan, ahead of them, had already surveyed the recently cleared area. He waited for MacRae and Len to approach. He was a small, thick man, but tough as rawhide and mean as a pit bull if you crossed him. Everybody in Colly knew about the time he'd rigged a shotgun to go off if anyone got into his watermelon patch. Killed a twenty-year-old Negro man. He'd rigged up the same kind of trap beside his woodshed with a similar result, but that fellow lived to tell about it. The community didn't take kindly to his self-styled justice for what they'd always tolerated to a certain extent.

But for all of his faults, Uncle Nathan knew how to find water. Even if you'd experienced his mean side, you'd respect him for that anyhow. "Right about here ought to be good," he said, digging the heel of his boot into the black sandy loam. "You could set the house right over yonder."

Len surveyed the setting at the edge of the woods and thought about the work involved in clearing new land. "If you don't mind my asking, Mr. Hugh, who're you building this house for?"

MacRae held his chin in one hand, his elbow in the other, his eyes roaming over the site. A rusty diesel tractor, its engine rattling noisily, idled at the edge of the field. "One of my immigrants wants ten acres for his brother who's coming over from Italy in a month or two."

"Right about here, then?" Nathan called out.

"I reckon that'll do, Nathan. How deep do you think you'll have to go?"

"Can't be more than eight or ten feet down to water—twelve at the most. We don't hardly even need that rig in these parts. Up there, the other side of Raleigh, we'd have to go down about two hundred or more feet." He spit tobacco juice over his right shoulder. "That granite and clay up there is the damndest thing you ever saw!"

"I know what you mean," MacRae said. "I say it'll be less than ten in this sand."

Sand-point wells were so common in this part of the state that most farmers Len knew drilled their own wells simply by driving down a pipe with a sand-point drill attached into the soil. It took some doing to hammer a pipe down straight, but Len had done it many a time with three pipes set up tepee fashion to plumb the pipe. One or two men might work up a good sweat, but cool fresh water was the result of their labor. Gentleman farmers like Hugh MacRae hired a driller like Uncle Nathan to do the job. Len wasn't complaining. Without the pay he earned working for Uncle Nathan, he was sure his parents, Maggie Lorena and Tate Ryan, would be on relief now.

Leaving St. Helena behind, Nathan and Len made their way back to Canetuck after crossing Black River at Still Bluff. "Just drop me off at the house and take the truck on up to Colly," Nathan said. "I'm too tired to run you down there this evening. Mr. Hugh said something about another well. You can come get me if need be." Len was tired too. His arms ached from keeping the heavy pipe straight as it found its way to water. But in his mind, he reviewed every word he'd heard today about Mr. MacRae's farm colonies. It all came back to him—the stories he'd heard when he was growing up about the immigrants who couldn't speak a word of English living over there in Pender County. Places like Van Eeden, Castle Hayne, and St. Helena sounded more like different countries than another part of the county. He recalled something his mother said about Mr. MacRae not inviting any Negroes, just white people from countries like Italy and Holland. Probably just as well, Len thought. He was sure he didn't know a single Negro who would want to live in a community where they didn't speak any English.

Chapter 2

When Hugh MacRae sent word to Uncle Nathan that he needed another well at St. Helena, Nathan drove his car up to Colly to tell Len it was time that he demonstrated all that he'd learned. "You know what to do. Mr. Hugh's going to have somebody there to help you. Hank Hudson's his name. He's the project manager at St. Helena—been there since day one."

"Why can't you go with me?" Len asked, astounded that his uncle was trusting him to do the job alone.

"Look at my hands, all swole up. They're killing me!" Nathan said. "You gotta go and do this for me. Mr. Hugh's counting on us. I'll pay you for it same as I would if it was me doing it. It's time you started putting a little aside—sort of a nest egg when you decide to go out on your own."

"I appreciate it, Uncle Nathan, but you know Papa is counting on me."

Nathan leaned in real close to Len. "You could make a living doing this for Mr. Hugh. He's like a god in these parts. What Mr. Hugh says becomes gospel. Besides, I'm counting on you, too." Uncle Nathan said. He stepped back a little, giving Len room to think about it. "You know there's not a one of my three boys that gives a damn about working in the well-drilling business. You think I care? No, sir. Suits me just fine for them to hire out to other farmers. When they're old enough, they'll go off to college anyhow. Your Aunt Kate will see to that."

"I never said I wanted to be a well driller, Uncle Nathan. I appreciate the work you've given me, but you always knew I had to be home...."

Nathan flashed his yellow smile the way a snake sticks his tongue out just before a strike. "You turning me down, boy?"

Len's stomach flipped over, but he managed to look his uncle in the eye. "No, sir. I'm just trying to tell you that Papa's counting on me to plow the lower field tomorrow. I can't be both places. What's he going to say when I tell him I'm going off to—"

Nathan leaned in again. "You let me talk to Tate. A man needs a trade to fall back on. Tate knows that."

At supper that evening, Tate was quieter than usual. He and Nathan had stood out by the well-drilling rig for a half hour or more while Len fed the hogs and watered the horse and mule. "I don't have to go tomorrow," Len said. "We could send word that I'd be there in a day or two after we—"

"No, you go on and go," Tate said. "Your Uncle Nathan has kept bread on the table the last few years. If it hadn't been for what you've been able to make and send home, Mama and I would've been mighty bad off."

Maggie shuffled in from the kitchen with a pot of grits. She plopped a wooden spoonful on each of their plates. "Kate tells me all the time how Nathan favors you, son. Those boys of theirs are scared to death of him."

"I'm scared of him, too, but I don't let him know it," Len laughed.

"Nathan's right," Tate said. "You need a trade. All these newfangled ideas they're coming up with don't make much sense to me. Nothing beats hard work."

"I believe in President Roosevelt's New Deal, Papa. Ray Wilkins said we'd likely get twenty dollars an acre for every acre of tobacco we *didn't* plant this year."

"Who's Ray Wilkins?" Tate said. "I've never heard of him."

"He's the new county agent, Papa." Len pushed his chair back. "Look, why don't you go to that meeting with me next week? Ray's going to explain everything then."

"No, you go, son. I'll do anything you say, but I don't want to go to any meetings and listen to a bunch of politicians tell me how to do my farming."

"But, Pa, they're not politicians. They're farmers like you and me. Some of them like Ray have been to college studying agricultural engineering."

"I know, I know, son. I'm not putting it down. Don't get me wrong. It's just that all this talk about new ways of doing things wears me out. I know it appeals to you, and I really want you to go. Old farmers like me are falling by the wayside."

Len fell asleep that night thinking about his options. Here was Uncle Nathan on the one hand offering him a trade, a way to make some real money—maybe even give up farming entirely. But, on the other hand, Tate was practically turning the farm over to him. Len had been to the meetings, and he liked what Ray Wilkins had to say. There were loans available from the government for seed and fertilizer, not to mention the allotment plan. If he could get a tractor next year, Len was positive that he could turn a profit.

In another room of the farmhouse, Tate's thoughts kept him awake long into the night. He'd likely lose Len to a trade like well drilling if he didn't give him control of the farming operation. Len was young—drawn to new ideas and new ways. Already in his short life, Len had been way off—to Boston first, and in the last year or two, he'd been all over North Carolina. Tate had never been any farther than Wilmington—not even to Raleigh.

In 1931, just two years ago, both of his sons had left home to find work in other places. Will was nineteen and Len was seventeen. Bladen County had been hit hard by the Depression. There weren't any big cities with mills and factories. The county seat at Elizabethtown had the courthouse and a few banks, and scattered throughout the county there were general stores where you could buy farm supplies and such, but you had to go to Wilmington or beyond for everything else. Most folks just worked their own farms, grew what they ate, and made do with what they had. But when the tax man came around, you needed some cold hard cash. Will, his oldest who had a knack for working on engines—automobiles, tractors, and such—couldn't even do that when nobody could buy tires or gasoline to run them.

Will had found work right away in Detroit, but he'd been laid off within a couple of weeks, only to find himself standing in long bread lines instead of working under the hood of one of Mr. Henry Ford's cars. He wrote that he was doing odd jobs until he could come up with bus fare. But the next thing they knew, he was hired by this real important man in Detroit to keep his fleet of cars running. Now, he sent a little money home right regularly.

Since he was fifteen, Len had worked with Uncle Nathan in the winter drilling deep wells in the upper part of the state. Last winter, when his jobs were finished, Nathan had gotten Len on with the Highway Department and left him up there to work a couple of months. Some weeks, Len sent five or six dollars home; other weeks there was nothing to send because bad weather prevented his crew from working. The Highway Department didn't pay you for sitting around waiting for it to fair off.

Unlike Will, Len was a farmer at heart. He'd come home this year all hepped up about an allotment program the government was offering as part of Roosevelt's New Deal for all Americans. Maggie had kept Len informed, sending him clippings and bulletins from the farm agent. She'd also told him that Tate didn't believe in it. But when he got home, Len took the bull by the horns and attended every meeting in Elizabethtown with or without Tate. Before he knew it, Tate was signed up for a program he didn't understand.

Tate was worn out with farming. He felt old, incapable of keeping up with the new and modern ways. Plant less, send the prices up? What the hell did they expect of an old-time farmer? The only way a man could survive was to plant enough to satisfy the tobacco worms and the boll weevils. If anything was left, it was a damn good season. But if Len wanted to do it, why shouldn't he? The land was his anyhow. A young man like Len could start new traditions, he could practice what the government was preaching, and maybe—just maybe—they'd be right and Roosevelt would be right: a new deal could be had by the farmers who'd gotten the short end of the stick for the last ten or fifteen years.

CHAPTER 3

Hank Hudson said he'd worked as project manager for Hugh MacRae since St. Helena was started. Hank was a tall thin man who wore a neat white shirt and khaki work pants. He also wore a wristwatch and a straw hat that looked brand new. When he lifted the hat occasionally to wipe his brow, his hair beneath it was thick and dark, matching a narrow mustache on Hank's upper lip. Len thought Hank was overdressed for the well-drilling job, but he proved to be an able hand and the two men accomplished the job before noon.

Following along at Hudson's heels had been a young eight- or nine-year-old boy. The project manager was a big talker, but the boy had never uttered a word. While they'd worked, the boy had squatted nearby catching Len's eye a time or two when Len reached for his wrench. He was a nice-looking little fellow, with blonde hair that hung from a cowlick over his brown eyes. Barefoot and wearing overalls and a long-sleeved muslin shirt, he seemed like a regular little country boy. "Don't he speak English?" Len asked. The boy stared at him.

"Sure he does," Hank laughed, ruffling the boy's hair with his hand. "Tell him your name." But the boy jumped up and half-ran, half-hopped to the edge of the woods. "Don't pay him any mind," Hank said. "He's real shy."

Len followed the child with his eyes, watching him scamper up the trunk of a bent live-oak tree. "What's wrong with his foot?"

Hank glanced away. "You don't want to know," he said.

"Why's that?"

"It's a sad story."

Len's heart quickened and he wanted to know more, but something told him not to ask. Maybe he really didn't want to know.

When they'd finished gathering the tools, Hank invited Len to his house. "My wife Maria said she'd have us a pot of boiled spring vegetables. I imagine she's got a piece of meat in there, too." He looked at his watch. "Ought to be ready about now."

The boy was sitting on the back steps of the small clapboard house holding a dog, not much bigger than a cat. "You can wash up there at the pump," Hank said. "I'll get us a towel off the line." He strolled across the grassy backyard and pulled a white towel off a line filled with what looked like a week's wash.

"Nice puppy you got there," Len said to the boy.

"That's Petey," Hank said, handing Len the towel.

Len dried his face and hands and walked to where the boy sat. He squatted in front of them and reached out to pet the dog. "Hi, Petey. You're a cute little fellow," Len said. The boy pulled the dog back, holding him close to his face. Taken aback, Len stood up. But the boy stood also and handed the dog to Len. "Oh, you want me to hold him? Okay."

"Colin loves Petey," Hank said. "Don't you, son?" The boy nodded and reached for his puppy. When he had him in his hands again, he sat down and nuzzled the dog against his cheek, fingering the dog's velvety ears. "Petey loves Colin, too," Hank said, affectionately.

A stout, dark-haired woman appeared on the back porch wearing an apron. She was younger than Hank and pretty as a picture. "Hey, Maria," he said. "This is Len Ryan."

Maria fluttered long, dark eyelashes. "Hello, Mr. Len," she said in a thick accent. "Welcome to our home."

"Maria's parents came here when she was just a baby."

"Yes, I am of very good fortune," Maria said, patting her husband's arm.

"Very fortunate, honey," Hank said.

Maria blushed and giggled, putting her hand over her mouth. "Oh, yes, very fortunate."

The kitchen was modest but clean. The small table was covered in a bright cloth, matching a ruffled curtain that moved slightly as a breeze drifted in the window. Len sat with his back to the iron stove, a good fire going in it. Colin kept glancing over at him, but he never opened his mouth except to eat. The little dog sat on the floor by the boy as if waiting for a scrap of food to fall his way.

Maria served them from the stove on heavy plates painted with sunflowers, loading each one with whole carrots, potatoes, cabbage, onions, and a sprinkling of garden peas. To one side, she added a thick slice of boiled, smoked ham. When she sat down to eat with them, she passed a large woven basket filled with a soft bread that smelled so good Len thought he couldn't stand it. "I declare, Miss Maria, that bread's liable not to make its way around the table."

Maria blushed and smiled. "*Grazie*," she said.

"What did she say?" Len asked.

"*Grazie*," Hank said. "It means 'thank-you' in Italian. Maria's was one of the first immigrant families to settle in St. Helena. All of the first homesteaders were Italian farmers."

"How long ago was that?"

"Way back in 1906. Most of 'em didn't have a pot to pee in over there in the old country. Hugh MacRae offered them ten acres of land and a three-bedroom house for 240 dollars."

"They had to pay it back, didn't they?" Len asked.

"Well, sure, but they had three years to do it in."

"Ten acres doesn't sound like much land to me," Len said. "I can't believe anybody could make a living off that."

"Oh, yes, a few did, but some left before they hardly got settled when they found out that they had to clear the land first. They thought they would go right to work farming. Maria's family stayed and proved it could work. After they died, Maria lived here right by herself until we got married."

"Who else lives on St. Helena now?" Len asked, puzzled by the strange language he'd heard when the field workers called out to one another.

"One or two of the Italians are left, but it's mostly Russians now. They're building a Greek church over yonder."

"How come they're building a Greek church?" Len asked.

Hank slapped his hand on his knee and laughed. "I asked the same thing," he said. "The preacher—I think they call him a priest—told me that the church was like they have in the old country. It's called Greek Orthodox, which means they changed it to Russian or something like that. It has a gold steeple—kinda squashed down, like an onion."

Len thought about it for a minute, trying to imagine the church. Pictures from a fairytale book his mother had read to him came to mind. "That'll be a sight to see in Pender County," he said.

"Would you like bread pudding?" Maria asked. "I have the custard sauce to pour over it."

"Yes, ma'am," Len said. "That sounds mighty good."

"She's a good cook, isn't she, son?" Hank said, winking at the boy across the table. Colin looked at him and smiled briefly before turning his gaze on Len.

"I can vouch for that," Len said, rubbing his stomach. The boy looked down at his bowl of bread pudding and rubbed his stomach and licked his lower lip. "You, too?" Len said.

While Maria cleared the dishes, Hank filled Len in on Hugh MacRae's farm colonies. He told him that Castle Hayne had been the most successful. "Most of them were Dutch flower growers when they came here. They were real good farmers to begin with. Some finished paying off their debt to MacRae's company on their ten acres and went on to buy twenty or thirty more," he said. "But that never happened on St. Helena. That's why he's all fired up about his new project up yonder the other side of Burgaw. He calls it Penderlea." Hank looked at his watch. "But wait a minute, I'm supposed to tell you to stop by his farm over there at Rocky Point on your way home."

"What for?" Len asked.

"His generator went out during that storm last night, and he ain't got no power to run all those fans in the barn."

"He's got electric fans in his barn?" Len asked.

"You bet he does."

"I don't know a thing about generators," Len said.

"Oh, he don't want you to fix his generator. He's got the co-op putting in a line direct to his house. He wants to talk to you about putting in another well and a new centrifugal pump."

"I'd best be on my way, then," Len said. "I'd like to say good-bye to the boy. Where'd he go?"

"I'm sure he's in the barn. The mama dog has some more puppies in there, but he's already picked his out," Hank said. He paused and glanced over his shoulder, looking for the boy. "You ever been to Castle Hayne?" he asked.

"A few times."

"That's where the boy come from. Thought you might've heard about him."

At supper that evening, Len talked nonstop about his day at St. Helena—all except the part about the boy. He knew better than to bring that up in front of Maggie. A name like Colin wasn't something you heard every day. There was more to it, and Len intended to find out what before he stirred things up.

Tate was tired from a long day in the field planting soybeans where he'd always grown tobacco. "Let's go on in the other room, son," he said. "I need to stretch out a bit." He unlaced his brogans and let them drop one at a time to the floor. Len pulled up a straight chair and sat near him, but it was all Tate could do to keep his eyes open..

"Ten acres is nothing, Pa. No wonder they couldn't make it," Len said, shaking his head. "We'll plant more than that in corn this year, won't we?

"Humm?"

"I said we'd plant more than ten acres just in corn this year."

"Need that much to feed the hogs and make a little cornbread for ourselves," Tate mumbled.

Len knew he was losing him, but he added, "A big storm could wipe out half of it. We have to think about that."

"Humm."

Maggie moved into the sitting room, leaving the dishes until morning. She pulled her rocking chair closer to a small stove, taking the chill off the cool spring evening. "I had the privilege of meeting Mr. Hugh MacRae at Wrightsville Beach when Abigail Montgomery was here a few years back," she mused. "We were in the dining room at the Oceanic Hotel, and he came directly to our table to speak to her."

"How did he know Miss Abigail, Mama?"

"Oh, Abigail had friends and acquaintances all over. She and Henry went to places like the Greenbrier up in West Virginia. That's what rich people do, you know." She pulled off her apron, laid it over the chair's arm, looked up at her son, and smiled. "Maybe she met him on the *Queen Mary.*"

Len chuckled. If his mama didn't know the answer to a question, she could readily make one up. "Will you write to her and ask her how she knows him?" he asked. "I sure would like to tell him y'all are friends."

"Of course, son. I cut the article out of the paper to send her."

"What article?"

"The one about Penderlea. It's that new government project over there near Watha."

"Well, I'll be. Hank Hudson called it that."

"My land, son, I've told you to read the paper. Look at all the interesting things you miss."

"That's what mamas are for," Len said, approaching her chair. He gave her a quick peck on the cheek. "What did it say?"

"It said Mr. Hugh MacRae is building another one of his farm colonies over in Pender County, except this time it's for the government and they're calling it a 'farm city.'"

Len took his seat again and leaned forward on his elbows. "Yep, that's what Mr. Hugh was saying to me."

"Some big outfit from Boston designed it. I thought Abigail might know him."

"What else did it say?"

"Well, it's not for immigrants this time," she said. "It's all a part of President Roosevelt's New Deal to get young farmers off relief. The government's going to provide the land and build the houses—furnish every single thing, right down to the hens in the henhouse." She shook her head and clucked her tongue. "I'm telling you, it all sounds too good to be true."

Len leaned back in his chair. "But they're not going to give it to them for nothing, right? What's the catch?"

"Practically," she said. "You get everything right up front to begin with. I guess they mean for a family to work it awhile before they start paying for it."

That's what the old man was talking about, Len thought. "When are they going to start it?"

"It's already started, son. Since March, I believe." She was sorting through a box of clippings on a small table beside her chair. "There was another piece in the *Star* just last week. Yes, here it is." Maggie read from the clipping:

> The project, known as Penderlea, is located on 4,500 acres of land purchased from Mr. MacRae who will be chairman of the board of directors of the corporation organized to assume responsibility for success of the project. All stock in the corporation, to be known as Penderlea Homesteads, Inc., will be owned by the government. Hugh MacRae of Wilmington, N.C., is widely known for his efforts in building farm communities.

"See there, I told you," Len said excitedly. "And he said I was just the kind of young farmer he was looking for." He hadn't meant to blurt it out.

Tate opened his eyes and sat up, wide awake now. "You'd leave all we've worked for here and go over to some government project in the next county?" he asked.

"I didn't say that. I just told you what he said."

Maggie stuffed the article back into her box and straightened her skirt. "Now, don't go getting yourself all upset, Tate. They're talking about families—marriage and children. Len's not married—he's not even courting anyone."

CHAPTER 4

Hugh MacRae's Rocky Point farm was a sight to see. Lush green pastures surrounded a compound of barns and slim round silos as tall as some of the buildings he'd seen in Boston. When Len drove up, MacRae stepped off the wraparound porch of a small one-story farmhouse. Len greeted the old gentleman eagerly, anxious to tell him all that he'd learned about the new project. But before he could get a word in edge-wise, MacRae slapped Len on the shoulder and started talking. "I've been thinking a lot about you, boy. Hank tells me you're a hard worker. Really smart. Know what you're doing. Says you know a lot about farming, too."

"Yes, sir, been at it all my short life," he laughed.

"I could use somebody like you on my new project. Have you heard about Penderlea?"

"Yes, sir. Mama told me about the article that was in the *Wilmington Star*. A farm city right there in Pender County. Sounds like a fairy tale."

MacRae looked annoyed. "Oh, it's no fairy tale, son. Penderlea will be something like you've never seen before, but for a man willing to work, it will be utopia."

Utopia? Len thought about the word. "Like I said, a fairy tale."

"Only in the sense that heretofore a place like Penderlea has existed only in the minds of men like Sir Thomas More." He was sure he was talking over Len's head, but the boy interrupted.

"That island wasn't real. It was a figment of his imagination. Mama read it to me."

MacRae smiled. "Well, sir, I'd say you are a smart boy. Did you ever think about going to college?"

"Yes, sir, I did. I met Mr. Rhyne up in Greensboro one time. He said he would help me get into Elon College. That was last year."

"Well, did you go to see him? Talk about it?"

"No, sir. I had to come home to help with the spring planting. My brother Will is working in Detroit, Michigan. Mama and Papa needed some help."

"Like I told you, you'll never rise up out of this Depression farming that worn-out land over there in Bladen County. Are you married?"

"No, sir."

"Got any plans to get married?"

"Not anytime soon."

"Well, you might start thinking about it," he said. "It'll take about a year to get this project ready. They'll have the electric lines over there by then. We'll need pumps—men to install them. People who can do things and farm, too. You're just the kind of young man I want on Penderlea."

"That might be tempting, Mr. Hugh, but my pa is counting on me to help him farm. The land belongs to him and my mama now, but someday it'll be mine and my brother's."

MacRae shook his head, exasperated. "I'm telling you, you can't make a living on that worn-out land. You need to get married, move on while you're young. With a government loan on a house at Penderlea and a job installing pumps on the project, you could probably bring in enough cash to help your parents, too."

"What about that new thing Congress just passed? Our county agent said we're going to get paid *not* to plant. It'll bring prices up. What do you think about that?" Len couldn't believe he was arguing with a man old enough to be his grandfather.

"Ah, the Agricultural Adjustment Act." The boy was up on things. He was smart. "Yes, allotments might work for awhile—bring prices up—but it's not a permanent cure. Crop rotation is better. Let your father give it a try," he said. He picked up a rusty bucket, turned it over, and propped his foot on it. "Listen here, son. Young men like you should get out of this old-fashioned cash crop way of farming. Truck crops are the way to go. Penderlea's the place for you. It's not a handout like those allotments."

"The County agent said allotments weren't a handout either. It's *recovery*. I've already signed us up for it."

MacRae shook his head. "That's fine, son. Let your papa take it. The government has a responsibility to its people. Roosevelt knows that. He's been privileged, but he understands the common man." MacRae leaned on his elbow propped against his knee. When Len grew quiet, he stood upright and kicked the bucket out of his way. "Penderlea is a whole new world. Your pa never had this chance."

"I can't let my parents lose their land," Len said. "Don't you think I'm obliged to help them hold onto it?"

"Of course you are, son. But you've got to think ahead. Penderlea is the opportunity of a lifetime. The soil is some of the finest in North Carolina. The people up there at State College in Raleigh say it's perfect for truck crops, and the fact that the thermal belt from the Gulf Stream dips in right there makes a growing season ten months long. In no time, you should be making enough money to send a little home." The old man had looked at him kindly. "This might be your only chance to help your parents, Len. The government's going to own their land, too, if they can't pay the taxes."

⌒

Mr. Hugh MacRae wasn't the only one putting marriage into Len's head, but Maggie Lorena's reasons had nothing to do with Penderlea. Maggie constantly played on Len's emotions, saying how poorly she felt—how she needed a girl—someone to keep her company, do the cooking. Tate had heard her talking to Len one night after he'd gone to bed. "Why, Len, if you were to get married, we could all pull together," she said. "Keeping you men in clean clothes and your stomachs full is wearing me down. I can hardly get out of bed in the morning." Maggie could generate a lot of sympathy from her sons when she talked pitiful like that.

Len was reading the paper, not paying much mind to her. "Pa said he'd been getting the fire started in the stove. I believe he makes coffee the way you like it, hot and strong."

"I know he does, son, but your pa is suffering with his joints, too. What we need is another woman around, a girl who's got some gumption."

"What about Will? He'll be coming home one of these days. He'll probably bring some little filly from up north with him."

Maggie adjusted her upper plate, trying to think of a better argument. "Will's always cared more about cars than girls. I thought you'd be the first to marry."

Len had laughed. "Don't you think I should get me a girl first, Mama?"

"Yes, I know, son. What about that little girl you spent so much time with up there in—where was it?"

"Greensboro. You can forget that one," he said absently, his nose in the paper.

"I know, she wasn't the right one, son, but you need to be thinking about it. How about those Devane girls? Everyone of them is pretty as a picture." She smiled, thinking he was mentally reviewing their faces along with her. He turned the page. She reached over and touched him on the knee. He looked up. "Listen, son, you're a good-looking boy. You could have most any girl in the county."

Len closed up the paper and put it on the table. He leaned forward, his elbows on his knees, and looked her straight in the eye. "Mama, I'll get married someday, I know I will. But right now, I don't know a soul I'd want to ask. When I do, you'll be the first to know." He started to get up, but she put her hand out to him. "What about Millie McBryde?"

"Mama, she's my cousin!"

"I know, son, but she's only your second cousin. Lots of folks marry their second cousins."

Len sighed and looked at her tenderly. "Mama, I know you've got my best interests at heart, but right now courting's the furthest thing from my mind."

What he didn't tell her—what he *couldn't* tell her was that he'd thought of little else since Mr. Hugh had talked to him about it. He should be settling down, getting married, raising a little family. Courting someone might take awhile. He'd need to build a house, carve out a few acres that were his alone. You couldn't ask a woman to marry you if you didn't have a place of your own. But he had no intention of announcing his plans to his mama or anyone else. Not until he'd found the right girl.

CHAPTER 5

AUGUST—BLADEN COUNTY, NORTH CAROLINA

The last of the tobacco was in the curing barn when Len tried to explain it to Tate one more time. "It's about supply and demand," he said. "If there's not as much tobacco available, the prices will go up and farmers will get more."

"That don't make a damn bit of sense to me."

"The government says it does, Pa. We can grow tobacco, just not as much of it. The best part is we'll get paid not to plant."

"I don't like somebody telling me what I can do and what I can't. I'd rather plant how much I want to and take my chances."

"Look, Pa, Ray Wilkins says we're going to get seventeen or eighteen dollars an acre for our allotments this year."

Tate had gone along with it because he didn't want to fight with Len. Watching and listening to Len made him feel old-fashioned and slow, but he was too tired to do things his own way. Len had told Tate how Hugh MacRae had leaned on him again. "He said every one of them houses on Penderlea are going to need a pump. He told me if I was to go live over yonder in one of them, I could farm my ten acres and make enough to send money home to you and Mama."

"Sounds like a bribe to me, son. You don't reckon he's just trying to set you up so's you'll come work for him."

"No, sir. I think he's genuine as the day is long. He's just got this crazy idea that our farms are too big. I reckon he's right to a certain extent." To Len's way of thinking, there were lots of things Mr. Hugh MacRae was touting that made sense, not the least of which was a new start. A little house with electricity and running water—a barn and a henhouse—and only ten acres to plow and plant was just what a young farmer needed. A man would want that if he was married and starting a family.

⁓

Tate knew Len was thinking about it, but he figured it would be awhile before Len reached the point where he'd take a wife. There weren't hardly any eligible girls around. He tried to imagine Len in Penderlea married with a house and barn, pigs in a hog lot—chickens running around the yard. *Hummph! If only it was that easy,* he thought, reflecting back to the time in Onslow County when he had built his own first home. Every board in it was hewn and sawn right there on the land his grandfather had been granted by the state of North Carolina. Nobody had told Tate he had to get married to have it. A man took a wife when he was ready. But that was in a day when men had pride, when wealth had to do with providing for your family. Nowadays, it was all about handouts, about being poor enough to get one.

⁓

Tate sat on the side of the bed, still as a mouse. "What is it, Tate? Go back to bed," Maggie said. "I didn't get a minute's rest last night with you snoring."

"Hush up, now. Something's wrong out there in the barnyard. I think it's Bess. Don't you hear it?"

Maggie held her breath until she picked up the loud wheezing sound. "What's wrong with her?" she asked in a whisper.

"I don't know. Might be one of them wildcats from over in the swamp after her. I'd better go see," Tate said, pulling on his pants over his night shirt. He reached for his gun in the corner of the bedroom. The temperature had been in the nineties in the daytime for the last two weeks, and the nights hadn't been much cooler. In the heat old Bess had been moving more and more slowly. She was ornery, too, even on her best days. But mules were like that. *Like some members of my family*, Tate thought. You had to love them even for their failings. Len was already out the screen door, heading across the backyard. Tate followed close behind. "She sounds like she's crying, Pa!" Len said.

They found Bess on the ground, her head near the watering trough. "Aw, Bess, git up," Tate said, tears in his eyes. Bess raised her head slightly and let it drop again. A whinny escaped from deep inside her. "What's wrong, shug? Git up now, you know you can do it," Tate said. He stood a little ways away from her, giving her room to rise. Buck, the workhorse, snorted and took off across the pasture.

"I don't think she can, Pa. She looks like she's give out."

"No, no, not my Bess. My daddy give her to me when I came to Bladen County. He said she'd outlive me!" Bess had been around as long as Len could remember. Nobody had been able to do much with her except Tate, who had more patience with her than with his own wife. Out in the field, his steady *Gee, Haw, Whoa*, meant he was having a good day with the old mule. Like a ringmaster in a circus, Tate could get Bess to do most anything.

Tate was on the ground now, his head against the mule's head. Bess took a deep snorting breath and exhaled, sinking deeper and deeper into the dust of the horse lot. "I think she's gone, Pa," Len said.

Tate looked up at him. "What're we going to do now?" he cried. "We'll never find another one like her—not in a million years."

"Maybe, it's best, Pa. I think it's time we got a tractor."

Tate looked up, startled out of his grief. "A tractor? You're thinking a little bit big for your britches, aren't you, son? Even if that allotment money comes through, we'll barely be able to make ends meet this year. We sure can't afford a tractor."

"I'm just saying that's what we need, Pa. I know we can't afford one. If Will was home, it might be different. He'd put one together for us, somehow or another. They've got them with these big ol' balloon tires now. I saw one up at Cotton Cove last week."

Tate recognized Len's dreamy look, one like Maggie Lorena got when she was wishful thinking. "Son, why don't you go on down yonder to Mr. Rob's and ask him if we can borrow his mule to drag Bess out where we can bury her? Buck's all to pieces. You know how high-strung he is."

"You're right about that, Pa. I've seen him spooked before. Might be a day or two before Buck's right again."

Before he left, Len covered the carcass of old Bess with a heavy tarpaulin. Buck had balked mightily when Tate tried to bridle him to lead him out of the corral. "Tell Mr. Rob if he don't mind we'll keep his mule a day or two," Tate called out. "If I can get hold of that horse, I'm going over to work the upper field."

Len waved his hand and set out down the road toward the McBryde place. The three-mile walk would give him a chance to reflect on some of the things he'd had on his mind recently. One of them was Millie McBryde. If she was home, it would be a good chance to look her over again. Mama had brought it up, and he'd be lying if he said he hadn't already thought about courting Millie McBryde. Trouble was, he never saw Millie. After they'd moved back to the country, Millie had finished high school at Long Creek. They were the same age, but Len had finished high school at Cotton Cove. Although the Ryans and the McBrydes only lived three miles apart, they lived in different counties.

Millie was born on Bandeaux Creek, in Bladen County, near Cotton Cove to be exact, but in the early twenties, Rob McBryde had sold his Bandeaux Creek farm land and moved to Wilmington where five of his older children had jobs. The two oldest boys, Hugh and Cal, worked for the Atlantic Coast Line Railroad; their other son Harry, worked for the Coast Line by day and went to law school at night. Rebecca, Millie's oldest sister, was a nurse at James Walker Hospital, and Belle had been a clerk in a store before she left Wilmington to work in Washington, D.C.

Maggie Lorena and Millie's mother, Miss Eva McBryde were first cousins. Mama loved to tell the story about how the McBrydes had run a boarding-house for awhile, but Miss Eva had made Mr. Rob promise that someday he'd bring her back to the country. Mama had told them about Uncle Jasper dying and his house being vacant and all. When the banks failed and Mr. Rob couldn't find work in the city, he'd brought his family back to the country to live in Uncle Jasper's house, honoring the promise he'd made to Miss Eva. Six months after they'd moved in, she died of a stroke.

Rob McBryde sat on the porch, his legs crossed and his feet propped up on one of the triangular posts of the mail order house that Len's uncle Jasper Corbinn had built just before the crash. He watched Len approach, coming up the lane between the young peach trees he and Eva had planted shortly before her death. He hadn't seen much of the Ryan family since then. Eva was the one to keep up with family. The Ryans were her kin, not his. *Looks like he wants something*, Rob thought. *Wonder what 'tis.*

Len threw up his hand. "Howdy, Mr. Rob," he called out.

"Howdy, Len. What're you doing out strolling this early in the day?"

"Not just strolling, Mr. Rob. I come a borrowing."

"Oh? If it's money you're needing, Len, you might as well keep on going. Your uncle Nathan's more likely to have some of that."

Len laughed. "No sir, I didn't come to borrow money. Pa's old mule died this morning, and we could sure use yours for a few days."

"Old Bess died?

"Yes sir, she must've been forty years old."

"Well, I declare. I sure am sorry to hear that. I hear tell her and my Jim came from the same mule trader over in Burgaw. Might've even had the same papa."

"I didn't know that."

Rob got up and stretched. "Well, come on around back and I'll get him for you." The frail old man took the steps gingerly. He looked mighty poorly to Len with his stooped back and unsteady gait. "One good turn deserves another," Rob said. "Zeb Corbinn gave me that mule when we moved here. I don't have much use for old Jim until it's time to plant my collards. Just keep him up there at your house. I'll let you know when I need him back."

"We'd be much obliged, Mr. Rob," Len said. "You getting along alright?"

"Fair to middling, son, fair to middling."

"I haven't seen Miss Millie since the—ah—the funeral," Len said. "How's she doing?"

"Millie's doing good," he said, his eyes watering up. "She's trying to take the place of her mama, you know. Works too hard. I sent her and Vera up to Wilmington yesterday. Rebecca's going to take them to the beach."

"Well, you tell her I said hello. Maybe I'll come down to see her sometime."

"You do that, son. She needs to be with some people her age. I told her that."

CHAPTER 6

Maggie questioned Len up one side and down the other about his errand down to the McBryde place. "You mean Millie wasn't even there?"

"No, ma'am. Mr. Rob said she'd gone to Wilmington to visit her sisters," Len said.

"Well, I declare. You'll just have to go back, son."

"Mama, I didn't go down there to visit Millie. I just went to borrow that mule."

"I know, son, but you could've killed two birds with one stone."

But Maggie Lorena was determined to get the two cousins together. The following week, on the first Sunday in September, she asked Len to take them to Singletary Lake where several of the area churches held their baptisms once a year. It was a big affair with picnic tables spread with a lavish assortment of country fare from chicken to chitterlings, every vegetable that had been cooked or canned, and an assortment of sweets that would require a taste of all. The Depression had wreaked havoc with what little people had in their bank accounts, but in the country good eatings were seldom in short supply.

Singletary Lake was a popular place for baptisms in the summer. One of Bladen County's bay lakes, it was cold and deep in places, but along the shore in the shallows, the dark brown tannic water was warm as a baby's bath. A quick dunk by a preacher with a strong arm was pleasant beyond its spiritual purposes on a hot day. After the services, most of the children present would slip out of their Sunday clothes and dash into the water to play.

The Ryans started out early that morning in the two-wheeled farm cart that served multiple purposes in a time when gas was unaffordable. Len had piled in several quilts and a couple of straight chairs along with the basket of food Maggie Lorena had prepared.

"I can pull up under those trees over there, and you won't even have to get out of the wagon, Mama."

"No, son, I want to be up close," she said. "You bring the chairs, and I'll show you where. Your pa's going to want to stretch out in the wagon before long."

"I see a good spot right there by the water's edge, Mama," Len said, helping her down from the wagon.

Maggie trudged along behind him using her parasol as a walking cane. She'd worn a long pale pink dress with a wide collar trimmed in matching lace. Her hat matched perfectly. Len often wondered at the stylish clothes that his mother wore, gifts he reckoned from Miss Abigail who always sent a new shirt for the boys and Tate as well. "Where's your pa?" Maggie asked. "He's got my fan."

"He's coming. He had to give the vittles we brought to the ladies who're putting things out." Len arranged the two chairs near the lake under a tree whose branches dripped long beards of gray Spanish moss into the water. Honeysuckle and wild azalea scented the air with a sweet perfume. "There you are, almost like being on your porch at home, isn't it, Mama?" Maggie sat down heavily, her large frame a bit too wide for the small chair. Len watched as the chair legs sank into the soft sand. She reached up and patted him on the cheek.

"I declare, son, you are such a good boy, always looking after Mama." When the services began, she tugged at Len's sleeve. "Look, son, that's Jeff Pridgen with the fiddle." A tall, slender, bearded man stepped up to the makeshift podium. Len had only met Jefferson Pridgen once before, but his deceased brother, Wash Pridgen, was a legend in the Ryan household. Maggie Lorena's frequent recollections of her days at BFU, later known as Meredith College, always included a tearful mention of Wash. Without so much as a glance toward her husband, she'd recall the love of her life with suggestive remarks as to his romantic approaches. Tate, more often than not, would shake his head and mumble that Wash was "that damn fool who stepped in a bear trap and blew his own head off!"

Jeff Pridgen lifted his fiddle to his chin and began singing "Shall We Gather at the River." The congregation followed his lead, sending a call to come forth throughout the dark woods that even hidden critters would find hard to resist. When Jeff ended the song, he bowed low and stepped back while the preacher from French's Creek made the call for all who were to be baptized to line up along the water's edge. "Come all ye fainthearted sinners as Brother Pridgen leads us again in singing *Just as I Am*." This time, instead of lifting his fiddle to his chin, Jeff Pridgen sang the invitational hymn a capella in a sweet high voice. Women, men, and young adults gathered, forming a line of gossamer white along the water's edge where the preacher waited.

Len had been baptized in this very spot when he was twelve years old, but he was mesmerized by the quiet beauty of the plaintive call and the line of people dressed in white who answered. To his surprise, Millie McBryde was the last person and the eldest in a line that began with the youngest candidates. Just in front of her was her twelve-year-old sister, Vera. Maggie tugged at Len's sleeve again and pointed to Millie. He bent to hear her whisper, "Poor girl hasn't been baptized yet because she took care of her dear mother all those years," she said. "There will be stars in her crown."

Len watched Millie's graceful steps as the line proceeded. She had her hands on Vera's shoulders. They were pretty hands, and he wondered if she played the piano. She reached up to brush away a flurry of gnats and revealed the slight curve of her breasts. *I wouldn't call that "skinny,"* he thought. His hands could reach around her waist! He kept his eyes on her. Every now and then, she attempted to push a wayward dark curl back underneath a broad white band that kept her hair off her face. *She is defi-nitely the prettiest one among her sisters*, he thought. In her flowing white dress, she looked like an angel—one he might want to ask to marry him.

⁓

When Vera McBryde sprang out of the water, she touched Millie's hand as she passed. Millie hesitated at the water's edge. "Come on, sister, there's nothing to be afraid of," the preacher said. "The Lord is holding thy hand." Millie continued timidly until she could reach out and touch his hand. The preacher guided her slowly, gently, until he had her in his arms. "You may hold your nose, sister," he said. She took a deep breath and pinched her nostrils closed. "I baptize thee in the name of the Father, the Son, and the Holy Ghost," the preacher said. He rocked her back until she was under water, then stood her up in one swift motion. Millie sputtered and the preacher gave her a little push toward the shore. "God bless you, sister," he said. The singing began again and the crowd started to move toward the food tables, but Len never took his eyes off Millie, whose white dress, stained a dark tan color from the lake water, clung to every curve of her slender body.

⁓

"You need to get out of that dress right now, Millie McBryde," Rebecca said. "It'll be ruined."

"I told you this would happen, Becca. I don't know why I had to be baptized anyway. I'm too old."

Rebecca put her arms around her sister. "You're never too old to be baptized, honey," she said. "Besides, I promised Mama."

Millie looked down at the stained dress. "Why couldn't it have been at White Lake like everybody else's in the family?"

"Singletary is a little closer," Rebecca said. "You're lucky they didn't have the baptism at Longview on Black River. It's full of snakes."

"Ooo," Millie said. "I'm scared to death of snakes."

"Look, there's Len Ryan. Go get out of that dress before he comes over here. You look downright vulgar."

Millie ducked into the bathhouse carrying a small satchel. Vera had worn a white blouse and a pair of culottes that she could wear to play in the water. Millie would need to soak both of their outfits overnight in the big Jasper tub to remove the stains. She loved having the big tub with hot and cold running water, she thought, slipping into a new dress she'd made just for the occasion.

Vera charged into the bathhouse. "Len Ryan's looking for you, Millie. Hurry up!"

"Well, he can wait just a minute," Millie said, adjusting her dry clothes.

"Hurry up!" Vera shouted from the doorway.

"What in the world is the hurry?" Millie said as she followed Vera out and came face to face with Len. "Oh, hey. I didn't know you were looking for me." He seemed taller, more grown up than she remembered. His red hair was darker, more brown than red, and he had combed it into sort of a pompadour. One loose curl hung down on his forehead.

Len laughed. "I saw you go in. Just thought I'd wait and speak to you."

"Yes, you did," Vera said. "I told you he was."

Millie narrowed her eyes and smiled. "Run and play, Vera," she said. "Have you had lunch?" she asked, turning back to Len. "Rebecca brought fried chicken."

"So did a lot of other people, including Mama," Len said. "There's enough fried chicken over there to feed an army."

Millie laughed. "Why does everybody say that. Who's ever seen an army fed?"

"I don't know, but come on, let's go get you a plate. We'll sit down by the water and catch up."

Avoiding his parents, Len led Millie along a path that circled the lake until they found a large rock that jutted out over the water. She followed along behind him aware that there'd be talk about them going off together, but she didn't care. Len was her cousin, and she had every intention of doing just what he said—getting caught up. The last time she'd seen him had been at her mother's funeral. He'd hugged her and said he was sorry, holding her in his thick arms, her head against his chest, rocking her a little. There'd been nothing more to it than that.

"Oh, this is a pretty place," Millie said. Len sat on the large rock and reached for her hand, his smiley brown eyes looking at her like he could eat her with a spoon. She smiled up at him when she took his hand. "Wonder where this big rock came from?"

"Way down under the earth, I guess," Len said. "You know they say all the lakes around here were made from big meteors shooting out of the sky." He reached above his head and let his balled fist fall toward the lake. "Boom! Like that."

She liked to hear him talk. "How long ago, I wonder?"

"At least a million years." He was staring at her as if seeing her for the first time. "Say, where've you been hiding yourself? Don't see you around much anymore."

Millie blushed. She'd always liked Len, but he'd never made her feel all jittery inside. He was doing that now. "I've been to Wilmington a lot this summer. Most of my friends are still there."

"They are? Who's that? Anybody I know?"

"I don't think so. Just some girls I knew in high school. Agatha and Mandy don't come back anymore since Miss Emily—since Miss Emily moved back to Onslow County." She didn't tell him about the boys, some like Rusty Ruark she'd hoped to see but didn't. She couldn't tell Len about that.

"I was wondering if you might like to go to the river sometime. A bunch of us are going swimming next Saturday."

"Do I know them?"

"There might be one or two there you went to school with." He reached out and pulled her close to him. "But I'll protect you."

Millie laughed and pulled away. "Is Hill Corbinn going? If he is, I'm not going."

"You're not going if Hill goes? Hill's my cousin and my best friend!"

"Yes, but he's got that motorcycle, and he's always trying to get me to go for a ride with him," Millie said. "I did it one time, and he liked to scared me to death."

He pulled her close again. She could feel the heat of him through his lawn shirt. "Like I said, 'I'll protect you, honey chile.'" He would have kissed her—she was sure of it, but someone was coming along the path and she stood up quickly, knocking her plate into the lake. When Len tried to reach for the plate, he slipped and toppled in. "Goddamn, look what you made me do!" he shouted, splashing around in the water.

"Len, I'm so sorry," she called out. "Give me your hand, I'll pull you out."

"I'll get him," a voice said behind her. Millie looked around to see Len's cousin Hill behind her. "On second thought, let's all go in," he said, plunging into the water with Millie in tow.

⌒

That evening, as she put their clothes into the Jasper tub to soak, she felt different. Something was happening between her and Len. She wasn't sure she wanted it to. They were cousins—just friends. But she'd been so lonely—so unloved since Mama died. Rusty had promised to find her again, but she couldn't wait around forever.

CHAPTER 7

Rusty Ruark had dropped out of Millie's life the summer of Amanda Evans's wedding when Millie had refused to go to the beach with him. He'd been drinking. Besides, Len was there and she'd been having too much fun at the reception. Rusty hadn't called her or come by the rest of the summer. She'd heard that he'd gone to Carolina. Then the bottom had fallen out, and she'd gone to work full-time with Miss Emily McAllister.

She'd seen Rusty from a distance in Wilmington several times after that. Once at the beach and twice downtown. Always, he was with a bunch of boys. Each time, their eyes had met in brief acknowledgment. Then she'd heard that he'd dropped out of Carolina.

Just before her family had moved back to the country, when they were living in the small Red Cross Street house and Millie was supporting the family on her small salary from the hat shop, she'd heard the jingle of the shop door bells, and peeped through the bead curtain and saw Rusty examining a hat. It was something she'd imagined, maybe even expected to happen one day.

"May I help you?" she asked him. He turned toward her, and she'd wanted to run to him and throw her arms around him. Instead, she spoke to him from the doorway to the workroom, one hand holding back the bead curtain. "Oh, hey, Rusty."

"Hey, Millie."

"I thought that was you," she said.

"Yep, it's me," he said, running his hand through wavy auburn hair. He was thin, much older looking, his face lined and his catlike green eyes sunken into dark hollows. A fastidious dresser when she had known him earlier, his jacket was rumpled and his shirt damp with sweat. A burgundy silk tie hung loose under his collar, looking as if it had been wrung out by hand. "I heard you still worked here. Thought I'd stop by and say hello—just for old times' sake."

"I've seen you at a distance," she said. "Are you still mad at me?"

Rusty laughed, and for a moment he was the eighteen-year-old boy whom she'd dated the summer of Amanda Evans's wedding. "You've grown up," he said, looking her up and down. Millie had never lacked for nice clothes, even with the Depression going on. Emily saw to that. Her problem was that she had nowhere to wear them except to work. When she didn't answer, he said, "I guess I have, too."

"No," she said, flustered. "You look just the same. I mean, you look nice." She turned away to keep him from seeing her blush, moving about the shop, arranging and rearranging the brightly colored hats that sat cocked this way and that on dull-faced mannequins. "Are you still in school?"

"No, I had to drop out. I'm working in Wilmington. Law school will have to wait." She detected bitterness in his voice. "My dad blew everything we had in the stock market."

"My brother Harry is a lawyer."

"I know. I see him all the time at the courthouse."

"You work at the courthouse?"

"Just in a government office," he said. "Nothing special."

"I remember how much you wanted to be a lawyer. Maybe you can do what Harry did. Go to night school?"

He turned and stared out the shop window. "My dad left my mom, she—" His shoulders sagged and his chest heaved. "She's sort of gone off the deep end. My brother and sister, they . . . I have to take care of them."

"I'm so sorry, Rusty. I didn't know. Things are not the same with me, either." She could tell him all that had gone on in her life, but nothing seemed as bad as what he was going through. She reached out to touch his arm, and he swung around and grabbed her, holding her so tightly that she gasped for breath. "Rusty, let me go, please."

He released her and moved toward the door. "I'm sorry, Millie. I shouldn't have come. I just felt like I needed to see you, needed to see someone who remembered what it was like when…"

"Wait, Rusty. I'm glad you came. It's just that you caught me by surprise. I didn't know about your father or your mother. When I thought about you, I figured you were finishing up college—maybe even married by now."

"You're the only girl I ever thought about marrying." His mood was suddenly dark. "But you went off with that hick at Mandy's wedding and I—"

There, she thought, *that's the Rusty I remember—cocky, sarcastic.* Maybe she liked him better that way.

"He was my cousin. I was a lot younger than you," she said. "You were drinking. You wanted me to—" She was stammering, and he stared at her.

"I was pretty bad, wasn't I?"

"I liked you a lot."

"Do you still?"

"I'm glad you came to see me," she said, her voice trembling. She tried to smile. "But I don't know if I still like you."

He looked at her askance. "Not even a little bit?" It was a game he'd played often, turning aside her disapproval by teasing her.

"Miss Emily is closing the shop tomorrow. I'm taking a new job at Belk-Williams. We may have to move back to the country."

"Why would you do that?"

"Papa promised Mama…."

"No!" he shouted, taking hold of her arm. "If you leave Wilmington, I may never see you again."

"Rusty, there's nothing I'd rather do than to stay here in Wilmington, but they need me to help—to hold things together for Vera and Rodney. I'll have to finish high school in the country."

"I see," he said, his mouth turned down. "We're in the same boat." He put his arms around her loosely and kissed her lightly on the lips. "I'm sorry, I guess I thought I was the only one whelmed over by life." She wanted him to kiss her again. "What's the use?" he said. "Nobody seems to have any control over their lives right now." He let her hand slide out of his and started for the door. "See you around," he said with a small salute. The door swung closed behind him, and she watched him go down the street until she could no longer see him.

The day her family moved back to the country, Harry told Rusty that Millie and his parents were moving that afternoon. Rusty ran all the way from Harry's office to the house on Red Cross Street. Millie had laughed when, out of breath, he thrust a piece of paper at her with his address on it. "Write me," he said.

After they'd settled into the Jasper Corbinn house, Millie wrote and told Rusty how much it had meant to her when he stopped by the shop. She told him about their house in the country and the county high school at Long Creek. She'd wanted to say more—like how she'd never had another steady boyfriend—like how she'd saved a box of little things he'd given her—a ring twisted into shape from a foil gum wrapper, a dried corsage of carnations from the junior-senior prom. But she decided that would sound forward. She'd wait to hear from him first. She never did.

CHAPTER 8

After Millie had graduated from high school at Long Creek, Rob McBryde pleaded with her to go on back to Wilmington. "You're eighteen years old," he said. "You ought to be with people your own age, shug. You stay down here in the country with me and you won't never find yourself a beau." She'd told him she didn't need a beau—she wanted to help him—help Rodney and Vera.

"Those young'uns are big enough to do for themselves," Rob said. "Eva never intended for them to be waited on hand and foot."

But they need a mother, someone to get them up in the morning... someone to tuck them in at night, she thought. Vera was only a little twelve-year-old girl. Rodney was sixteen and wild as a hare. "I don't want to go back to Wilmington, Papa," she'd said. "My home is here, with you." She'd felt so grown-up saying that.

But at the same time that Len began to show an interest in her, things changed that summer. Rebecca, her oldest sister, asked Vera to come and live with her and Mr. Jones. Then, Rodney declared that he was quitting school and signing up with the new Civilian Conservation Corps. Millie was horrified—thought that her father would be too. But he'd surprised her by taking it in stride. He said Rodney understood that times were hard. He had a right to do his part to keep them off relief.

Whether she wanted to admit it or not, Millie felt like a bird out of a cage. Here she was at courting age, someone was interested in her, and there was nothing to keep her from showing a little interest herself. That was not to say she had any intention of marrying the first guy who came along, meaning Len of course, but it was nice to be courted under any circumstances.

⌒

Len Ryan had already crossed that bridge. Having a girlfriend—someone who thought he was the cat's meow—changed his perspective on some things—like Penderlea, for instance. When he stepped into Ray Wilkin's office and saw a large map of Penderlea pinned up on the wall, he felt as if he'd been struck by lightning. "Damn, that's something else, isn't it?" he said to Ray.

"Sure as hell is," the county agent said. "North Carolina has never seen anything like it."

Len traced the outline of the horseshoe-shaped plan with his finger, stopping in the center. "Look how it's laid out—just like a city map." He turned his head this way and that, examining the roads and the small farms drawn in the plan. "You been over there yet?"

"Hell, yes," Ray said. "It's the damndest thing you've ever seen. There's these bulldozers and tractors all over the place, digging ditches and strewing trees around like in a stew pot. I wouldn't of set my foot out of the truck. There was snakes everywhere. I couldn't tell what was what, but they say Hugh MacRae has already selected some of the homesteaders."

"He has?"

"Hell, yes, he's over there right now building some temporary office buildings and such. They're even going to have a Civilian Conservation Corps camp to help with the construction. After the roads get built, they're going to start building the houses."

Len tried not to sound too excited. "But did you see any of the farms? What does the soil look like?"

"They ain't even got the roads built yet. It won't nothing but swamp and woods," Ray said. "A few old places scattered here and there. They say a long time ago, Indians camped there on their way to the coast each year. The only dry land was this hill where they found arrowheads and pieces of pots. I saw 'em in the project manager's office."

"Did you see Mr. Hugh?"

"Nope, he won't there the day I went. This fellow that runs the office said he was there most every other day." He looked askance at Len. "What you so interested in it for? I don't need to remind you that your daddy's counting on you. Besides, you ain't even eligible unless you're married and got a passel of young'uns."

"Just curious," Len said. "That's all."

That's about the time that Len Ryan started coming around to see Millie more and more. Sometimes he was on the motorcycle with Hill Corbinn. They'd pull up into the yard, cut the engine, and wait for her to come out. One time he was in a long wagon, hauling a load of late corn to his Uncle Nathan's. Said he just stopped by to say hello. "I brought you and your pa some corn, too," he said, handing her a toe sack of sweet-smelling roasting ears. Impulsively, Millie had asked him to stay for supper. He'd done so without the least bit of hesitation.

That Saturday evening, as he'd promised, he drove up in a big three-axle truck. She'd been sitting on the porch with her father shelling peas. A crowd of boys and girls she knew from school were hanging out the back of the truck. "We're going swimming over at Longview," Len said. "Come on and go." She'd jumped up and almost spilled the peas out of the blue enameled colander she held in her lap.

"Papa, is it alright?"

Rob surveyed the truck and its six or seven occupants, not especially pleased with the sight of some older boys. "Y'all wouldn't be drinking any hard stuff, would you, fellas?"

"No, sir, we're not into that," Len said.

"No, siree," another boy called out.

At the time, they weren't. But by the time they'd reached Longview on Black River, the jar of whiskey had been passed around a couple of times. Millie was furious. "You told Papa you didn't have any liquor," she said.

"Aw, honey, this isn't liquor. This is fine whiskey, made right here in Bladen County."

After the girls changed into swimsuits under the tarp-covered back of Rupert's truck, the crowd swam and played all afternoon in Black River. The swimming area had been cleared and white sand brought in to make a beach. Along the riverbanks on either side, trees dipped their branches into the tannic water. In places, fallen trees provided a resting place for turtles and snakes. As pretty as it was, Millie had never liked the river, preferring the clear water of White Lake instead. Len tried to get her to take hold of a long vine and swing out over the water and drop into the dark river. She'd told him she couldn't swim, and that was no lie. She also refused to take a drink of the white lightning that he continued to offer her. When the light of day began to fade, Millie reminded Len that she'd promised her father she'd be home before dark.

"C'mon, Millie, that's when the fun begins. Mr. Newby left us some hot dogs, and we're going to roast them over a fire." One eye drooped slightly and his complexion blazed red, more from the drink, she suspected, than from the sun.

"I can't, Len. I told Papa—"

Len had grabbed the keys from Rupert Hicks and told her to get in the truck. On the way, he said she was "no damn fun," that she'd embarrassed him in front of his friends. "Taking a drink now and then never hurt anybody," he said.

Millie shivered, wet and cold, clutching her dry things to her chest. When they reached the McBryde place, she jumped out of the truck and ran into the house without saying good-bye. She never expected to see Len again, but the next morning, he'd walked the three miles between their houses to apologize.

When she told Rebecca about it at Sunday dinner the next weekend, her sister had laughed. "You should have *pretended* to take a drink. That's what I do. Mr. Jones hates it when I won't take a drink with him."

"I don't like to pretend, Becca. Besides, I'm not sure I even like Len that much."

"I'm not meaning to sound like Belle, little sister, but I don't see a whole lot of other boys hanging around your door."

"I know. Maybe I should go back to Wilmington and live with you."

"If you wouldn't mind sharing a room with Vera."

Millie thought about it. "No, I'm not going to do anything as long as Papa needs me. I'd like to come more often though. Have you been downtown lately?

"Vera and I went to the Bijou last Saturday. We saw a triple feature—at least Vera did. I'd worked the night shift and couldn't stay awake."

"Did you walk by the Beau Monde—you know, Miss Emily's hat shop?

"Of course we did, but it's still all boarded up. Why'd you ask?"

"I don't know. I just think about what it would be like to live there again—to have a little hat shop of my own."

"Why, Millie, honey. I didn't know you'd even thought about such a thing."

Millie laughed. "Just wishful thinking. I'd need a rich husband first, and like you said, there aren't a lot of boys hanging around my door. Besides, Papa would be so lonely without anyone here but him."

Rebecca put her arms around Millie. "You're lonely, aren't you?"

"I have a few friends. Len's not bad. I think he's kinda cute in a countrified way."

"Watch out now, little sister, those country boys can be awful fresh. I'd hate for you to get knocked up and *have* to marry him."

"Becca! Don't say such a thing!"

Since they'd lived in the country, Millie had started attending the small Bethlehem Church in Colly where all the Corbinns had gone for a hundred years or more. The cemetery was practically nothing but Corbinns and Moores. There were a few Keiths scattered about here and there, but the Corbinns claimed the majority of the gravesites. Rob McBryde was not one to go to church on a Sunday, especially since Eva died. But Millie felt it was important for her to go even without him. Most Sundays, she'd start out walking and meet up with Cousin Kate and Cousin Nathan Hill, who had a wagon load of children like stair steps. They'd make room for Millie, and she'd ride several miles to the church with all of them packed in like sardines.

Len usually arrived late in the company of a bunch of boys who'd rounded up his crowd in a truck of some sort. You could hear them coming a mile down the road. Millie stood on the steps to the church with two of the Hill girls watching them unload. "They may as well not even come in the church," Geraldine Hill said. "One or two of them always sneak out for a smoke during the service."

"Look at Len," her sister Sadie said. "He's the cutest one. I wish he wasn't my first cousin." Len looked around until his gaze stopped on Millie. His eyes lit up and he headed over toward her. "Hummn, I think he's looking for you, Millie," Sadie said.

"Oh, you know Len," she said, "he's always friendly."

"What? Aunt Lorena told Mama that he's got a terrible temper. She told her he has these tantrums and throws things."

"Well, I've never seen it," Millie said. "He's always sweet as pie to me." She turned and smiled at Len as he approached. "Hush, now, don't let him know we're talking about him."

"I declare, just look at all these pretty girls standing on the church steps," Len said. "I might have to take one of you inside and sweet talk you right under the preacher's nose." He burst out laughing. "Which one's it going to be?" he asked, pretending to look them over.

"Cut out that mess, Len Ryan," Geraldine said. "We know who you want to sit with."

"You do?" He turned to Millie. "Why, here she is. Good morning, Miss Millie. How're you today?" He removed his hat and bowed a little. "Might I have the pleasure of your company for church services today?"

"You'll have to stay for the whole service," Millie said. "No sneaking out for a smoke."

"Well, gol dern, I don't know if I like that or not," he said, his eyes twinkling. "But I don't imagine I'll be able to leave the side of such a sweet girl anyhow. What d'you say? Let's go in and see what happens."

Millie really liked Len. He could be so funny with his quick wit and expressive eyes that danced over her when he cracked a joke. In church that day, he had reached for her hand and held it all during the service. If she hadn't liked it, she would have pulled her hand away.

After church, Len's aunt Kate invited Millie and Len to Sunday dinner. "I'll send one of the boys down in the wagon to get Mr. Rob. I've been wanting to have y'all to dinner for some time."

"Thank you, Cousin Kate. That's mighty kind of you."

At the house, Geraldine handed Millie an apron, and they went into the kitchen to help get the meal on the table. Cousin Kate had a big roast of beef in the oven and a pot of beans and Irish potatoes already cooked. "I'll make a pan of biscuits, and one of you girls can make some Johnny cakes," she said. "Sadie, you open those jars of succotash." A third teenage daughter, Katherine, set a long table that ran almost the full length of a screened-in porch.

Outside, the weather was warm and bright, typical October with the sun not too hot, but warm enough for shirtsleeves. The younger children, four boys, chased about in the well-swept yard, climbing trees and swinging on long ropes. The Hills were a typical country family, Millie thought, with lots of children, a big house, and plenty of food to go on the table. Len said that his Uncle Nathan might be gone two or three weeks at a time on well-drilling jobs, but Aunt Kate kept the home fires burning.

That evening, Millie lay awake thinking about what a life might be like with Len in the country. He was coming on pretty strong. Aunt Kate had taken her aside and said she wanted to put a bug in her ear. "Sister told me that Len asked her to talk to Dr. Bayard. See what he thought about him marrying his second cousin."

Somebody better be asking me, Millie thought. She liked Len well enough, but she'd always seen herself marrying someone like Rusty Ruark. If not him, someone *like* him and living in a small house in Wilmington. She might even have that little hat shop down on Front Street. She was only nineteen. She wasn't in a hurry to get married.

As if her own doubts weren't enough, she got up the nerve to ask Rob McBryde what he thought of Len courting her. At first, Rob hedged a little. "There were some other fellows that used to come around in Wilmington," he said.

"That was a while ago, Papa. I haven't lived there for over a year."

"I just hate to see you put all your eggs in one basket," he said.

"Don't you like Len?

"He's alright."

"Just alright?"

"Look here, shug. Len's your cousin. You can't help who you're kin to, but you sure don't have to—" He'd stopped short of saying "marry them."

"We're just friends, Papa. You said you wanted me to have friends."

"I did, shug. I sure did," he said, looking a little rattled. "Now, you go on and have your fun. Your mama would want that."

But Millie had known then that Papa had some doubts about Len. She had some, too.

CHAPTER 9

NOVEMBER 1933

Her birthday was on Saturday. She'd be nineteen. Four days later, Len would be twenty. Millie decided to ask Len to spend the afternoon with her and stay for supper. "I'll make us a cake. You can help me. We'll celebrate together," she said.

"I don't know much about making cakes," Len said.

"Well, it's time you learned," Millie said as she tied an apron on him. "All of my brothers know how to cook. Not that they do much of it."

"I'll just sit here and watch if you don't mind," he said, taking a chair at the table.

"Alright," Millie said. "I learned how just watching. I guess you can, too."

Millie wore a pretty little frock, one she'd made by putting together several patterns. She did that real often and liked the way she could make her dresses fit her perfectly. The fabric was gingham, woven into a maroon and black plaid, a piece she'd found in Eva's sewing chest, a huge wood storage box left over from the days when Papa had a store in Bandeaux Creek. Around the neckline and down the buttoned front, she'd piped it with white poplin. She'd made a sash to match and tied a band of the fabric around her head, allowing her black curls to fall over her face.

Len watched her closely as Millie placed a pound of butter in a large mixing bowl that her mother had always used for her cakes. The bowl was cream colored with a brown stripe around the rim. Just the feel of it in her hands brought back memories of her mother. As she rubbed the butter into three cups of sugar, Millie watched Len out of the corner of her eye. "Did you ever watch Cousin Maggie Lorena make a cake?"

"Not hardly," Len said, laughing. "Mama never liked me and Will around much when she was cooking."

"No wonder you don't know much about cooking," Millie said. After she'd added the eggs, one at the time, she added the flour and milk, alternately, ending with the flour.

"Why can't you just dump everything in there all at once?" Len asked.

"Because that's not how Mama did it," Millie laughed.

"What kind of cake is it?"

"What kind of cake do you want? I meant to ask you that. The batter is all the same."

"How about caramel? That's my favorite," Len said, licking his lips.

"Mine, too."

"Looks like you're beating the devil out of it now," he said. "You want me to tell you some more about Penderlea while you're doing that?"

"Sure, when I'm finished, you can lick the bowl."

"I'm going to go over there and see it when I get me a truck," he said.

Millie buttered three round cake pans and cut circles of brown paper to go in them. "I can't believe they'd give you a house and everything to go in it, just like that."

"Oh, you'll have to pay for it after you get the farm producing. Mr. Hugh MacRae's got it all figured out."

"I heard his name a lot when I lived in Wilmington," Millie said. After pouring the batter evenly into the three pans, scraping the bowl clean, she held up her hand. "Want to lick my fingers?"

Len smiled. Taking one finger at the time, he licked each one while holding his eyes on hers. When he finished, Millie stood there as if unable to move. He moved in closer and started to kiss her, but she pushed him away.

"I'd better wash my hands and get these pans in the oven, or else we won't have that cake."

Len sat down in his chair. "I'd say I've already had my cake—gonna get to eat it too," he chuckled.

While the cake baked, Millie fried chicken in a black iron skillet and put on a pot of rice to boil. They'd also have sweet potatoes and collards, a mainstay of their diet when fresh vegetables were no longer available. Len excused himself to go out in the yard and talk to Cal and Rob. Cal spent most weekends in the country. Millie thought it was as much to free her up as it was to visit with his father. There were always chores to be done around the small five-acre farm, chores Rob was no longer able to do. Earlier in the day, Cal and Rob had straightened up the tool shed and brought in the sweet potatoes to protect them from a frost that was expected before the month was out.

At supper, Len talked of nothing but Penderlea. "You ought to go look at it, Cal. Might be something you'd be interested in."

"Not me," Cal said. "I'm no farmer. Besides I have no intention of getting married anytime soon. What about you?"

"I've thought about it," Len said, "but right now, I've got my work cut out here. Pa and I are signed up for that allotment program. He's turned most everything over to me."

"But if you were married, things might be different?" Cal asked.

"Well, sure," Len stammered. "I might consider it, but until—" He looked at Millie and then at Rob McBryde. "Listen to me, doing all the talking. I declare, Millie, you have put on one fine supper."

"Thank you, Len," Millie said, pushing her chair away from the table. "I'll get everybody a piece of cake. Papa, why don't you and Cal go out on the front porch and I'll bring yours out there? Len, you can help me with the dishes."

When the dishes were done, Millie rummaged in a drawer and found a small candle to put on the cake. "Just for us," she said, lighting it with a kitchen match.

Len laughed. "Don't tell me we're going to sing happy birthday to each other."

"No, we're not, Len. I can't carry a tune in a bucket with a hole in it. Just say it and blow out the candle. No need to even tell them about it," she said, kissing him on the cheek. "Happy birthday, Len."

He kissed her back—on the mouth. Just a sweet little kiss, but the look in his eyes told her that he had more in mind. "Happy birthday, Millie."

Millie took a deep breath. She'd told herself not to get too involved with Len, but she hadn't been able to help herself. She liked him a lot. She might even love him. But things were moving too fast. She needed more time to think about it. After all, they were cousins.

"I'm thinking about getting married," Len said, as if reading her mind.

"Really? Do you have anyone in mind, or are you just contemplating it?"

"Both," he said, a smile curling up the corners of his mouth. Len was such a big tease, but that smile always gave him away. "Would you like to hear more?"

Millie blushed and her heart did a little dance against her ribs. "I guess so. Go take this cake to Papa and Cal so they'll stay out front. I'll get us a glass of milk, and we can sit on the back porch." When Len returned, Millie handed him the milk and she picked up the plates of cake. He held the screen door for her.

"I'll need to speak to him about it sooner or later," Len said.

"Who?"

"Your papa. I'll need to ask him if I can marry you."

The china plate Millie was holding crashed to the floor when she threw her hands up to her face. "Oh?"

Len bent over in front of her and picked up the broken dishes and the caramel cake. "Now, look here, you can't start breaking dishes and all." He put the pieces of dish in the sink and turned around to find Millie sitting down again in a chair at the small kitchen table. She looked as if she might cry. "Are you alright?"

"Len, I don't know what to say. I hadn't thought about us getting married." It was a lie, and he probably knew it.

"Get us another piece of cake, and let's go out on the porch," he said.

Millie brought the cake out and sat down in a small armless rocking chair. Len pulled a larger rocker, the old cane-bottomed one that Rob usually sat in, over close to her. "Looks pretty wore out. Reckon I better not sit in it?"

"It's okay," Millie said. "It's been like that as long as I can remember."

Len ate his cake and drank a full glass of milk while Millie hardly touched hers. When he'd finished, he wiped his mouth on a napkin and sat back in the chair. "You see, I figure it like this. I'm Colly's most eligible bachelor, and you're about the prettiest little girl between here and Bandeaux Creek." He chuckled. "If me and you was to get hitched, we'd make a nice couple, maybe start a little family." He glanced at her to see if she was following him, but Millie was looking off into the distance, her gaze taking in a flock of magpies diving in and out of the hayfield stubble. They were yapping and shouting at one another. She often watched them and wondered why they did that. "You listening?" he asked.

"What?" She turned to give him her undivided attention. "Yes, I'm listening."

"Well, I'm just saying that if we got married, we could…"

"You're not forgetting that we're cousins, are you, Len?"

"Hell, no. That's another thing I was going to tell you. Dr. Bayard told Mama that lots of people marry their second cousins."

"Rebecca says it's not a good idea. Sometimes the children are a little off."

"Mama said Dr. Bayard said he didn't see why—"

"I can't believe Cousin Maggie Lorena talked to him about us," she said, full of indignation.

He stood up and pranced before her. "No, no, you're jumping to conclusions. Mama just asked him about cousins getting married and all. She didn't say who!"

"But she was talking about us, wasn't she?"

Len smiled, his eyes crinkling at the corners. "I reckon Mama thought we were courting pretty heavy. She thought we might be talking about it." He studied her, more serious now. "You do want to talk about it, don't you?"

Millie stood up so quickly that she almost knocked him backward. "I reckon it wouldn't hurt to talk about it, but I..."

Len put his arms around her and squeezed her. "How about this instead of talking," he said, pulling her in closer and touching his lips to hers. He kissed her hard, his breath coming fast, his lips tasting of caramel and vanilla flavoring. Something loosed itself inside her. Something warm and exciting.

Len saw him first. Just the top of his white-haired balding head as Mr. Rob came around the house. He stepped back from Millie in the nick of time, but Millie had not recovered as quickly. Her father stopped on the bottom step and took one look at her. "What're you doing, Millie?"

"Nothing, Papa. We were just coming around there to the front porch. Thought you might want another piece of cake."

"You look like the cat that ate the canary, shug. Why's that?"

Len had backed off from Millie, but he was red-faced, too. "I just asked her to marry me, Mr. Rob. That is, if you don't mind."

Rob ascended the remaining steps slowly. Len thought he looked to be a hundred years old. He went to his chair and plopped down. "I reckon that's up to Millie, Len. She's nineteen years old today. Ought to be able to decide for herself."

Len reached for Millie's hand and pulled her toward him. She put her hand in his and held his arm with the other. "Well, I guess that settles it," Len said. "Let's go tell Cal."

⌐

Later that evening, just after her papa had turned off his bedside lamp, Millie tapped on his door. "Can I talk to you a minute?"

"Come on in," he said. She left the door open and a shaft of light spread across the iron bedstead where he lay under a light coverlet. He was on her mother's side of the bed, and she wondered if he slept there on purpose to feel his deceased wife's closeness.

Millie sat down on the bed beside him. Reclining like that, he looked smaller. "Papa, you like Len, don't you? I mean, you think it's okay to marry him, don't you?"

"He don't have a pot to pee in, but neither do we," he said. "I don't know what he intends to do about it, do you?

"Len says after a year or two, we might move to that place over in Pender County. Len says Mr. MacRae invited him personally. We'd have our own little ten-acre farm."

"Ten acres?" Rob sat up in bed. "That's what he gave those immigrants in Castle Hayne. All they could grow on it was flowers."

"Len says Mr. MacRae talks like Penderlea will be different."

"How?"

"I don't know exactly, but Len says it won't be immigrants this time, it'll be just regular farmers like him. They'll give you your own little house and everything."

"Nobody *gives* away a house and land, shug. You oughta know that."

"But Len says this will be different. Mr. MacRae called it utopia."

"Call it what you will, nobody's giving land and houses away free. Not this day and time." Millie didn't say anything. She'd upset him, and she was sorry. Rob reached out and took her hand. "Shug, all I can say is if you make your bed hard, you're the one's going to have to sleep in it. Just remember that."

CHAPTER 10

They'd decided to marry at Thanksgiving. Millie's family would be there on the holiday, and she'd asked her brother Cal to drive them to Dillon, South Carolina, on Saturday. A real wedding was out of the question. Things might have been different if Eva McBryde had been alive, but as it was, there was simply no money for extra things, and no one really expected it, most of all Millie. They wouldn't be the first couple to cross the state line for their nuptials. With the Depression going on, it was considered the smart thing to do. Two of Zeb Corbinn's daughters had done it in the last year. It wasn't like running away and not telling anybody, although some had sure enough done that when they'd met with opposition from the family. Some girls had good reasons for it.

Belle, Millie's second-oldest sister, had arrived in Wilmington by bus from Washington on Wednesday. Cal had picked her up. She'd slept until eleven o'clock Thanksgiving morning, getting up just in time for a soaking in the Jasper tub before the rest of the crowd from Wilmington arrived. She sat on the kitchen stool in her mother's old pink chenille robe touching up her bright red nail polish. Her hair was perfectly combed and pinched into waves from a center part.

"I can't believe you'd accept living in a camp house, Millie McBryde," Belle said. "Mama would have a fit!"

"I can't see where it makes much difference where we live," Millie said, irritated that she was having to defend Len. "We're just starting out. Len may be a country boy now, but he has plans."

Belle held her littlest finger up and blew on it. "Heap big plans, but no money," she sneered.

Millie juggled the pots and pans on the iron cookstove, making Belle's breakfast while she prepared the holiday feast for her family. *You'd think she was the bride*, Millie thought. She'd barely had enough time herself to slip into a dress and tuck her dark curls beneath a ribbon headband. Belle would be dressed to the nines by dinner time, standing out as a little better off than the rest of them. Actually, Millie was the prettier of the two girls, who favored the McBryde side of the family with their large noses and slightly flared nostrils. Both had beautiful brown eyes and dark, almost black hair. Millie was the taller one with a thin but curvy figure and long graceful legs. Belle was petite and slightly slew-footed, best described as cute, but her smart clothes and beauty tricks made up for any shortcomings. Millie was worried that Len might not be able to resist Belle when she turned on her charms.

She slipped two eggs into a small skillet and scrambled them around with a fork. "Len's not the only one with no money. Nobody has any," she said, scraping the eggs into a plate. "Do you want grits?"

"Sure, with lots of butter."

"I've made some curtains," Millie said. "The camp house looks real nice. You'll have to come see us." Maggie Lorena had insisted that Len fix up the camp house, saying she and Tate had spent many a wonderful night there. Under his breath, Len had expressed some doubt as to the truth of the statement. He said he remembered quite well the scenes in the cramped quarters after the fire had burned Aunt Mag's house down to the ground. But the other option was for the newlyweds to live with Rob McBryde for the time being. Millie had wasted no time in saying she preferred the camp house. The thought of honeymooning in her own bedroom with her father in the next room had embarrassed her no end. Len had insisted that either option would only be temporary.

Belle buttered a biscuit and spread it with bright red strawberry jam. "Can I have a jar of this to take back to Washington? Did Mama make it?"

"No, I made it, and yes you can take a jar back with you. Have you heard about Penderlea?"

"Pender what?" Belle asked.

"Penderlea. It's Mr. Hugh MacRae's newest farm project over in Pender County. You know, like Castle Hayne."

"I dated a boy from Castle Hayne," Belle said, smiling. "Met him at the beach. He was cu-yute!" She hurriedly wiped her mouth and threw her napkin on the table. "Look, hon, I've got to finish getting dressed. You can tell me about that later," she said, rushing out of the kitchen.

Rebecca and Junius Jones came in the back door with their youngest sister Vera following a few steps behind. "Here comes dessert! I canned these peaches myself last summer," Rebecca said. "This is the last jar."

"I helped make the cake," Vera said, placing a warm pound cake on the kitchen table.

Junius Jones pulled Millie into an elaborate hug, rocking her from side to side, causing her feet to leave the floor. "Mr. Jones, you're embarrassing Millie," Rebecca said. She pushed him aside and reached out to embrace her sister. "I'm sorry, honey," she said, "he just loves to hug."

Vera grimaced and rolled her eyes. "I'll say he does." Millie detected a tone behind the remark that caused her to wonder if there was more to it.

"Hey, little sister," she said, embracing Vera. "Don't you look pretty today? I love that dress."

"Mama made it for my birthday last year, remember?" She twirled around for all to see. "It was too big then, but look how much I've grown." Millie remembered the dressmaking effort on the part of her mother. Eva left it lying on the sewing machine for weeks at the time, too tired to finish it. The day before Vera's birthday, Millie took up her mother's sewing and finished the dress.

"Well, it's perfect for you now, honey. Why don't y'all go on in and say hey to Papa and the boys? Becca, you can help me here in the kitchen. I'll get Belle to set the table."

"Where is Belle, anyway?" Rebecca asked "I'm surprised she could tear herself away from Washington to be here."

"Oh, Becca, don't start that, you know..."

"You know I wouldn't miss this for anything in the world," Belle said, making her grand entrance. Fully dressed now with her face powdered and rouged, she resumed her perch on the kitchen stool. Without giving her a hug, Belle looked at her older sister. "Where's old baldy?"

"Belle, you are so mean," Rebecca said. "Let's not spoil today." She smiled and her tone softened. "Come and give me a hug. I've missed you."

"Hmmfp," Belle said, but she hopped off the stool and gave her sister a less than warm embrace. "Nobody misses me."

Millie wiped her hands on her apron and reached out for Belle. "Why would you say that? You know I miss you."

"You won't after you get married. All you'll think about then is Len."

"Listen to you, Belle. You must be lonely up there in D.C.," Rebecca said. "Aren't those Yankee guys beating down your door yet?"

"Oh, hush up, Becca. At least I haven't married the first man that ever paid attention to me, an... an old *fuddy-duddy* at that."

Rebecca turned her back to her sister. "Say what you will about Mr. Jones, Belle. He's the sweetest, most loving, and gentle man you could ever imagine."

"Yeah, what's he like in bed?"

"That's none of your business, Miss Priss."

In an instant, Millie was closing the swinging door between the kitchen and the dining room. "Will you two hush? They can hear you."

"Oh, poot, they can't," Belle said. "Say, Rebecca, I hope you told Millie the facts of life. She probably still thinks that Aunt Rhoadie found all of us in a stump."

Millie blushed, aware that Belle was not far from right. She'd believed that old wives' tale until her friend Mary Avis took her aside when she began her periods and told her how babies were made.

"Maybe I ought to explain it to you both," Rebecca said.

"I don't have to be insulted like this," Belle said. In a pout, she went out the swinging door, pushing it so hard it came back and hit her shoulder.

"Why does she have to be so mean?" Rebecca said.

"Mama always said not to pay any attention to it."

"Speaking of Mama, you do know the facts of life, don't you, Millie?"

Millie was blushing again. "Mama didn't tell me anything, but Mary Avis did."

"Mary Avis? Your high school friend? I'm surprised she knew."

"I was too," Millie said.

⌒

Millie had gotten up before daylight to start Thanksgiving dinner. Rob had killed two chickens, cleaned and defeathered them before Millie got into the kitchen. She'd boiled one hen to make chicken and pastry, and roasted the other one in the oven with a large pan of dressing. There were turkeys out in the woods, but Rob said they'd be tough as shoe leather. He'd rather have chicken. The day before, Millie had baked her sweet potatoes for candied yams and made a pan of savory cornbread for the dressing. At the last minute, she'd also cooked the collards, remembering that her mother never cooked collards the day company was coming. For good measure, she'd dropped in a whole pecan to staunch the smell. Rebecca retrieved the pot of collards from the back of the stove, drained off the broth, and chopped them with the sharp edge of the egg turner.

"Cousin Maggie Lorena sent snap beans and corn," Millie said. "Len never comes empty handed."

"Mama used to say she wasn't much of a cook, but Cousin Maggie was generous with what she had."

Millie shook her head. "Don't let Len hear you say anything bad about his mama."

Rebecca dumped the chopped collards into a deep bowl, pressing and smoothing them into a dome shape. "That wasn't anything bad, Millie, it was the truth."

"I know, but just don't tell it in front of Len."

"I won't, but I hope he knows what a good cook he's getting in you, honey," Rebecca said. "You cook just like Mama." She put her arm around Millie and hugged her. When she let her go, she saw that Millie had tears in her eyes. "What's the matter, did I say something wrong?"

"No, Becca. I just miss her so much. I love to cook, but I'd rather have Mama here doing it." She didn't tell Rebecca that earlier that morning she'd bawled her eyes out, suddenly overcome with grief—thinking that her mother would never be in the kitchen again—how it was all up to her now.

After dinner, Harry brought out a bottle of sweet wine and Rebecca retrieved her mother's long-stemmed sherry glasses from the china cabinet. The tall pastel-colored glasses with twisted stems were never used except at Christmas and Thanksgiving. "Let's toast our little sister and Len on their forthcoming marriage," Harry said.

"Here, here!" Cal said. "May they have a long and happy life together."

"You may kiss the bride," Rodney said.

"Rodney, you hush up," Rob said. "That's a private matter between Millie and Len." He turned to Harry. "You oughtn't be giving that boy strong spirits. He's too young."

"I reckon if I'm old enough to work in the CCC, I ought to be old enough to have a sip of wine," Rod protested, his face beet red.

"Now, Rodney, don't be talking back to your papa," Rebecca intervened. She walked around the table and put her hand on her father's shoulder. "Papa, he's almost seventeen—bringing in the only money y'all have now. That twenty-five dollars from the government helps out pretty good, doesn't it?"

Rob stood up, still imposing at the head of the table despite his years. "It won't enough to give Millie a proper wedding, but I guess this will have to do." He raised his glass to Millie, then to Len. "May the Lord be at your side. You're going to need him in this day and time."

Millie squeezed Len's hand under the table. "Thank you, Papa."

⟋

Most of the Wilmington crowd had headed back in Harry's car right after dinner on Thursday. Len excused himself also, saying his mama had asked him to be home in time for their Thanksgiving supper. "You'll come back tomorrow evening, won't you?" Millie asked. "We'll need some help with all of these leftovers."

"To be sure, to be sure!" Len said.

⟋

After Millie finished putting away the sherry glasses and her mother's good china, she joined her father on the porch. She wished she hadn't invited Len to supper the next day to help finish up the leftovers. They'd be spending the rest of their lives together. She wanted to have some time with Papa, and she would need the day to get the house in order before she left.

"Cal's out yonder splitting wood," Rob said, puffing on his pipe. "I declare, you can't get that boy to hardly sit down."

"He told me he wanted to set a good example for Rodney," Millie said.

"Won't do no good. Rod's got too many other things on his mind."

"What things? He's not even seventeen, Papa."

"What every other boy his age this day and time has got on his mind: girls and driving too fast."

"Oh, Papa, don't worry about Rodney, he doesn't even have a car."

"I'm not worried about automobiles, sister, I'm talking about that motorcycle he rides around on with Quinton."

"Who's Quinton?"

"He's one of your cousin Archie Corbinn's sons. You'd know he was a Corbinn if you was to see him."

"Maggie Lorena is a Corbinn," she said, laughing. "Does he look like her?"

"Sort of," he said.

She put her feet up in the swing and wrapped her arms around her knees. "Papa, can I ask you something?"

"Ask. I'm listening."

The swing had slowed almost to a stop. Millie put her feet on the floor and looked at her father. "You don't think I'm making a mistake, do you?"

He sighed. "Sister, I told you what I think. I'm an old man. Times are different."

She crossed over to him and kissed him on the cheek. "I love you, Papa. Please don't worry about me."

"I'm supposed to worry about you, shug. I worried about all the rest of my young'uns. Since your mama's gone, I need to do it double." He chuckled, relieving the tension.

"Okay, worry about me a little," Millie said. "Guess that means it's all right for me to worry a little about you, too."

"I reckon that'd be all right. Just don't make a habit of it."

CHAPTER 11

L en was there promptly at supper time the next day. She'd expected he would be. The Corbinns and Ryans were known for their big appetites. She'd peeped out the living room window and seen him coming up the lane, swinging one arm with each stride and carrying a package tucked under the other. He handed Millie a jar of sorghum syrup and a box filled with his mother's tea cakes. "Mama said it wasn't much, but it might satisfy a sweet tooth." He leaned over to peck Millie on the cheek. "Sweets for the sweet," he said, his eyes lighting up. She loved the way he laughed a little when he said something nice. Len had a flair for the dramatic, too, often drawing a crowd when he told stories about the antics of some of the local folks, whom he could mimic to a fault. Sometimes he got so tickled at his own stories that he'd have to stop and catch his breath.

"I saved you a piece of lemon pie," she said.

"Well, now. I'd say we'd better get to it."

Rob was quiet at supper, and the space the lack of conversation left in the room was hard to fill even for Len, who was seldom at a loss for words. "Mama said to tell you to come on up to the house if you get lonely, Mr. Rob. She's still a pretty good cook."

"Nothing ever been wrong with Maggie Lorena's cooking, son. I hear she just don't do much of it."

Len laughed and slapped his knee. "You're right about that, Mr. Rob." He slid his chair back from the table an inch or two, and leaned toward Millie's father. "Is that what you want me to call you, sir?"

"What?"

"Well, now that we're about to be kinfolk, maybe you want me to call you…"

Rob took a long swig of tea and wiped his mouth. "*Mr. Rob* is fine, just fine," he said, getting up from the table. "That was a mighty good supper, Millie, shug. I'm going out to the barn and smoke my pipe. I'll see y'all directly."

Millie covered the food and stacked the dishes in the sink while Len waited on the front porch swing. "I declare, it's like a summer night, and here it is almost December," she said, slipping in beside him.

Len lifted his arm and put it around her shoulders. He smelled like sweet soap. "The paper said it's going to be cool in a couple of days, but I've got wood stacked up against the camp house. You don't have to worry one bit about getting cold," he said, squeezing her.

Millie leaned into him, liking the way she fit under his arm. "I've got a few quilts I can bring."

"Sure thing, honey. By the way, Mama has a lard stand full of quilt scraps. She's been saving them for years. Y'all can have a good time making quilts this winter."

Millie laughed, more to herself than anything. "I've never done much quilting, but I love to sew. Papa said I can take the sewing machine with me."

"Oh, Mama's got a sewing machine. Belonged to Aunt Mag." He jumped up, excited. "Hey, that's an idea. You and Mama could take in some sewing. Might help out a little."

"Yes—I guess we—I could do something like that. Right now, down here in the country, I don't think many folks have money to have dresses made. Most seem to make their own."

"There's a few that still have a little money coming in."

"I'd rather make hats," she said. "I used to think I'd have a hat shop on Front Street in Wilmington. You know, like Miss Emily McAllister."

"Hats? Women down here in the country don't wear them fancy hats like they do in Wilmington."

"I'll bet they would if they had somebody to make them."

"No, I don't think so," he said, shaking his head. He stood up and faced her, pointing his finger. "But dresses? Now, you and Mama could make some nice dresses. Yes, ma'am, we can put the word out that you're taking in sewing." So entranced was he with this idea that he backed up and fell over the rocking chair and nearly tumbled off the porch. "Goddamn!" he said.

She saw a small cut on his forehead where he'd hit the arm of the chair. "Oh, my goodness. Are you hurt?"

Len righted himself and the chair. "I could've broken my neck!"

"I'm so sorry. Let me get a cloth. You've cut your head."

He reached up and felt the knot, inspected his fingers for blood. "It's not serious. But it could've been!"

Millie covered her mouth, attempting to stifle her laughter. "I'm sorry, you had such a funny look on your face," she said.

"I don't think it's so funny, me falling and almost breaking my neck. The only thing that's *funny* is your damn sense of humor."

Millie cringed. "I didn't mean it like that." No, she surely hadn't meant to make him mad—not on the night before their wedding. "I'm sorry. I shouldn't have laughed," she said.

"No, I don't rightly think you should've," he said. She watched him go down the steps limping slightly. He turned and threw his hand up half-heartedly. "I'll see you tomorrow."

⌒

That evening, she lay awake long into the night wondering what she might have done differently. It was her nature to laugh when something struck her funny. What would life be like with someone so easily provoked? It wasn't the first time she'd seen Len fly off the handle. She made a promise to herself right then and there to be more careful, knowing full well you can't change the stripes on a zebra. But her stomach was in knots. The last two years of her life had set her in a direction that she had little control over. When the Depression hit her family hard, all of her choices in life—college, career, marriage—had gone down the drain along with the stock market. Miss Emily had offered to help her, to make her part owner of the hat shop, but that had gone away when Emily's life crashed, too. Then, Mama had died, and just like that, her rock, her foundation had been kicked out from under her. Marrying Len was a chance for a whole new life. *Or was it?*

CHAPTER 12

Cal was quieter than usual on the drive to Dillon. Ordinarily, he would've been cracking jokes with Len. He really seemed to like Len, but Millie wasn't so sure he approved of her marrying him. She guessed that was natural. All of her brothers were overprotective sometimes. But when they crossed over the Pee Dee River, she found out what was really bothering Cal. He stopped on the other side of the bridge and parked the car on the edge of the embankment. "Y'all can stay here if you like," he said. "I'm going to walk down to the water."

"I think this is where Davy got killed," Millie whispered to Len.

"I'm going with him," Len said. Millie sat and watched from the car as the two men slipped and slid down the sandy bank. She heard Cal tell Len that the Bladen County sheriff had shot Davy three times from the bridge. Millie cringed. It had happened almost ten years ago, but she remembered it like yesterday. Davy had been an ordinary guy, her cousin, Cal's best friend. But he'd gotten mixed up with a bad woman. Patty Sue Jackson had ruined Davy's life. Cal had never been the same since Davy died. She'd ruined Cal's life, too, but at least Cal was alive.

When they climbed back into the car, both Len and Cal were somber. Millie was afraid to say anything. She didn't want to upset either one of them. "Well, that's it," Cal said. "I just wanted to see it again. Davy's car was parked right over there. He'd left that package in it for me." Len looked at Millie, puzzled.

"Davy left his journal—one he'd written at the insane asylum in Raleigh. He wanted Cal to have it."

"Oh," Len said, wishing he could get hold of it. "Was it like a true confession?" he asked innocently.

Cal stopped the car and stared straight ahead. "No, Davy had nothing to confess to. He was framed by Patty Sue McBryde. He was a good person. What happened after he escaped was an accident. He told me that himself."

"Oh, I'm sorry," Len said. "I didn't know." Cal pulled out again and Millie was relieved when nothing more was said about it.

⌒

The justice of the peace was in his garden digging sweet potatoes when Cal pulled into the yard near a Model-A coupe parked inside an open shed. Signs along the road had led them to the small cottage. A few late roses still bloomed on an arched trellis that framed a path leading to the front door. Len hesitated, his hand on the car door. "I reckon that's him in the garden. Maybe I ought to go over and speak to him before we go inside."

"Go on, then," Cal said. "We'll wait in the car until you find out if this is the right place."

"The sign says it's the right place," Len said. "I'm just wondering if he's the right man."

Cal laughed. "You're not getting cold feet, are you, Len?"

Millie, who was riding in the back seat, slapped him on the shoulder. "Go on with you, Cal."

Len got out of the car, leaving the door open. Cal reached over and pulled it shut. "Good way to get a door knocked off," he said. Her brother was particular about his car. Len would have to learn.

"I hope you're going to be happy, honey," Cal said. "This is a big step you're taking."

Millie looked down at her hands and adjusted her gloves, pushing the cloth between each finger. She'd worn a wine-colored swagger suit passed on to her from Aunt Lilibeth. It was much too elegant for church in the country, but she thought it was perfect for her wedding suit. Her blouse was a brilliant fuchsia color, and her gloves and hat matched. Just a few days ago, she'd cut her hair into a short bob, and it curled nicely around her face. "I know it's a big step, Cal," she said, glancing out the car window. Len was at the garden fence talking to the man in an animated way. Len could talk to anyone. He had a good personality, and most people took to him right away. "Do you like him?"

"Who, Len?" He turned around to look at Millie over his shoulder. She looked more timid than usual. "Of course I like him. You do, don't you?"

"Yes."

When Cal turned back, Len was walking toward the car. "Well, that's good enough for me, honey," Cal said. What he didn't say, couldn't say to his sister, was to tell her about a conversation he and Harry had with their father on Thanksgiving while the women prepared dinner. Rob was concerned that Millie was too young. She'd turned nineteen only a few weeks earlier. "I've been trying to get her to go back to Wilmington," Rob said. "She had some nice beaus in Wilmington. Rusty Ruark, for one. Remember him? Your mama sure liked him."

"What's wrong with Len?" Cal had asked. Rob puffed on his pipe, but Harry answered for him.

"Nothing's *wrong* with Len, Cal. I think Papa was hoping Millie would marry somebody with a little more money behind him."

"Hush up, Harry. You don't know what I'm thinking," Rob said sharply. "I only want the same for Millie that I want for all you children. These are hard times. Farming may be a thing of the past."

"Are you sure it's not the Corbinns you have something against?" Harry asked.

"They're your mama's kin, not mine," Rob said.

"I reckon there's not much difference between the Corbinns and the Ruarks now," Harry said. "The Ruark boy was in my office last year looking for a job. Said his family lost everything in the stock market. I heard his pa turned to alcohol. Rusty was going to law school, but he had to go to work to support his mother and the other children."

"What was he doing in your office?" Cal asked.

"Looking for a job like everybody else. He got laid off by the city of Wilmington. Wanted a job with the government. Thought maybe I could write him a letter of reference. I've known him since he used to hang around Millie over there on Princess Street."

"Did he get it?"

"I guess so. I still see him around every now and then."

"Nice boy. Had red hair," Rob said.

"Len has red hair," Cal said.

Harry had avoided further conversation on the matter by changing the subject. "I've got a bottle of hooch in my car. Anybody want a swig before dinner?"

⌒

Len was grinning from ear to ear when he came back to the car. His wavy red hair was darker now, smoothed down with hair oil. He'd worn a beige suit and a crisp new white shirt. He opened the door for Millie. "C'mon, honey," he said. "The judge is going to meet us in the front room. I reckon it's time to get hitched." He laughed and took her hand to help her out of the car. When she stood up next to him, he slid his arm around her waist and pulled her into his arms. "I'm excited. Are you?"

"I guess so…. I mean, I am, too."

"You sound nervous, honey. Don't be. People get married every day," he said, sounding as if he knew all about it.

She adjusted her hat with one hand and put the other on his shoulder with the slightest pressure, increasing the distance between their lips. "Do I look all right?"

"Honey, you look like you just stepped out of a band box." Millie cast her eyes downward and blushed. "I mean it!" Len said.

When Millie had awakened that morning, frost was on the ground. Rebecca had told her to go through their mother's wardrobe and take the things she needed with her. Millie had found the black coat that Harry bought Eva only months before she died. Rebecca had left a box on her bed containing a peach satin brassier and camisole. There were drawers to match. That's where she also found a package from Mama wrapped in tissue and tied up in pink ribbon. Tears ran down her cheeks. and her nose dripped on the ivory satin gown and negligee trimmed in Alencon lace. The note had been written shortly before Eva died.

> *Dearest Millie,*
>
> *Your Aunt Lilibeth sent me this lovely bridal set just before your papa and I were married. You're just the size I was then. Although I have no idea at this time when you will marry, I know that my days are numbered and I want to make sure that you have the most beautiful thing I own if I am not present when you vow your heart to the one you love. Please don't be sad—I will be there in spirit.*
> *Love, Mama*

When she'd tried the gown on, it had transformed Millie into the blushing bride she'd read about. Her skin tingled and her breasts took on a new firmness. Below, in her privates, she felt excitement. There was no other way to describe it.

Walking toward the rose-covered trellis that formed the entrance to the justice's house, Millie's breast brushed against Len's arm. He squeezed her arm tighter. They stepped up on the porch, and the justice's wife opened the screen door and invited them into the parlor. Millie was sure the woman was thinking about all the things a new bride would be doing before the evening was over. The woman smiled coyly, as if to prove Millie right. "Well,

well, another young couple wants to get married," she chirped. "You've certainly come to the right place. The reverend will be here directly. You just sit down and fill out these papers."

Len was all smiles, sort of bowing and scraping as he was prone to do in such situations. He inquired of the justice's wife just how many couples her husband had married. Was this a favorite time of the year to get married? Did they have a family gathering at Thanksgiving? How many children did they have? All the while he was filling out the paper as if it didn't require his full attention. Millie wanted to yank it away from him. Shouldn't he study it more carefully, considering the seriousness of what they were doing? It was then that she remembered something her older sister had said. "Men don't like bossy women. You have to make him feel like he's the most intelligent person in the world, even when he's not."

Their first night, they stayed as planned in the little three-room camp house. When she'd first seen it, Millie almost died. It was nothing more than a shack, a lean-to of sorts where the Ryans stored their discarded junk—not that anyone had much junk these days. Nobody ever threw things away. They might become useful again in harder times. Len had worked alongside her tacking down boards and repairing cracks while she swept and cleaned the little make-do house. Before the week was over, Millie had made feed-sack curtains for the small window in the kitchen, a tablecloth, and a little skirt to go around the sink. A smaller room that had been the boys' room when the Ryans lived there was now a storage room filled with boxes of junk that belonged to various members of Len's family. Millie had pushed and piled the boxes into a corner away from the door and draped sheets from the ceiling to form a small bathroom. From home, she brought a commode chair that she'd found in Jasper's barn, a table, and a stool for her vanity. Above it, she hung an oval gilt-framed mirror that had been her mother's.

The bedroom, partitioned off from the kitchen by a colorful quilt, was only large enough for an iron bedstead and a small bedside table. Maggie Lorena had surprised them by asking Lizzie's daughter to remake an old goose down mattress for their bed. She'd stitched up another large sack that Tate had filled with corn shucks to make an under-mattress. The last thing Millie brought for her trousseau were the linen sheets and a light blue embroidered coverlet. Only the spiders spinning their webs in corners of the camp house saw her blush when she smoothed them out on the bed.

It was after dark when Cal dropped them off that evening. Tate saw the headlights poking through the oak grove then flash across his ceiling. An hour before, he'd lit the bedside oil lamp and placed a drinking glass filled with the last of Maggie's chrysanthemums on the little kitchen table. When he'd gone out and closed the door to the camp house, he'd said a silent prayer. *God go with them. They're going to need you, to be sure.*

Relieved that the lights were off in the big house, Millie and Len went straight to their new home where Millie slipped into her dressing room. She took a small satchel with her, and when she returned to the bedroom, she was wearing the satin gown that clung to her like the wet baptismal dress. Just before she slid under the covers, she blew out the lamp.

CHAPTER 13

Maggie Lorena Ryan felt she had died and gone to heaven when Len married Millie McBryde. Having a girl around the house, one she could bare her heart to—a young woman not unlike herself when she'd married Tate Ryan in Onslow County—one who could help her as much as Maggie felt she had helped Tate's mother, Miss Sally Catherine, was an answer to her prayers. But that changed when Millie began to show signs of being in a family way. At first, morning sickness kept her away from the breakfast table; then she stopped coming over for dinner. At supper she showed up pale and weak, and would often excuse herself before the meal was over. Pretty soon, Len would be off to chew the rag with his friends up the road at Eddie Lee's general store.

Maggie counted up the days and months more than once, anxious to figure the time of conception—suspicious, if the truth were known. But it was more than eight weeks after they were married that Millie's sickness began. Prior to that, her new daughter-in-law had spent a pleasant part of each day with Maggie, helping out in the kitchen, stirring the wash-pot, whatever was the main chore of the day or week. It was just what Maggie had wanted, a companion and a helper. But Millie's pregnancy had turned her into a sickly girl not worth her salt. Now she spent most of her time in bed.

"I'm worried about that girl," Maggie said to Lizzie. "I think something's wrong, don't you?" They were sitting in the kitchen close to the cookstove shelling black walnuts.

"No, ma'am. She be all right," Lizzie said. "A bad beginning make for a good ending."

"Maybe she doesn't like me?"

Lizzie stood up and shook her apron into the wood box. The old Negro woman came after breakfast each morning, and more and more often, she'd stay the whole day. She'd clean the kitchen, including the supper dishes from the night before, cook a big dinner with whatever was on hand. Maybe she'd fry a squirrel or two that Tate had bagged and cleaned the afternoon before. Reluctant to go out in the chill, Lizzie would spend the afternoon by the kitchen stove shelling walnuts or the like until she could go home for good and crawl under her own patchwork quilts. Once a tall, strong colored woman with an agile step, she was now bent and stooped, and shuffled along with a wobbling gait. "Miss Millie be all right," she said. "Young girl like her missin' her mama most at a time like this."

"Well, I reckon I'm the next best thing," Maggie said, feeling a touch of resentment. "I could tell her a thing or two about having a baby, and she could be over here keeping me company while I did. I'm telling you what's the truth, this younger generation doesn't know a thing about what we had to put up with."

Lizzie made a little snorting sound. "Now, you know she don' mean nothin' toward you. When you's feeling poorly like her, you jus' want to sleep. Don't you 'member how it was when you was carryin' Mr. Will?"

"I remember, I helped Tate build that chicken house out there after we moved into Aunt Mag's house." She remembered further back, but she didn't tell Lizzie. No one would ever know that secret. How she'd spent her days feigning the flu holed up in her room. But Reese Evans had stormed into her room one evening, ending the nightmare. "Mama said every pregnancy was different," Maggie said, shutting out memories of more than twenty years ago.

As winter settled in, the weather turned bitter cold and the old camp house was drafty, no match for the small stove that burned wood night and day. Despite Maggie's invitation to come over to the big house, Millie wrapped herself in a pile of quilts and kept the chamber pot close by. She cried herself to sleep almost every night, remembering their wedding night. She'd been so shy and afraid, saying, "Wait, please wait." Finally, Len, worked into a frenzy, forced himself upon her. He was like an animal, grunting and groaning, jamming his organ into her. "That hurts, Len," she cried. "You're hurting me!" But he'd ignored her cries. Finally, she'd given up and yielded to him. To her surprise, her hips began to move in rhythm to his and the pain subsided, replaced by something vaguely pleasant. But Len had rolled off her and lay on his back panting. "God, that was good. I needed that," he said.

"It hurt," Millie said.

"It's supposed to hurt the first time. A man calls that 'picking the cherry.'"

"That sounds so coarse."

He started to laugh. "Damn, I didn't know I was marrying a *virgin*." She'd sobbed in silence, her tears soaking the pillow. When his breathing fell into a shallow rhythm, she shifted away from him, feeling the stickiness between her legs and on the sheets.

"Don't be rolling away from me, honey," he'd said softly. "I've been waiting a long time for this night." The room was pitch black except for a shard of moonlight that slipped through a gap in the curtains. She resisted when he took her hand and put it on his still engorged member. "I guess this big ol' boogey bear scared my girl, didn't it?" He said it so gently, as if talking to a child, that she laughed despite her discomfort at touching him there. "What?" he asked, propping up on his elbow.

"I never heard it called a 'boogie man,' but you did scare me."

It became a private joke between them. He was her "boogie man," and she was his "fraidy cat," but despite his attempts at gentleness after that first night, she continued to dread his advances. One night, he'd begged her to have a little whiskey to make her "relax," telling her that women learned to like it, too. "How do you think your mama came to have all those children?" he asked. "She enjoyed it!"

Without giving it any thought, she snapped back, "Is that why your mama only had three?" They were sitting at the small kitchen table, a full glass of whiskey in front of her and his empty glass before him. He glared at her, his lips curled in a half smile. "Don't you be talking about my mama, now."

"I just wondered why Cousin Maggie only had three children if she liked it that mu—" He had stood up so quickly that the table turned over in her lap, its sharp edge cutting into her legs. He glared at her, wagging his finger in her face. "I said, leave my poor mama out of this." Without bothering to right the table, he stormed out of the camp house. She didn't see him again until the next morning.

After that, she tried her best not to rile him—to be ready for his advances. More often than not, he would have been out drinking with some of the fellows he ran around with. The "boys," as he called them, hung out by the few cars or trucks parked at Eddie Lee's store, nipping at jars of homemade liquor. Millie always left the lamp burning low. Len would come in, strip off his clothes, and slide under the covers. If she pretended to be sleeping, he'd start rubbing her arm and feeling for her breast. It became a pattern and she prepared herself for his advances, thinking that this was what she was supposed to do. But it all changed when she told him about the baby. Len was afraid to touch her, saying he'd never do anything to harm the baby in her womb.

Oddly, Millie missed his nightly persistence, the way he'd get all worked up, sort of out of control—*hell bent,* Papa would say—nothing stopping him until he'd satisfied himself. Sometimes she liked that. Not that he ever paid much mind to what she did or didn't like. Now, at a time when she felt so unattractive, when she wanted to be loved, held in his arms—caressed more than anything—he kept his distance. Occasionally, he'd press himself against her buttocks at night, grunting like a pig, and she'd feel the stirring, the wetness in her privates, and want him to touch her there. He never did.

Millie confided in her sister, Rebecca, who didn't have any children, but who knew a lot about what went on in the marriage bed. "Is that the way it's supposed to be, Becca? I mean, could he hurt the baby?"

"That's hogwash, Millie, a backwoods notion that he probably overheard from some ignorant..." She stared at her younger sister, feeling sorry for her. "Honey, you need to tell him that I said we learned in nursing school that some couples do it right up until the last."

Millie looked incredulous. "Oh, I could never tell him you said that. He'd be mad as the devil that I'd been talking about his private business."

"Look, honey, just tell him that you'd like to try a different position. Offer him the back door."

"The *back door*?"

"Yes, you know, get down on your knees like this." Rebecca hopped up on the bed and kneeled with her rear end up in the air.

Millie threw up her hands to cover her face. "Oh, no, that's terrible! That's how animals do it."

Rebecca slid off the bed and hugged her sister. "Look, honey, it's fun to do it different ways. Just because you're pregnant, it doesn't mean that you can't enjoy it."

Millie smiled, attempting to overcome her embarrassment. "You sure do know a lot about...it. Does Mr. Jones...I mean, does he want you to...to enjoy it, too?"

"Of course, he does," she giggled. "He knows right where that little sweet spot is, and he can pure tee make me purr."

Millie knew what she meant. She'd discovered her sweet spot when she first became a young woman. And she'd learned in the short time since she'd been married that all of her bodily joy was linked to it. But Len had no idea where her sweet spot was, or what would happen if he chanced to touch her there.

CHAPTER 14

Maggie Lorena trudged out to the road each day as soon as she saw the mailman pull up beside the rickety old mailbox that had housed her correspondence for twenty years. Mr. Bell had been their mailman since rural delivery began. Occasionally, there was a letter from Will or a distant relative, but what she was really after were the newspapers. the Wilmington Star, the Bladen Journal, and the Pender Chronicle—each one filled with intriguing news. Maggie thrived on the news. Newspapers were her link to that other world beyond the mundane existence that had become her way of life. She was no longer a correspondent, faithfully gathering the news of her community and reporting it to a readership that included the three counties. She hadn't written a story since the Depression hit and what little they had became even less. But Maggie Lorena never failed her family. She kept them informed.

When the Lindbergh's twenty-month-old baby was kidnapped the year before, she'd hardly slept between the *Wilmington Star* editions that came only three times a week.

"She's got more time on her hands to sit around reading the newspaper than I do," Tate said to Len at dinner when Maggie alluded to some big news she'd heard that very day.

"Well, somebody around here likes to educate themselves," Maggie replied. "You two wouldn't know a thing about Hitler over there in Germany plotting to take over the world if I hadn't told you."

Tate yawned. "I'm not one bit worried about what's going on way over yonder. It's all I can do to keep up with what's going on right here," he said, jabbing his finger on the dinner table.

Len scraped his chair back. "You can tell me, Mama. What did you hear that was so important?"

"It was in the paper. Came out of Washington. It's about Penderlea. Here, I'll read it to you."

> Materials will soon be on the grounds for immediate construction of ten of the 200 houses eventually to be built on the 4,500 acres in the development. The Subsistence Homestead Corporation here reported that a cannery already is in operation at Penderlea, and between 800 and 1,000 acres are now under cultivation.

She looked up, expecting an immediate reaction. When none was forthcoming, she rattled on. "I declare, the more we hear about it, the better it sounds," Maggie said, picturing something akin to Boston Commons.

"Does it say if any of the houses are ready yet?" Millie asked.

"I know they're not," Len said. "Ray Wilkins told me they were just now building the roads." Tate kept quiet. So Len had been looking into it—talking to the county agent. He'd been playing dumb, but when Maggie pointed out the news to him, Tate went back and read it sooner or later. When she wasn't looking, of course. Len was more obvious about his interests. "Cut that out for me, Mama. This is history, the biggest thing to hit North Carolina in a long time."

"That's what I'm trying to tell you," Maggie said. "Mr. Hugh MacRae's project is getting national attention. FDR says these subsistence projects are going to save the nation. They've established a camp for transient labor, and here's a long list of all kinds of jobs available. Maybe there's something Will could do."

Millie picked up the paper and scanned the article. Len had told her not to appear too interested. "It says John Nolen, a big-city designer from Boston, is laying out all of the roads. There's to be a community center with a lake and a park." She looked up and smiled. "We've got that right here at White Lake, haven't we?"

Tate could've kissed her right then. The girl had a good head on her shoulders. He'd thought she was stepping down right much, moving into the camp house when she'd been living in Jasper's house. But Millie was smart, and she was strong. She'd made a nice little nest to start a family in. Hadn't he and Maggie Lorena started out the same way? Better, when he thought more about it, but it was easy to put the fires out of his mind.

Maggie took an even more personal interest in Penderlea after Abigail Montgomery replied to her recent letter saying that she was on the American Friends Service Committee whose work with destitute mining families in Morgantown, West Virginia, had caught the interest of Eleanor Roosevelt.

> *You simply must get involved, Maggie, dear. There is so much women can do without being in smoke-filled board rooms. I'm also sending you a subscription to the Women's Democratic News. The reports on the progress of the new resettlement project you mentioned, Penderlea Homesteads, have been nothing short of spectacular. I read that Emily McAllister—whom I'm sure I need not remind you was the woman our dear Jon was engaged to—is very involved. You two were such good friends in the past, I'm sure that Emily would welcome your help.*
>
> *How exciting that Len has met Hugh MacRae. That contact may be all he needs, should he want to apply. I assure you that if Hugh MacRae and Eleanor Roosevelt are involved, the project*

will be utopian. One thing I must tell you, however, is that Eleanor Roosevelt differs drastically on one point with MacRae. She put up a real stink about subsistence housing projects whose applicants are "hand picked." She says that the communities should be an experiment in ordinary life, and an ordinary community contains people of every race and ability. I understand that Mr. MacRae does not share that view.

Abigail's news that Emily McAllister was involved in Penderlea struck a sour note with Maggie, who was already suffering from pangs of melancholia. There was so much going on in the world, and here she was stuck in the backwoods of North Carolina. She had hardly a penny to her name, while women like Abigail Montgomery and Emily McAllister were hobnobbing with the rich and famous and not doing without a thing. All Maggie had ever wanted was to be recognized for her talents as a writer, to be *somebody*. But here she was, one of the poorer citizens looking for relief from the ravages of the Depression that had been brought about by the greed of the very ones who were now on boards of advisors and such as that. Maggie could only imagine what Aunt Mag would have to say about the sorry state of things. On second thought, she knew Aunt Mag would likely have chastised her for feeling sorry for herself.

Maggie spent several hours a day on her cot with her eyes closed, letting her thoughts drift to happier times. Wash Pridgen, Reece Evans, Jon McNamara—all conjured up the romantic moments in her life—sweet *and* sour moments. Wash and Reece, both dead now. Jon McNamara was a heel, undeserving of much thought, but she was sure that he had been in love with her. Secretly, she'd admit to a speck of satisfaction when Millie told her that Dr. Jon McNamara had jilted Emily McAllister. But she did feel sorry for Emily—closing up shop like that and leaving Wilmington for good, all because of a thankless child.

PART TWO

Many Are Called

CHAPTER 15

ONSLOW COUNTY, NORTH CAROLINA

In her last conversation with her daughter in early December, Emily McAllister had bitten her tongue rather than ask Jeanne if she might be coming home for Christmas. "I have some good news," Emily said. "Shall I save it for Christmas?"

"Oh, do tell me, Mother. You know I don't like games."

Emily had been tempted not to repeat the joyous news, but she relented, knowing it was petty on her part. "I had a letter from Maggie Ryan. Len Ryan and Millie McBryde were married at Thanksgiving."

"Oh, I knew that would happen some day. Isn't it wonderful, Mother?"

"Yes, Maggie was ecstatic. I'm very happy for all of them."

"Did you go to the wedding? Millie must have been a beautiful bride."

"They were married in South Carolina, a justice of the peace."

"Too bad. It seems I've missed out on a lot of things, haven't I, Mother?"

"It's all right, Jeanne. Be happy." There was a pause at the other end of the line.

"Ashley has asked me to come to Savannah again for Christmas," Jeanne said.

"Oh, really? Will you go?"

"Yes, I think so."

"Oh? Well, I guess that settles it. I'll miss you," Emily said.

⌐

Despite her feelings of rejection, the old excitement of Christmas shopping had come over Emily a few days after her conversation with Jeanne. She'd seen no reason why she shouldn't indulge herself and take a Pullman to Philadelphia. For the last few years, she'd routinely given Darcy and Gardenia a large check and asked them to buy for themselves and the children. She'd missed the joy of buying presents for children, a part of Christmas that she'd loved more than anything. In the past, Jeanne had been fun to buy for. She loved lavish presents and gave them in return. Emily decided she'd do the same, with or without Jeanne.

After Emily had made her arrangements for the train, she'd called Amanda and Agatha, the precious nieces whom she'd practically raised, asking them to join her. They had husbands and children—families of their own now—but they loved the idea of meeting their aunt in Philadelphia where both girls had spent most of their childhood. Except for the few times Reece had sent for them to come to Onslow County at Christmas, they'd grown up knowing the magnificent stores in Philly and memorable Christmas gatherings with their mother's family. On this trip, they would stay in the same hotel as Emily, have lunch together, and shop to their hearts' content in stores like Wanamaker's and Gimbel's, beautiful stores they'd known in the past.

⌐

The reunion was just what Emily needed to restore her spirits. She held to her resolve to put Jeanne completely out of her mind and enjoyed every minute with her nieces. On their second afternoon, they'd stopped for tea at the Mayflower Hotel, an elegant old hotel that had been the setting for many family wedding receptions, including Emily's. "I can just see Cousin

Mary Madeline propped up over there on that settee," Agatha said, laughing. "She was always about two sheets in the wind."

"She was the only woman I ever saw my father cater to," Amanda said.

"Jeanne was fond of her, too," Emily said. "Birds of a feather," she added reflectively. "At least she was around for the good times."

"You worry too much about Jeanne, Aunt Emily. She's out on her own now. Some girls are like that."

Oh, the wise Amanda, Emily thought, *a mother with children of her own.* She hoped that Amanda would never suffer the rejection of a child. "But I miss her," Emily said. "We were so close for so many years. Can you imagine such distance from one of your children?"

Amanda had gotten out of her chair and put her arms around her aunt. "I know you've forgiven Jeanne, Aunt Emily, but I think there's another reason she doesn't come home. Most likely she hasn't forgiven herself for what she did to you. I'm not sure she ever will."

"But it was so long ago. She probably did me a favor. She's much more important to me than Jon could ever have been."

On Christmas Eve, Emily had gone about her last-minute chores with a lump in her throat. It was dusk outside when she lit the candles. She should be happy. Christmas had always been her favorite time of the year. In the last few days, she and Boss's wife, Nellie, had tied greenery and wound it on the staircase banister, entwining red velvet ribbon and a bow at every third spindle. The Christmas tree was a fat cedar that Boss had marked in the woods months earlier and cut only two days ago. The fragrance of the tree was enough to bring back her memories of Christmas when the old house had been in its glory. Then, there'd been tiny red candles scattered about on the branches. The glass balls were the same ones that Reece had bought in Venice to replace the tin vintage ornaments that had been a part of her grandparents' collection. She'd hung them along with strings of electric lights and ropes of popcorn and cranberries. Beneath the tree were dozens of presents, gaily wrapped in colorful paper. In an upstairs locked closet was "Santa's stash," as Darcy called it, deposited by him over a month ago.

Emily heard the horn as someone turned into the lane, making little toots as they drove the quarter mile to the grand old house. *Darcy must be in a festive mood. I guess it's no different than sleigh bells,* she thought. But she also knew it was uncharacteristic of Darcy, the staid storekeeper who maintained his poise at all times. *Maybe he's getting mellow—or maybe it's just that it's Christmas.* It was more like something Jeanne would do.

Emily was in the dining room before the breakfront mirror, pinning a sprig of holly just above her ear when Nellie had called out to her, "Miss Emily, it's yo' Jeanne! She's come home for Christmas!" Emily glanced into the foyer just in time to see Jeanne in the doorway, wearing the coat with the white fur collar, staggering beneath a load of brightly wrapped presents. Boss followed behind with another stack. They started for the parlor when Jeanne looked up to see her mother standing speechless before her.

"Surprise, Mother! I decided at the last minute that I couldn't bear to miss Christmas. The trains were booked. Ashley let me—she let me drive her car."

Emily hugged her, releasing her hold only to look into Jeanne's eyes, her own full of tears. "You said you'd never drive again."

"I know, but there was no other way."

"You wanted to come home that badly?"

Jeanne wrapped her arms around Emily and held her. "Yes, and I promise I'll never miss Christmas again."

⌒

The grand old plantation home had not seen such a Christmas since Reece Evans had last entertained at one of his Christmas soirees. After the children were put down for the night, Darcy opened a bottle of vintage champagne, toasting Jeanne in a shaky voice, welcoming her back home. Emily could only watch as brother and sister hugged and kissed. This was what she had wanted. Some things would never change, but after she was long gone, Darcy and Jeanne would carry on the traditions. At midnight, she slipped up to her bed, a little toddly from the champagne, or was it nostalgia, she wondered, remembering her husband, Duncan, whose life had been cut short by cancer, and thinking of Reece who had probably shortened his own life with wine and tobacco. She even thought of Jon McNamara and what might have been. Downstairs, she knew that Jeanne was assisting Santa, and for the first time in many years, all had seemed right with the world.

At Christmas dinner, Emily proudly announced that Hugh MacRae had asked her to be chairwoman of the selection committee for his new farm colony in Pender County. When Emily had first learned of the project at her Democratic Women's luncheon in December, she'd hoped for an appointment to the Board of Visitors of Penderlea Homesteads, but Hugh MacRae had other ideas. "I want you to chair that selection committee," he'd said. "We only want the cream of the crop, Emily, and you know people."

Darcy smirked, in his typical fashion. "I thought he'd given up that sort of thing after his last project failed at Van Eeden."

"Well, he didn't," Emily said, "and look how successful they've been at Castle Hayne and St. Helena."

"Maybe Castle Hayne," Darcy said, "but not St. Helena. There are only a few Russian farmers left."

"Penderlea is quite different," Emily said. "It's going to be a *farm city*. Hugh has learned from his experience. The entire project will be self-sufficient. Homesteaders are being selected from among local farmers. They'll have their own community center, a cannery, and a cooperative or general store where individual farmers can buy and sell what they produce. It sounds wonderful to me, son."

"I think it sounds rather boring, Mother. Imagine, not ever going to town. What'll happen to stores like mine?"

"Darcy, you're being very narrow minded. Penderlea is nowhere near

Jacksonville. It's a resettlement community for homesteaders—a place where young farmers can make a fresh start. They'll be able to buy their homesteads by working these small ten-acre farms. You should go and see it."

"I've been to Arthurdale," Jeanne said. "It's a mining community, but the same kind of thing in West Virginia. Mrs. Roosevelt has taken a personal interest in it. The little houses are wonderful. We made window boxes and curtains for the windows. It was great fun watching the people when they saw their new homes for the first time."

"When were you in there?" Emily asked.

"A while ago, but it's not important. Tell me about Penderlea."

But, it is important! Emily thought. *I know so little about you.* "Oh, Penderlea?" she answered, trying to get a grip on her thoughts. "Yes, Penderlea is marvelous. John Nolen, a city planner and landscape architect from Boston, is involved in it. They have planned and developed so many cities and parks up north. Here they are down south in the middle of nowhere making a *farm city* with three hundred homes out of land that once belonged to the Indians."

"Didn't it all at one time, Mother?" Jeanne asked.

"What?"

"Didn't it all belong to the Indians at one time?"

"Yes, I guess it did," Emily said. She couldn't argue Jeanne's point.

"Last summer, I was in Atlanta working with a women's rights organization. I became friends with a close friend of Mrs. Roosevelt who had been sent to the South to report on the progress of the Public Works Administration. You would have gotten a kick out of her, Mother. She was very outspoken about how poorly the Negroes were treated down south, yet they were getting all of these jobs with the WPA making scads of money while decent white men were desperate for jobs."

"Yes, we've heard that around here, too. I'm afraid it will take many years to change attitudes."

"I'm curious about the selection process at Penderlea," Jeanne said. "Will it be racially diverse?"

Emily laughed. "I would hope so, but with Hugh MacRae involved, one can't be sure. I'm afraid he thinks there are already too many Negroes in these parts. On second thought, maybe that's why there's a selection committee."

Jeanne jumped up from her chair. "Don't be too sure. Look at what happened at Arthurdale." Nervously, she lit a cigarette. "Mrs. Roosevelt worked so hard to get the project approved. She put her own personal money into it with the idea that this resettlement community would reflect the diverse ethnic background of the miners in West Virginia. But you know what? When the *committee* was given the names, they only picked the white Christian applicants. Mrs. Roosevelt was sick about it."

"Yes, I'm afraid we'll have the same sort of thing at Penderlea."

CHAPTER 16

Jeanne had left before news of a devastating fire on Wrightsville Beach was broadcast on the morning of January 29. The fire had begun before midnight in Kitty Cottage and spread northward, claiming everything in its wake, including the grand old Oceanic Hotel and 103 private cottages. The beach home that Emily had prized so highly was among them. With mixed emotions, she recounted her summers there with Reece's children and the McBryde girls. Dinners at the Oceanic were among her happiest times. Jon had loved the beach house. He said he could live the rest of his life there. So much for that, she thought. Those dreams had gone up in smoke long before the fire.

Shortly after the Wrightsville Beach fire, an article appeared in the *Wilmington Star* announcing that applications for the new homestead community in Pender County could be obtained either from county agents or from an office on the fourth floor of the Federal Building in Wilmington. Emily had been told that she and her committee would be provided with an office near MacRae's in the Southern Building where they could review the applications as they arrived.

MacRae's instructions were clear. Applicants were to be selected for their industry as well as their need from among local farmers. He said he expected these early selectees to be highly skilled. Many might already be working in construction at Penderlea, hoping that it would improve their chances of being selected. The Civilian Conservation Corps had set up a training camp on the project, and boys from all over the state were asking for applications for their parents. Left unsaid was the fact that the least likely candidate would be a young black tenant farmer who had never had any opportunity in the first place.

After obtaining an application, those who could fill it out themselves would likely be ahead of the game; then there would be the need for references. A county agent was the first objective; next, the family preacher; and then an upstanding member of the community whose name might be recognized by someone on the selection committee.

When the selection committee had approved the application, it would be given to a government representative who would make a personal visit to the home of the prospective homesteader. Since the first ten houses would not be ready until about the end of June, only ten families would be chosen initially, and only with Hugh MacRae's approval.

⌒

Emily McAllister had grown up on both sides of the Mason-Dixon line. She and Reece were born in Philadelphia, but their mother died young, and their father felt he could not raise them alone. He'd taken the children in 1920 to their grandparents in rural Onslow County, where they'd been educated for a time by a governess. In their teen years, they were sent to Philadelphia for higher education. Emily had met the young Duncan McAllister on a packet boat on a return trip from school after her last semester. They fell in love and decided to marry. Her grandfather endowed the couple with a home and the keys to a general store in the bustling little town of Jacksonville, North Carolina.

Although she was less provincial than many of her neighbors, Emily felt that she'd had a good life in Onslow County. In college up north, she'd had many friends of different nationalities. She'd seen the difference education made. In Jacksonville, where she'd become a matron with her own home and business, she'd endeavored to provide education and opportunity to the large community of Negroes who were in her employ, many of whom were descended from the slaves of her great-grandparents before the Civil War. She did not get up on a soapbox in the middle of town to proclaim her beliefs of racial equality; she just tried to improve life for them in her own little world. Hugh MacRae might be asking more of her than she is willing to give.

⌒

When Emily approached MacRae shortly before the first Board of Visitors meeting at Penderlea Homesteads, she found him in a foul mood. "Excuse me, Emily. I've just had some bad news," he said, putting his hand on her shoulder. He turned to a man who stood beside him. "You get the president on the phone. He's given me his personal authorization to build this project. Ickes can go to the devil." The aide hurried off, and MacRae turned back to Emily. "I'm sorry, dear, they want to federalize all of the subsistence projects, including Penderlea. I'd have to go to the secretary of the interior before I could spend a dime."

"I'm sorry, Hugh, I've caught you at a bad time. I only wanted to thank you for appointing me to chair the selection committee." She'd also planned to tell him that her committee had met and chosen the first ten homesteaders. Letters were ready to be sent out based upon his approval.

"You may not thank me after these bureaucrats get involved," he said. "They're already talking about increasing the size of the farms to twenty acres and cutting back the number of homes to 150."

"I'm so sorry, Hugh. They must not understand—" But MacRae had stamped off, making his way to the head table where North Carolina Governor Ehringhaus, Alvin Johnson, and Dr. Elwood Mead, director of reclamation of the Department of the Interior, watched him approach. He stopped at each dignitary's chair to greet them. Emily suspected that the many other distinguished men and women in the room were part of the Penderlea project because of their admiration for this one man. Until now, Hugh MacRae had controlled all aspects of the project's development.

Could it be that certain individuals in Washington were now saying he was a multimillionaire spendthrift?

After he had introduced the Board of Visitors, MacRae picked up a sheaf of papers, looked at them briefly, then appeared to set aside his prepared speech to speak extemporaneously. It didn't surprise Emily. He was a commanding speaker in any circumstances, his Scottish brogue not the least of his attraction. Wearing a dark suit, white shirt, and string tie, he posed a striking figure against the burgundy pleated curtain that had been quickly arranged as the backdrop for a stage.

MacRae's words were measured at first. "This project was, we believe, wisely started as a corporation under government ownership and control. Possibly, because of unsatisfactory results in other localities, and in projects quite different from this in character, it is now contemplated, if not decided, that direct control be transferred to a bureau in Washington. The effect of such a change deserves the careful consideration of all who are deeply interested in the eventual success of a movement for improving rural life conditions. It should be realized that there is a fundamental difference between a subsistence homesteads project united to industry and a rural community dependent on diversified farming. These cannot be classified together or treated alike."

Emily surmised that he was talking about projects like Arthurdale, connected to the coal mining industry in West Virginia. Penderlea was a horse of a different color. These homesteaders would be providing their own food; they'd be self-sufficient. MacRae then asked the Board of Visitors to look at what had already been accomplished on Penderlea in less than ninety days. He invited them to take a half-hour drive down the road to see for themselves the prosperous, self-sustained community at Castle Hayne where a program of intensive diversified farming had been successfully followed.

Emily glanced about the room. Most of the board members were eagerly finishing up their fried chicken and potato salad, but a few were listening in awe to MacRae's remarks. Had the government pulled the rug out from under him? There was little doubt left when he announced that although he would continue in the role of project manager, Dr. Alvin Johnson would be given control as chairman of the board. Exactly how this all came about no one knew, but Emily was certain that it was meant to be a comeuppance for the wealthy gentleman who was accustomed to putting his money where his mouth was. The difference this time was that it was the government's money.

Emily had heard some of the criticism—*talk* as it were—by some of her Democratic women who had husbands in Congress. MacRae had already spent $325,000 of the original million-dollar loan on clearing, ditching, and building roads, not to mention the operations center. He'd also spent $18,000 of the federal funds for a transient labor camp and $24,000 to establish an experimental farm at Willard; yet not a single house had been built. He'd caused even more talk by putting his brother and his son-in-law on the board and giving them management positions.

After the meeting, the Board of Visitors was shown through the head-quarters buildings, which included sleeping quarters for the operations staff, offices, warehouses, a fabricating shop, sawmill, and garages. MacRae was noticeably absent. A young woman, attractively tanned and wearing a neat flowered dress, asked them to assemble under a grove of trees where she told them that the community gardens, supervised by an expert from North Carolina State College, were being planted to provide for one hundred families during the coming winter. She explained that by the time the vegetables were ready for use in June, a cannery would be ready for prospective farm families to process the produce.

Hank Hudson, who introduced himself as the farm manager, explained that as the land was being cleared, farm crops were being planted. Buck-wheat, sweet potatoes, velvet beans, Sudan grass, and lespedeza would not only condition the land, they would also either provide food for the farm families or feed for their livestock. The board had been advised to wear sensible shoes, especially the ladies, who were instructed that "galoshes would even be appropriate." Although sand had been scattered in the very wet areas, Emily wished she had chosen her galoshes instead of the pair of brown oxfords she changed to after lunch.

They were taken next to the poultry farm, where three thousand purebred chickens were being raised as foundation stock for farm flocks. The farm manager explained proudly that by standardizing on one breed, selected for proven laying and weight-building qualities, the management was demonstrating the possibility of additional income for every homesteader.

Following some light refreshments served by ladies from Pender County, the board witnessed demonstrations of methods used in clearing, stumping, and preparing new ground for cultivation. Watching the monster machines—two seventy-five-horsepower Caterpillar diesel tractors—pull up several stumps in succession, the board members were told that they averaged eighty stumps an hour. If they ran into a particularly difficult stump, it was dynamited. An estimate was given that thirty-five tons of explosives would be used before the project was finished. To the amusement of all, one of the visitors stripped off his coat and asked to give it a try. Although he was a rugged-looking fellow of considerable size, when he tried to climb up onto the giant tractor, his foot slipped and he sank almost to his knees in the mud.

In another field, a smaller thirty-five-horsepower Caterpillar tractor pulled a four-ton disc with thirty six-inch blades, plowing through roots and small stumps left by the clearing crews. A Farmall tractor followed, demonstrating, with smaller discs, the method for pulverizing the soil and making it ready for cultivation. In an adjacent field, a Fordson tractor pulled a large ditching plow mounted on wheels, showing the method used to dig the one hundred or more miles of farm ditches. After a ditching line was established, a large knife was run down the center line to slice roots, followed by the plow which cut a ditch three feet deep—a foot wide at the bottom and three feet wide at the top.

By the end of the day, Emily was exhausted, not only from marveling at the new technology used in clearing the cut-over woodland, but from the thought of the task still at hand to build a farm city. On a large poster of the landscape plan, architect John Nolen had indicated where trees would be left for shade along the highways and service roads. Each home site would be surrounded by trees. Wooded reservations were to be left along the drainage courses and at other strategic points to provide parkways and windbreaks. Near one boundary of the project, within a short distance of the community center, Nolen proposed a large park with a lake for boating and bathing. Playgrounds and athletic fields were also indicated.

Jane McKimmon, a member of the Board of Visitors who had been introduced as assistant director of the North Carolina Agricultural Extension Service, walked up behind Emily.

"Magnificent, isn't it?" Jane said. "It will put North Carolina way up there in the eyes of all of those naysaying politicians."

"Yes, it's wonderful," Emily said. "This plan for a farm city makes me want to take up a whole new life."

"Not me," Jane said. "My little backyard garden in Raleigh is enough farm for me." She laughed, looking around. "I'm surprised Hugh is not here. He loves to show off Penderlea."

Emily glanced toward the project center. "He's probably over there in the office rolling heads. He was pretty agitated."

"Can't say as I blame him," Jane said. "He's put his heart and money into this project. They ought to let him do it the way he sees fit. He always does things right."

"Have you worked with Hugh before?" Emily asked.

"Oh, yes. If it has anything to do with agriculture in North Carolina, Hugh's usually involved. They adore him at State College. His experiments with grasses have revolutionized pasturing."

"Yes, I've heard about that."

"Come, sit down over here and tell me about *you*, honey," Jane said, leading Emily to a rough-hewn bench. "I need to sit a spell. My feet are killing me."

Emily followed along, agreeing with her new friend that she needed to get off her feet, too. They sat in the shade of a cluster of tall pines. In a distant field, the tractors moved back and forth across the rough terrain, dragging stumps and roots into a huge pile for burning. "Do you think the government is really going to cut back on the project?"

"There's no telling. This New Deal President Roosevelt has offered us has a lot of kinks in it. They're still working them out. But it doesn't matter. Hugh MacRae will find a way to keep those big Caterpillars out there running. What I'm concerned about is the gardens. People can't work if they don't eat."

Emily extended her hand. "I'm Emily McAllister, Mrs. McKimmon. I live in the next county—over in Onslow."

"Wonderful to meet you, Emily. Are you involved in home demonstration?"

"Oh, no. I'm helping review the applications, but I do love gardening."

Jane McKimmon's eyes twinkled merrily. "Maybe you should start a tomato club or two? Where 'bouts in Onslow County are you from, Emily?"

Emily laughed, aware that Jane McKimmon had already sized her up as an unlikely farm woman. "Over near Jacksonville."

"Would you like to help me set up the home demonstration clubs on Penderlea?"

"I'm afraid I don't know anything about home demonstration clubs."

Mrs. McKimmon laughed. "Oh, honey, all I want you to do is to be a liaison of sorts between the new homesteaders and our agents. We'll do the rest."

"I'll be happy to do what I can."

"Wonderful, Emily. Maybe you'll learn something, too. You can teach others. We'll only overcome this Depression if we all learn to make the most of our resources."

⌣

Emily's car was but one that day that had to be pulled out of the mud in the rain-soaked field where cars were parked. On the main road, she followed a long line of cars making their way back toward Wallace. Although the main roads in Penderlea had been cut, and a few fields cleared of the heavy timber, it was hard to imagine homes or crops under cultivation where she looked out today. It would take a magic wand to ready the land for even the ten homesteaders who had been chosen and told that their homes would be ready by June.

CHAPTER 17

After her first visit to Penderlea, Emily made the sixty-mile round-trip at least once a month to see the progress and to pick up any applications that might have been turned in at the project office. Building roads and clearing and draining land was a slow process, but it had to be done before any of the houses could be started. Seeing the plan develop as Nolen had laid it out was thrilling. Because she was embarrassed to drive her new Buick automobile onto the project when there were so many in need who were working there, she'd purchased a farm vehicle for Boss to drive her over the rough roads. She'd also acquired an ankle-length khaki-colored skirt and jacket that came with a matching pair of jodhpur-styled riding pants like Amelia Earhart wore. A crisp white shirt and a pair of sensible shoes completed her outfit.

If the weather was hot, and it often was on early spring days in southeastern North Carolina, she wore a shaped straw hat or tucked her brown wavy hair under a colorful scarf. Her shoes were stylish sturdy brown leather with a flat heel and an elastic insert that allowed them to come up slightly on her ankle. Emily did not feel her age, but the calendar did not lie. In two months she would celebrate her fiftieth birthday. She'd never put on the extra pounds that made women her age look so much older. A good figure was important to her, and she refused to leave her house without foundation garments that held her figure in place. When she looked in her mirror each day, she was still quite happy with herself. She had a pleasant face, an aristocratic nose, and good teeth. On the streets of Jacksonville, she'd seen a lot worse in women her age.

Emily did not come empty-handed on her jaunts to Penderlea. More often than not, she and Boss brought along pimento cheese sandwiches and pint jars of cold sweet tea. As required, she always stopped in at the project office first. She hoped she would run into Hugh MacRae, but she had not seen him since the Board of Visitors meeting. She surmised that most of his duties on the project itself had been turned over to his assistant, the farm project manager. The offices were located on the outskirts of the project near what the workers called "Camp Penderlea," a series of barracks and a mess hall built by the Civil Works Administration to house the Civilian Conservation Corps. In addition to the housing for the young men and the project offices and shops, there was a ball field with bleachers built by the men, and a canteen at the end of the mess hall.

Emily soon became great friends with the farm manager, Hank Hudson, who introduced her to Gordon Van Schaack, the Boston landscape architect who was implementing John Nolen's design. In a grove of stately oak trees, Van Schaack showed Emily the ten-acre site that had been set aside for a picnic area. "No doubt this is the most beautiful spot on Penderlea," he said, adding that the site probably had once been an early settler's home place. There were several other open areas on the forty-nine-hundred-acre project where old farms had been, but most of the land had never been cleared or cultivated since the beginning of time. "There are wild azaleas and native gardenias all over the place," Van Schaack said. "See, someone had daffodils over there," he said, pointing to a clump of spent leaves. "They're long gone now, but we saw them bloom when we first started clearing."

Van Schaack went on to explain that a nursery had been established to provide landscaping plants for the homesteads and community buildings. As the land was being cleared, a crew of men went ahead of the bulldozers and tractors, digging small trees, shrubs, and other natural plants that might be used on the grounds. "Of course, we'll use some commercial nursery stock, but the majority of the plants will be native to this part of eastern North Carolina," he said. "By next spring, you'll see nothing but gorgeous azaleas, dogwoods, and those wonderful native gardenias you folks call Cape Jessamine."

"Are those men over there building fireplaces?"

"Oh, yes, and the picnic tables are being built in the wood shop. I had one brought here for you to see today." Van Schaack led Emily to a sturdy picnic table with attached benches. "Mr. MacRae wants to open the picnic grounds to the public soon. He's anxious for the world to see what's going on here."

Emily looked around at the tranquil setting, the care with which the landscape was being preserved. "If everything else is done this well, we'll be overrun with applications—not that we haven't been already."

Van Schaack accepted a sandwich from a tin box that Emily offered to him. "Mrs. McAllister, these delightful picnics are the very essence of what I'm trying to create here at Penderlea. Your southern charm and the sweet tea make it seem all the more worthwhile," he said.

"You are most kind," she replied. Van Schaack's old-fashioned manner might have been wasted on a younger woman, but Emily found him charming. "It's been a pleasure seeing the plan executed. I can hardly wait until my next visit."

"Nor can I," he replied, with a brief sensuous smile. "Your pimento cheese sandwiches have moved me to new heights of production."

Emily laughed. He really was flirting with her. "An exaggeration, I'm sure, but I'll do anything to help," she demurred, surprised that she felt like returning the flirtation. She'd promised herself that she'd never allow another man to enter that part of her mind—the part of her that expected something in return, but she found his flirting contagious. "Your expertise has brought great dignity to this part of the South, Mr. Van Schaack," she said, deliberately trying to make the conversation more formal.

"Gordon, please. May I call you Emily?" he asked, his bright blue eyes twinkling beneath bushy eyebrows.

"Of course," she said, unable to hold back her smile. Quickly regrouping, she asked, "Is a farm city an entirely new concept in landscape design?"

"Yes, and you can thank John Nolen and Hugh MacRae for that." He glanced away, reflectively. "Actually, I believe an associate planner of Mr. Nolen's first sketched the plan in 1923 for another site near the MacRae colonies. That project never received the support needed by investors."

"When do you expect them to start the houses?" Emily asked.

"A good question, my dear, one everyone is asking; however, the roads must come first. In a planned community such as Penderlea, considerable thought and attention must be given to the design of the road system. Roads cost money to build and to maintain and they take land out of cultivation, yet they are essential to the well-being of the community. Each piece of property must be serviced by a road so that the homesteaders can have direct access to the rest of the community."

"Penderlea really is like a city, isn't it?"

"Oh, yes, my dear. A farm city," he emphasized.

"I hope the state will do its part and get the roads leading into Penderlea fixed. I have to go around my elbow to get to my thumb getting here."

"Oh, yes, that's an issue over which we have no control, but the approach roads are under construction. The one from Willard is rough graded, with two bridges yet to be built. The one from Watha has been surveyed, but that's all. The road from Burgaw will be the only hard-surfaced road. It's being stumped and cleared now. By the first of next week the grading crew will be at work on it."

Emily listened with rapt attention. There was no bluster or hyperbole in his tone, only confidence that the plan was being carried out expeditiously. "I understand that two of our first homesteaders are already working here. Have you met them?" she asked.

"Yes, that would be Mr. Van Bruggen and Mr. Alden. Handpicked by Mr. MacRae."

"Yes, of course. I reviewed their applications. Do you know the status of their houses?"

"There've been delays, as you know—politics and all—but we're still optimistic that at least ten houses will be ready in a few months."

"If you see either of them, would you point them out to me? I'd like to meet them in person. Their interviews are conducted by government personnel."

"Oh, I see. Do they have to come into the office in the Federal Building in Wilmington for that?"

"Oh, no, someone from the office visits them in their homes."

He smiled, knowingly. "Sounds as if the government wants to do a little snooping around."

"I hadn't thought about it that way, but I suppose you're right," she said.

⌒

The farm manager, Hank Hudson, was an equally likable fellow. He'd been MacRae's overseer at St. Helena until Penderlea had gotten under way. "I guess Mr. Hugh wanted someone in here besides a government man," he told Emily. "He knew I'd know how to do things the way he likes them done." Hank seemed very comfortable with Emily, delighting in driving her over the project where the roads were taking shape very quickly around Nolen's elongated horseshoe design. "Thought I'd show you some of the farmhouse sites today," he said. "They're putting in some driveways. Doing some site grading, too." She approached the truck and, as usual, Hank's boy hopped into the back. He was a likable little fellow. Blonde and fair skinned, he didn't look at all like the dark-haired farm manager. Emily had tried to strike up a conversation with him on several occasions, to no avail. But she tried again.

"How are you today, young man?" she said, but the boy had ducked his head and turned away.

"Mind your manners there, Colin. Mrs. McAllister is our guest," Hank reprimanded.

Emily got into the truck. "Please don't embarrass him. I'm sure he's just shy."

"Maybe a little too shy," Hank said. "I was hoping he'd get over it if I brought him here to the project. I figured he'd get to meet more people. Mr. MacRae even offered him a job running errands, but he won't leave my side."

"How old is he?"

"I think he's ten, maybe close to eleven. I'm going to put him in the new school when they get it built."

Emily couldn't hide her consternation. "You don't know how old your son is?"

Hank laughed. "Oh, he's not my real son. I sort of adopted him when I was working for Mr. Hugh over at Castle Hayne. He's been with me since before my wife died. Don't hardly talk to nobody else."

On Crooked Run Road, they stopped to observe workmen maneuvering the huge plow rigged up on wheels. Terra cotta pipes were strewn at intervals every now and then where a driveway over the ditch was intended. "Just imagine these pretty little white cottages with green shutters at every place you see a driveway going across the ditch. Like that right there," he said, pointing to a lot that was being cleared. "The house will go toward the front; the barn over there, the chicken house there, and the hog lot over yonder." His excitement was contagious, and Emily easily pictured the house and outbuildings. "See that stump? There'll be a washhouse with the pump in it right there. Soon as they get the lot cleaned off, the well-drillers come in."

Emily shook her head. "So much to be done," she said.

"Yes, ma'am," he agreed, "but Mr. Hugh has asked the employment service in Wilmington for a whole bunch more relief labor. No telling how many will be out here next week."

"Mr. Hudson, do you mind my asking how long it will take to get the farms ready to start growing things?"

"I guess it all depends on how hard a man wants to work pulling stumps and roots. Can't do much until you can get a plow in the ground. I expect some of the homesteaders are going to have to make a choice as to whether they get their land ready, or pay somebody else to do it while they're working in construction. You see, there'll be a little grace period in there before the government will expect them to start paying off their loans."

CHAPTER 18

AUGUST 1934

In early August, Emily made her weekly trek to Wilmington to pick up new applications for the Penderlea Homesteads project. She had a long list of things to do before she returned to Onslow County, and she was anxious to take care of the Penderlea business first. When she stopped by the federal office, she found Rusty Ruark sipping coffee and chatting with several fellows around a water cooler in the hallway. "Mrs. McAllister, I wasn't expecting you today," he said, stepping over to greet her.

"Hi, Rusty, I had a few other things to tend to in Wilmington. Thought I'd stop in and see if you had any Penderlea applications."

"Yes, of course. I'm delighted to see you," Rusty said. "Come on in to my office." He ushered her into a drab government office with nothing but a metal desk and two chairs. "I had a bunch of new applications, but Mr. MacRae asked me to bring them over to his office. He said you could pick them up there—wanted to make sure *he* saw them first."

Emily remained standing. "That's fine," she said. "I don't mind running over there."

"Sit down, please sit down." He held the chair for her, and she felt obliged to sit. "While you're here, there's something I think I ought to tell you. I heard some talk that the government's going to stop everything on the project until they do more studies."

"Yes, I heard," she said. She liked Rusty, had known him since he was a young boy, but there was something about him that made her hesitate to share her knowledge with him. "One can't blame the government for being cautious," she said. "There's a lot of money involved. People's lives, too."

"Yeah, but the boss better watch his step," he said, strutting in front of her in a professorial manner. "You know, the bigger they are, the harder they fall." He flashed a cynical smile.

Emily stood up, preparing to leave. "I don't think there's a big problem, just a disagreement over the pace of the project. Hugh—Mr. MacRae—has had this project in mind for a long time. He's anxious to move forward. That's his way of doing things."

"Oh, I think there's more to it than that, Mrs. McAllister. Please, just a minute more of your time," he said, offering her the chair again. He took his seat behind his desk. "There's something I've been wanting to ask you."

Emily wasn't prepared for an interrogation by this would-be lawyer. "Really, Rusty, I do need to go. So many things to do today." But she slipped into the chair and sat on the edge of the seat, more out of curiosity than politeness. "You had something to ask me?" He smiled and folded his hands under his chin. Hugh MacRae would be furious if it got back to him that she had been chit-chatting with a government employee, even one from Wilmington they'd both known for years. "I really don't know much about what's going on in Pender County. I'm just handling the applications that come into the project office."

"Of course, and doing a fine job. I heard through the grapevine that the president's wife is taking a great interest in our little project. They say she's planning to visit us when the first ten houses are complete. That's what I wanted to talk to you about."

"Excuse me?"

"That's what I wanted to talk to you about," he repeated. "When, or if, ER comes, I wondered if I might offer her the hospitality of your home."

"I'm sorry? I don't quite know what you're asking. Is Mrs. Roosevelt planning a visit to North Carolina?"

"We don't know. There's talk of it. I just wanted to be able to say I'd mentioned it to you—if you'd be willing and all. You know, being the social-type person you are."

Emily stood quickly. "Oh, my, I'd certainly be honored to have Mrs. Roosevelt in my home, but I don't need . . . I wouldn't want you to . . . I'm sure when the time comes, Hugh will want—" Annoyed that she'd allowed him to unnerve her, she looked at her watch. "Oh, I'm really late. Thank you, Rusty," she said, edging toward the door.

Rusty stood and walked around his desk to open the door for her. "Yes, it might be best to wait on that, but there's one more thing I wanted to ask you." He kept his hand on the doorknob, preventing her from opening it herself and disappearing down the hall. She had no choice but to pause.

"Yes?"

"What do you hear from Millie McBryde?"

At the sound of Millie's name, Emily relaxed, remembering that Rusty and Millie had been friends. "Oh, you probably know she's married now."

His chin dropped slightly. He forced a smile. "No, I didn't. I used to see her brothers around town, but since I've been working for the government, I'm either stuck in the office or out on the road visiting Penderlea applicants." There was a touch of bitterness in his voice, and she remembered that he'd been unable to finish law school because of his family's misfortune.

"That's not always a pleasant job," she said. "I know some who've been turned down after the interview. It's a shame, but not everyone meets the criteria for a homesteader."

"You bet they don't. I've seen some pretty sorry people hoping to get on the government's gravy train. Had to deny their applications."

"Really?" But she stopped short of telling Rusty that she was thinking that Millie and Len Ryan would be the perfect candidates for a Penderlea homestead.

Hugh MacRae's secretary met Emily in the hallway, handing her a stack of applications rubber-banded together. "He wants to see you in his office," the secretary said. "He's in a terrible swivet, honey. A bunch of big shots are coming here from Washington, and the regional director from Atlanta wants Mr. MacRae to take them up to Penderlea and show them around."

"Well, I'm sure he'd be glad to, Betty. Just tell him I was here."

"No, you'd better go on in. He'll tell you."

Emily tapped lightly on the glass in Hugh MacRae's door before turning the knob. "Come on in, Emily," he said. She stepped inside the office expecting to see only Hugh, but an attractive gentleman about her age sat in a leather chair opposite Hugh's desk. "Emily, this is Reginald Ashworth from the division's regional office in Atlanta. He's got some folks coming down from Washington on the train tomorrow, and he wants you to meet them in Willard, take 'em over, and show them the project."

Ashworth rose to take Emily's hand, bowing slightly. "Mrs. McAllister, I'm delighted to meet you."

"Thank you, Mr. Ashworth, the pleasure is mine," she said. The gentleman was wearing a dark pin-striped suit and looked more like a Wall Street banker than a government employee. His hair was slicked back like that of an old-time movie star, but he wore sturdy black shoes that needed a good polishing ... *from traipsing around resettlement projects,* she thought. Emily turned to Hugh MacRae. "You'll be there, of course?"

"No, I can't go. I told Reggie you'd take them around, show 'em the project." He smiled at her, a little twinkle in his eye. "I hear you've gotten yourself quite a reputation with those pimento cheese sandwiches and that sweet tea."

"There's always one for you, Hugh, but I keep missing you on your rounds."

He approached Emily and put his arm around her shoulders. "Look here, honey, I know this is a lot to ask, but you've taken such an interest in the project. It's really important for the government men to see that we're not all a bunch of country bumpkins down here." He gave her a little hug. "You'll do this for me, won't you?"

"I'd be most appreciative of your company, Miss Emily," Reginald said. "You won't have to do a thing but show us around. I'll have my car, and I'll bring the gentlemen back here for our board meeting the next day."

"I suppose I could do it. I'd planned to go to Penderlea again the first of next week. We're getting applications there as well as here in Wilmington. My committee meets next Wednesday."

Hugh hugged her again. "Wonderful, Emily. I knew you'd do this for me." He turned to Reginald Ashworth. "Do you have that train schedule, Reggie?"

"Yes, sir. The train is due a little after two in the afternoon. Unfortunately for us, that's enough past the lunch hour that we won't get any of those pimento cheese sandwiches." He smiled, revealing perfect white teeth.

Emily laughed. "Wouldn't be a problem," she said gaily, "but we may need to worry about that storm out in the Atlantic. I heard on the radio that a hurricane is bringing some rough weather off the coast for the next day or two."

Hugh walked over to one of the large windows in his office and looked out over the Cape Fear River toward the ocean. "I think it's still a ways off. Everything's on the ground to start the first ten houses—the last of the lumber and supplies was delivered yesterday. We don't have time for a storm, not now," he said, sounding as if it might be within his power to hold off bad weather. "We're hiring new men every day. Some are future homesteaders. Already got about 150 CCC boys stationed at the camp there."

"I wish I could tell you when those studies will be finished, Hugh," the director said. "I'm afraid Harold Ickes is convinced that it'll take twenty acres or more to make those farms work."

"Yes, I know, and he's a damn fool. Been sending agents to Castle Hayne—asking questions, filling out forms. But folks like Ludeke will tell them how it's done. A man like him knows how to be smart about farming."

"I thought he'd bought some more land, enlarged his spread."

"Well, he has," Hugh said. "And there's nothing wrong with that." He pointed his finger at Ashworth. "That's what he was supposed to do!" Hugh MacRae was mild mannered—maybe even grandfatherly until you said something that riled him. Then the Scotsman in him reared up, and one could almost see smoke coming out of his ears. He walked around his desk and sat in his chair, rocked back, and put his feet on the corner of his desk. "Listen here, I expect every one of these folks at Penderlea will want more land. But they'll have to pay for a house and ten acres first. It's reasonable, and every one of them will be able to own something because we gave them the opportunity."

"You've got a lot of confidence in these people, Hugh. I hope they don't let you down," Ashworth said.

MacRae put his feet on the floor and sat up, staring hard at the government man. "They won't be letting *me* down, they'll be letting themselves down. But you watch. One or two might not make it, but the rest will. These folks are handpicked. With a little help—and I'm going to see that they get it—Penderlea will be the utopia of resettlement communities. The government is going to wish Hugh MacRae was running all of their projects."

"I was afraid you were disappointed that Harold Ickes put Alvin Johnson over you as president of the Penderlea Homestead Board," the director said.

"Hell, no! I'm managing it. On the project is where I belong—seeing that things get done the way I want them done."

Emily stood by the window overlooking the river. She had the feeling that they had forgotten she was in the room. She started toward the door. "Excuse me, Hugh," she said, "I'd best be on my way."

Both men stood simultaneously. "Sorry, Emily," Hugh said. "We were neglecting you."

"No, not at all. I'll be at the Willard station tomorrow, a little before two. The Coast Line is usually right on time."

Ashworth reached out to shake her hand. "I'm much obliged, Mrs. McAllister. I'll be driving a black Dodge. See you there around two o'clock."

Hugh hugged her. "Thank you, honey, I knew I could count on you."

⌐

Emily wished she had not chosen that particular day to come to Wilmington. She felt like an object of convenience for Hugh MacRae. Entertaining a bunch of congressmen from Washington was not her cup of tea. She'd be the only woman in a pack of politicians who were smoking cigars and laughing about the fact that they were off on a jaunt to backwoods North Carolina.

CHAPTER 19

Emily arrived at the Willard train station promptly at two o'clock. Reginald Ashworth was standing beneath the shed that covered the loading dock. There was no train station as such in Willard, but the North Carolina Agriculture Department had established a test farm there and Willard had become a regular stop on the Atlantic Coast Line route to Wilmington. Just down the line was Van Eeden, St. Helena, and Castle Hayne, all farm colonies built by Hugh MacRae, who knew that rail access to markets was essential to the success of truck farming.

She straightened her hat and tucked a few wisps of hair behind her ears. Emily loved the short cut she'd worn since Christmas when Jeanne had taken the scissors to her hair. The thick bouffant style that had been hers for twenty years was "outdated," Jeanne said. Emily had enjoyed the way her hats had sat atop her luxuriant tresses, but the style was no longer the fashion and she realized it had made her look much older.

Reginald Ashworth's hand was on her car door. "Mrs. McAllister, your looks need no improvement," he said.

"Goodness, Mr. Ashworth, you beat me here. Have you been waiting long?"

"Only a minute or two," he said, opening her car door. "Please, call me Reggie."

"Of course, Reggie." She straightened her dress and adjusted her hat again. "I'm afraid we're in for some wet weather. The radio said we'd likely have rain most of the day."

"That shouldn't matter. These fellows that are coming down just need to get a general idea of the scope of the project. They're politicians. That's where the money comes from, you know."

"Yes, I understand. But only the main road is paved. We're liable to get into some mud."

Reggie laughed. "I hear the project manager keeps a tractor close by, just for that purpose."

Emily cringed. She had avoided getting stuck on Penderlea again since the Board of Visitors meeting. Gordon Van Schaack had given her a lengthy description of the soil types found on the project. He said the very fine-grained soil was heavy sand as long as it was dry, but turned into deep mud when it was wet. He'd warned her to stay off the project in rainy weather.

"Just stay on the main road," she cautioned. "I'm glad you're driving."

"Yes, of course," he said, looking somewhat dubious. "Well, we'll just do the best we can, won't we?"

The train was over half an hour late. Emily and Reggie had watched the skies darken and the rain move in. As several passengers disembarked from the train, they pulled their suit coats about them and held their hats against the wind. "You get in the car, Emily, and I'll direct the gentlemen. There's no need in us all getting wet."

"There are five of them, Reggie. We can't all get in one car."

Ashworth looked distressed. "They told me there would only be three or four," he said. "Would you mind taking your car, too?"

She smiled. "Do I have a choice?"

"Emily, I am so sorry. Please run to your car before you get soaked, and I'll work this out with the gentlemen."

Driving in rain didn't usually frighten Emily, but the wind was ferocious.

Three of the five congressmen, smelling of cigar smoke and whiskey, had piled into her car without introductions. To them, the experience was something of a joke. "Nothing like a train ride to North Carolina in a hurricane to break up the week," she overheard one of passengers say as he hefted himself into the back seat and slammed the car door. Another got in on the other side, and another in the front seat beside Emily.

"You must be Mrs. Hugh MacRae," the man beside her said.

Emily smiled, icily. "No, I'm afraid not. I'm Emily McAllister. Just a good Democrat from Onslow County, North Carolina."

"Well now, I'd say this was our lucky day, wouldn't you, gentlemen?"

There was some mild chortling in the back seat, but the man beside her reigned in his humorous asides. "Forgive us, Mrs. McAllister, we've had a long ride and looked forward to stretching our legs looking at your new subsistence project. Perhaps we should find a dry spot and wait until this blows over."

"I'm afraid the forecast calls for a lot of rain. There's a tropical storm off the coast," she said, attempting to hide her dread of what lay ahead. Determined to maintain her demeanor, she pulled up beside Reggie's car and rolled down her window a few inches. "Do you still want to go to Penderlea? It might be better for you to go on to Wilmington and come back tomorrow," she suggested.

"Can't do it," he shouted over the pelting rain. "They've got a full day of meetings tomorrow. Would you mind leading the way, and we'll just see what we can see?"

"I guess so, but you can't see much from the main road." She closed her window, pulling out onto the Penderlea Road. "We'll just see what we can see," she repeated, slightly under her breath.

Once they were on the highway, the man in the front seat next to her introduced himself. "I apologize for the imposition, Mrs. McAllister," he said. "I'm Harold Cooley. I'm on the Agriculture Committee in the House. Looks like those fellows in the back seat have fallen asleep. I'll introduce you when we reach the project. There *is* somewhere we can stop and go inside, isn't there?"

"Yes, it's only five miles to Penderlea. I'll try and pull into the construction site. That's where the project manager's office is."

"Would you like for me to drive?"

"No, thank you. I've been here before. I think I'd better lead the way for Mr. Ashworth."

Emily maneuvered her car onto Garden Road, which would take them to the operations site. Just ahead of her car, two trucks were parked in the middle of the road, front end to front end. She pulled up behind the truck nearest her and tooted her horn. The driver raised his head up from under the hood. He signaled for Millie to go around him. She edged toward the side of the pavement, praying that her tires were on solid ground. But just when she was almost around the truck, the car began to slide sideways into the ditch. The weight of the men in the back seat did not help the situation. Before she knew it, the car came to a sideways stop in the ditch. Reggie Ashworth was directly behind her watching the disaster unfold.

Once Emily's car settled into the ditch, all seven men, plus the two truck drivers, got out to try and assess the damages. The rain was coming down in fine blinding sheets. In minutes they were all soaked to the skin. Emily stayed in the car. One of the truck drivers recognized her and opened the passenger door a crack to speak to her. Water poured off his hat into her car. "You might want to just stay in there, Miss Emily. I'll take these gents over to the project office. We can't pull your car out until this rain lets up."

"No, I want to get out. If you'll just help me, I can get out that door."

Ashworth was by the man's side. "You go on, take the others to the office, I'll get her out," he said to the man. "What a mess. I'm so sorry, Emily." He held the door while she slipped across the seat. When she was by the door, he pulled her the rest of the way out until she could stand on the soft ground. "Your shoes and dress will be ruined," he said.

She pulled off her hat and threw it onto the seat. "I'm more worried about my car."

"Don't you worry 'bout your car, Miss Emily," the other truck driver said.

"I've got my tractor right over yonder. I'll get you out and back on the pavement soon as I can."

Suddenly, to her surprise, Ashworth swept Emily off her feet and into his arms. "I'm not going to let you ruin your shoes," he said. "Hang on," he said, and dashed toward the project office.

"Wait! Put me down, you'll hurt your back!" She felt like a silly schoolgirl, protesting as Reggie sprinted across the slippery pine needles that covered the ground under the swaying pine trees.

"Hush! You're talking to a running back for the 1904 Oak Ridge football team."

"I think I weigh a little more than a football," she cried.

"I said hush. We're almost there."

And hush she did, enjoying for a brief moment the warm scent of an excited man. How long it had been since she'd felt that!

It was almost dark when the truck driver came into the office with the news that he had Emily's car out of the ditch and parked just outside the office. "We brung yours over, too," he said looking at Reggie.

The small office that had been hastily built during the first construction phase was rank with the odor of damp wool and perspiration, but the rumpled dignitaries had dried themselves out while playing cards around a small potbellied stove. Unfortunately, they'd seen little else of the Penderlea project. "I think we can all cram into Ashford's car for the trip to Wilmington, Mrs. McAllister," Representative Cooley said. "We've troubled you enough for one day."

"I can't say it was a pleasure, Mr. Representative," she said, "but I don't imagine any of us are worse for the wear. Please come back in drier weather," she laughed.

Ashworth began assembling his crowd for the drive to Wilmington. "I've got the car running outside. You fellows climb in while I put Mrs. McAllister in hers."

"No, please go on, Reggie. I'll be fine."

"Do I have to hog tie you again and throw you over my shoulder?"

Emily laughed. "No, I'll go willingly," she laughed.

Ashworth held her umbrella over them as they half-ran to her car, which stood idling near-by. The truck driver held the car door open. "Thank you, kind sir," Ashworth said. "I'll take over now," he said. He slipped a bill into the man's hand. The truck driver stared at the twenty-dollar bill and walked away shaking his head.

"That was nice of you," Emily said. "In fact, you're just a nice fellow," she said, realizing that she was a little addled, not only by the day behind them, but by the man who'd slipped his arm around her.

"You were wonderful, Emily. Most women would have fallen to pieces under those circumstances. I'd like to see you again, if I may."

"Oh? Well, yes, I'm sure we will." Flustered, she brushed her skirt behind her knees and tried to sit down in the car.

But Reginald Ashworth pulled her in closer, forcing her to look up at him. "No, I mean, I'd like to see more of you. More than just a chance meeting. Is that possible?"

"I guess so."

He touched his lips to her forehead. "Thank you. I'll be in touch."

⌒

The rain had washed most of the mud off Emily's car, but the tires threw thick clods of mud against the inside of the Buick's fenders as she drove along the dark road toward Onslow County. Her mind whirled around the events of the day. She should be upset, irritated that she had gotten herself into such an ordeal. She had no business driving in this weather. She did not work for the government, nor for Hugh MacRae. She should have spent the day at home reading a good book. Instead, she was smiling. All the way home, she was smiling.

CHAPTER 20

SEPTEMBER 1934

Millie's water broke in the wee hours of the eighth day of September. Her contractions were mild at first, then stopped completely. After Len had notified Lizzie and Maggie Lorena, he went to Eddie Lee's store and called Rebecca. When he got home from making the call, Lizzie had changed the bed linens and gone back to the big house to cook breakfast.

"Lizzie said you might as well go on with your work." Millie said. "If things don't start right away, it might be awhile."

"Are you all right? Can I do anything?" Len asked. He sat down on the bed and took hold of her hand. She wasn't accustomed to this much attention from him. It was nice.

"I'm fine," Millie said. "You could bring me some breakfast after you have yours."

"Don't you need me to stay with you?" he asked, nervously. "It'll be awhile before Rebecca gets here."

"I don't think so." She thought this exaggerated concern was comical, but she dared not giggle.

"Don't you know? I mean—aren't you afraid?"

"Sure I'm afraid it's going to hurt, Len. But I think about all the other women who've survived birthing babies. I reckon I can do it too."

"Well, all right, but I'll be back as soon as Lizzie gets your plate ready."

Millie smiled, thinking it might not be so bad having babies. It was almost pleasant to be laid up in bed—everybody waiting on you. For the last few days she'd been about to pop, waddling around the house and yard feeling like she could lay eggs. The Scuppernong grapes were dripping from the vines underneath the grape arbor, and she'd tried to pick some to make jelly, but her legs hurt so badly that she'd had to sit down in an old chair that Maggie kept under there for herself. Millie had come by her varicose veins proud. Eva had warned all of her girls that they'd likely inherit the curse that made the veins in her legs stand out like knots of bluish ropes. Unfortunately, varicose veins didn't go away after the baby was delivered. They might not hurt as much, but Millie knew her legs would look just like her mother's, black and blue for the rest of her life.

⁓

Rebecca had insisted that Len call her. She'd told her supervisor that she'd need a day or two off when the time came. The birth of the first grandchild in the family—the birth of her first niece or nephew was so thrilling. Mr. Jones wanted to go with her, but she said he would just be in the way. She'd fixed him an attractive dinner plate and put it in the refrigerator and told him he could have his supper at the café down on Front Street. If she was gone overnight, there'd be no problem. He cooked his own breakfast every day anyway because she was often on night duty.

Rebecca arrived at the camp house about noon with a package of stew meat. "I stopped at Uncle Duncan's butcher shop. He sends you his love and best wishes."

"That was nice," Millie said. "Did he have all of his fingers?" She burst out laughing. "Oh, oh, oh, I shouldn't have done that," she cried, holding her belly.

Rebecca was laughing, too. "All except that one." She reached for a Dutch oven hanging on the wall. "That was Mama's favorite joke." She touched the stove. "How come the stove is cold?"

"Lizzie said it would get too hot in here to cook. When the time comes, she'll bring a kettle over from the big house."

"Well, let me go over there and put this stew on. When things start to happen, they'll go fast."

"I feel, I feel...I feel like pushing down" Millie said, her eyes opening wide. "Am I supposed to?"

"No, not yet! Just take some deep breaths until it passes. I'll go get Lizzie."

"Wait, Rebecca. I'm scared," Millie said.

"Oh, don't be. You've got another hour or two yet. But I'll tell Len to call Dr. Bayard over in Atkinson—just to let him know we might need him."

"What if he doesn't get here in time?"

"For goodness sake, Millie. Lizzie is a midwife and I'm a registered nurse. Besides, this is your first baby. They always take their sweet time coming. Nothing's going to happen."

⌐

And nothing untoward did. In fact Annie Louise defied logic and came into the world before the doctor arrived and long before the stew was done. Millie's labor had lasted only two hours. By three o'clock in the afternoon, the ordeal was over and she was able to eat a little of the rich stew at supper. Rebecca sat with her, holding the baby in the makeshift bedroom of the camp house. "She's beautiful, Millie, honey. Look at this head of black hair! I'm surprised it's not red like Mama's and Len's, aren't you?"

"I'm just glad she's got all of her fingers and toes," Millie said.

"Yes, she does have all her little fingers and toes," Rebecca cooed to the baby. "She's going to be mama's little helper and daddy's big girl. Yes, she is." She nuzzled the baby and looked up at Millie. Her eyes were full of tears.

"I know you want a baby," Millie said, her own eyes weepy.

"I guess it wasn't meant to be," Rebecca sniffed. "It's not that Mr. Jones and I haven't tried."

"I know," Millie sympathized. "Cousin Maggie says that Aunt Mag

McFayden never had children of her own. They say she just claimed all of her nieces and nephews. Uncle Archie was way older than her. Do you think that has anything to do with it?"

"Heck, no! Look at Papa. He and Mama were still having babies when she was in her forties and he was in his fifties. It's just a matter of chance. There's no way to tell."

"Nobody is having as many children as they used to," Millie said. "They can't afford them."

Rebecca moved over to the bed and sat down next to Millie. She tucked the baby under her sister's arm. "You will be careful, won't you, honey?"

"About what?" Millie asked, thinking she might mean caring for the baby.

"About having another baby. Men don't give a hoot. It's going to be up to you. As soon as you start having your periods again—probably after you stop nursing—keep up with your periods. Write them down. When you know your average cycle, right in the middle will be when you can get pregnant. Stay as far away from him as you can for three or four days. Or else you'll have yourself a new baby every two years, just like Mama. One is really enough."

"Oh, I want more than one!" Millie said. "And Len really wants a boy. He's going to be persistent about that."

"Well, it's all up to you."

⌣

"Are you disappointed, Len?" Millie asked after everyone had left them that evening.

"No, honey, not a'tall." But of course she knew he was. "They say a man always hopes for a boy—someone to carry on his name."

"She's just our first baby," he said. "I reckon we'll have a passel more."

⌣

Annie Louise was colicky and cried through the night for the first three months. That's when Len began to sleep in his old room at his mama's house. "My nerves just can't take it, Millie. I have to get up at sunup." So the first few months after the baby was born, Len was seldom in the camp house at night. But often, once the baby was asleep, loneliness overcame Millie and she'd wrap the baby in a blanket and slip in the back door of the big house and into bed with Len.

"We need a place of our own," Len whispered. "A place with more than one room, where the baby could yell her head off and I could get some sleep."

"She'll soon be sleeping all night," Millie said.

"But there's hardly room to turn around in the camp house with the crib and all. Mama said we could move over here for good if we want to. You could take Annie into Will's room."

Len's childhood bedroom in the big house was sparsely furnished with a three-quarter iron bedstead, a chair, and a small table. A narrow doorway separated it from Will's room, which Maggie had kept just as Will had left it in anticipation of his return. A curtain was all that separated the two rooms. A door would have to be added to do any good. She tried to imagine what it would be like—Len in his own room, her and Annie in Will's. In Cousin Maggie's house? "You wouldn't want that, would you?"

"I don't know, it wouldn't be too bad. You're over here all the time anyhow. Mama says once she gets to sleep, nothing bothers her."

"We'd move the baby's crib over here?"

"I reckon so."

"What about Mr. Tate? He needs his rest, too."

Len chuckled. "Pa's deaf in one ear and can't hear out of the other."

His back was to her and the baby was between them. She wanted to snuggle closer, wrap her legs over his, tell him he'd miss her, miss their privacy. She lifted the baby and placed her under her other arm, afraid Len might roll back on her. She'd heard of babies being smothered that way. "Len?"

"What?"

"What about Penderlea? You said maybe we could—"

Len sat up on the side of the bed, his hair tousled and his eyes bleary. "Damn, I was almost asleep." He reached for his cigarettes, lit one with a wooden match, sat hunched over on the side of the bed looking as if he had the weight of the world on his shoulders. "I've been thinking about it, too. But Ray Wilkins said things were at a standstill over there. The government's been changing the rules right and left. Mr. Hugh is fed up. He's threatened to resign."

"He wouldn't do that, would he?"

"Why not? He practically gave the government the land. He planned the whole damn thing. Those fellows up in Washington say he picked sorry land, soil that wouldn't drain if you dug ditches from here to China. They say he's already spent too much money—ten-acre plots aren't big enough to piss on, much less make a damn living. I tried to tell Mr. Hugh that, but he's hard-headed as the devil. Said he's already proved they could at Castle Hayne."

"Your mama said she read in the paper yesterday that Mr. MacRae was asking everyone in the county—not just those interested in moving to Penderlea—to come and use the picnic grounds he's built for the home-steaders. Does that sound like he's giving up?"

"I don't know, but something's not right. I'm not willing to pull up stakes and move over there before it's ready. Besides, I can't go off and leave Mama and Papa right now. If Will was home, it might be different, but he's got a pretty good job working for some man that owns a whole fleet of cars. He might never come back home. I can't say as I blame him."

Millie closed her eyes, put her arm across her forehead. There, he'd said it. He was giving up. She felt as if the rug had been pulled out from under her. She'd accepted a lot of things because of Penderlea—the camp house, no electricity or running water. Now a baby. She'd told herself that she could put up with anything as long as she knew there was going to be an end to it. As long as she knew there'd be that little cottage at the end of her rainbow. Now Len was backing up? "You promised me," she said quietly.

Len jerked his head around. "What? I did what?"

"You said we'd only be here a year or so. You said Will would come home and then we could go."

"Goddamn, Millie, you really know how to kick me in the damn teeth when I'm down." He said it in a loud whisper, but she was sure they could hear him in the other bedroom.

"I have feelings, too. I'm disappointed."

"You're disappointed?" he said sarcastically. "Well, goddamn, I am so sorry to be such a sorry husband and disappoint little 'Miss McBryde' who has always had everything handed to her on a damn silver platter!"

"Hush, Len. They'll hear you and that's not true!"

"Don't hush me! I'm going back over to my own damn house where I can say what I want to say and say it as loud as I want to say it." He jerked on his pants and put on a jacket. He stopped in the doorway. "You coming with me?"

She was afraid not to.

CHAPTER 21

L en tacked another room onto the camp house, stuffing corn husks and cotton batting between the joists as insulation before he nailed on particle board he'd found that had fallen off a truck headed for Wilmington. The new room would be their bedroom, and the alcove where their bed had been would be the baby's room. The old cookstove, in its thirtieth year of service to the Ryan family, was sufficient to heat the small house, but Tate had suggested that a chimney would add an element of style to the exterior and be safer as well. He said he knew of a brick mason who'd owed him a little money for years. After Len put up cypress siding on the exterior, the little camp house seemed more like a real house, but it really didn't change how Millie felt.

The project kept both Len and Tate busy between chores until Thanksgiving. That evening at dinner in the big house, Len had commented that they'd likely seen the last of warm weather for awhile. The wind had been blustery all day, and Tate could tell by his rheumatism that they were in for some bad weather. "You better check those barn doors when you go out, son. I've already got my shoes off."

"I will, Papa. I'm looking forward to putting mine under that bed in our new room tonight." He glanced at Millie. "Tomorrow's our anniversary, you know."

"Is that a fact?" Tate said, smiling. "Well, y'all better go on then, and get to it."

"Land sakes, Tate. You'll be embarrassing Millie," Maggie said.

Millie laughed, thinking she'd heard more bawdy remarks than that from Maggie Lorena. "I'll take the baby, Len. You go on and look after the barn," she said. "We'll see y'all after breakfast."

Millie wrapped the baby in a small quilt and braved the wind crossing the short distance between the house and the camp house. She'd seen the gleam in Len's eye and knew what was in store. He'd settled down in his demands since the baby had been born, to the point that she looked forward to the intimacy of married life. When she reached the camp house, Annie was asleep and she decided that she'd wait to nurse her again when she woke up. With a little luck, she thought, this might be the first time the baby slept through the night.

⌒

The wind had roared all night long, shouldering against the flimsy shelter like a heavyweight intent on moving a mountain. But the little house held its own until just before dawn when the older part of the tin roof had blown off, exposing the baby in her crib and pelting her with sleet. Len grabbed the baby and told Millie to run for the big house. Barefoot and in their nightclothes, they'd made their way into the kitchen before waking Maggie and Tate. By the time his parents were up, Millie had made a pot of coffee and a pan of biscuits. Annie was still fretting on her shoulder.

"Can't you do something with her, Millie? My nerves can't stand it," Len said.

"I think it liked to have scared her to death," Millie said. "I hope she doesn't take a cold."

"Babies are tougher than you think," Tate said. "Here, give her to me. I'll quiet her." He took the baby and jiggled her in his arms, humming a flat tune as he did so.

Maggie gritted her teeth. "I'm going back to my bed," she said. "Tate, you bring me my coffee."

"In a minute. Poor little darlin' must've thought the world had come to an end," Tate said, rocking her back and forth.

"Thank you, Mr. Tate. Look, Len, she's quieted right down."

Len took a long swig of his coffee. "He's got more patience than I do. That's for sure."

⌒

When the cold rain stopped, Len and Millie went out to see what they could salvage from the camp house. By afternoon, the weather had faired off, and they were able to get some of their things outside to dry in the sun. Len plopped down in an overstuffed chair still damp from the rain. "Come here," he said. "I need to talk to you."

"Just a minute," Millie said. "Let me finish hanging Annie's things on the line. They won't dry if I don't." When she'd hung the last piece of clothing, she walked over to where he was sitting. He grabbed her arm and pulled her into his lap. "Whoa!" she said.

"Look, I know you were scared last night. It scared me too. I don't want to live like this. I know you don't either. I'm not promising anything, but I just want you to know that if you can put up with this a little while longer, I'm going to do something. I'm not exactly sure what it's going to be right now, but things have got to change. We can't let something like that happen again."

"All right, Len," she said. "I can put up with it." She almost added "spoiled Miss McBryde that I am." Instead, she kissed him, and he kissed her back.

"Thank you, honey. I'll make it up to you, one way or another."

⌒

Len devoted most of his time in the next two weeks to putting the camp house back together. Tate wasn't much help, he noted to Millie. "He's awful slow, sort of short of breath."

Millie was outside boiling diapers in the wash pot and rinsing them in a tub of water. "Do you need me to help?"

"No, it would hurt Pa's feeling if I let you help me instead of him. But I am worried. This morning he was standing on the ladder passing tin roofing up to me. He turned white as a sheet."

"Maybe you ought to take him over to Doc Bayard's. It might be his heart."

"I just wish Will would come on home and help us out."

Millie dried her hands, red and raw from the water and the strong soap. More and more often, she'd had the same thought. *If Will was home—*"Wishing won't bring him home," she said. "Why don't you write to him?"

Len walked over to the boiling pot and warmed his hands. "I'm not writing to him and begging him to come home. He knows what we're going through down here."

"But if he knew your pa was sick."

"Now, goddamnit, don't you start telling me what to do. I've got all I can do on me, and I don't need you to start nagging at me about getting Will home."

"I'm sorry, Len. I didn't mean it like that."

"Yes, you did. You think I don't know what to do." She started to walk away from him, wishing she'd kept quiet. Len followed behind her. "Don't go sulking off. You listen to me. I'm sick and tired of working my fingers to the bone for you. You don't appreciate a thing. You're no better than that outlaw cousin of yours that chopped up his wife with an axe."

She whipped around to face him. "Len, that's not true! Davy didn't—"

"Don't talk back to me. I know what I'm saying." He started toward her.

"Your mama is at the window," Millie said. "She can hear you."

"I don't give a damn who hears me. I'm mad as hell and I just don't care who knows it!"

Maggie appeared on the back porch of her house. "What's wrong, Lennie?"

"Nothing's wrong, Mama. Just go on back inside before you catch cold."

CHAPTER 22

JANUARY 1935

The weatherman said that so far January had been the coldest on record. Snuggled up in bed under a pile of quilts in the drafty camp house, Millie and Len had no doubt about it. Beside them, the baby rattled with each breath. Millie stepped out from under the covers long enough to pull a blanket over Annie's shoulders. "Poor little thing, no wonder she has a cold."

Len sat up in bed and lit a cigarette. "I'll bet those houses Mr. Hugh is building are tight as a tick. I sure would like to go take a look at them."

Millie snuggled against him. "Oh, could we, Len?"

"Not yet, honey. I'm dying to see them too, but I don't want to upset Mama and Papa. Dr. Bayard called that spell Papa had something like a little heart attack. Besides, we don't have a way to go." He took a long drag off his cigarette and flicked the ashes on the floor. "Damn! I wish Will would get his ass home."

"I'll bet Cal would take us. I could ask him."

"No, no, don't do that. I don't want anybody getting all hepped up about it. Let's just keep it between us now. You start telling everybody you're thinking about something, and they think you're wishy-washy if you don't do it."

Millie fluffed up the big feather pillows against the head of the iron bedstead and sat up beside him. "Tell me some more about what it would be like over there."

Len smiled. He loved to dream about it too. "Well, now, we'd have electricity for one thing. You know, lightbulbs on the ceilings and all. Just flip a little switch and light up the whole room."

"And running water?" she said.

"Yep."

"Hot water?"

"I'm sure of it. They make these hot water storage tanks now that are hooked into the stove." He reached over and tickled her. "You could take a hot tub bath anytime you like."

"Maybe they have washing machines, too. If they have electric lights and running water, we could have a washing machine."

"Somebody said they were going to have a separate little washhouse," he said.

"Did you say we'd get a barn and a corn crib, too?"

"Yeah, and the paper said they'll give you a start on some livestock, even chickens."

Millie pictured a flock of black and white Plymouth Rocks kicking up dust, pecking at microscopic bugs. "When Annie is a little older, maybe she could have a real cat," she said.

"What do you mean, 'a real cat'?"

"Those old perish-gutted yard cats your mama feeds are eaten up with fleas. I'm talking about a house cat." She felt him tense up.

"Mama loves those cats," he said.

"Oh, I know she does, Len. I just meant a pet cat, one Annie could name and call her own."

"Maybe we'll have a horse for Annie," Len said, relaxing again. "You know like a pony with a saddle. You could ride it too."

But Millie had closed her eyes and drifted off to sleep while Len's restless mind continued to toss and turn like a young man's will. The Depression had only made bad things worse for farmers. What was it MacRae said? *This might be your only chance to help your parents, Len. The government's going to own their land too, if they can't pay the taxes.* But MacRae had been wrong when he said the land was worn out. Land could never be worn out. It might be depleted of nutrients, but a modern farmer like Len knew there were ways to rebuild the soil if a man was willing to work it. Len was already a leader in the community. People looked up to him, and he liked the feel of it. If he left, Tate and many others would give up. Some would leave. If he stayed, they might all have a new deal—maybe a better life.

But Len couldn't say this to Millie. When he tried to tell her how he felt about things like that, she got all upset and sad. That made him mad. A man ought to be able to say how he felt. But he'd decided to make an effort to keep his thoughts to himself—tell her about the good things—his plans—the things he had in mind for them when things were better. If the truth be known, he was afraid to go to Penderlea—afraid of the government having a hold on everything he owned.

Roosevelt's New Deal held some promise in Bladen County, too. A man right here could have a better life. He could borrow the government's money—rob Peter to pay Paul—work from sunup to sunset each day—go to bed dog tired and get up and do it all over again the next day. He didn't have to go to Penderlea to do it; he could do it just as good in Bladen County as he could there. But there was one difference—one *big* difference. Here in Colly, the land was his. His Corbinn ancestors had acquired it by land grants in the early 1700s—their bones now part of this ancient soil. How could he ever feel that way about government-owned land on Penderlea? If Millie could see that, he'd just put Penderlea completely out of his mind.

⌒

"I hear they've got the first ten houses almost finished," Ray Wilkins said. "They told me that several are being built by the folks who'll live in them."

"Yeah, I heard," Len said. He'd stopped in the Bladen County agent's office to take another look at the drawing pinned up on the wall. Everybody was talking about MacRae's farm city now. There it was with all the little farms laid out in a horseshoe pattern around a community center. A school was right in the middle.

"Would you believe, they've got a big cooperative store where home-steaders can sell their stuff? Even got a cannery. Been operating it since last summer."

"You been over there lately?"

"Nope, been thinking about doing just that. You want to go with me while you ain't got much to do outside?"

"I reckon I could," Len said.

"Tell you what, you get Millie or Miss Maggie Lorena to pack us a lunch, and I'll pick you up about seven o'clock tomorrow morning."

At Eddie Lee's store that night, Len kept quiet about his plans for the next day. The camaraderie that existed among the young farmers who spent their evenings there was very important to him. He was afraid that his interest might be seen as pulling away from all they had been working for together. And not everyone shared his enthusiasm or his admiration of Hugh MacRae. Josh Henry, a neighbor, had suggested that the community center was intended as MacRae's new country estate. "Pen-der-lea," Josh said, putting on airs. "Don't that sound like one of them damn mansions in Wilmington? I bet he'll move in with a bunch of servants by the end of summer."

"That's bullshit and you know it, Josh," Eddie Lee said. "Why in the hell would he want to live way out there in the boondocks of Pender County when he's got all them big houses in Wilmington?"

"MacRae mansion or not, a couple of my cousins who live over that way found jobs on Penderlea," Roland Rooks said. "They're paying carpenter's helpers fifty-five cents an hour. My cousin said they've got this big labor camp built by the CCC where you can live while you're working there." He hopped up on the counter to sit, lit a cigarette, and blew smoke over his audience. "I'm thinking if things don't get better soon, I might go looking for a job."

Len listened to the banter, laughing along with the rest of them. But he intended to see it for himself tomorrow, and not the least of his intentions was a visit with Hugh MacRae. Later that evening, he told Millie about his plan to go with Ray Wilkins to Penderlea. "I just want to see it for myself," he said." He pulled Millie close. "Don't get your hopes up, shug," he said. "I know you'd like to have one of those little houses with electricity and running water. I would, too." He was quiet for a minute, and Millie was afraid to say anything. "You know, we need to be thinking about the long run. What if Penderlea is a big flop? Where would we be then?"

"I suppose we could always come back here and live in our little camp house."

"You're damn right we could," Len said. "And I could build you a house you'd be proud of. One of these days, we'll have electricity. We could have a pump and running water—everything your little heart desires. I could do it all myself."

"I know you could, Len," she said. She believed it. Len could do anything. He had a knack for building things—look at the camp house. Out of need, he'd worked on it until it could stand up to cold weather and storms. He'd even made it pretty with the brick chimney on one end. Just yesterday, he'd dug a hole for her to plant a climbing rose to tie against it. And he'd already plowed a small garden near the house where she'd plant a row of cut flowers and a few kitchen vegetables.

"Maybe you'd rather have that?" he said, "You know, a big house with everything you want in it right here on land that already belongs to us?" Millie didn't say anything. He leaned over her, trying to see her expression in the darkened bedroom. "Is that something you'd want?"

"I guess so. I'd just always thought we were going to Penderlea. It all sounds so good. Something we could have right away."

"I know it does, honey. That's why I'm going over there tomorrow to see what it's like. We might not even want to go."

Tate stepped out onto the porch when he heard Ray Wilkins's horn. A cold wind out of the north had brought a few flakes of light snow overnight. Ray poked his head out of the truck window and waved. "Better come go with us, Mr. Tate."

"Naw, I'll stay here and keep the womenfolk company. Won't do for the fires to go out with the little one around." He looked across the way and saw that Len was pulling the door to the camp house shut and Millie was at the small kitchen window waving the baby's hand. "Y'all have a good time," Tate said, swallowing a lump in his throat.

"You take it easy today, Pa," Len called out.

"Can't get into too much trouble with this wind. I might go in the woods later—bag a squirrel or two, if I'm lucky."

"Be careful, then."

"I will." He watched until the truck's tail lights faded into the distance, went back into the house, and slumped in a chair next to the stove. Maggie poured him a cup of coffee and handed it to him. "You reckon this means they're going to go to Penderlea?" she asked.

Tate glared at her. "Is that what you want?"

"I don't know what we'd do without Millie and Len around here," she said. "But we can't stop them. I reckon Len's a grown man now. I wish he'd just go on and go if that's what he wants to do."

Tate was pensive. He had given over most of the responsibility for running the farm to Len. In his mind, it was Len's farm now. If Len should leave, it would all fall back on him, and he didn't feel like he could do it anymore. Dealing with the farm agent—with the government—was a new way, and he was sot in the old ways. "I reckon you haven't thought about what I'll do if he goes," he said.

"You can't hold him back, Tate." She gritted her teeth at the thought. Maggie had a habit of doing that when things didn't suit her. "Millie said he was just going to go with the farm agent. He might look into some work for the rest of the winter. She hasn't said a word about going herself. Millie's not even thinking about it."

⌐

While Len was away for the day, Millie decided to bundle up the baby and take a basket of laundry down to her father's house. Rob kept the old washing machine they'd brought from Wilmington hooked up on the back porch. Tate hitched up the horse and cart for her. "I'll put a load of manure on your little garden while you're gone," he said.

"Thank you, Mr. Tate. Tell Miss Maggie I'll be back before supper."

"Take your time, shug. We don't need a thing," Tate said. "Tell ol' Rob to take care of hisself." He reached over into the cart and patted the baby. "You sure you don't want us to keep Annie so's you can come and go a little quicker?"

"No, sir, I know Papa will want to see her."

⌐

When Millie returned, with her hair washed and every inch of her skin scrubbed, it was obvious that she'd enjoyed a good soak herself in the Jasper tub. "You're looking all scrubbed and polished—clean as a whistle," Maggie said. "Does Cousin Rob use Jasper's tub?" Maggie still referred to the house and its furnishings as her brother Jasper's, even though Jasper had been dead a number of years.

"I reckon he does," Millie answered. She didn't say how often she observed that the bathtub was as clean when she arrived as when she left it.

"You stepped down right smart, marrying Len, didn't you?" Maggie asked.

"Oh, no, ma'am. We didn't have indoor plumbing in Bandeaux Creek. Just in Wilmington. I knew what it would be like."

"Now, you're not fooling me one bit, Millie. I've had nice things—been places. It was hard to come back here, but I did."

"One of these days, we'll have electric lights and indoor plumbing, Cousin Maggie. Doing without makes me appreciate what I used to have even more."

"I thought you didn't miss it." Maggie loved to do that—chide Millie into saying something she didn't mean to say. But Millie ignored her and tickled the baby, giving all her attention to Annie. "I needed you today," Maggie said. "Couldn't get my corset hooked. Tate was off in the woods hunting squirrels. My back was killing me."

"Oh, I'm so sorry. I should've helped you on with it before I left."

"No, no, it's all right. It's just that I know Len counts on you helping me."

"You need to let me know ahead of time, Cousin Maggie," Millie said, straining to keep the irritation out of her voice. "Will you be needing anything this afternoon? I can stay for awhile, if you like."

"Just put one of my BC headache powders and a glass of water on the table before you leave, honey. I reckon I'll be all right."

Millie did as she asked, but she couldn't help but wish even more so that Len would come home and say he'd signed up for one of those houses. Already, in the little over a year they'd been married, Millie had taken over most of the housekeeping chores. She did all of the cooking except breakfast, which Maggie Lorena managed perfectly well. If Maggie helped with the baby—listened out for her, or played with her on the bed—at the end of the day, her mother-in-law slanted her report to Len and Tate to make it sound as if Millie had neglected the child.

Sometimes Millie wondered how in the world she had gotten herself into such a predicament. But she felt she had no one to blame but herself. Papa had warned her. Living in a camp house had sounded like an adventure. Maybe even a challenge. Her own mother had lived without the conveniences of electricity and indoor plumbing. She'd raised eight children without such luxuries. Eva McBryde had never complained; more often, she'd bragged about how good life was—how devoted Rob was to her and her children. But Eva never had a mother-in-law to look after, and she'd always had a decent house and one or two Negro helpers. Even after Len had fixed it up, the camp house still wasn't much more than a chicken coop.

Millie liked to believe that she'd taken everything in her stride. She'd believed in Len before Annie was born—believed that the camp house was only temporary. She'd played the part of a dutiful wife. She'd washed diapers and chopped wood in freezing weather, suckered and handed tobacco in the scorching heat of August. She'd gardened and canned vegetables, helped slaughter hogs and stuff sausage. And she'd waited on his mother hand and foot. She'd done it all with the belief in mind that there would be a better life coming when they moved to Penderlea.

CHAPTER 23

Ray Wilkins gripped the steering wheel as he plowed his truck through the deep mud ruts on Pender Road. It was all he could do to keep it from sliding into the deep ditches. Bulldozers worked back and forth like ants in the fields on either side of the road, tugging and pushing huge piles of roots and debris and loading it into trucks. Now and then, a loud boom signaled the destruction of a stubborn stump. "Look at that," Len said. "I've never seen so much going on at one time in one place. Have you?"

"I can't take my eyes off the damn road," Ray said. "Damn things so churned up, we're liable to need one of those big boys to pull us out."

"Hell, I'll drive," Len said. "A little mud is nothing to me. I worked on the highway up there near Greensboro last year, just a slippin' and slidin' all over the damn place." He laughed at his own joke, completely missing the dirty look Ray sent his way. "You just have to gun it and keep on going," Len said, skidding one hand against the other.

"Keep an eye out for a road to the left," Ray said. "The project manager's office is over that way somewhere."

"I reckon that's where we'll find Mr. MacRae. Don't you?"

"Might be, but they say he's likely as not to be driving one those bull-dozers." Ray laughed. "If you see him, let me know and we'll pull over and speak to him if there's a dry spot." They turned left and made their way on a road that cut through plowed fields. "Look, I'll bet that's the cannery up ahead. Those must be the community gardens over there."

"I saw some collards," Len said. "That's about all."

"What did you expect? It's January. You ain't got much more than that and a few turnips growing in your pa's garden, have you?"

"No, I reckon not," Len said. "Millie told me the other day that we were running low on what she'd canned last summer. She said the baby would soon be eating table food."

"That looks like the construction office," Ray said. "I'll pull in over there. See those men standing around the fire? Go ask them where the houses are."

Ray and Len got out of the truck, and Len approached the cluster of men. "Howdy," Len said, extending his hand to the first man to look his way. "Name's Len Ryan."

"Pleased to meet you," the man said. A huge smile seemed to cover his entire face. "Dutch Van Bruggen here. You looking for work?"

"My county agent was coming over to take a look. I just came along for the ride."

"Not too much going on today," Van Bruggen said. "Rain's about ruined us this week." Dutch Van Bruggen's blue eyes were set into a very round face above a well-trimmed dark beard. He was a short, stocky man—wearing the usual garb of the area farmers—rough denim overalls and a plaid flannel shirt—but his speech revealed a slight accent. "Well, if you wanted some work, there's plenty of it here," he said.

"You wouldn't know if any of the houses are finished, would you? I'd sure like to see one."

Dutch let out a big laugh. "So would I. I've been living in a tool shack while they're building mine."

"You mean you're living here already?" Len asked.

"You might call it that, but it's more like camping. My wife and I have been here almost a year. I've got my ten acres, but it's still not cleared and the house isn't finished yet."

"How'd that come about?"

"My daddy lives over at Castle Hayne. He was talking to Mr. Hugh MacRae last year right after I'd gotten married. Mr. Hugh told Daddy that I ought to apply. I wanted a place of my own, so I came over here and talked to the project manager, got an application, and Mr. Hugh himself signed it. After that, I got a letter saying I'd been accepted."

"I heard they come to your house—look around—ask a lot of questions."

Dutch caught Len's eye, his likable grin lighting up his face. "I guess when Mr. Hugh signs off on you, nobody else needs to."

Len smiled back at him, acknowledging this bit of inside information. "He's a fine fellow. He sure is. If I decide to put in one of those applications, I might need to renew his acquaintance." They both laughed loudly.

"Have you met Jesse Alston? He's that fellow standing over there. He was already here when I came. Land wasn't even cleared, much less the houses started. The project manager hired us to work in the gardens at fifteen cents an hour. Of course, there was no place for us to live, but they said when they started the houses, we could hire on. That's how we come to camp out in those tool shacks. The roads weren't even built."

"When's your house going to be finished?" Len asked.

"It's almost done, but the rain slows things down."

"How're you making out?"

Dutch laughed again. "Fine, 'cept when it rains. Trucks get stuck trying to bring in supplies. It's a damn mess."

Len looked up and saw Ray motioning to him. "Excuse me, Dutch," Len said, pointing to Ray in the distance, "he's calling me to come over yonder. I'd like to talk to you some more after awhile." Len shook his hand and proceeded over to the project manager's office, excited at the prospect of finding Hugh MacRae inside.

"Come on in here, Len," Ray said, pulling Len inside. "I've got somebody I want you to meet." Len stepped in directly in front of a man who sat behind a large desk that nearly filled the narrow room. "This here's Len Ryan, Mr. Lucas. Personal friend of Hugh MacRae's."

Len removed his hat. "Howdy, Mr. Lucas," he said. The project manager studied Len for a moment, working his mouth around. His upper lip curled into a half-assed grin, revealing a row of small yellowed teeth. Len had seen that kind of look on another man, one of his teachers who was handy with a paddle.

"Personal friend of Mr. Hugh's, huh?"

"I can't say I'm a personal friend of Mr. Hugh's, but I've done some work for him."

Lucas leaned back in his swivel chair and propped his feet on top of the desk. "What kind of work do you do, Ryan?"

Len shifted from side to side. He wasn't sure he wanted Mr. Lucas to know that much about him. Ray spoke up. "Len's done some well and pump work. He's farming now."

"Let the man answer for himself, Wilkins."

"I'm farming with my daddy over in Bladen County. I did some pump and well work with my Uncle Nathan," Len said. "Brought a little extra money in for a time. That was before I was married. Got a little girl now."

"Well, if you were looking for work, I might could use you. We've got ten wells and pumps to put in before these folks can have water. You interested?"

"I reckon I might be. Can't say for sure right now, but I'll take an application."

Lucas swung around in his chair and ruffled through a stack of papers on a shelf behind him.

Len peered over his shoulder. "If you have one of them homesteader applications over there, I reckon I could take one of them too."

Lucas stood up and turned around, a paper in his hand. "You'll have to go to Wilmington to get that. We're all out here. But if it's hard work you're interested in, instead of a handout, mail this back to me. We've got more homestead applications than you can shake a stick at. It's pump help I need right now."

Len didn't like Charlie Lucas, neither his manner nor the way Lucas talked down to him. He reached for the paper. "Thank you, I'll take a look at it. C'mon, Ray, there's a couple of fellows out there I want to talk to."

"Much obliged, Mr. Lucas," Ray said. "Tell Mr. Hugh that Len Ryan stopped by."

"We don't see him around here much," Lucas said.

Len had his hand on the door, but the tone in Lucas's voice stopped him. "Doesn't he work here anymore?" he asked.

"Mr. MacRae never did *work* here, Ryan. He ran the place. There's a difference."

When Ray had closed the door and they were outside, Len said, "Why'd you tell him Mr. MacRae was a personal friend of mine?"

"Don't get all hotheaded. You have to know how to handle these bureaucrats. Lucas thinks he's a big shot. I just wanted him to know that you knew MacRae. Might make a difference."

"Well, don't tell anybody about this. I don't want Mama and Papa worrying that I might be about to leave," Len said.

"You could use the work though," Ray said. "Admit it. Everybody does."

⌒

"Millie's gonna ask me about the houses," Len said. "Wonder where they're at?"

"Did you ask those fellows over there?"

Len looked for Dutch Van Bruggen, but when he didn't see him, he approached the man that Van Bruggen had called Jesse. "Excuse me. My name's Len Ryan. Dutch Van Bruggen said you fellows were helping build your own houses. I don't see him around now. You reckon we might see yours?"

"Name's Jesse Alston. You shore can. I'm picking up some lumber off that truck that just come in. If you don't mind hauling it in the back end of your truck, we can get back over yonder to the house, I'd be glad to show you mine." On the drive over to his house, Jesse told Len and Ray that he'd moved to Penderlea one month after the project was started. "Me and my wife and son came here with nothing much but the clothes on our backs—the first homesteaders. I was sick and tired of not owning anything, tired of farming somebody else's land. The government was offering me a chance to buy a farm of my own, and forty years to pay it out. Why wouldn't I come?" Jesse shook his head. "No, suh! I wasn't going to turn that down."

"Forty years? That's a long time," Len said, mentally calculating that he'd be in his sixties before he paid for a homestead on Penderlea.

"How much interest?" Ray asked.

"Three percent," Jesse said. "That ain't bad. You figure, you get a five- or six-room house, a barn, corn crib, hog pen, smokehouse, and a chicken house," he said, laughing and counting them off on his fingers. "Wait a minute there's another one—oh, the washhouse and pump house."

"You going to help build those, too?" Len asked.

"No, suh, won't have to. Them boys from the camp over yonder are doing that. I told them where I wanted everything, but them guys from the government are supervising it right down to the last nail."

"How come they let you build the house?" Len asked.

"I didn't build it all by myself, son, I just helped out. The government's paying me as a carpenter's helper. Making fifty cents an hour," he said, proudly.

Len was driving the truck now, keeping his eyes on the ruts, thinking how easy it all sounded. But didn't he already own land? At least, he just as good as owned it. As if reading his mind, Jesse took a different tack. "You know, I could've waited until my daddy died. He's promised me and my brothers a hundred acres each over there in Duplin County." He rolled a chaw of tobacco around in his mouth and spit out the window. "But, hell, it's worn-out land—been worn out for forty years. Penderlea has never been farmed before. Look out there at those fields. They got stumps in them now, but one day soon, there'll be the prettiest corn you've ever seen out there."

They turned in a lane off the main road, and Jesse told them to pull up near the house. Odds and ends of the construction littered what appeared to be the front yard. On either side, the roughly plowed fields were strewn with stumps and large roots. Deep holes where stumps had been dynamited pocketed the yard. "Watch where you step," Jesse said. "As soon as they let me use a dozer, I'll push some dirt into those holes."

Len and Ray got out of the truck and helped unload the lumber. "See that tool shed over yonder? That's where me and my wife, Katie Belle, lived until a couple of weeks ago. Of course, when you come in, you'll see that there's still lots to be done. But the house is mostly finished. My wife is working at the cannery now. Nick—he's my boy—he's staying with some of the other children while his mama is working. Come on in, I'll show you around."

Jesse led the way through a screened-in porch, and into a kitchen that had a small table at one end with three chairs. "Look in here at the living room. They haven't brought all of our furniture yet."

"Furniture comes with the house?" Len asked.

"Yes, suh, and fine furniture it is! Look at that there settee. Isn't it a nice one? We're getting a chair to match it too. They make them right here at the shop on Penderlea."

Len studied the dark-stained oak furniture. It sure looked better than anything he could make. The paneled walls were pine tongue and groove, and the floors were polished oak. In the two bedrooms, the walls were real plaster, not the particle board that had come into fashion in the last few years. There was a tiny room just for the toilet, and another larger room for a claw-footed tub and a lavatory. "Turn on that spigot there, Len. Feel the hot water. It's straight from that tank beside the wood stove in the kitchen."

One bedroom had a double bed, a large walk-in closet, and a lavatory in one corner. The other had two closets and two single beds. "Nick loves his room. He's gonna get a chest of drawers, too."

"Are all the houses just alike, Jesse?"

"These first ten are, but there's a rumor going around that up in Washington, they think they're costing too much money. I'm glad I got one first."

"How about electricity?" Ray asked. "I see you've got kerosene lamps and electric light fixtures."

"Oh, we've been wired, but they're not finished building the line. It's coming though. Tide Water Power Company is building it, and the Pender County Rural Electric Cooperative is borrowing money from the government to help pay for it. We've got Hugh MacRae to thank for that, too."

"I was hoping to see him here today," Len said. "You see him around much?"

"No, suh, not much. He's usually up there in Washington with all them government men—even knows the president himself. That's how he gets so much done."

⌒

When Len returned from his trip to the homestead project, he told Millie that he could never see them living on a project like Penderlea where everything belonged to the government.

"Did you talk to any of the homesteaders—see any of the houses?" she asked.

"Yeah, one or two."

"What were they like, Len?"

"Who?"

"Not *who*. The houses. What were they like?"

"Everything was knee deep in mud, but I did get to go inside one house. It was real pretty with polished wood floors."

"Is that all you saw, the floors?" Millie asked.

"Look, honey, the houses were real nice, but everything was half-finished. They didn't even have the lights on yet. To tell you the truth, I was kind of disappointed."

"What do you mean you were disappointed? How could anything be worse than living in the squalor we live in right here?"

Len stared at her in disbelief. "What did you say?"

"I just said that I don't see how you could think Penderlea would be any worse than living here."

"That's not what you said."

"I did, too."

Why he had not killed her right then and there, she'd never know. But instead of turning on her, he had put on his jacket, gone out, and slammed the door. She didn't see him again until the next day. Where he'd slept that night, she couldn't imagine, but he had shown up for breakfast.

"Len, look, I'm sorry about last night," Millie said. "I shouldn't have ... said that."

"I've got to go," he said. "I'll be home before dark unless that old truck breaks down on me." He kissed her tenderly on the cheek. Watching him drive out through the oak grove, she wondered at his sudden change. Maybe she should speak up more often—say what she was *really* thinking.

CHAPTER 24

L en climbed four flights of steps before he reached the offices of the Division of Subsistence Housing. A man waited on a bench beside the door. "Is this where you get an application for Penderlea?" Len asked.

"Yup, that's what they told me," the man said. He was at least ten years older than Len, and wore a pair of soiled overalls and a well-creased straw hat that was stained with perspiration. Len had nearly scrubbed his skin raw, and was wearing a new pair of khaki work pants and a white dress shirt, anxious to appear clean-cut, a term Wilkins used when he described what they'd be looking for.

"Len Ryan," he said, extending his hand.

The man pulled a stubby pipe from his mouth, leaving a deep impression in his lip. Saliva bubbled in the corners of his mouth and he slurped at it, taking a breath. "Doyle Mulcahy. Pleased to meet you," he said in a pleasant voice. He held up a sheaf of papers. "Got mine all filled out except for my medical examination."

"I thought you had to go to Burgaw for that."

"No, sir. Not unless you live in Pender County. I live in New Hanover, but he has to tell me which doctor to go to if I want it free. That's what the young man said. Said he'd take me over to the county clinic soon as he finished up with t'other fellow that was here when I come in."

"How long have you been here?" Len asked, anxious to get back home before dark. The old truck's headlights were out.

"Hour or so," Mulcahy said. "You in a hurry?"

"I can wait if I have to."

The door opened, and a man about Len's age escorted an older man out of his office. "Your papers are in order, Mr. Mullins, but like I said, it may be awhile before you hear anything."

"I can't wait much longer. My wife's expecting, and I'd like to get settled before the new one comes."

"So would everyone else, sir. So would everyone else." He nodded to Len. "If you're waiting for me, I'm closing for the day."

"You can't close," Len said. "I drove all the way...." He pulled out the pocket watch Aunt Mag had given him for his sixteenth birthday. "It's only three o'clock. The paper said you'd be open until five o'clock."

"Look here, fellow. I've got to show Mulcahy the clinic, and I'm not coming all the way back over here for half an hour or so."

Mullins smiled, his face deeply tanned beneath his pale forehead and bald head "I'll show him where it is," he said. "I'm headed out of town. Going right by there."

"All right with me," Mulcahy said.

Obviously irritated by the change of plans, the government man motioned Len to come in. "I've been in this office since eight o'clock this morning. Let's make it quick."

"Yes sir, I won't trouble you a'tall," Len said. "I just want to get an application for Penderlea."

"You and everybody else," he said. Len glanced at the nameplate on the desk. Rusty Ruark. It rang a bell—not exactly a pleasant one. Where had he met this redheaded snoot in a rumpled seersucker suit who looked as if he'd just come off a binge? Ruark plopped down in his chair and ruffled through some papers. "You'll have to answer some questions first."

Len settled back in his chair. "All right, shoot."

Rusty looked at him askance. "Are you an American citizen?"

Len smiled. "Yes, sir. Free, white, and twenty-one."

"Look, don't get smart with me. Just answer the questions."

"Are you married?"

"Yes, sir."

"Farmer?"

"Yes, sir."

"All right, fill these papers out and bring them back with two letters of reference and a medical report from your doctor that shows you're in good health."

"Why's that? Can't you look at me and tell there's nothing wrong with me?"

"Look, I don't make the rules," Ruark said. "It's the duty of my department to eliminate any tuberculosis-ridden riffraff from making it any further than my desk."

"I don't have TB, and I'm not riffraff. My people—"

Ruark stood up. He handed Len the application papers. "Look, here, Ryan, I'm sorry, but you'll have to have your medical exam just like everybody else," he said. Catching his eye for the first time, Rusty recognized Len. *This is the hick who danced with Millie the night of Amanda's wedding. She was his date* and he was leaving for college the next day, but she'd refused to leave with him. *Now Millie's married to the jerk?* Rusty showed Len the door. "The project's as good as dead anyhow."

"What do you mean?"

"Look, you can read about it in the paper, Ryan." He gave Len a little shove, closed the door behind him, and pulled a small flask from his breast pocket. A chuckle escaped from somewhere deep inside him. *Misery loves company,* he thought.

Outside Ruark's office, Len was blinded by a flash of light. When he regained his sight, a young man in an unpressed suit and wearing a hat shoved a card into his hand. "Bucky Smith, with the *Star*," he said. "You one of the Penderlea applicants?"

"I … I came to get … an application, but…"

"Yeah, I know. We just heard the news. I'm here to interview this Ruark fellow. What did he say to you?"

"I don't understand. He said—"

"Look, I can tell you what the bottom line is. Hugh MacRae told the government they could take Penderlea and shove it."

"No, I don't believe you. Mr. Hugh wouldn't do that. He loved his farm city. He told me…."

"Yeah, yeah, I know what he told a lot of people. Mr. Hugh MacRae is used to doing things his way. But the government has decided to do it *their* way. They've federalized the project—put it under the Resettlement Administration—say he works for the government now. He'll have to do things according to their rules." The reporter chuckled. "Mr. Mac's not used to working for the government or anybody else. He told them that Penderlea was his idea and he was best suited to see it through. Besides, he'd practically given them the land to build it on. He figured that alone entitled him to a big say."

"Why'd you take my picture?"

"I came over here to interview Ruark, saw you charging out of his office, I figured you'd heard the news. Want to tell me about it?"

"No, sir. I haven't even told my wife yet."

Len had been to the new A&P grocery store and bought two cans of salmon and a loaf of white bread before he left Wilmington. "Maybe you can fix some salmon croquettes for supper," he'd said, as if nothing had happened before he left that morning.

"Go over and tell your mama," Millie said. "I think she was planning on me cooking dinner over there."

"You go tell her," he said, reaching for his whiskey bottle. "I'm not in the mood to get the third degree."

"All right, watch the baby for me. I've got her ready for bed."

Millie crossed the yard wondering where Len had been all day. She suspected that he might have gone to talk to Mr. MacRae, but she dared not ask him. Len was mixed up about Penderlea. She thought he really wanted to go. Len wanted a better life as much as she did. But when she returned to the camp house, he was pouring himself a second glass of whiskey and his eyes were glazed over. He looked to be almost in a trance. "Sit down a minute. I want to talk to you," he said.

"Don't you want me to start your supper?"

"No, I want you to sit down here and have a damn drink with me. There's something I want to tell you."

"All right, but I need to put Annie to bed first."

"Go do it."

Millie didn't like his tone. There was more to it than just the argument they'd had the day before. She picked up Annie and took her into the bedroom and pulled the curtain. After she'd nursed her, the baby fell asleep in her arms. Millie tucked her in the crib and returned to the kitchen to find Len in a stupor.

"I'd better fix your supper," she said. "You look tired."

"Wait a damn minute," he said. "I want to tell you something."

Millie sat down in her chair, her heart in her throat. Maybe he was going to leave.

He looked at her through droopy eyelids. "You know that government project they call PEN-DER-LEA?" He was drunk, sarcastic, accenting each syllable.

"Yes, I've heard of it a time or two," she said, almost laughing.

"Don't get smart-mouthed with me," he said, his tone threatening. He took a swallow of his drink. "Now, I just want to say it loud and clear so's there's no misunderstanding. I give up on Penderlea. If it was the last piece of dirt on this goddamned earth, I wouldn't have it. I'd rather own a hundred acres right here in Bladen County, and not make a damn dime on it, than to go over yonder to Pender County and owe my soul to the damn government."

Millie swallowed hard, but she kept a promise she'd made to herself. "All right, Len. I'll fix your supper now."

The next morning, Len got up as usual, had his breakfast with Maggie and Tate, and went out to work on the farm. Maggie Lorena knew something was wrong. She called to Millie when she saw her in the yard hanging out wash. "Is everything all right, Millie? Len looked a little piqued this morning."

"Everything fine, Miss Maggie. How're you feeling today?"

"Every bone in my body hurts. This cold weather has stirred up my rheumatism. I'd be much obliged if you'd keep an eye out for the mailman and bring me the *Star* when he comes. I don't believe I'd be able to make it out there and back. I'd hate for the menfolk to find me sprawled out in the oak grove."

When Millie saw Mr. Bell's car stop, she waved to him and he waited for her to get to the mailbox. "Morning, Miss Millie," he said. "How're you today?" She leaned forward to speak to him through the car window.

"I'm doing good, Mr. Bell. How about you?"

"Fine, just fine," he said, flipping open a newspaper that had lain on top of the stack of mail. "I didn't know Len was thinking about going over to Penderlea," he said.

"What?"

"Maybe you didn't either," he chuckled. "But here it is on the front page of the *Star News,*" he said, jabbing at a large picture. Millie reached for the paper and stared at Len's face. He looked so scared.

"Thank you, Mr. Bell." That was all she could manage before turning to walk toward the house.

CHAPTER 25

Hugh MacRae's threats to resign from the Penderlea Project had been well publicized, but they had remained just threats until February, when he'd sent word to the Board of Directors and the Board of Visitors that he had tendered his resignation to President Roosevelt. The next day, the announcement came out in the *Wilmington Star* with the picture of a startled young man captioned: Len Ryan, young Bladen County farmer, reacts to the news that Hugh MacRae has resigned from the Penderlea Homesteads Project. Ryan was in the Federal building to obtain an application for the project.

Emily McAllister was as shocked as anyone by the news. The bull in the woods had obviously met his match in Harold Ickes, secretary of Department of the Interior. The two had butted heads over the Pender County project, and Ickes had come out the victor. Although her views differed from MacRae on several aspects of the planned community, Emily couldn't imagine anyone besides MacRae continuing the project. Penderlea was his from the beginning. She tried to reach him by phone, but was told by his housekeeper that he was not accepting phone calls. The paper had said that his resignation was pending President Roosevelt's approval—that he would stay on until a replacement was found.

A subsequent article with a Washington byline cited a long series of disagreements with Washington authorities. "Unofficially," the article stated that MacRae was said to have resented "instructions and red tape." MacRae's successor was to be his son-in-law Julian Morton, a fact that was pointed to as evidence that the disagreements were impersonal.

The news was even more disturbing than Emily feared. Just as predicted, the Division of Subsistence Homesteads had announced that farm management studies at Penderlea indicated that the ten-acre plots were insufficient. But worst of all, plans for the farm city would have to be completely revised. Everything would be put on hold. The article also said the number of houses would be reduced to 150, and the resized farms would be approximately twenty acres each instead of ten.

Further reports in the paper said that legislators in Washington were conferring daily as to the future of the project. The consensus was that Penderlea's nine-hundred-thousand-dollar appropriation would not be sufficient to complete the work as originally proposed. Only ten houses had been completed to date. Already, Emily had heard Hugh say that the government wanted the remaining houses made smaller and of lesser material. He'd been furious about that.

⌒

When she couldn't reach Hugh MacRae, she telephoned Jeanne. "There must be something I can do. He was so passionate about Penderlea. It was the culmination of all of his ideas, the utopian farm colony. He was so close. Why has he resigned?"

"Mother, I'm surprised that you haven't figured it out," Jeanne said. "This new government doesn't like the laid-back way southerners go about doing things. Especially wealthy southerners like Hugh who are used to doing things their way. Obviously, he's stepped on some toes."

Emily was pensive. "Yes, I suppose you're right. Hugh is downright arrogant when it comes to getting his way."

"He and Eleanor Roosevelt would get along just fine. She wanted the very best for the homesteaders in Arthurdale. Secretary Ickes fought her tooth and nail. Like Hugh MacRae, she took it personally. She didn't want to be a part of some slipshod housing that was no better than the shacks they were living in."

"I think I could be friends with Eleanor Roosevelt."

"She's your kind of woman, all right," Jeanne said.

"Were you there very long?" Emily asked. "In Arthurdale, I mean?"

"A few weeks. I was traveling with some of Eleanor Roosevelt's friends. She'd asked them to go there and look things over. Sort of undercover, you know." She heard Jeanne light a cigarette. "I saw some need so I stayed on with a family that I met. I helped with sewing the curtains I told you about. We planted some bushes and flowers."

Emily couldn't imagine Jeanne sewing or gardening. When she didn't respond, Jeanne burst out laughing. "Oh, Mother, go on and say it. You didn't know I could do that."

"No, that's not what I was thinking."

"Isn't it what you would have done?" Jeanne asked. "Maybe I want to be more like you."

PART THREE

Money, Marbles, and Chalk

CHAPTER 26

DECEMBER 1935—BLADEN COUNTY, NORTH CAROLINA

There'd been a light flurry of snow the Saturday before Christmas. Not enough to hardly blink at, but it had put Tate in the Christmas spirit. He'd gone out by himself that morning in search of a dense cedar he'd seen the day he'd buried Bess near the old Croom place. He'd found it right where he left it and Buck had towed it home on a tobacco sled. It was a little too much for Tate—he'd had to sit down and rest several times during the cutting and loading of it—but this was the first Christmas Annie would remember. He was determined to make it special for her.

Tate brought the tree into the house and stood it in a tub of sand so Millie could decorate it. "It's the most beautiful tree I've ever seen, Mr. Tate," Millie said.

"Had my eye on it for some time," Tate said, proudly. "I shot some mistletoe out of a tree, too, and there is a toe sack of running cedar. I reckon you'll find something to do with it."

"Oh, yes. I see some holly, too." She threw her arms around his neck and hugged him. "You are the best granddaddy in the world."

"You're not forgetting about old Rob, are you?"

Millie laughed. "Well, next to him, which reminds me, I ought to go and put a little something on his mantel."

"Reckon he'd like a tree? I saw another one not far from this one."

"No, sir. Cal is coming to get him to spend Christmas in Wilmington. Papa said he wants to see that big old Christmas tree in the park one more time."

"Well, I hope he's not thinking it will be the last time."

"No, sir. I don't think so. But he did give me all of Mama's glass balls. They're over in the camp house. I'll go and get them while Annie's in the kitchen with Miss Maggie. We'll surprise both of them."

Together, Millie and Tate trimmed the tree with the assorted ornaments that had been in Millie's family for as long as she could remember. "Papa said I was the only one who cared about them."

"Maggie Lorena had some pretties—before the fire," Tate said. "Old Aunt Mag loved to decorate for Christmas."

"Let me go fetch her now. Annie might like to hang some tinsel on the low branches."

"My stars, look at that, Annie!" Maggie said. "We must be dreaming."

Millie held Annie up to touch the delicate balls. "Pretty. Can you say 'pretty,' Annie?" The child pursed her lips and said something like "pity." "That's it, 'pretty,' darling."

"I haven't seen anything so pretty since Aunt Mag used to decorate her tree," Maggie said, her voice softening. "You should have seen it, Millie."

"Mr. Tate told me about it."

"He did? And did he tell you that they melted in the fire?" she sobbed.

"Don't even think about that now, Cousin Maggie. You sit right here in this chair and hold Annie while I put some of that running cedar on the mantel. We'll stand the Christmas cards up there."

"If y'all don't need me, I'm going out to the barn," Tate said.

"He's got something up his sleeve," Maggie said. "Wants Christmas to be real special for you-know-who." She pointed to Annie who was sitting in her lap.

"Umhum," Millie said. "I know what you mean." She finished arranging the cards on the mantle. "How does that look?"

"You really know how to fix up things," Maggie said. "Oh, I almost forgot there was another one that came today." She reached into her apron pocket. "It's from Emily McAllister, There's a letter, too."

The card was the most beautiful thing Millie had ever seen. It was cut in the shape of a large wreath of holly and evergreens. There were tiny little glass balls in bright colors pasted to the wreath, and in the center at the bottom, a bow made of real ribbon. The card was addressed to the whole family. "She's always remembered us at Christmas," Maggie said. "I still can't believe Jon MacNamara deserted her. What a scoundrel!"

"You met Jon when you were in Boston, didn't you?" Millie said. "Emily said you liked him then."

"Well, yes, but I never let on that I was drawn to him," Maggie said. "I was a married woman, you know."

"Well, of course, I didn't mean to suggest anything."

"Oh, that's all right, Millie. I was quite an attractive woman at the time, and a womanizer like Jonathan MacNamara found me hard to resist."

Millie stifled a chuckle remembering a conversation she'd had with Emily who related a different story. Emily said, according to Jon, that Maggie threw herself at him in Boston. "Did you say Miss Emily enclosed a letter?"

"Yes, I put it there by Len's chair."

"May I see it?"

"Of course, I just thought Len might want to see it first. It has something about Penderlea in it."

Millie reached for the letter, trying to hide her irritation. "Len's not very interested in Penderlea since—" She picked up the baby and started for the door, slipping the letter into her apron pocket. "Since that picture was in the paper. Maybe I'd better read it first. We don't want to provoke him, do we?"

"My stars, no!" Maggie sputtered.

"I'll put Annie down for a nap and bring it back at supper."

Maggie did not give up easily. "I don't see why Len would get mad if he has no intention of going anyhow," she said.

"That's true," Millie said. "I'll still bring it back after Annie's nap."

Walking across the yard, Millie had misgivings. Len's mama always wanted to be the center of attention, especially when it came to giving any news to the menfolk. "Pecking order," they called it in the chicken yard. A pile of logs caught her eye, reminding Millie that they'd need to split some more firewood soon. There were only a few sticks left beside the stove. After the first frost, the community hog killings had started, and Len had been gone nearly every morning from dawn to dark to help their neighbors. She couldn't complain about things when he came home bringing fresh meat, but today a cold wind was blowing in from the north.

In the camp house, Millie put the sleepy baby on her bed and laid down beside her, snuggling them both under a quilt. Emily's letter consisted of two folded sheets of fine linen paper. The fragrance that emanated from the thin sheets reminded Millie of her friend and former employer. Just the sight of Emily's handwriting warmed Millie's heart. She wished she'd stayed in touch with Emily. But Emily had withdrawn completely from everything about the same time that the McBrydes had moved back to the country. After that, Millie had simply lost touch with her. What could she have said anyway? She and Emily had been great friends, but out of respect for the difference in their ages, Millie never asked about her personal life.

CHRISTMAS, 1935

For my dear friends, the Ryans,

Here's wishing all of you a Merry Christmas! How I've missed you! These past few years have been difficult for all of us, each in our own way. Resettling in Onslow County was not easy at first, but I have found I love being here in the country near Darcy and his family. His wife Gardenia is delightful, as are my precious grandchildren, Alison and David. I'm sure you share my sentiments, Maggie, as I can't imagine a more wonderful daughter-in-law than Millie McBryde. Little Annie must be a joy as well. Jeanne is living in Hyde Park now, working with some women who are

well-acquainted with Mrs. Roosevelt. It's not likely that we will see
her at Christmas, but we have our fingers crossed.

Len, I just wanted to let you know that I saw your picture in
the paper—almost a year ago now—when Mr. MacRae resigned
from the Penderlea Project. Some time later, he told me that you
had worked for him at St. Helena. He called you the "perfect
young farmer," and lamented his inability to help you find your
place at Penderlea. Of course, his resignation was quite a setback
for the project, but since July, when Washington transferred
it to the Resettlement Administration, and we got rid of that
curmudgeon, Harold Ickes, the project has been continued and
plans completed for one hundred and forty-two units of twenty
acres each. I tell you this to encourage you and Millie to apply for
one of the new houses if you're interested. I 'm not sure how much
I can help, but every application that comes in goes across my
desk before it reaches the Federal office. If you apply, I promise
that I will do everything I can to make sure you are chosen for
one of those farms.
Merry Christmas to each one of you, with love,
Emily

Millie's heart skipped a beat. Maybe this was what she'd been waiting
for. A word from Emily might be all that was needed to fire Len up about
Penderlea. She closed her eyes and took a deep breath. Annie was sound
asleep. Millie nuzzled her cheek and whispered, *We must say our prayers,*
little one.

⌣

On Christmas morning, Maggie banged on the door of the camp house
at five-thirty. "It's your pa, son. He says it's just indigestion, but I think it's
worse than that. You better come."

Len found his father sitting on the edge of the old feather bed, pale as a ghost. "Just a little too much of your mama's fruitcake last night, son. I'm all right. Help me get my britches on, and I'll go to the kitchen."

Millie was standing near, the baby in her arms. "I'll get you some coffee, Mr. Tate. You wait right here."

"No, ma'am. Just step on out now. I'll be in there as soon as I get my clothes on. It's Christmas morning, isn't it?" He looked tenderly at the baby. "Her first little Christmas. We've got to make it special for her."

"I think Santa did that already," Maggie said. "I reckon you stayed up a little later than usual to give him a hand." She looked at Tate, and then at Len who both ducked their heads and looked the other way. "Come on in now and get your breakfast. I'm sure there's not much under the tree that it can't wait a little longer."

There was more under the tree than any of them had expected. Len surprised his mother and Millie with a box of chocolate-covered cherry cordials. For Tate he'd bought a plug of tobacco and a large cigar. They were still in the paper sack from Eddie Lee's store, but his cousin had wrapped a piece of red string around the sack and tied it in a bow. Millie had made a new apron for Maggie and flannel nightshirts for Tate and Len. Both put them on over their clothes and paraded around, proud as peacocks. Tate held up a small reindeer he had carved out of apple wood for Annie. He jostled it up and down in front of her face. "Lookie there, Annie, it's one of Santa's reindeer. He left it just for you."

Millie sat back and watched the joyous expressions on Maggie and Tate's faces. Even Len was all smiles. She was sure this was the real Len, a man who found happiness in the simple pleasures of things like Christmas. The monster that came out in him at other times was just that, a monster that he had no control over—a monster that would probably never go away completely—one that would always lurk there in the shadows waiting to rip her heart out.

CHAPTER 27

M illie missed her second period the end of January. On their wedding anniversary in November, she'd made Len a pear pie, using the last of the hard pears from the old Croom place. She'd stored them since September in a basket of Spanish moss, just for the occasion. Most of the time, Len was satisfied with a little cane syrup and a biscuit for dessert, but he called it a real occasion when she made him a pear pie. A present was out of the question, but she knew the pie would make him happy.

The evening had been ruined when Len had forgotten it was their anniversary. She'd told him that morning, but he'd left for Eddie Lee's store while she was putting Annie to bed. The pie was intended to be a surprise—not something to share with Tate and Maggie until Len had received the full benefit of having it all to himself.

"Did he say how long he'd be gone?" Millie asked.

"No, he didn't," Maggie said. "He just said he'd see us in the morning."

"Oh," Millie said. "Well, I guess that's it."

Tate looked up from his paper. "Is something the matter, Millie?"

"No, sir. It's just that it's our second wedding anniversary. I thought he might have stayed home tonight."

"Well, I declare," Maggie said, throwing her mending into a basket beside her rocking chair. "Tate, go in yonder and get your jug out of the pantry, and we'll have a little toast to the occasion."

"Without Len?" Millie asked.

Maggie sat back in her chair. "That's right. I guess it wouldn't be much of a toast without Len."

"No, no, let's *do* all have a toast," Millie said. "I'll get the glasses."

"Well, all right," Maggie said, hesitantly. Tate hadn't moved from his chair, watching and listening to the scene unfolding. "Tate Ryan, are you going to just sit there?" she said. "Go get that Scuppernong wine. It ought to be good and potent by now."

Tate shuffled off to the pantry, still confused about what was happening. But after they all had a few sips of the wine, it really didn't matter. "I want you to know, Millie, that you are the best thing that's ever happened to Len," he said.

"Thank you, Mr. Tate," she said, choking back her tears. He was always so kind to her, much more so than Len. She hugged him, inhaling his warm woodsy scent. *Why couldn't Len have been more like Mr. Tate?* she thought.

"I wish we had a radio. We could turn it on and have a little music," Maggie said, leaning her head back on the rocker.

"Better still, I could get out my fiddle," Tate said. "Actually, it was my pa's fiddle, but I used to play it a little."

"Oh, do!" Millie said, pouring herself another tumbler of wine. "Some fiddle music would be perfect."

So Tate had fiddled while Maggie and Millie patted their feet and clapped their hands until Maggie had fallen asleep in the chair. Millie began waltzing around the small room bumping into things, but Tate was having so much fun that he paid little attention to her. Neither of them heard Len come up on the porch and open the door. "What's going on here?" he said, looking around the room.

"We're celebrating our anniversary," Millie said, her slurring unmistakably the result of strong drink.

"You look drunk to me," he said.

"Look, here, now, Len," Tate said. "Millie remembered that it was your anniversary, and I thought a little of my wine might be appropriate. Don't you want some? Your mama's sound asleep over there."

"I'll take mine back to the house, Pa. Millie needs to get home and check on Annie." He gave her a dirty look and picked up the wine jug. "Come on, Millie. Good night, y'all."

Millie was positive: that was the night she'd gotten pregnant with their second child.

CHAPTER 28

Early in the new year, Millie had fainted at the sight of blood when she'd chopped the head off a live squawking hen. There was no time this go-round for morning sickness or lying about. In fact, she was, more often than not, amazed that she could do all that she could do.

"I feel wonderful, most of the time," she'd told her sister. Rebecca always seemed to show up when she was most needed. "Did Papa send for you?"

"No. I just wanted to check on you both. Mr. Tate said he found you resting your head on the wood block. It could've been your head instead of the chicken's if you'd fallen on the axe."

"Oh, I'm all right. And you don't have to worry about Papa," Millie said. "I see him right regularly. Take him a pot of beans, or something like that every few days. He likes to make his own cornbread. Says nobody but him can make it like Mama did."

Rebecca sat on the linoleum floor playing patty-cake with the baby. She looked up at Millie. "I told you to keep up with your periods. Now here you are pregnant again."

"My goodness, Becca, I'm really happy about it. Len's excited, too. He's sure it's a boy."

Rebecca came often, bringing clothes for Annie Louise who was growing like a weed. "I won't need a thing for the new baby," Millie said. "When Annie outgrows something, I put it away instead of passing it on to Lizzie's grand-daughters like I used to."

"What if it's not a girl this time?" Rebecca asked.

"Len will be disappointed," Millie said. "I'm sure it's a girl. Look how high I'm carrying it." She rubbed her hand over her slightly distended belly. "Remember Mama used to say that."

"Oh, pshaw! There's absolutely no way of knowing if you're carrying a boy or a girl," Rebecca said. "Those are old wives' tales." She was an experienced nurse now, and the whole family turned to her for advice. But Millie thought she was wrong about this baby.

"What about you, Becca? Are you and Mr. Jones still trying?"

"Of course, we keep hoping, but since he's been laid off, we've only got my salary to pay the bills. If I couldn't work, we wouldn't be able to make it."

Millie laughed. "That's funny. I've never stopped *working* since Annie Louise was born. In the country, a woman never stops working to have a baby."

"Well, they won't let nurses waddle around the hospital as big as the broad side of a barn."

They were sitting at the small table in the cramped kitchen. Rebecca had brought a pot of black-eyed peas she'd cooked with a ham hock that morning. At the stove, Millie chopped another pot of collards with a long-handled egg turner. "Reach up there on that shelf and get the jar of pepper vinegar," Millie said. "I know how you love anything hot."

Rebecca removed the jar from the shelf and opened it, inhaling the pungent smell of the vinegar and hot peppers. "Oowee! That'll take the top of your head off!" She sat down in her chair again, crossed her legs, and folded her hands in her lap. "Honey, is Len good to you?"

"Of course, he is," Millie replied. She didn't look directly at her sister.

"I know you said he has a terrible temper. I mean, has he ever hit you or anything?"

Millie's face was damp from standing over the steaming collard pot and her black hair hung in tendrils around her face. Rebecca thought she looked liked an angel. She couldn't believe that anyone, especially Len, could hurt her.

"Well, no," Millie said. "But he's made me think he was going to." She sat down at the table opposite Rebecca. "Sometimes he gets so mad, he acts crazy—struts around yelling and shaking his finger at me. He'll hit the table or the door frame, but not me. It's almost funny."

"Honey, I think he's dangerous. You can't talk back to him when he's like that—say things that aggravate him even more. "

"Len's not dangerous, Becca. He's fractious, to be sure. But please don't worry. You've never seen him act ugly to me, have you?"

"No, and I'd better not! It's just that Cousin Kate told me that Len was hell on wheels when he got mad."

"She ought to know a thing or two about bad tempers. I hear Mr. Nathan's is worse."

"Yes, but what worried me was that she said Mr. Tate told her that you have a way of provoking Len without even knowing you're doing it."

"Why in the world would Mr. Tate say that?"

"I don't know, honey, except that he was worried about you, too."

⌣

Nathan Hill was a frequent visitor to the Ryan household on winter after-noons. He'd come near lunchtime and stay, if invited, to chew the rag for another hour or so with Len and Tate. His gnarled hands had forced him to retire sooner than he'd planned. Nathan was more and more involved in flower farming, and he encouraged Tate and Len to do the same. "I declare, it's the easiest kind of farming for an old man like me," he said.

"Old-man farming, huh?" Tate said. "You're a good ten years younger than me, Nathan."

"You know what I mean. Of course, if you want to keep on doing what you do, it's all right with me." He smiled that little half-assed smile that they all understood was Nathan's way of saying, *then kiss my foot.*

"I reckon if I had a passel of girls like you do, Nathan, I could keep 'em busy with it," Tate said. "As 'tis, Len's got all he can do, and Will's off up yonder in Detroit. Flower farming is about the last thing I need."

They'd just finished a big dinner, and Tate excused himself to go out back to the toilet. Nathan looked around for Maggie. "Where's your mama?" he asked Len.

"She hits her bed right after dinner, come hell or high water," Len said.

Nathan lowered his voice another notch. "Look here, now. You saw that article, didn't you?"

"What article?"

"You know, the one that was in the paper yesterday. The one about the government needing another 175 men?"

"Where?"

"What the hell do you mean, *where*! You know what I'm talking about. Penderlea!"

"I saw it, but I'm not interested. Not anymore."

"Len, you ought to think again about that. I told you Hugh MacRae knew what he was doing when he started that project."

"I reckon he did, Uncle Nathan, but the government's not listening to him anymore. He quit, remember?" Len passed one hand over the other to emphasize his meaning. "Kaput!"

Nathan grinned, took off his glasses, and wiped them with his handkerchief. "I don't like to hear you talk down on a man I admire, son. It's not right."

He sounded more ornery than usual. Len decided to back off the subject of Penderlea. "How many acres are you planting in gladiolus this year?"

"Now don't go changing the subject on me, son." Nathan grinned again, another half-assed grin. "There's something I ought to tell you about Hugh MacRae. He don't back out of something unless it's gone sour. He's a winner, that man is. He tried his best to get the government to do things his way. They'll be sorry, you mark my words."

"You know I have a lot of respect for him, Uncle Nathan. I'm just disappointed that he's not in on it anymore."

"Well, that may be so, but there's plenty of work to be had over there if a man needs work, and I know you need work, the kind of work I taught you to do. They say the government's bought another four thousand acres of land. They're going to make it even bigger."

"I know," Len said. "Mama cut the article out. Read it to us. It's over there on the table."

"That means more houses and more wells and pumps whether Hugh MacRae's in it or not. I'm telling you, if I was a younger man, damned if I wouldn't go."

Len hung his head. "I know they're hiring, Uncle Nathan, and we sure need the money," he said. When he looked up his eyes glistened. "But I can't just go."

Uncle Nathan jumped up from his straight chair, almost upsetting it. "Why the hell not? Your ma and pa have been taking care of themselves for a long time. They'll make it. Millie will too. Kate raised all of our young'uns. But she sure couldn't have done it if I hadn't been bringing home the bacon." He put his hand out to Len. When Len stood up, Nathan pulled him into an embrace. "Listen to me, son. You know I never misled you. You just put everything else aside and go on over there and get some of that work they're paying so high for. I can't hardly stand it, knowing I can't go with you."

⌒

Len wondered how come everybody except him knew just what he ought to. Hadn't he thought about nothing else since Mr. Lucas had given him a work application? That's why Millie had gotten to him so easily after he come home from looking at Penderlea. He *wanted* that work—knew it would be a way of checking out Penderlea without obligating himself to the government. But when MacRae had backed out, Len considered it a wake-up call. He had no business taking on a whole new life when he had more than he could do in the one he had. He'd even thought that maybe it was the Lord's way of telling him it wasn't right to leave Maggie and Tate to fend for themselves. Children were supposed to help their parents.

In the last year, Maggie had been taken to the hospital in Wilmington three times. It had been a terrible time for Len and Millie with Will gone and all. The last time, the doctors had taken her gall bladder out. She'd stayed in the hospital for two and a half weeks. Tate was with her at the hospital several nights before the doctor told him he was going to have to go home or they'd admit him, too. Every time Len thought about going to Penderlea, he thought about that. The gall bladder incident had made them all realize how bad off they were without a decent vehicle. Zeb Corbinn, Maggie's brother, had loaned them his car the first two times. Len had felt like a two-cent piece with a hole in it when he'd asked his uncle. He'd rather die than do it again. That's when Len had written to his brother and told him about it. Will had sent him two hundred dollars and told Len to go buy a used car.

Len loved having a car—not that it was much of a car. It was a 1929 Ford Fordor Sedan, one of the first of its kind to come off the assembly line. "This fellow I bought it from over in Rowan said somebody told him it might've been used to run whiskey," Len said. "It's got four of them Houdaille shock absorbers that they use in real expensive cars."

Tate inspected the car. "I never saw it around Will's garage."

Len smiled, catching his drift. "I reckon it's been painted over several times."

Tate laughed. "I'd say so. Fenders are pretty beat up, too. But it don't make a whole hell of a lot of difference if the engine runs good." He kicked a tire. "Tires are pretty good. Remember that old Chandler I bought for your mama? The engine was like new. It'd just been setting in Miss Bessie's garage for ten years or so." He began to laugh. "But after your mama driving it for two or three years, it give completely out."

Len laughed so hard, he had to hold his sides. "I believe it's still out there behind the tool shed," he said. "Will said she tore that engine all to hell."

⌒

"I don't know what we'd do without you and Len," Maggie told Millie. "I wish Will would get married and bring us another girl home. I always wanted a girl like you. Two would be nice."

Millie was folding freshly washed clothes on the couch while Annie played with her blocks on the floor. *Another girl to wait on you hand and foot!* she thought. "What do you hear from Will?" she asked. "Has he said anything more about coming home?"

"My stars, no. Will loves his work. He's making good money."

"Yes, I know. Sending money for the car was a real blessing."

"Will's a good boy—a mighty fine boy. He looks after his folks."

It was a bitter dose to swallow, Will getting all that glory while Len sacrificed his hopes and dreams—their hopes and dreams—to take care of his parents. True, if Will hadn't sent the money for the car, Miss Maggie Lorena might have died. The doctor had warned them that they'd think she was dying, even if she wasn't. She'd rolled in the bed like a worm in hot ashes while Mr. Tate had tried to comfort her. Len had gone to Zeb's and called Doctor Bayard. "You'd best take her to James Walker Hospital in Wilmington," he'd said. "That gall bladder is going to have to come out."

That had been the end of Len's peace of mind—not that he'd had much for the last year. But Millie saw a big difference in Len after he got his car. For one thing, he was gone a lot more.

CHAPTER 29

Winter was hard on everybody. Tempers flared in close quarters. Colds and flu passed from one to the other. When he was in the camp house, Len was nervous and underfoot. He complained constantly about the lack of money to do this and that on the farm. He wanted a tractor in the worst way—talked like he wished he'd bought one instead of the car. "A tractor would've made a whole hell of a lot more sense come spring planting time," he said.

"I don't think a tractor was what Will had in mind," Tate said.

"Will don't know the half of it," Len said. "There's work here for him. Everybody keeps asking me when he's coming back. There's a little more money with some of those CCC camp boys sending a few dollars home. Folks are getting their vehicles running again. They need a mechanic. Will could make a lot of money right here."

Millie put a plate of pork, dried lima beans, and canned applesauce in front of him. "We needed that car, Len," she said, looking down the table to where Tate sat. "We don't know who might be next to go to the hospital." She'd wanted to list a half-dozen other things, like what if Annie came down with pneumonia? Or—something just as bad in her mind—what if there was trouble with the baby inside her? She'd heard of terrible things happening. Rebecca told her that babies died if they couldn't be taken by an operation.

Later in the day, Tate called Len aside. "Maybe if you was to go over to Penderlea and work a couple of months, you could get us a tractor," Tate said. "That work won't last forever."

"I've thought about it, Pa. You know I have."

"I've told you before, I can keep things running in the winter. I can get Troy and his crowd to help me with the tobacco seed beds. Lord knows, I've been doing it all my life."

They were out by the barn, shoveling manure into the cart. Len noticed how Tate was straining with each shovelful. "You're pale around the gills, Pa. You ought not to be doing this. The doctor said—"

Tate leaned on his shovel and wiped sweat off his pale upper lip. "I'd rather wear out than rust out, son. You can't do everything."

Len climbed up on the fence and sat on the top rail. "Pa, you know I can't go and leave all of you, not with Millie expecting. What would her folks think of me?"

"I know, son. You have a responsibility to Millie, but your mama and I can take care of ourselves." He smiled up at Len. "Been doing it a pretty good while."

"That's what Uncle Nathan said. But it wouldn't be right, Pa. You know it wouldn't. If something should happen to Millie, or the baby—or even Mama, you wouldn't have a way to go after the doctor, or even call him."

Tate looked off into the distance. How could he convince Len to go whether Will came home or not? He couldn't. Not with the spells he'd been having. "I'm going to write to Will. Ask him to come home, but you gotta know, son, he might refuse."

"I don't think he will. I know I wouldn't."

"You'd better talk to Millie first," Tate said. "She might not like the idea of you going off to work now that she's carrying another baby."

"I don't mind, but your mama's not going to like it," Millie said.

"That's what Pa said about you."

"No, Annie and I will be fine. Mr. Tate takes real good care of us. But your mama may not want to—change things."

Len's ears perked up. "Why not?"

"I thought you knew," Millie said. "Will's sending her a money order every week or so. Just recently, she ordered some elastic stockings from the Sears and Roebuck catalog. She got a new kettle for me and some clothes for Annie. She might not want things to go back to like they were before he left."

"Well, I'll be damned," Len said.

"Maybe if Will comes home, I could go, too," she said, hesitantly. "You said some of the people were living in the outbuildings. If you liked the work, we could get an application from Emily and maybe move there." It was the wrong thing to say.

"Goddamnit! I'm not talking about moving to Penderlea, I'm just trying to find a way to put bread on this table," he said, punching the table with the forefinger of his right hand until she thought he'd break through it. A jar of whiskey peeped out from behind the curtain on a shelf above the sink. She wished she had seen it in time to dash its contents down the drain, but that would have only made him madder.

"I just thought—"

"Hell, I know what you were thinking about. You were thinking about yourself—about Millie McBryde whose family thinks *you* stepped down when you married this poor old country boy who can't give you a pot to pee in."

"That's not true. They all like you!"

"They don't look down on me? Ask your pa—ask Rob McBryde, whose own nephew murdered a woman, then got shot down in the river by the goddamned law. Ask him what he thinks of Len Ryan. I'll tell you what he thinks. I'm a damn son-of-a-bitch who doesn't know his ass from a hole in the ground."

"Len, why would you say that?" she cried. "It's not true. You're drinking, and I don't like you when you're drinking."

"You don't like me?" he said, in a mocking tone. "You don't like me, much less *love* me, and you're wondering why you married this son-of-a-bitch." His face was scarlet now, and he was wagging his finger at her.

"Len, please, you're going to wake the baby."

"To hell with the baby, I'm talking to you, woman!" He'd continued to rant and rave, following her from chore to chore while she straightened up the camp house. Finally, he picked up the Mason jar of white lightning, went out, and slammed the door behind him.

Tate Ryan was not one to write letters, but he did know how. He'd rather say what he had to say on a penny postcard, but he might as well make an announcement in the newspaper as to write Will on something that could be read by most anybody from here to Wilmington. While Maggie fed the chickens, he tore a piece of lined paper off her writing tablet and took a postage-paid envelope from her writing box. The letter was brief and to the point.

> *Dear Will,*
> *Soon as you can, you need to come on home. There's work here for you. We need a tractor. Len can go work at Penderlea if you come home.*
> *Love, Pa*

CHAPTER 30

Will Ryan's four-day bus ride from Detroit to Rocky Point was enough to make him never leave home again, which was something he didn't intend to do anyhow. He'd forgotten how sweet the air was on a spring morning in Colly. Walking along, he reminisced about days gone by when he'd driven his pa's mule and cart along the sandy road, never imagining that he would go as far away as Detroit, Michigan. Will sniffed his jacket sleeve. He still smelled like Michigan—chimney smoke and automobile grease—smells that might never wash off.

He'd gone to Detroit in the fall of 1932, hoping to get on with one of the big automobile manufacturers, but he soon found that he was but one of thousands who were out of work. With only pennies left in his pocket, he'd slept in an abandoned boxcar and stood in lines for bread and soup—something he'd been too embarrassed to write home about. Finally, he'd gotten a job with a man he'd recognized on the street as one of Patty Sue's friends. Dusty called him "Bud," just like his mama and Patty Sue had done.

Dusty Miller had hired Will as his boss's personal mechanic. The job came with a room on the first floor of a brick building adjoining an attached wooden garage, much like his own garage at home. In the shop, Will had available to him every mechanics tool he could imagine.

"I sure would like to meet the boss," Will said to Dusty soon after he'd been hired. "Like to tell him how much I'm obliged to him for this job. There are still men out there on the street standing in line waiting for handouts."

"The boss don't like to get *too* personal with the employees," Dusty said. "He's real shy ... stays to himself. Let's just say he don't like questions. Know what I mean, Bud?"

"Well, sure thing, Dusty, to be sure."

Cars came and went all during the day and night. Some needed an oil change; others four new tires; some rings and pistons. Dusty was the only driver Will ever saw. "That's my job," Dusty said. "The boss runs a big company. Lots of cars."

Must be traveling salesmen, Will thought, but he'd been warned not to ask questions, and he didn't.

When the letter from his Pa had come, Will wondered how in the world he'd tell Dusty that he had to go home. The work had never slowed down one bit since he'd been there. Dusty depended on him. Could he get somebody else? He had his mouth all set to ask Dusty, but that day, Dusty hadn't shown up as usual. Will kept the radio on all morning, listening to cowboy music while he straightened up the shop. He was caught up, just waiting for Dusty to bring him a car. In the afternoon, the radio programs came on and he pulled a chair close to the potbellied stove, propped his feet up on a crate and listened to *Amos and Andy*. He was getting uneasy. It wasn't like Dusty not to show up at all. At five o'clock, the news came on. The announcer talked loud and excited. It took a while for the news to sink in that the biggest gangster in Detroit had been shot and killed just a few blocks away. "Also arrested were a dozen or more of the gangster's henchmen, including his driver, the notorious Dusty Miller," the announcer said. "Authorities reported that Miller was a master car thief who stole cars to be used in the mob's business, and then dumped them into the Detroit River."

Will had been terrified. How could he have been such a dumb country hick? That's all he was—a dumb country hick from North Carolina. But he was a country hick with money in his pocket; he closed up the shop and never looked back until he reached the bus station. Four days later, he'd arrived in Burgaw with a small satchel and a lot more smarts.

When he reached Moore's Creek Battleground, a car passed Will and stopped a few yards ahead. Betty Bloodworth put it in reverse and backed toward him. She opened the door and stuck her head out. "Well, as I live and breathe, is that you, Will Ryan?"

"Yes'um, it's me."

"C'mon, get in this car and I'll give you a ride home."

Will jogged the few steps to her car and got inside. "Morning, Miss Betty. M-m-much obliged for the ride. I'm 'bout wore out from w-w-walking."

"You coming home from Detroit for good, Will Ryan?"

"Yes'um. I was awful homesick. B-b-been gone almost three years."

"Well, you didn't miss much here," she said. "We're all still poor as church mice. But your mama sure will be glad to see you. Len's working over yonder in Pender County, and she's 'fraid he won't never come back." She pulled over beside the mailbox in front of the oak grove. "Here you are. Give my regards to Mr. Tate and Miss Maggie Lorena."

Will noticed first thing that his Coca-Cola sign with Ryan's Garage on it was right where he'd left it. In fact, nothing seemed to have changed much except that the camp house had been painted and it looked a little larger. The oak grove was still littered with rusted vehicles—tractors, old farm machinery, and an old truck he had a special fondness for. As he passed Patty Sue's truck, he rubbed his hand over it tenderly. *Hello, old girl. I'm going to fix you up one of these days.*

He slipped around to the back of the house, wanting to surprise his mama, and found Millie bending over the wash pot stirring a load of diapers. "Howdy, Miss Millie. How're you today?" Millie looked up to see her brother-in-law. She hardly recognized him. Will had been at her mother's funeral.

That was the last time she'd seen the large man who resembled Tate down to a gnat's toenail.

"Will? I declare, is it really you?"

"S-s-sure is." He was trying hard not to stutter. The affliction had almost disappeared while he'd been in Detroit.

"Well, as I live and breathe," Millie said, grabbing him by the shoulders. "You're an answer to our prayers."

"Well, now, that's a m-m-mighty nice welcome home, Millie." He stood back and looked her over. "Looks like Len's been b-b-busy while I've been gone."

Millie blushed. "It's due in August," she said. "We're hoping for a boy this time."

"My goodness, I haven't even met Annie yet."

"Hold on a minute and I'll run get her up from her nap. I want to see your mama's face when she sees you."

"Okay, I'll w-w-wait right here, and we'll go in together." Millie was only gone a few minutes, but Will had glanced around and could see her marks on everything. Beds of pink thrift were mounded in old tires that had been painted white. A red rosebush covered the fence and reached up over the roof of the camp house. Will thought he might like that. A woman in the house. Someone to make things pretty.

⌐

"Sakes alive, Will Ryan, you almost gave me a heart attack!" Maggie exclaimed. She sat up on the bed and waited for him to embrace her. "Am I dreaming?"

"You're not dreaming, M-m-mama. It's me, in the flesh. I brought you a present." He rifled through his valise and came up with a shiny black figurine of a sultanlike character wearing a black turban and carrying a curved knife. "It's the S-S-Sheik of Araby," he said, proudly.

Maggie examined the curiosity. Tears came into her eyes. "I declare, son, it's the most beautiful thing I ever did see. Did you bring it all the way from Detroit."

"Yes, ma'am, I d-d-did. I thought it w-w-would be real pretty up there on your shelf over the bed."

"Oh, no, I want it where I can see it. Millie, put it there on the dresser where the baby can't reach it."

While Maggie refreshed herself on her chamber pot, Will and Millie took the baby and went into the kitchen to find something for Will to eat. "I declare, I'm about perished," Will said.

"When did you eat last?" Millie asked.

"I think it was last night, m-m-maybe in Tennessee somewhere. After awhile, I lost track of where I was. I slept, m-m-mostly."

Will was a good bit lighter than he'd been when he left Colly for Detroit. He was two years older than Len but more like Tate's side of the family. With his black hair and dark eyes, he looked nothing like the Corbinns. Millie poured Will a glass of buttermilk and sliced him a chunk of pound cake. "This ought to stave off hunger until supper time."

"When's Len c-c-coming home? I heard he was w-w-working at Pend-erlea."

"He's supposed to come home on Friday evening. That's payday."

"Are y'all going to g-g-get one of them houses over there?"

Millie looked down, afraid she'd say the wrong thing, something that would get back to Len. "He's just working right now, Will. They've got a big crew over there. Len said over a thousand men. I expect all of them are looking to get a house. I think we missed our chance when Mr. MacRae was the project manager. He'd taken a liking to Len."

"Well, I can't hardly w-w-wait to see him."

"Me, too, Will."

⁓

Millie didn't make a point of telling Will that Len had not come home *every* Friday night—nor that he didn't always bring his paycheck home—at least not the whole paycheck. Len said he slept in a bunkhouse with a lot of other men. There was a bathhouse nearby and a canteen—a place that sold chewing gum, cigarettes, and toiletries. He said they also had beer. Len said that sometimes he had one or two to relax at the end of a hard day. A couple of weekends, Len had not come home until Saturday, about midday. She'd thought maybe he'd gotten drunk, slept it off. When he'd come home, he'd divided up what was left of his pay between his mama and Millie.

⌐

For Will's homecoming dinner, Millie picked turnip salad from the garden and sliced the last of the smoked ham down to the bone. That morning Tate had shot three squirrels, dressed them, and put them in a pan of salty water. For supper, she'd cut them up and season them with lots of black pepper, and fry them to a dark brown. As Cousin Maggie suggested, she'd cover them with water and let them stew for several hours. Millie did not like the wild taste of squirrel or venison, but she knew Will and the others would enjoy it. A jar of Maggie Lorena's big hominy completed the menu.

Rebecca had taught her that a meal should be balanced and colorful. Her sister would always be the best cook in the family. She'd cautioned Millie not to fall into the ways of country people, lacing vegetables with too much grease. It was bad enough, she said, that they gorged themselves on cornbread and biscuits, fat meat and chitlins. But Millie found it was hard to change old ways.

⌐

After dark, Maggie Lorena suggested that they go ahead and eat. "Len's probably tied up on one of those pump jobs," she said. "Just put a plate aside for him, Millie. He'll be perished when he gets home." Millie had put the plate in the oven, but Len didn't come home that night or Saturday morning. By Saturday afternoon, Millie was sure that Len had gotten hurt in a wreck, or maybe on the job.

"No news is good news," Will said. "Len can take care of himself." He was worried about Len too, but he didn't let on that his fear was more that

Len just might have found something or someone to keep him there. Will had seen that kind of thing before. "If I can get that old blue Ford truck running, I'll go to Penderlea on Monday and check on him. Maybe you and Annie would come with me, Millie." She'd jumped at the chance, like he knew she would.

CHAPTER 31

Millie had hardly slept at all Sunday night. She'd gotten up before light and prepared food for the baby and a picnic lunch for Len, Will, and herself. "Want to go in the truck with Uncle Will?" she asked Annie as she dressed her.

"Da-da," Annie said.

"Yes, we're going to see Daddy, darling. Mommy's excited, too." Annie was eighteen months old now, and every day she seemed to be accomplishing something new. Millie longed to be with Len. The fun in having children was watching them grow together.

Will tapped on the door. "Ready when you are, Millie." She opened the door and handed him a basket and a cloth bag she used to carry Annie's diapers. "I'll be right with you as soon as I say good-bye to Cousin Maggie and Mr. Tate." She crossed the yard carrying Annie and went into the house through the back door. Tate and Maggie were sitting at the table, finishing their breakfast. Maggie didn't look up. "Morning, y'all," Millie said. "Will's ready to go. It may be after dark when we get home. Go ahead and eat without us. I'll fix something for Will when we get back."

"Give Granddaddy a hug," Tate said, reaching out for his granddaughter.

"Do you have something for supper, Cousin Maggie?"

"I reckon we'll be able to scrape together a few rations. My rheumatism is acting up, but I can always make a little gravy—if it's out of nothing but squirrel's tracks." She looked up and smiled. "Y'all just go on. Tell Len Mama sends her love."

Millie gave her a peck on the cheek and reached for Annie. "Give Grandmother a hug and tell her bye-bye, Annie." Annie waved her hand. "Doesn't Grandmother get a hug?" Millie asked.

Annie drew back, clinging to Millie. "You'll hurt Grandmother's feelings." Annie drew back again.

"That's all right," Maggie said. "She's peeved with me because I wouldn't let her touch my Sheik of Araby." In the truck, Millie couldn't help but mention it to Will. "Your mama doesn't like children very much. Has she always been like that?"

"Mama's just n-n-nervous, that's all. She don't m-m-mean nothing by it."

"Lord-a-mercy, I know that. I just wondered if she had always been like that."

"They say it started when Yancey died."

"Oh," Millie said. She couldn't imagine how awful she'd act if Annie died.

⌐

Len had left Colly soon after Tate had told him that he'd written to Will and asked him to come home. He'd decided that working for wages would be a hell of a lot better than doing without a tractor for another growing season. He'd been gone only a week when he came home to pick up clean clothes and to tell his family that he had been welcomed by Mr. Eugene Autry, district manager of the employment office. "He hired me on the spot as a pump installer. I'll be making seventy-five cents an hour for a five-day week and an eight-hour day. That's more money than I've ever made in my life," he crowed.

"Are there lots of houses now?" Millie had asked.

"Right many. You've never seen anything like it," he said, chuckling. "They come in there with the timbers already cut by the mill. In two and a half hours that house is up and ready for the next crew. Another crew comes in and they do the partitions, plumbing, and wiring. Then another crew does the paneling and the floors. I might put the pump in one day, go back the next day, and everything's finished, right down to those little green shutters you're so crazy about."

"Have they got electricity yet?"

"The line's built, and they're wiring the finished houses." Len had pulled her to him and hugged her. "Honey, I know what you're thinking. We could have one of those houses as good as anybody, but I don't think that's what we want. They're set on these tiny little farms. The fields are full of roots and stumps. The soil is wet and sour. If a house and everything to go with it sounds too good to be true, it is!"

They'd been sitting at the kitchen table. She'd prayed that Len would come home all hepped up about Penderlea. Instead, he was about to light into all the things he'd found wrong with it. She didn't want to hear it. She got up from the table and started washing the dishes. Len came up behind her and put his arms around her. He nuzzled her on the neck and kissed her ear. "Look, honey. I'm looking out for us. I see those folks barely making it. Dutch said every dime he makes goes to the government. There won't ever be any spending money just to go to a show or something."

"Not much of that anyhow, is there?" She prepared herself for the assault, but Len had turned his attention to the baby, who was playing close to the heater. He scooped her up and swung her up to his shoulders. "You're playing too close to that old stove, Weezy. One of these days Daddy's going to build you a new house where you'll have plenty of room to play."

Millie closed her eyes. *History repeats itself,* she thought. He wants to stay right here and build a house. She'd heard the tales from Maggie Lorena about how Tate had procrastinated about a new house—how everything else came first—how Maggie had done without things because there was no running water or electricity. She'd thought to herself then, *things can't get much worse.*

The blue Ford pickup that Will drove to Penderlea had been a truck he souped-up for Patty Sue McBryde before she was murdered in 1928. After her death, the truck fell into Geneva McBryde's hands. Geneva had the tires taken off it, and put it up on blocks in her yard. Some time later, she mentioned to Will that he could have it if he'd haul it away. Will had plenty of worn-down patched-up tires he'd salvaged off junked vehicles. He'd taken four of them up to Cotton Cove and given Miss Geneva two dollars for the truck. That's how it had come into the Ryans' possession.

All had not been happy over Patty Sue's truck sitting in the yard. To Maggie Lorena, it was an evil thing in itself. She hated the old blue truck sitting out there in her oak grove. She'd taken matters into her own hands late one evening and set it afire. Will put the fire out and moved the truck before any real damage was done. He'd parked it out of her sight after that, knowing the truck would run like a scalded dog when he tuned it up and had good tires to go on it.

Will loved working on the old truck again. He thought he could make it like new if he had the mechanics tools he'd left up in Detroit. Every now and then a touch of sadness seeped into his heart. Patty Sue had loved her truck. Sometimes he imagined he caught a whiff of her in it. But his sadness was even more for the boy. *Wonder where Colin is now? He must be ten or eleven years old*, he thought. Sadly, he felt sure that Colin had forgotten them. He'd thought the old woman who'd come to fetch him looked mean as the devil—not much different from her sister, Patty Sue's mama.

⌒

The area around the Penderlea project office, set back in a tall pine grove, was teeming with workers going this way and that. Millie and Will sat in the truck for a few minutes looking around to see if one of them might be Len. "I'll go ask somebody," Will said. "I doubt if there are too many tall redheaded fellas around here named Len Ryan." He went into the project office and came out shortly. "Pretty little lady in there said Len was working at a house over on Crooked Run Road. She told me how to get there." Will backed the truck out and swung around to head toward the road. A large construction truck coming up behind him braked to avoid hitting Will. The truck's load of lumber shifted and in a flash rolled over on its side, spilling lumber all over the road. Will grasped the steering wheel when he saw though his rearview mirror what had happened. "Gol dern!" he shouted. "That truck turned over!"

"Oh, my gosh," Millie said, craning her neck out the window.

Will parked the truck and got out just as the driver of the construction truck crawled out of his cab. "Damn hick!" the driver shouted at him, shaking his fist. "Why don't you look where you're going!"

Will approached him. "I'm s-s-sorry. I didn't see you c-c-coming."

A man came out of the project office to see what the commotion was about. Taking long strides across the construction site, he looked to be someone in charge of things. He went straight to the driver of the overturned truck who was sitting on the ground unhurt. "I might have known you'd be involved, Carson. I've told you a dozen times that you drive too fast."

The driver stood up and brushed himself off. "He pulled out in front of me!" he shouted. "Damn hick!"

"That's enough out of you!" the man said. Millie, holding Annie, had gotten out of the pickup and stood beside Will. "You could have killed this man and his wife."

"Oh, we're not married," Millie said. "This is my brother-in-law."

"He wasn't paying a bit of attention to where he was going," the truck driver fumed.

"Eugene Autry," the other man said, extending his hand to Will.

"Will Ryan." He shook Mr. Autry's hand and turned to the truck driver. "I'm m-m-mighty sorry, mister. I hope you didn't get hurt." The truck driver threw up his hands in disgust and walked off.

"Not your fault, Will. He's been warned several times about his driving." Mr. Autry called out to the truck driver. "Get somebody to help you pick up this lumber and wait for me in my office." He turned back to Millie. "I'm sorry, Miss...?"

"Mrs. Ryan," Millie said. "Maybe you know my husband, Len? He works here."

"Len Ryan? Sure I know Len Ryan. I hired him. I didn't know he was married."

"Yes, sir," Millie said. "This is our daughter, Annie. Annie, can you say hey to Mr. Autry?" Shyly, Annie lifted her hand.

"She's a cute one," he said. "Wait a minute and let me get my car. I'm headed over that way. You can follow me, and I'll show you where Len is working."

"Thank you. Thank you very much," Millie said.

Will tipped his hat. "Much obliged, Mr. Autry, but I hope that man w-w-won't lose his j-j-job because of this."

"Don't worry about it, son. See that line over by my office?" He pointed toward one of the white buildings beneath a tall stand of pine trees. Men were lined up near the door. "They're all looking for jobs—just waiting to take his place," he said.

They drove about a mile and a half over the project before Autry pulled into a site where a house was under construction. The ground was littered with building materials and the remnants of trees and stumps. "Your husband is a mighty good pump man," Autry said, opening the truck door for Millie. "Let's go around back." He reached for the child and she went right to him. "C'mon, Annie, let's go find your daddy." When they rounded the corner of the house, they saw Len standing next to a young woman. Millie's heart skipped a beat. Len was handsome even in his faded overalls.

The woman's hair was swept up on top of her head, and she wore pancake makeup with bright lipstick and nail polish on her fingers. In a slim straight skirt and a long-sleeved blouse that she'd tied at the waist, she definitely did not look like a homesteader. *A working girl,* Millie thought. *In those high-heeled shoes, she's got to be!* Len leaned against the side of the pump house, looking down at the woman with a great big smile on his face.

She had her hand on Len's arm, gazing up at him like she could eat him with a spoon. Mr. Autry called out to him. "Look who's here, Len."

"That's the lady who told me where Len was," Will whispered to Millie.

"God-a-mighty!" Len said, stepping quickly over to Autry and taking his daughter. "It's Annie Weezy! And you brought your mama and Uncle Will with you." He reached out to pull Millie to him as his eyes met Will's. "You son-of-a-gun, you finally came home."

"Yep, sure did," Will said, extending his hand to Len. "Good to see you, little brother."

"This here's Mazie. She works in Mr. Autry's office. She came to tell me y'all were here."

"Pleased to meet you," Mazie said. A piece of pink chewing gum poked out the corner of her mouth.

Autry threw up his hand. "I need to get back to the office." He looked at the girl. "You coming, Mazie?"

"Oh, yeah, Mr. Autry, I'm coming," she said, starting toward a light green Chevrolet coupe parked close by. She smiled, all the while keeping her eyes on Len, smacking her gum. "I just came over here because I was afraid Len would be worried if he heard about the wreck." She slipped into the car and started the engine. "See you later, Len," she called out, her wheels spinning in the sand.

"Mazie is real nice," Len said. "You'd like her a lot, Millie."

"Yes, I'm sure I would."

Len grabbed Will by his shoulder. "When did you get home, brother?"

"The m-m-middle of the week. We looked for you on the weekend. You m-m-must have gotten t-t-tied up?"

Len glanced at Millie. "Yep, Millie knows I don't always get home."

"I brought us a picnic," Millie said, looking up at him. "Your mama sent some of her grape hull cake. Can you stop for lunch?"

"To be sure, to be sure," Len said. "I'll pull up some boxes to sit on over there around that stump. C'mon, Annie, Daddy's going to fix us a table."

After they'd finished their picnic, Len walked them through the house, dodging workmen left and right. The partitions between rooms were going up, and the floor was littered with bent nails and lumber. Millie tried to place the different rooms, but Len was uneasy that Annie was going to get hurt. "Let's step back outside. It's not a good time to be in here," he said. They walked around the yard where Len pointed out the different structures. "There's the washhouse. It can double as a smokehouse. Over yonder is the barn and the corn crib. The man that's getting this one came yesterday. You should have heard him talking about all the things he was going to buy with money the government was going to loan him," Len said, laughing.

"M-m-maybe I ought to get m-m-married, come over here, and get me one." They both laughed again.

Len was getting fidgety. "Look, I've got to get back to work," he said. "Here comes the farm manager, Hank Hudson. I want to stay on his good side."

"How come?" Will asked.

"He's one of the bosses. Might need a good word from him sometime." He picked up Annie and gave her a hug. "Daddy'll be home soon. We've got money, marbles, and chalk—streetcar tickets and won't have to walk," he laughed, holding her over his head. But when he hugged Millie, she stiffened. "I know my girls miss me, honey. I'll be home soon."

"This weekend?"

"Soon. I'm going to take off a few days to help with the tobacco planting. Mr. Autry said I could."

"I'll help," she said. *But my heart won't be in it now that I've seen Penderlea.*

The farm manager waited for Will to back out before pulling into the parking space. Will threw up his hand and the manager waved back. A young boy, ten or twelve years old, sat in the back of the truck with a large white dog. The boy smiled, and Will threw up his hand again. Millie waved too. "Could we stop at that store up on the main road and get some Pepsi-Colas?" she asked "I'm dying of thirst." But Will wasn't listening. He was looking in the rearview mirror, watching the boy, who was watching the blue truck pull away. "Will?"

"What?"

"I said, could we stop and get some drinks?"

Will continued slowly down the road, trying to clear his thoughts. *Millie asked me to stop. Get drinks.* "Sure we c-c-can, Millie. I could use one, too."

On the way home, Millie pretended to sleep along with Annie, but bad thoughts raced about in her head. Len had made excuses about last weekend, but he'd been very vague. He said the project manager had a fishing camp over by the river. He'd invited some of the men there for a fish fry on Friday night. Len had been afraid they'd think hard if he didn't go. Plenty of white lightning was passed around. Some of the fellows bunked down in the camp to sleep off the liquor. Len was among them.

Millie tried to picture the fishing camp. Her brothers often went to places like that with other men. She'd heard them laugh and talk about what went on. Wives weren't allowed, but often some of the fellas would bring girls. She opened her eyes and peered out into the darkness. Annie was still sleeping. "Where are we, Will?"

Will was lost in thoughts, too. "What? Oh, we just passed over Colly Creek."

"I hope I can get Annie in bed without waking her."

When they reached the oak grove, Will pulled in right beside the camp house. "Let me take her. You open the door and get her bed ready."

Millie handed him the child. "I'll fix us some supper after I get her tucked in."

Will sat at the kitchen table while Millie brought out some cold sweet potatoes and warmed a bowl of stew for both of them. The camp house felt cramped and makeshift to her after seeing the nice houses with their partitions and open rooms. There'd been windows in every room, and she'd imagined making curtains for them. "Thank you for taking me, Will. It really meant a lot to me. It's going to be real nice over there, isn't it?"

"I reckon so. Mama says Len's not interested in calling it home. How about you?"

"I don't know. I feel like we'd be better off over there, but if Len doesn't want it—"

"I know how I'd feel if I was Len," Will said. "It's one thing to work for wages and get paid, but another thing to borrow ahead and always be owing somebody."

"You mean the government, don't you?"

"Yes'um, I do."

"It's only twenty acres. I know we could do it. We could pay for it with Len's wages, and he could farm too."

Will reached over and patted Millie's hand. He was so much like Mr. Tate. "Just give Len a little time," he said. "He might come 'round to it." He stood up and started toward the door. "I'd better get on over to the house. Ma and Pa'll wonder why I haven't come in." Will hesitated at the door. "Let me ask you something. Did you see that boy in back of the farm manager's truck?"

"I saw him, Will, but I didn't pay much attention to him. Why?"

"He looked awful familiar to me. I thought you might have noticed, too."

"I was getting Annie settled. Who'd you think he looked like?"

"I thought he was the sp-sp-spitting image of Patty Sue McBryde."

CHAPTER 32

H ank Hudson, the farm manager at Penderlea, had carved a small cubicle out of his large office for Emily McAllister. She was playing a large role in the resettlement project, and he felt it only fair that she had a place to hang her hat. "You ought to be on the government payroll," he said. "I need an assistant, not just a volunteer. Besides, you ought to be getting paid for all you do."

Emily laughed. "I don't do that much," she said. But she knew she did. Over the past few months, she'd become a one-woman welcoming committee for the Penderlea project, spending more and more of her time greeting the new homesteaders. By April 1936, 142 houses had been completed. A few still lacked hinges, door fastenings, and other hardware, but fifteen families had moved into Penderlea by the end of the month. In May another fifty families moved in. As each new family arrived, Emily would step out onto the small landing outside the project manager's office and say, "Welcome to Penderlea." Then, she'd offer to show them where their homestead was located and instruct them on the use of the plumbing fixtures and the appliances.

Prior to each of their arrivals, Emily saw that a quart of milk, a loaf of bread, and a bushel basket of whatever produce was being harvested at the time from the community garden was in the refrigerator or on the table when families saw their homesteads for the first time. In addition, she made sure a roll of toilet paper was in the bathroom. Most families came with everything they owned in the back of a pickup truck. Some of the them were standoffish when they first arrived—skittish and afraid to accept the handouts, mistrusting Emily as much as the government even though they'd come to Penderlea with that in mind. Others came with high expectations, only to find out that all that was promised was either slow to come or not available at all. But Emily observed that the real misgivings and distrust came when the homesteaders were given the very detailed arrangement of a home and farm management plan predetermining how all income would be spent, and enforced by a joint checking account arrangement whereby the project manager was required to countersign all checks. She found she could help them very little with that discovery.

"I'm sorry, Hank. After the next batch of houses is finished, I intend to take some time off, visit my daughter up in New York. I think the Wilmington office can handle the applications from now on, don't you?"

"I expect so. We're about full up with what's built anyhow. They're talking about buying more land—building even more houses—making 'em thirty acres each."

"Well, I don't want to review that many more applications, so it's just as well," Emily said. "When the project was federalized, the number of forms doubled. Most were incomplete when I got them. It was a real mess." She confessed to Hank that what bothered her more than anything was the invasion of privacy by field workers who'd been sent to applicants' homes to follow up on the various forms detailing family history. They questioned neighbors, friends, and employers to the point of rudeness, causing some of her favorite applicants to completely abort the process. "I think they all blamed me," Emily said.

"You sound frustrated," Hank said. "I know that feeling. It comes from all the red tape."

"That's another reason I want to get away," Emily said. "The homesteaders that have moved in think I know all of the answers. I don't." She looked down at her hands, wondering why she was admitting to this. "Nobody does."

"You'll come back, though, won't you, Emily? We'd be lost without you. You know more about what's going on in Penderlea than I do."

Emily laughed, but she knew it was true. When Hugh MacRae started Penderlea, he'd asked Hank to be the first farm manager. Hank and the boy had been there ever since, living in a small house that had belonged to a tenant farmer on the original tract. But Hank was often bumfuzzled, as he called it, by exactly what the government meant by some of their lengthy directives. When he'd arranged for Emily to share his office, homesteaders found it convenient to pay her a visit if Hank was out. Sometimes they just needed to air their concerns with her. But when Hank was in the office, she sympathized with the frustrated homesteaders who could never get a straight answer from him. "Well, now, I'll look into that," he'd say, or "I'll have to see about that."

Emily was sure the only reason homesteaders felt they could confide in her was because she *wasn't* a government employee. For the most part, they were wonderful people who were there because they wanted the chance to make a better life. They were truly grateful for a house with electricity and running water, but the big questions were never answered. How would they come up with the first year's rent? When would they be able to own their homes? No one, especially Emily, had the answers. She could only sympathize with the confusion and uncertainty in their lives. She was afraid of what they were getting into, too.

"I won't leave you just yet, Hank. There are a few more families coming in that I'm curious about. Some of the applicants have touched my heart. I'd like to meet them," she said.

Hank looked pleased. They'd become good friends in the last year. She liked him as a person, his ready smile, and the way he stopped and really listened, like now, to what she had to say. "There's something I've been wanting to ask you, Hank. You don't have to tell me if you don't want to."

"Shoot."

"Your boy? Colin?"

Hank smiled. "You like him, don't you?"

"I do, I really do, Hank. Tell me about him."

"He's at the house today, plowing the garden."

"He's a smart boy. Tell me how you came to adopt him."

"Oh, that. I don't think he'd mind me telling you. We were living over at St. Helena then, me and my wife. Didn't have any children. We tried, but I think it was her. You know she died of cancer—something about her female organs going bad." Hank blushed, but he continued when Emily lowered her eyes. "One day I heard some of the immigrants talking about a woman who lived over near St. Helena. They said she had this little boy that she kept tied to the bed all day long while she worked in Burgaw."

"She tied him to the bed?"

"Yes, by his foot."

Emily thought she'd faint from the thought of it. "That's how he hurt his foot?"

"I think so. He won't talk about it much. Just says he broke it one time. Didn't grow back right. I don't make him talk about it. When I heard about it, I went and got the sheriff, took him over there, and we got the boy. The woman came to get him at the sheriff's office that evening, but the sheriff had already gotten an order from the magistrate saying she couldn't have him back. She had a fit, but she left, and the next thing I heard was that she'd moved away, lock, stock, and barrel."

"Have you ever heard from her again?"

"Never."

Emily was quiet for a few minutes, composing her thoughts. "Hank, I think his foot could be fixed by an orthopedic surgeon. I could arrange it, with your permission."

"Oh, my goodness. I don't want him to have no surgery. He's been hurt enough. No, don't even think about it, Miss Emily."

CHAPTER 33

L en had only obligated himself to work at Penderlea through the end
of May. Charlie Lucas was leaving and soon would be replaced by a
new project manager. There was no love lost between him and his surly
boss. On his last day installing pumps on Penderlea, Len went straight to
the cashier's office to pick up his pay rather than have any last words with
Lucas. Along with the little bit that Millie had managed to save from week
to week, his pay would have to hold him until September when he'd go
to the tobacco market in Clarkton and sell the tobacco. He was afraid a
tractor was out of the question for this growing season.

A month ago, as the farmwork had picked up, Len had cut down his
number of working days on the homestead project to two a week. The rest of
the week he was back in Colly farming. No one, except Mr. Lucas, had seemed
to mind. There were always jobs and plenty of men looking for work. Len was
good at pump work, and Lucas knew it. It made the manager look good when
he could send a man out to take care of a situation, and the man took care of
it. Len did that. There were times when Len thought he could make a living
installing pumps and keeping them running, but he sure as hell didn't want
to obligate himself to a puny little twenty-acre farm to do it. He'd seen what it
would be like, heard the talk. Penderlea sure wasn't utopia! Not yet, anyhow.

Len was hopeful about his crops this year. Tate, Will, and even Millie had done much of the work in early spring, watching over the tobacco seedlings as they came to life beneath the gauze coverings. Now the seedlings were growing strong in rows in the field. Yet to come was the suckering and topping, and removing the great horned tobacco worms. The corn looked good, too. There'd been plenty of rain this spring. Too much in Pender County. But when a man had his crops under way, rain was a blessing.

Hank Hudson was talking with the cashier inside the caged office. He threw up his hand to Len. "Howdy, Hank," Len said.

Hank waved. "I heard this was your last day, Len. How about leaving us a way to get in touch with you? We might need some help from time to time."

"I'm not going to have much time for awhile, Hank, but they've got my address in the office. When's the new project manager coming?"

"I imagine in another week or so."

The cashier handed Len his pay envelope and unlocked the door for Hank, who reached out to shake Len's hand. "I wish you'd consider staying here with us, Len."

Len smiled. "No, sir, can't do that. Got to get back over yonder and take care of my business in Bladen County."

"All right, but keep it in mind. The new project manager, Melvin Harrell, sent word that he wants his own servicemen on the project."

"That so? Probably a good idea," Len said. "After a year or so, some of those pumps are bound to break down from time to time."

They left the cashier's office, and Len started toward his truck while Hank headed toward the administrative office. He stopped short and called out to Len. "Hey, wait a minute. There's someone in my office who's asked me about you. You mind stepping over there for a minute before you go?"

"Who is it?"

"A lady," Hank said. "C'mon, you'll see."

Len was slightly taken aback. He couldn't imagine who wanted to see him. He followed Hank into the project office. "Let me see if Miss Emily is here."

"Miss Emily McAllister? Well, I'll be damned. Where is she?"

"Right here," Hank said, sticking his head into Emily's cubicle. "Somebody to see you, Miss Emily." Emily's delight overwhelmed Len. He'd always liked her, but thought of her more as Millie's friend than his. She hugged him and took a step back to look him over.

"My goodness, look at you, Len, all grown up. If you get any more handsome, we're going to have to send you to Hollywood."

"Thank you, Miss Emily," he said, blushing. "I was hoping I'd catch you one of these days. It sure is good to see you. Millie will be tickled to death. She's been worrying me to death about getting an application."

"I know, Len. Millie wrote to me and said you'd changed your mind after Hugh MacRae resigned."

"Well, now I didn't *change* my mind, I just—maybe I did, but Millie shouldn't have—"

She recognized irritation when she saw it. "Oh, Millie just said that you all were better off where you were." Emily reached for her hat on the rack. "I was just going over to check on the Mullinses. Dan says he knows you. Why don't you come with me and say hello? You'll be halfway off the project and on your way home."

⁓

Len thought Dan Mullins would never let his hand go. He was shaking it up and down, up and down, his round face all smiles. "I declare, I never thought to see you again. Are you near us? Where's your house?"

"No, sir, I never did apply. Been working here since January though. Putting in pumps." He nodded his head toward Dan's pump house. "Put that one in right there," Len said, chuckling.

"If that don't beat all," Dan said, a wad of chewing tobacco stretching his smile even more. "C'mon in the house, meet my wife Sula. We've 'bout got what little we brought with us in place. Expectin' a baby most any day now. Got two girls already. They say the new baby will be the first one born on the project."

"That so?" Len asked, a little envy surfacing. He could've been moving into Penderlea himself, and Millie having one of the first babies on the project. "My wife's expecting, too," he said. "Looks like an August baby."

"That so?" Mullins asked.

Emily was standing near her car. "Will y'all excuse me? I need to run back to the office a minute. I promised Sula I'd bring her some things from the cannery the next time I was over this way. I'll be right back."

"Sure thing, Miss Emily," Dan said, pulling open the screen door for Len. "Come on inside, I'll call to Sula." As Len stepped inside the screened-in porch, he looked out over the little farm and imagined he was just arriving and planning for his future as a Penderlea homesteader.

"Come on in, Len," Dan said. "She's up and about. We've got two other young'uns. She can't rest for long."

Len followed Dan into a small neat kitchen with linoleum flooring and a tiny black and white enameled cookstove and matching cabinet. A sink with a flowered curtain draped around it was underneath the window. On the opposite wall was a drop-leaf table and two chairs. Len thought it looked a little like a dollhouse kitchen. "This is real nice, Dan."

"It's tiny, Len, to be sure, but we don't care about that. It's a lot better than what we had." He stuck his head into the adjoining living room. "Here she is. Honey, this is Len Ryan from over in Bladen County. He installed our pump."

"Pleased to meet you, Len," she said, her voice a slow, pleasing drawl. She struggled to get up from the sofa where she'd been sitting, her belly swollen with child. Her face was pretty as a picture, childlike, framed by short, wavy brown hair, held in place at the side by a hair clip.

"Pleased to meet you, Miss Sula. This is a mighty nice place you've got. First time I've been inside one exactly like this."

"Thank you, Len," Sula said, her hands on her enlarged stomach. "I don't know where we'll put another child, but we'll manage."

"It's a little bigger than some—one of the first ten houses they built. I guess the fellow that had it didn't make it." Dan said. "Only ten acres of land came with it, but after Mr. Hugh resigned, they changed it to twenty acres. I guess you know that the government has cut back right much on the size and quality of the houses too."

"Yeah, I heard that," Len said.

"Ten acres was nothing. I might be able to grow a little tobacco on twenty. You can't make any money off vegetables and flowers!"

"Better not let the farm manager hear you say anything about tobacco," Len said. "He told me the other day that the whole principle behind the project was truck farming."

"Well, just don't mention it," Dan said. "Once I get this place paid for, they can't tell me what to grow."

"How long do you reckon that'll be?" Len asked.

"No telling."

Dan's two little girls stood in the hall doorway. "I told you girls to take a nap," Sula said. "Come on in and speak to Mr. Len. Did I hear you say you had a little girl, Len?"

"Sure do. Hey, girls. Maybe I'll bring my wife and daughter over one day, and y'all can get to know each other. Millie's dying to see one of the houses now that they're about finished."

"Please bring her, Len. I don't know a soul here except Miss Emily, and she's not a homesteader."

As if on cue, Emily poked her head in the door. "I brought those things from the cannery, Sula."

"Thank you so much, Miss Emily. I don't know what we would do without you."

Emily and Len said their good-byes, and Emily walked Len to his truck. "Things are falling into place around here, Len. I think it's going to be real nice when they iron out the kinks." She handed him a piece of folded paper. "Why don't you take this application and put it aside? There may come a time when you'll want to come to Penderlea."

Len smiled. "I declare, Miss Emily, you and Millie are gonna get me over here whether I want to or not. But I guarantee you, it won't be anytime soon. I got my crops to bring in first."

"Just keep it in mind, Len." She reached up and gave him a hug.

Len put the application into the glove box of the truck. He didn't want Millie to see it. The more he had seen of Penderlea, the more confident he'd become that he and his family were better off in Bladen County. He wasn't like the men he'd worked with, either. They were hard-up, down-and-out farmers who'd either lost their land or never owned any in the first place. Some were relief workers who carried their paycheck home every weekend, but there were more who drank and gambled away every penny they made. They weren't all like Dan Mullins and Dutch Van Bruggen.

When Len had first started to work on the project, he'd met a braggart who said he was on the list to get in Penderlea. He said when he did, he was going to take everything the government gave him. "I might never do a lick of work," he said. And he didn't. A few weeks after he'd moved in, the project manager gave him his start-up money and the fellow packed up, bought a car with the money, and left. The FBI was after him the last time Len had heard.

Len had also met homesteaders who couldn't do the farming. Some thought truck farming would be like having a big garden. Trouble was, even gardens took decent soil. You couldn't rush new ground. Good soil took years to make. Farmers knew that. Even the government knew that.

There were women, too, that hung around the camp cantina. Some like Mazie Rivenbark worked in the project office. Mazie had been after him since the first day he met her. She was fast and razor sharp. Slipping around was just her thing. Len didn't want to fall into that way of life. Once or twice, she'd cornered him, came right out and asked him if he was *interested*. He managed each time to laugh and slough it off, but she had some cunning ways he might find hard to resist the next time.

Will watched Len's car pull into the oak grove at a fast clip and skid to a stop in the sand a few feet from him. "You son of a gun," he said when Len climbed out. Will had tuned up the car to a fair-thee-well the last time Len was home.

Len grabbed Will by the shoulders and gave him a bear hug. "If you hadn't been here to keep things running, I never could have gone to Penderlea. Look at this," he said, pulling a narrow metal box out from under his arm. "There's enough cash in here to carry us until we sell the tobacco. Maybe we'll have enough to buy a tractor if we get some allotment money."

"Money always did p-p-put a smile on your f-f-face."

Will had made things seem right again. The burden of taking care of everyone and everything no longer fell on Len alone. Millie was happier. Mama and Papa were happier. Yes, the money he'd made at Penderlea had put them back on their feet. Now he could put his heart into farming.

Despite her pregnancy, Millie had been willing to do just about anything to help with the farming. Back in the winter, she'd helped burn off the weeds and rubble in the tobacco seed beds. That's how you sterilized the soil, leaving the heavy ash to nourish the seedlings. When Len had left in March, the tobacco seedlings were already up and growing in their beds beneath gauze coverings. Millie and one of Lizzie's girls watched over them faithfully, pulling weeds and weak seedlings to encourage the others to grow strong and healthy. After six weeks or so, they'd removed the gauze and allowed the tender plants to harden off in the warmth of the sun.

Will had done his part, too. Tate alone could never have accomplished the heavy plowing and discing of the fields to get them ready for the plants. Will had rigged up a makeshift tractor, a funny sight to see, an engine setting on a four-wheeled platform with a drive shaft pulling an eighteen-blade disc, but it sure as hell got the job done a lot faster and better than a man and a mule. And, Len, taking a day or two at a time, had come home from Penderlea, bringing fertilizer and lime to turn into the newly plowed fields. Will had also rigged up a mule-drawn transplanter. The old way had taken three people walking along—one to make a hole in the furrow with a hand peg, another to put it in the hole, and another to pour a fertilizer and water mix to get the seedlings started. The new transplanter was mule drawn and still took three people, but it was a lot faster, and Millie could sit on it and ride while helping to do the planting.

"You could get a patent on that machine and make a fortune," Len said.

Will laughed. "They've got transplanters already up there in Michigan. I went to one of them farm machinery shows and saw it. I figured out how I could make one."

⌒

Unfortunately, in June and July, a long drought set in. Lack of rain meant they'd had to replant the tobacco three times and tote water to it for weeks to keep it from burning up in the fields. Will had rigged up a galvanized tank on the back of the farm jalopy, which helped some. But even then, they'd had to abandon about half of the acreage they'd planted. "It's a good thing we signed up for the allotments," Len said. "After we top and sucker, there might not even be enough left for the damn horn worms to feast on." His face and hands were black from the sticky gum that covered the tobacco leaves. He'd been in the field all morning, cropping the first leaves—the heavy lugs that lost their green color first, indicating that the tobacco was ready to be harvested.

"Don't give it up, son," Tate said. "I've seen a lot worse and still got a few good barnings. That's one thing you learn about tobacco. It likes the heat, and it don't mind some dry weather after it gets on up there."

In July and August, the tobacco barn teemed with neighbors and friends helping with the barning. As soon as a mule-driven sled full of tobacco leaves was pulled under the shed and unhooked, an empty sled was attached to the mule's harness and one of the youngsters in the neighborhood jumped in and took the reins to head out to the field for another load. The smell of tobacco and horse sweat perfumed the air like nothing else could on a hot summer day.

Despite the heat and the fact that her legs were swollen and thick with varicose veins, Millie worked in the tobacco right up until the last of her pregnancy. She loved being at the barn with all its activity. Neighbors helping neighbors harvest and barn the sticky green leaves was a lot of work, but everyone seemed to have fun while doing it. Millie had missed out on that. Rob McBryde had never grown tobacco in Bandeaux Creek. His main crops had been cotton and corn. To Millie, tobacco barning was more like a celebration with all the laughing and carrying on. Men and boys, colored and white, were back and forth to the field all day, their tanned bodies slick with sweat when they skidded by on a sled, sometimes reaching out to put a juicy horned worm on a squealing young girl who was handing tobacco. The women sang and gossiped, handing and tying the green gold onto sticks to be passed along to the barn for curing.

"You out here working in tobacco, that baby's liable to come into d'world black as I am." Minnie laughed, a large contagious laugh that caused the three girls handing her tobacco to laugh, too. Minnie was Lizzie and Troy's youngest daughter, a girl who had come along at a time when Negro children were beginning to receive a proper education. Tall and thin, her dark brown skin glistening, she was lovely in a simple feed sack dress that clung to her slender body.

"Please teach me how to tie tobacco," Millie said. "I just want to see if I can do it."

"C'mon over here, shug, I'll show you," Minnie said. "We need another looper anyhow." She showed Millie how to stand beside a hip-high tobacco stick held up by a wooden frame. A string from a ball of tying twine that rested in a rusty tin can on the ground was brought up over the stick through a notch in the top of one end of the frame. "Hold the string between these two fingers," she said, indicating her thumb and forefinger. One of the young girls handed Millie five leaves of tobacco. Millie twisted the twine around the stems, and in one motion, flipped the bunch over and around the stick. To a bystander unfamiliar with the tying process, there appeared to be some sleight of hand or trick involved, but Millie had watched long enough that she grasped the process quickly, tying and flipping one bunch to the right, another to the left, until the stick was filled end to end.

"Not bad for a city girl," Len said, removing the stick when it was filled. He'd taken the job of hanging the tobacco that day, a job that required the younger men to climb up into the barn rafters to hang the sticks.

"I'll bet you didn't think I could do it," she said, laughing.

"Looks like you're good enough to have your own stick," Len said. "I'll set you up and we can get this field in the barn in no time." Millie was pleased that she was able to work the next three days, keeping one eye on Annie, and getting faster by the day, encouraged by the Negro women. Some jobs like tying tobacco were worked up to over the years.

Chapter 35

The tobacco barning was almost finished when Millie woke during the wee hours of the morning with contractions. There had been no time to call Rebecca until after Lizzie had brought the baby into the world at ten o'clock that morning. Dr. Bayard stopped by later in the day to look the baby over and to record her birth. "She's a beautiful baby girl, Len. Just keep it up, and you'll have a boy one of these days."

Again, Len said it didn't matter one way or the other, as long as the baby was healthy. He remembered well the death of his little brother Yancey, who had come into the world bald and sickly looking. Dr. Bayard heard the whooshing sound in Yancey's chest early on and had announced the hole in his heart before he was a year old. Cathleen Marie not only had a head full of red hair, she weighed over nine pounds and looked to be several months old at birth.

"I declare she's the prettiest baby I've ever seen, even if she is ours," Len said.

"Shhh. Don't let Annie hear you say that. We don't want her to be jealous."

"Oh, honey, Annie is beautiful, too. She could never be jealous."

But Millie knew differently. She'd been raised with three sisters—three entirely different sisters, who each had their merits and shortcomings.

The camp house became even more cramped with all the baby's paraphernalia. Although toward the end of the month Len was spending most nights at the tobacco barn keeping the fires going, they decided that the best thing to do was change places with Will, and move into the big house with Maggie and Tate.

"I'm just getting to be an old bachelor anyhow," Will said. "I can let my things pile up and there won't be nobody to say a thing to me." He eyed his mother.

"You can do your own cooking, too," Maggie said.

"Awe, M-m-mama, Millie does most of the cooking anyhow. You'll feed me, w-w-won't you, Millie?"

Millie was folding a basket of freshly laundered diapers while Cathleen slept beside her on the settee. "You know I will. I always cook enough to feed an army."

"She's a g-g-good cook, isn't she, Mama?"

"I reckon one of the best, like her mama. Cousin Dick used to say he'd rather put his feet under Eva McBryde's table than any other in the world."

"Where is he now?" Will asked.

"He's still in Oklahoma," Millie said. "I imagine he'll be in Bandeaux Creek for homecoming."

"I never will forget that time he came to the church wearing those Indian feathers," Will said. "All he needed was a little war paint with that big red nose of his."

"Don't go making fun," Maggie said. "Cousin Dick is famous out there in Indian Country."

Millie picked up the baby and placed her in a wicker basket that had been lined with a soft quilt. "Miss Maggie, if you'll watch Annie and the baby, Will could help me bring a few of our things over. Len will help bring the rest tomorrow."

Walking across the yard, Will told Millie that the more he'd thought about it, the more he was convinced that the boy he'd seen at Penderlea was Colin McBryde. "Len said he'd had the same thought."

"You mentioned it to Len?"

"I sure did. He'd seen him over at St. Helena before y'all got married. Hank told Len he just calls him 'Boy.' Said he adopted him."

"Did Len see the boy while he was working at Penderlea?"

"Once in awhile, but he must've been in school back in the winter." Will picked up a wooden box Millie had packed. "Len says we'd better let well enough alone 'cause of the way Mama felt about Patty Sue. I don't know if I can do that."

Millie placed her hand on his arm. "Maybe we should, Will. No one knows for sure if he's Davy's boy."

"Well, I know for sure he was Patty Sue's," he said, adamantly. "That little boy loved me and Papa. We were the closest thing he had to family. I can't let that go."

Len and Tate Ryan took turns tending the fire in the barn. They'd rigged up cots under the shed and found the outside night air a blessing compared to the confines of the house in August. Sometimes, Minnie's husband, Troy, would sit with them. Tate and Troy would take turns telling stories from long ago. The bear stories were Len's favorites. He'd act as interlocutor, reminding Tate or Troy of tales he'd heard as a boy. He knew most of them by heart, but hearing the old-timers tell them again was like music to his ears.

"How big was that bear, Papa?"

"At least as big as you," Tate said. "Maybe bigger."

"Maybe three hun'erd pounds," Troy said. "I was with Mr. Tate. We climbed dis tree, but dat bear come right up there wid us. Mr. Tate, he kicked at him an' dat bear pulled off Mister Tate's shoe and chawed it up like it was a ham bone."

"Yep, that seemed to satisfy him for a little bit." Tate said. "He shuffled off into that huckleberry patch over yonder, enough time for me and Troy to take off and run like hell for the barn."

"What did you do then?" Len asked.

"Well, sir, we knew he was still out there, 'cause ol' Bess was shivering and snorting," Tate said. "Troy knocked the ladder down so's the bear couldn't climb up there in the hay with us."

"Yas suh, we'uns spent de whole night up dere."

A storm had been brewing in the distance for some time, convincing Tate that another night on the army cot in the damp night air would put him down for good. "Just come and get me if need be. I'll make sure your ma has a good breakfast for y'all in the morning." He started toward the house, turned around, and pointed his finger. "Watch out for them bears."

Len laughed. "We've got that old hound dog over there. He's full of fleas, but that won't stop him from running off a bear." Tate glanced at the hound, who looked to be almost as old as he was. "Don't count on it, son," he said, laughing as he walked away.

Thunder continued to rumble in the distance across the flat sandy terrain that had once been a dense pine forest. Len moved his cot to a nearby shed and drifted off to sleep while Troy fed a few sticks of firewood to the barn furnace. He stirred a little when Troy closed the barn door and found his makeshift bed on a bundle of burlap sacks. "Believe that storm's comin' dis way," Troy said.

"Maybe," Len mumbled. He had taken a long swig off a jar he kept hidden under the tobacco sticks, and he was drowsier than usual. Sharp cracks of lightning lit up the sky as the thunder moved closer. When the wind picked up, Len welcomed the breeze that brushed over him, drying his damp skin. A light rain would come first, settling the dust; then the hard rain that would beat the daylights out of the tin roof. A real frog strangler, he hoped, that would leave the air clean and fresh. But what came next was not the rain, but a loud crack that shook the earth and lit up the sky. He was looking right at the barn when the bolt of lightning hit the tin roof and ran down the log post that held up the shed roof attached to the barn. "Troy! You all right?" Len called through the pelting rain, answered only by another crack of lightning. "Troy, do you hear me?" He stared into the black rain, afraid to move, afraid of what he would find when he did. Finally, he'd crawled through the driving rain, smelling the smoke and burnt flesh, until he reached Troy propped against the post that held up the barn shed. Troy's head was split wide open, and his overalls were still smoking. The frail old Negro who had been a part of his family for sixty years was dead and gone.

Inside the house, Tate had laid awake trying to judge the closeness of the storm. The weather report had said a change was in the forecast. Storms were predicted, but Tate had never been afraid of lightning. Instead, he always looked forward to a cooling thunderstorm on a summer night, though he'd seen the danger of it many times. His thoughts drifted briefly to the night his house in Onslow County had been struck by lightning and burned to the ground. When he heard the loud crack of lightning, he'd sat up in bed and listened, thinking it might've struck something—maybe a tall pine.

Tate hurriedly pulled on his clothes as rain beat down hard on the tin roof and the wind picked up again. He was on the back porch looking out toward the barn, but could see nothing through the blinding downpour. Millie was suddenly by his side. "Do you think it struck something, Mr. Tate?"

"I don't know, shug, but I think I'd better go find out. You stay here until the rain lets up. I'm sure Will heard it, too." Tate could smell the smoke as he got closer. When he reached the barn, he found Len crying, cradling the dead man in his arms. All he could do at first was stare in disbelief. Troy's head looked like he'd been hit with an axe. He and Len both were covered with blood. "Are you hurt, son?"

"Oh, Papa, " Len cried, patting the bloody corpse, his face distorted by grief. "Look at him—poor old Troy, poor old fellow."

"Are you hurt, son?" Tate grasped the side of the barn for support, averting his eyes.

"No, sir, but poor old Troy, he—"

"C'mon, son. Get up," Tate said, spreading out a burlap sack to receive Troy's body. "We'll wrap him up in this. I don't want Minnie or Lizzie to see him until they have to."

Millie and Will arrived one after the other. Millie began to cry. "Mama always said, 'One comes in, another goes out.' He was the dearest old colored man."

Len didn't say a word to her, to anyone. He'd opened the door to the barn, looked in, and saw the smoldering efforts of a third of his labor for the last three months. When the lightning struck, it had knocked a hole in the roof and the sticks had collapsed on top of the furnace. "It's all gone, Pa."

Tate sat down on a wooden bench next to Troy's body. "It could've been worse, son. Might've gotten you, too." He looked out across the darkened fields thinking about the corn that was yet to be harvested. "There's still the corn, if it ain't gone too."

The *Wilmington Star* called it a tropical storm. The thunder and lightning that preceded it was but one of the damaging results. In other places nearby, tornadoes had touched down with profane disregard of life and limb, shattering ancient trees and flimsy buildings with like fury. The rain continued for two days, drowning crops and filling ditches to overflowing.

Len had tried covering the hole in the tobacco barn roof with a tarpaulin, hoping he and Will might salvage the tobacco by rehanging it and getting the fire going again. But it was no use. The barn had lost its dry seal, and by the time the storm moved on up the coast, the tobacco had already begun to mold. Selling it at market would be a joke.

The corn situation was even worse. After the rain stopped, Tate took the mule and cart to the field and picked up load after load of corn, hoping to salvage the soggy ears by spreading them out on tobacco bed netting in the yard. Millie was his only helper. The colored folks were all mourning the loss of old Troy, Tate's best friend since he had come to Colly in 1910.

While the rest of them attempted to salvage the tobacco and the corn, Maggie Lorena watched over the sleeping baby girl, lovingly stroking the red curls while Annie entertained herself with a Sears & Roebuck catalog. *How different little girls were from boys,* she thought. Annie would spend an hour or more with the catalog or a picture book. Maggie picked up the *Star.* It was a day old, but she often laid it aside until she had time to read every last page. There had been no magazines around for several years. Subscriptions were too expensive. Because of her "Rambling 'round Colly" articles, which she wrote only on occasion now, the *Star* kept her on their list and she received her papers a day late in the mail. She read the front page, only scanning the headlines. Adolf Hitler made her head ache. Britain and France would stand up to him—show him a thing or two. Wallis Simpson and the Duke of Windsor were to be married despite the consequences. Maggie read every word of that. *Love conquers all,* she sighed. She turned the pages wishing her column was there.

"What's this?" Maggie said. Annie looked up from the catalog. She tugged at her grandmother's long skirt, pulling herself up to see. "Hush, now, let Grandmother read the paper," Maggie said. "'Penderlea Farm Manager Killed.' My stars! Daddy needs to see this." Annie watched her closely.

"Da-da?"

"Yes, your daddy needs to read this."

> An important official of the Penderlea Homesteads Corporation, Farm Manager Hank Hudson was killed yesterday morning when explosives he was using to dynamite a stump failed to go off.

"Oh, my goodness, Annie." The child appeared to be listening to every word.

> Spectators said that Hudson had gone to inspect the failed ignition when it suddenly went off. A pinewood knot struck him directly in the head and killed him instantly.

"Oh, dear!"

A young boy, reported to be his son, was thought to be standing at a safe distance, but was hit by flying debris. The boy was rushed to James Walker Hospital in Wilmington where his condition is unknown.

"Poor little fellow," Maggie said, shaking her head.

"Da-da?"

"No, honey, not Daddy. Hush, now."

Hudson was a widower who had spent the early part of his adulthood at St. Helena in the employ of Hugh MacRae.

"There! I knew it. Len told us he'd met that man at St. Helena." She folded the paper carefully and put it on the table beside Len's usual chair.

Will came inside before the others wanting a glass of iced tea to quench his thirst before supper. He picked up his niece and set her down on his knee. "Do you want a sip of Uncle Will's tea?" Annie put her small mouth on the rim of the glass and sipped.

"Ummm," she said, licking her lips.

"Look at that article there," Maggie said, indicating the folded newspaper on the chair. "I want Len to see it. I think it's the man who used to work for Hugh MacRae."

Will read the first few lines. "Oh, my God!"

"Did you know him, son?" Maggie asked.

"I knew him. You d-d-did, too!"

"What? I don't believe so, son. I—"

Will caught himself just before he said Colin's name. It wouldn't do to let on to Maggie that he knew the boy. "We met Mr. Hank when Millie and I went over there. I'd better go tell Len."

Will stopped by the pump outside, soaked his head with water, and washed his arms and hands. With a soiled towel that hung on a nail on the shed, he wiped himself dry and clean. "I was just coming after you," he said, seeing Millie, Tate, and Len approach.

"Is something wrong?" Millie said, rushing toward the house.

"No, wait," Will said. "I'll tell you, but it's nothing about the young'uns." He glanced toward the house, but kept his back to it in case Maggie was watching. "Mama showed me this article in the paper. Hank Hudson over at Penderlea was killed in a dynamite accident. The boy was hurt, too."

"My God a'mighty," Len said. "Hank got killed?" He went pale as the inside of a cucumber. "The boy, too?"

"That the man who used to work at St. Helena?" Tate asked.

"Yes, sir," Will said, looking down at his feet. "Pa, there's something I've been meaning to tell you. We think the boy with him was Patty Sue's little boy."

"Damn! You mean—"

"Yes, sir—he's about the right age."

Tate looked at Len, then at Millie. "Did y'all know?" Len nodded.

"We don't know for sure," Mr. Tate, Millie said. "Will thinks the boy favors her. Len said Hank always just called him 'the boy.'"

"Was the boy killed?" Tate asked, his voice tender.

"No, sir. It just said the boy was hurt. He's in the hospital in Wilmington."

"Who's with him?" Len asked. "Hank said he didn't have any people."

"I don't know, but I'm gonna go find out."

"I wish I could go with you," Millie said.

"You can't leave these young'uns," Len said. "If anybody goes with him, it oughta be Papa."

Tate was sullen. "No, I can't go. Your mama would have a fit. Besides, some of us need to be here for Lizzie's family. They've got Troy laid out over yonder at her house, expecting us to come pay our respects."

"Go on, Will," Len said. "I'll tell Mama you had to fix a truck that's broke down up at Eddie Lee's store. She won't question it." Len hoped he was right.

CHAPTER 36

W ill poured a can of gas into the truck and added a quart of oil. He'd piddled with the engine all summer and knew it would run like a scalded dog. With both door windows open, he tore out of the oak grove and mashed the gas pedal to the floor. Flying along the sandy road, he imagined he was a bootlegger outrunning the law. The old Ford was made for this, he thought. He even imagined that Patty Sue was looking down on him from wherever she was. She'd always been like an angel to him. All the questions he wanted to ask Colin went through his mind. Where had he been before Hank had taken him in? How had he hurt his foot? Will slowed the Ford down to the speed limit when he hit the Wilmington highway. The last thing he wanted was the law after him. He laughed to himself, thinking how close he'd come to being an outlaw up in Detroit.

He was at James Walker Hospital by three o'clock in the afternoon. Taking a deep breath, he parked the truck, got out, and found the entrance underneath a tall portico. There were two balconies above the center door. He made a note to find his way to the top balcony so he could look out from that height. Will had always loved high places. He laughed to himself, thinking maybe it was because he was a flatlander. Stopping at a large desk in the foyer, he took off his cap and cleared his throat. A nice lady in a white uniform and a nurse's cap looked up at him. "May I help you?"

Will smiled back, shifting his weight from side to side. "There was a b-b-boy about twelve years old brought in here a day or two ago. M-m-may I see him?"

"What's his name?" the nurse asked. She was scanning a typewritten list attached to a clipboard.

"Not sure w-w-what he goes by. I knew him as Colin." He hesitated. "M-m-maybe Colin McBryde."

"We have a Colin Jackson?" Will was confused for a minute. Patty Sue's aunt was an old maid. Her last name would have been Jackson.

"Y-y-yes, that's him."

"I'm afraid that's not possible. Mrs. McAllister said he was not to have any visitors."

"Mrs. who?"

"Mrs. Emily McAllister. I believe he's her ward."

"Well, I'm his... I'm his uncle, and I n-n-need to see him." Will's face turned scarlet. Lying didn't come natural to him.

"Why didn't you say so? Just a minute, and I'll go and tell Mrs. McAllister." Will watched her go down the hall, her rubber-soled shoes squeaking with each step. He'd never been in a hospital before. He smelled wood alcohol and liniment, things he associated with hurt.

Within a few minutes, Emily McAllister came rushing down the hall. "Will? Will Ryan? You're Maggie's other son. I can't believe we've never met."

Will smiled, and a dark blush spread over his rugged complexion. "Len seems to find all the pretty w-w-women first," he said.

"I'm so glad you've come. Did Millie send you?"

"Millie?" He was confused. "Oh, Millie. No, mum. We all decided I should be the one to come."

"I don't understand, Will. How do you know Colin Jackson?"

"I might ask you the s-s-same thing," he said. "How did Colin c-c-come to be your ward?"

Emily led him over to a seating area where a man was sleeping, his head on his arm. "Let's sit down, we can talk here," she whispered. "You want to go first?"

"All right, but I'm not as good a storyteller as Len is." Will told her as best he could how he and Tate had befriended Patty Sue while Maggie was in Boston. "Her husband, Millie's cousin—his n-n-name was Davy McBryde—got arrested for m-m-murdering her mama. She was a hateful old w-w-woman and everybody said she deserved it, but Davy shouldn't of d-d-done it. Anyhow, I worked on s-s-some of Patty Sue's vehicles. I hate to say it, but she told us she was running a t-t-trucking business, and we believed her." He didn't admit that he'd had some suspicions. "It turned out she was b-b-bootlegging. She had this little boy she brought with her—just a baby at first and her trying to t-t-take care of him and his d-d-daddy in the insane asylum."

"I know about Davy McBryde. It was awful hard on Millie's family. He was her double-first cousin."

"Is that a fact? Well, anyhow, that w-w-went on a year or two before Davy escaped and came down to Cotton Cove and k-k-killed her. It just about tore me and Papa up. Len never knew her that g-g-good. He was gone a lot back then helping Uncle Nathan. Me and Papa wanted to take the boy, r-r-raise him, but this hateful old lady came and got him. Had the l-l-law with her, said she was Patty Sue's aunt. That's the last we saw of him until—until I saw Colin at P-P-Penderlea."

"You recognized him after all these years?" Emily asked.

"I reckon I did, s-s-sure enough. He looks j-j-just like her." Will glanced down the hall in the direction Emily had come from. "When can I s-s-see him? Is he hurt b-b-bad?"

"Not too bad. A cut on his forehead and some bad bruises. He got a lot of dirt in his eyes."

"Oh, my stars, that must've hurt."

Emily put her hand on Will's arm. "He's had a bad shock losing Hank. I think Hank was all the family Colin ever had. I got to know them both at Penderlea. Hank asked me if I would take care of him if anything ever happened to…" She took a deep breath, holding back her sobs.

"Well, we could t-t-take care of him."

"You don't really think Maggie would take him in, do you?"

Will thought about that for a minute. "I don't think she'd be t-t-too ornery about it. I could take him in to my p-p-place—the camp house. We could—"

"Will, this little boy has been badly abused. His aunt tied him to the bedpost with a strap. She'd leave him food like a dog, and go off to work." They both were in tears now.

"My God a'mighty! I knew we shouldn't have l-l-let him go with that old woman. I knew it!"

"That's not the worst of it," Emily sobbed. "He broke his foot trying to get loose. She never took him to a doctor."

Will was furious. "Why didn't anybody know? There must have been somebody. I would have killed her."

"Somebody did know," Emily said. "They told Hank about it, and the sheriff got a magistrate to write an order. They went over there and got Colin. The old aunt moved away and left him. That's when Hank got custody of Colin."

The man who had been sleeping in a chair near them roused up and stared. Emily led Will a ways down the hall. "Maybe you shouldn't see him—not today. It might bring back some unpleasant memories."

"But I came here to see him," Will pleaded.

"I know, but he is so hurt and confused," Emily said. "He trusts me. Let me take him home and care for him. I have the papers. They say I can keep him as long as he's happy about it. I'm thinking of sending him to Oak Ridge Military Academy. I have a friend who went to school there. He says it's a wonderful place for boys—even those with parents who love and care for them. Colin will be able to make friends. Someday when he's older I'll tell him about you and Tate. He'll probably want to come and see you."

"What about the McBrydes? Mr. Angus's f-f-family?"

"They never claimed any kin. Hank said he went to see Miss Geneva, told her he thought he had Davy's son. But she told him no, she didn't think that was possible."

"Could I maybe just s-s-speak to him? See if he recognizes me?"

"They've got him doped up, Will. He was so upset about Hank." She thought for a minute, reconsidered. "I suppose it won't hurt. Come with me. I'd like for you to meet my friend." Emily opened the hospital room door slowly, and they entered the darkened room. As his eyes adjusted, Will saw a gentleman sitting in a large chair in the corner. The man rose to meet them. "Will, this is Reginald Ashworth," Emily whispered.

"Pleased to meet you, Mr. Ashworth," Will said, but his eyes were on the boy. Colin had thrown back his cover and his naked chest was exposed. One arm was above his head. "He's sound asleep," Will whispered. "Don't wake him."

Emily and Will stepped outside the room, and Mr. Ashworth followed them into the hall. "Thank you, Miss Emily," Will said, hugging her. "Colin's a lucky boy to have you."

Reginald Ashworth slipped his arm around Emily and pulled her toward him. "He is at that," he said. Tears filled her eyes, and Ashworth handed her his handkerchief.

"I'm all right," she said. "We just came so close to losing him."

Emily walked along with Will on the way out. He told her about the storm and the death of old Troy. "We lost the whole barn of tobacco, t-t-too. Len's real upset. He's talking about going b-b-back over to Penderlea to look for work after cold weather sets in."

"There's lots of work there," Emily said. "Tell him that the Resettlement Administration recently allotted half a million dollars to expand the project to more than twice its size. There'll be about 150 new homesteads in addition to a school. They're working on the plans right now."

"Gol dern! That's a lot of pumps," Will said. "Work like that would tide him through the winter. Thank you, Miss Emily. I'll t-t-tell him."

"I wish he and Millie would go over there to live. I think they could have a homestead if they wanted it," she said. "Hank mentioned Len to me several times. Said Len was the kind of homesteader they needed—someone who knew how to do something besides farm. He called Len a 'jack of all trades.'"

"I'll tell him that, Miss Emily. I'll t-t-tell him that for sure."

"Please do, Will. And tell him I'll put in a good word for him with the new project manager."

Timidly, Will leaned over and kissed her on the cheek. "You're just about the nicest lady I ever did see. One of these days, bring Colin to see his Uncle Will, w-w-won't you?"

She smiled. "You can bet on that."

CHAPTER 37

CHRISTMAS 1936—BLADEN COUNTY

In the weeks following the barn fire and the loss of old Troy, Len had been almost impossible to live with. He drank himself into a stupor almost every night. But one day Tate had gotten hold of him and told him they were going to lose everything if Len didn't pull himself together. Millie heard Mr. Tate raise his voice to Len for the first time. "I never thought I'd see the day that one of my sons would abuse himself the way you're doing, Len Ryan."

"You don't know how it feels to have the life go out of somebody while you're holding them in your arms, Pa."

"Watching you like this is just about as bad," Tate said. "You need to go on back over to Penderlea and get some of that work Miss Emily was telling Will about."

Len pretended not to hear him. "Ray Wilkins says there won't be any tobacco allotments next year," Len said. "First you do, then you don't. It's a sorry state of affairs, if you ask me."

"I told you," Tate said. "But you were all hepped up about it."

Len was disappointed all right. He'd not only talked up allotments to Tate, he'd been instrumental in convincing all the farmers in his district that the Agricultural Adjustment Act was going to change the way they farmed.

"It was a good program, Pa. Ray Wilkins says they'll bring it back. Not that it'll do us any good now."

Ray Wilkins, usually loyal and enthusiastic about the government's agricultural programs, applauded when the U.S. Supreme Court declared the Agricultural Adjustment Act unconstitutional. In order to make the demand higher than the supply, the government was destroying food crops all over the place at a time when people were starving. "It just didn't make a whole hell of a lot of sense," Ray said.

Not many things the government did made a lot of sense to Len, but he'd thought the tobacco allotments helped farmers like him. "We'd of been in the poor house last year if we hadn't of had that allotment check."

"You and a lot of others," Ray said. "But they're talking about making some changes. Congress is going to take another look at it. FDR is mighty disappointed. I think we'll get 'em back."

⌒

The new project manager at Penderlea, Melvin Harrell, hired Len immediately, giving him a government pickup truck and the necessary equipment to make service calls. The first job he sent Len on was to his own home in Willard. "I've got this here new pump in my truck. I want you to replace the old one out there in the pump house with it. Damn thing knocks off every now and then. My wife Lela sure gets unhappy when she has to do without water." He laughed, slapping Len on the shoulder, then gripping him hard before removing his hand. "I can count on you keeping that to yourself, can't I, Len?"

Melvin Harrell had a reputation for being a stickler for the rules—his own rules, mostly. Like Charlie Lucas, he'd been a Pender County farm agent before the government had asked him to be the new project manager at Penderlea. In nearby Willard, he had a fine home and a lovely wife who was the model of a good homemaker. Everybody said she kept the prettiest house you've ever seen, had a showplace of a flower garden. and wore beautiful clothes and jewelry. Melvin himself was a handsome, clean-cut man. Len thought he had the tall, rugged good looks of a gentrified cowboy who rode around on a horse all day overseeing his spread. Melvin's horse was a brand-new Dodge pickup truck.

Not all of the homesteaders liked him. Some said he was uppity, thought he was better than they were, but Melvin Harrell had a reputation for getting things done and there were a few—Harrell's chosen few—who thought Melvin Harrell was the best project manager they'd had on Penderlea. Len Ryan was allowed into this elite group when he mentioned that he'd put in five or six pumps for Hugh MacRae, including the one at Invershield. Melvin Harrell liked that sort of information. It gave him some boasting material for impressing the division administrators to whom he had to report. "I've got us a pump man right here on the project," he'd say. "Knows more about water pumps than anyone in these parts." Then he'd tell them that Len used to work for Hugh MacRae, adding, "You know how particular he is."

Len's homecoming on Christmas Eve from Penderlea was like a gift in itself. He'd been gone most of the fall. With him home only four or five weekends since he started on the project, life had been easier for Millie. Neither Mr. Tate nor Will put fear in her like Len. They were menfolk just the same; they had to be waited on. The good part was that both Tate and Will were content to hold the baby, or play with Annie, which was something neither Len nor Maggie Lorena was disposed to do.

"Mama, here come Daddy's truck!" Annie cried.

Millie pulled the front curtain a little further to the side, her heart doing a flip-flop when she saw the headlights on the pump truck bouncing along the sandy lane through the oak grove. "I believe it is, honey. Let's go out and meet him." Annie turned the doorknob with both hands. She was two and a half now and becoming very independent. "Wait, you need your sweater," Millie said.

Len was excited, too. He'd anticipated his reunion with Millie and the girls all the way home. Before he'd left Penderlea, he'd stopped at the general store and told Joe Beasley that he needed some presents. "What you want, some candy?" Beasely asked.

"No sir, I told you, I want some presents," Len said. "I got the money, right here in my pocket." *I got marbles and chalk, too, if you want them,* he'd thought, but Joe might not understand the quip. It was something that Len's Uncle Zeb always said when he wanted to indicate that he was wealthy in more ways than one.

"Your wife might like some piece goods," Joe said.

Len looked around to see who was in the store with him. Several homesteaders lolled near a potbellied stove in the center of the store. Two long counters flanked either side of the large room. Behind one were shelves full of groceries, canned goods, and such; behind the other was an assortment of household items, piece goods, and some ready-made clothing. Len leaned over the counter and signaled Joe to come closer. "You got any silk panties back there?" he whispered.

"How much you want to spend?" Joe Beasley asked.

"I want some silk britches for my wife if you got any back there," Len said out of the corner of his mouth. "Don't matter how much they cost."

"Two dollars all right?"

"Yep," Len said, "if you wrap them up real pretty."

While Joe retrieved the silk panties, Len peered through the glass top of the display case. "Let me see them two little sock dolls right there. How much are they?"

"They're a dollar each. Made right here on Penderlea by one of them Home Demonstration ladies."

"Let me have them and a pack of chewing tobacco for my pa. I'll take two of those bandana handkerchiefs for my brother." Len scratched his head. "How much are them handkerchiefs with the lace on them?"

"Seventy-five cents each."

"I'll take one of those for my mama. Could you wrap it up and tie a string around it?"

"Sure thing, Len. Your mama will love it. It's fine Irish lace."

⌒

Len hugged Millie like he'd really missed her. "I thought you'd never get here," she said. "You won't believe how the baby has grown, just in the last few weeks." Len reached for his second child. "Well, I declare, little Callie Reecie," he said jostling the six-month-old child who kept her eyes warily on her mother.

"She's a good baby. She hardly ever cries," Millie said.

The Christmas tree was brushing the top of the ceiling. Tate and Will had gone together deep into Colly Swamp to find just the right one. Millie had spent hours decorating it with her mother's glass ornaments. "My God, that's a pretty Christmas tree," Len said. "Where'd you find it."

"I told you I know where all the pretty Christmas trees are," Tate said with a sly grin. "I've been traipsing these woods for a mighty long time. I mark 'em when I see 'em. Might be two or three years before I see them again, but I know where they are."

"Sounds like voodoo to me," Len said. They all laughed, but they knew Tate had a sense about those things.

After supper, when they'd all settled in the living room, Maggie announced that she had a surprise. "There's syllabub for those that want it. Pa's wine is pretty potent this time of year, so beware if you partake."

"I made sugar cookies," Millie said.

"Well, sir, I'd say this is a real homecoming," Len said, jiggling the baby on his knee. "But we better get these children to bed so Santa Claus can come." Tate and Will looked at one another wondering if Len had done his part. "I heard some jingling when I went out to fetch the wood. Did you hear it, Annie?" Annie covered her ears with her hands, a look of terror on her small face.

"No hear Santa Claus," Annie said, clinging to Millie. "He not come tonight. Annie scared."

Millie pulled her into her lap. "Don't be scared of Santa Claus. He's good," she said.

"No, he scare Annie," the child said.

"You better not be scared of Santa," Len said. "He might not leave you anything."

Annie sat up straight in Millie's lap. "I not scared," she said.

⌐

"I thought you'd never get here," Millie said, snuggling up against Len under the covers. Len ran his hands up her legs, over her hips and across her breasts. Millie sat up and peered across the room to the small bed beneath the windows. "Wait, I'm not sure Annie is asleep," she whispered.

"She better be," Len said in her ear. "This old Santa Claus wants to give you your presents right now. He can't wait another minute." He pulled Millie down into the feather mattress and rolled on top of her.

"Mama?"

"Wait, Len. What is it, Annie?"

"I can't go to sleep. Can I get in bed with you and Daddy? I'm cold."

Millie held her breath, waiting for Len to explode. But he rolled off her and sighed. "Come on over here, shug," he said. "Mama and Daddy will get you warm." But before the night was over, Millie put the sleeping child back into her bed and woke Len to give him his Christmas present.

⌐

On Christmas morning, the hearth was cold and the house silent when Annie crept into the living room and spied a Raggedy Ann doll sitting in her little chair by the stove. A big teddy bear was on the mantle, and two stockings stuffed with oranges, apples, and raisins hung above the potbellied stove. Tissue-covered presents peeped out from under the tree. "My goodness, look what Santa brought," Millie said. "And we didn't even hear him come."

Tate looked on amused as the little girls squealed, tearing open the tissue-wrapped presents. Within minutes, Annie had gone through hers and was eyeing the other presents under the tree. "Look here, now, Annie. Those presents might be for somebody else," Len said. "Why don't you give this one to Grandmother? And here's one for Mama and one for Uncle Will," Len said.

"What about Gandaddy?"

"Oh, here's one for Granddaddy, right here."

Annie sniffed the paper sack. "Tinks like bacca," she said.

"Well, let ol' Gandaddy have it, and I'll put it to good use," Tate said.

Millie opened her present and held the silk britches up before she realized what they were. "Oh, my goodness," she said, blushing. "Len, you're embarrassing me in front of your mama and papa."

"Just don't be trying them on, and it'll be okay," Len said, laughing. "You can do that later on in private." He'd already whispered to her that he intended to make Annie a pallet under the Christmas tree that evening.

CHAPTER 38

Len learned quickly that Mr. Harrell liked to keep a lot of things to himself. He wouldn't call him dishonest, but Melvin Harrell had a way of working things to his own advantage. "I'm sure I'll have to ask Joe Newsome to get off the project by the first of January," he said when Len returned to work after Christmas. "Didn't want to do it before Christmas," Harrell said. "Joe hasn't been able to meet his payment in almost a year."

"Couldn't he get another one of them loans?"

"No, sir. He hasn't been able to keep up. He was supposed to start paying his first loan off, but he just keeps getting deeper in debt."

"Maybe he could come work with me awhile. I could use a helper."

"Nope. He's done some construction, but I'd have to get a work order for him to work in your department. Joe's finished here as far as I'm concerned." Len couldn't believe it. A man's life was decided just like that by the government. "You could have that house, Len," Harrell said, adding insult to injury.

"What are you getting at, Mr. Harrell?"

"I'm saying that if you wanted Joe Newsome's house since you're my pump service manager, you could have it."

"Now, wait a minute. Joe still lives there. I saw him the other day. He says he's going to make it."

"Well, sir, he isn't making it, and no one knows it better than I do, Len. I have to co-sign every check he writes. If you want that house, I can see that you get it. We've already done a little looking into your record. You don't have a thing to worry about."

Len knew Joe Newsome. He'd put in his pump and met him when Joe came to select his house. He was probably just now getting his soil in good enough shape where he could make something of it. He'd been working twelve or fourteen hours a day in construction on the project to make enough for his payment. Now he was going to lose his house.

"I can't take Joe's house," Len said.

"It's not exactly *his* house," Melvin Harrell said. "Belongs to the government until he pays for it."

"I don't think I can do that, Mr. Harrell. No, sir, I can't do that. I know Joe."

⌒

But Melvin Harrell didn't give up easily. Instead of making a direct request to the office of the Resettlement Administration in Wilmington, he'd contacted the district administrator in Atlanta, explaining that he was in desperate need of a water management coordinator, a title that Harrell had created himself. He said that he had the perfect man for the job, but the only way Len Ryan would consent to come to the project was if he could come as a homesteader. Harrell said he'd already given Len a work grant, but he might leave if he had to wait too long in the application process. The district administrator telephoned Harrell a few days later and said that the project manager could waive everything except for the field worker's report as to character and reliability. If Ryan had a reputation for not paying his debts, they would both be in hot water with Washington.

⌒

Mr. Harrell called Len into his office. "That house is yours, Len. I had to pull a few strings, but you'll get it and twenty acres under the usual terms.

You can move right in as soon as a field worker visits your folks in Bladen County and fills out the necessary forms."

"I told you I didn't want—"

Mr. Harrell put his arm around Len's shoulder. "Look here, son, I know how you feel about Joe. I feel badly, too. But it's happening over and over. Penderlea is not a handout. Joe couldn't make his payments. He lost this opportunity."

"But he must feel like—"

"He took it like a man, Len. He's already gone."

Len was stunned. Not that he hadn't thought about it since Mr. Harrell mentioned it to him. But he wasn't one to take advantage of somebody's hard luck. He would rather have given Joe some money—even a dollar or two might've helped him. He took a deep breath, tried to think what was best. Now that Joe was gone and Mr. Harrell was telling Len that the house was his, maybe he should think about it. "I need to talk to my wife. I don't know how she'd feel."

"I've already turned in the paperwork, Len. These field workers are real nice fellows. They just stop by your pastor's house—maybe the general store—ask what kind of a fellow you are."

Len stood up very straight. "I'm not a bit worried about anything anybody would say about me."

"Of course you aren't," Harrell said. "He'll just stop by, meet your wife and your parents. I *know* you're not ashamed of them."

"I'm not ashamed of nothing or nobody, but I sure as hell don't like the idea of some government field worker nosing around asking questions about me."

Mr. Harrell leaned back on his heels, hands on his hips. He removed an unlit pipe from his mouth and pointed the stem at Len. "You better think about that, son. I'm offering you a homestead that's the envy of half the people on this project. You wouldn't turn that down because of a few questions, would you?"

"No, sir, I didn't mean they didn't have a right to—"

Harrell walked over to his desk chair and sat down, propping his feet on his desk. "You're damn right, they do."

"I still need to tell Millie they're coming."

"Does she have a telephone? You can call right here from my office."

"No sir, we don't have a telephone. I'd have to go home and tell her."

"No, there's no time for that. I've already talked to the Federal Office in Wilmington. They've got a man that can go up there tomorrow. We'll know in a day or two if you're *accepted*," the project manager said, winking at Len.

<hr>

Millie saw the car drive up. A tall man wearing a suit and a hat got out and looked around. Will was in his garage, and she figured the man was most likely looking for a mechanic. Millie took the last of the Christmas tree decorations off the tree, nestling them carefully in a box of cotton. She'd tried to give them back to Papa, saying that her sisters might want some of them. "None of the others have children," he said. Millie reminded him that Belle was married and had a little boy now. "Belle never cared much about family things," he said. "You take them."

She wanted to protest that Belle did care, but Papa was angry with Belle because she hadn't told him she was getting married. "I'll keep them for now," Millie said. "Maybe some day one of the others will want a few of them, just because they were Mama's."

When she'd taken the tinsel off and wrapped it smoothly around a piece of cardboard, she lifted the tree out of the sand-filled water bucket and carried it outside, leaving a trail of cedar needles behind her. She tossed the tree on the trash pile and started back to the house. "Millie, wait up," the man called out. She stopped, watching him approach. "It's me, Rusty," he said.

"What?"

"It's me, remember, Rusty Ruark?"

Millie looked around him to see if Will was within earshot. If Len had any idea that Rusty had stopped to see her, he would be mad as a hornet. "Hi, Rusty." She tried to look pleased to see him. In a way, she was. "What are you doing out here in the country?"

"Well, now. You don't seem very happy to see me. Len's brother thought you would welcome an old friend."

"Sure, Rusty, I mean, it's good to see you." She imagined how she must look to him in an old dress and a rag tied around her head. "Please come in. If I know Cousin Maggie Lorena, she will remember you from Amanda's wedding."

"Yes, I'd like to see her, Millie. Part of my job, really."

"What?'

"Let's get you inside. You must be freezing in that flimsy dress," he said, running his eyes over the dress. She felt as if he could see right through it.

"I am," she said, hastily opening the front door. "Let me go get her. She's in the kitchen looking after the girls."

"Oh, you have more than one?" he asked, following her through the dining room. She stopped and turned to face him. "Why don't you sit down in the parlor while I get her? I'll poke up the fire."

"Oh, no need to do that. I'll come with you. It's my job to see how people live."

Millie put her hand up, gesturing for him to stop. Maggie was just a few feet away behind the kitchen door. "Why are you here, Rusty? You keep saying something about your *job*."

His smile was sarcastic, a thin mustache twitching nervously above small white teeth. "I thought you knew. I'm from the Resettlement Office in Wilmington." He gave her a sly look. "You do want that little homestead on Penderlea, don't you?"

Millie could hear Annie in the kitchen. The baby was fretting, too. Probably a dirty diaper. Maggie never changed dirty diapers. The kitchen would be a mess. Dishes from the night before were in the sink. "Len said he told the project manager *no*. I don't understand. Why are you here?"

She tried to steer him back toward the front room, her hand pushing against his chest, but he grabbed her and spun her around, pulling her into his arms. "I never thought I'd see you again," he whispered. There was whiskey on his breath.

"Rusty, let me go!"

"No," he said, holding her tighter.

She wrenched away from him and stood in the middle of the parlor. "I think you ought to go."

"Now, now," he said. "That's no way to act when the only thing standing in the way of you and Len and that little government house is me."

"Rusty, what do you want?" she asked, trying to keep the fright out of her voice.

"Just you," he said. "Wanna trade favors? We could go for a little ride. Run down the road and see your papa. Will said it wasn't far. Could stop along the way for a little poon tang." It was a coarse expression, and she realized he was more drunk than she'd thought.

The back screen door slammed, and she heard Will coming across the porch and into the kitchen. He asked Maggie where Millie was. The kitchen door opened, and she could see Will through the French glass doors coming toward them. He stuck his head in. "Millie, Mama said you'd better come see about the baby." But one look at her and he realized something was wrong. "Everything all right?"

Millie looked at Rusty. "He was just leaving," she said.

"Millie wants to go for a ride with me," Rusty said, smugly.

"I do not! Will, please make him go!" she cried.

Will reached behind him and picked up an ancient shotgun that Tate had always kept in the corner of the dining room. The trigger was busted and the handle cracked. "This old thing ain't been fired in many a year, but it'll sure knock the hell out of somebody if he was to mess with Miss Millie."

Rusty eyed the rugged man who stood several inches over him. He knew better than to tangle with a big country boy. "I'm leaving," he said, lifting his hat to tip it slightly to Millie. "Don't say I didn't warn you."

Rusty spun his car out of the sandy lane and onto the road. Will was on the porch, and Millie stood just inside the screen door. "He said he knew you from Wilmington," Will said, inviting her to tell him more. "I shouldn't have told him where you were."

"I did know him a long time ago in Wilmington. Now, he's one of those field workers who come around asking questions."

"What about?"

Millie was still stunned. "The project manager over at Penderlea wants Len to work for him permanently. He wants to give us a homestead. Rusty works for the government."

"No wonder he was such a b-b-bastard," Will said. "Excuse me, Millie."

Millie looked down, embarrassed to tears. "He wanted me to go off with him. Said we wouldn't get the homestead if I didn't."

"God amighty! Len will kill him."

"Please don't tell him, Will. Just let Len think we were denied. If he knows Rusty was here, and we don't get a homestead because of it, he'll blame me the rest of my life," she cried.

⁓

For the next few days, Millie lived in fear of Len's reaction. When he'd told her before Christmas that he'd refused Mr. Harrell's offer, Millie had been sick about it, but she'd agreed with Len that it wasn't fair to take advantage of another family's hard luck. They'd figured that somehow Joe would be able to make it. But Rusty wouldn't have been there if Len hadn't accepted.

Will kept his word. Nothing much was said about the government man at all. Maggie had complained that she should have introduced him to her. "After all, I am the mistress of the house," she said.

"I'm sorry, Cousin Maggie, he'd already caught me in my house dress. I knew you were still in your nightclothes. The kitchen was a mess. I didn't want to embarrass you."

"That was real thoughtful of you, Millie," she said.

⁓

Len wanted to pack up and leave for Penderlea early the next morning. "I didn't have time to come and tell you, honey. Mr. Harrell had already set things in motion. I couldn't argue with him."

"Do you know for sure we've been approved? What if we go and find out—"

"You don't know Mr. Harrell, shug. Nobody tells him *no*."

"I'll need time to pack our things," Millie said.

"I'm supposed to be back at work tomorrow afternoon. Mr. Harrell is expecting me to get in half a day's work on the project. We won't need to take much in the way of furniture," he said. "Maybe the high chair and that little crib Pa made when Annie was born for the baby. She'll have her own big bed." He picked her up and sang, "Mama, Mama, have you heard? Daddy's going to get you your own big bed."

"Big bed!" Annie said, laughing and stretching her small hands out wide.

"Yes, ma'am, your own big bed."

Maggie and Tate observed the happy scene. How could they not be happy for Len and Millie? But each had their separate thoughts about what they'd lose when the little family moved out of their home. "You'll be back from time to time, won't you, son?" Maggie asked.

"To be sure, Mama, to be sure," Len said.

Will assured them that he knew the way to Penderlea. "One pretty Sunday afternoon this spring, we'll take a ride over there and see everything." After they'd piled the last of their things into the truck, Maggie, Will, and Tate watched the pump truck pull out onto the road.

"They might not even stay," Maggie said.

"Mama! What makes you say that?" Will asked.

"Len's heart wasn't in it. That man Harrell acted like he was doing Len a favor, but he worked things out more to suit himself."

Takes one to know one, Tate thought.

PART FOUR

A Better Life

CHAPTER 39

JANUARY 1937—PENDER COUNTY, NORTH CAROLINA

Despite Len's earlier reluctance to take advantage of Joe Newsome's failure, he was more than happy with his new place. Joe had done something no other homesteader had done. At Len's suggestion, he'd built a white running fence around the barn. A year ago, when he'd put the pump in, Len had said to Joe, "If I was you, I'd put me a board fence around the barn and pasture—paint it white." Joe had loved the idea. *Spending his time and effort on the fence might have cost Joe his homestead,* thought Len. *He'd worked his ass off on that fence.*

A horse and colt looked out over the fence from the pasture. Inside the hog lot, piglets squealed in unison, running for a sow who'd plopped over contentedly in the mud. Here and there chickens scratched in the sand while an arrogant rooster looked on. Except for the lane leading back to the barn, a thick carpet of coarse green grass covered everything. The house itself had green and white striped awnings over the front windows and the side entry to the screened-in porch. Len had never seen awnings used in the country, but he'd been told that the house would be much cooler inside because of them. A pale green shingled roof would have the same effect. Awnings and dark green painted shutters set against the white siding of the house completed the little cottage that looked to have been taken right out of a picture book.

"Let's go in the front door," Len said. "Do you want me to carry you over the threshold?"

Millie knew it was meant to be a joke, but she wished he would. This all felt like a dream to her. She'd waited and wished for a better life for so long, nothing seemed real. "You'd have to carry all three of us. It's their new house, too."

Bricks were stacked neatly on either side of a path that led up to the small covered porch. "Looks as if somebody started a walk," Len said.

"I could finish it," Millie said.

"You may have to, honey. It'll be a while before I can get to that sort of thing."

"Look, there are lattices for roses on either side of the porch," Millie said. "I can bring some cuttings from Papa's house." Everywhere she looked, Millie saw potential projects that enticed her.

But a different feeling came over her when she stepped in the front door. The house was cold and filled with sadness. If misfortune had a smell, it was there in the trash scattered about on the floors. Rags had been stuffed into a broken pane of glass, and dirty dishes were in the kitchen sink. The stove and the mattress off the double bed were missing. Annie picked up a ragged doll with no hair from the bedroom floor. "Somebody forgot their dolly," she said. "It's boken."

"Mommy will fix it," Millie said, wondering if she'd ever be able to fix the brokenhearted house.

They went out through the back door and walked around the yard. Millie spied a black iron kettle setting over the remains of a small fire. "I thought we'd have a washing machine."

"There's supposed to be one in that little house," Len said.

"I don't see it."

"I reckon they took that, too," Len said. "We ought to be thankful they left the horse." He held Annie up to touch the chestnut-colored horse and colt, both of whom had white stripes down their long noses. The colt nibbled at Annie's hand, eliciting a squeal of delight from the child.

That night, they made pallets out of quilts on the floor for the children. Len and Millie slept on the twin beds meant for the children, but they both lay awake wondering what had happened to Joe and his family, wondering how they would fare in this house that had held the Newsomes' hopes and dreams. "We'll make it our house," Millie said.

"What?" Len was almost asleep.

"I said, we'll make it our house. It feels lonely now, but we'll fill it up with our children and us."

"Miss Emily used to bring food and supplies to everybody that moved in," Len said. "I wonder if she knows we're here. As close as y'all were, I would've thought she'd have been here with bells on."

"Maybe she doesn't know. It all happened so fast," Millie said. *Maybe too fast*, she thought. She cringed every time Len mentioned anything about their good fortune. *Maybe Emily has seen Rusty's report. Maybe we'll have to leave.* "I'm sure she'll come when she can. She's never seen the girls."

"Emily is one of the blue hen's chickens. Be *real* nice to her." Len said.

"I wouldn't be anything else but nice," Millie said.

"You can't say anything about anybody, especially the project manager. He has folks who don't do anything but listen out for talk about him."

"I'm not worried about getting along with people, are you, Len?"

"Just be careful, honey. There's a pecking order. You can mark my words on that."

She sat up in her bed and looked over at him. "Len, I'm so proud of you, so proud that they wanted you to come. I don't ever want to leave, Len."

"Let's hope we don't have to."

Emily was there the next afternoon. One of the secretaries in the project office had called her to tell her that Len had asked for her in the office when he'd arrived. "I don't get over here as often as I used to," she said, "but I wouldn't miss seeing these little girls for the world." She'd brought with her a wrapped gift for the baby and one for Annie, who tore it open to find a Didee doll. A tiny baby bottle was also in the box.

"Look, Mommy, a bobble like Cathleen's." Annie sat down on the floor and put the bottle in a small hole in the doll's mouth.

"Yes, and she has a diaper on. You have to remember to change it when she gets wet."

Annie turned the doll upside down and felt the diaper. "Not wet."

"No, Mommy has to put water in the bottle. Then the baby gets wet."

They were sitting at the small kitchen table. Millie got up to fill the tiny bottle from the spigot in the kitchen. "Len has gone to the project office to see if we can get a kitchen stove. I guess the Newsomes knew we could get another one."

"I'm really surprised they took it," Emily said. "A lot of families take things they shouldn't when they leave."

"There are a few other things missing, but Len said we would just do without. He doesn't want to get them in trouble. It must be awful hard to leave everything you've worked for after a year."

"I know, but Joe knew when he signed on that everything was his as long as he made his payments," Emily said.

"Len says a lot of people are confused about that."

"Some of the early homesteaders like the Aldens and the Van Bruggens are getting along fine now, but they had to do without new clothes and shoes to make that first sixty-dollar rent payment at the end of the year. Someday, they'll own their homes."

"I know Len and I can do it, Miss Emily. Thank you for all you've done to help get us here."

"I'm afraid I didn't do a thing. You have Mr. Harrell to thank for that," Emily said. "But I do have a basket of things in the car for you. I included a few extras from home." She reached out to hug Millie. "You're like family, you know."

"Thank you, Miss Emily, you've always been like family to me. Speaking of family, I want to invite Papa and all my people from Wilmington for lunch on Easter. Could you come, too?"

"Oh, dear, Millie. I've promised Jeanne that I'll be in Hyde Park at Easter. There's someone I want her to meet. He'll be going with me."

"Hmmm," Millie said. "Do I know this someone?"

Emily blushed. "If you'd been around Penderlea a little longer, I'd say 'maybe.' Reggie Ashworth is a regional director with the Resettlement Division. That's how I met him."

Millie hugged her. "Oh, Miss Emily, I can't believe it. That is so wonderful."

"Well, we're just friends," she said, smiling. "We're both really busy with our own lives, but it's nice to have a man around the house now and then."

"Are things all right between you and Jeanne now?"

"Jeanne keeps her distance. We're not as close as we used to be, but that's all right." Emily looked at the sleeping baby. "You're lucky to have two girls. Maybe one will be close to you."

Emily encouraged Millie to join one of the Home Demonstration Clubs. "They're very active on the project. If you don't, I'm afraid you'll really feel left out."

"But there's so much to do," Millie said. "I want to make curtains and some furniture for the yard." Millie paused, picturing all the work cut out for her. "It'll soon be time to start a garden."

"My goodness, you'll likely need some help," Emily said.

Millie thought a minute about the colored help that her mother had over the years. There was always a Rhoadie or a Mae to help with housework and take care of the children—not that Eva McBryde had been a lady of leisure. Even Maggie Lorena had decrepit old Lizzie to help out. "Len says that modern wives here at Penderlea do most everything themselves. I don't mind."

"I know, dear, but trust me. It's very important to be one of the 'girls.' It will make things easier for Len."

"How's that?"

"Oh, I don't know, but you'll see. The women on Penderlea take a lot of pride in their homes. I've heard the menfolk brag about all the new things their wives have learned at Home Demonstration Club. I guess they feel that it shows teamwork."

About midday, Len stopped at the house followed by two men in a delivery truck. "They've got the mattress and a stove with them, honey." He grabbed two slices of bread from the basket Emily had brought, and spread one with peanut butter. "This will hold me until supper. Maybe you could make us a pan of biscuits."

"But the stove won't be hooked up."

"Those fellows will do it." He gave her a peck on the cheek and headed for his truck while the delivery truck backed up to the screened porch. A black and white enameled stove showed though the cracks in two wooden crates. Millie picked up the baby and told Annie to sit in her chair and watch while she held the door open for the men.

"Where you want this to go, Missus?" one of the men asked.

Before she could answer, his helper spoke up. "Can't go but one place. Right over yonder," he said, nodding toward the flue hole that had been stuffed with rags. They sat the crate down and stood looking at it. "What about that other piece out there in the truck. Don't it go on top?" the helper said.

"Yep. Go get it. Get that stovepipe, too." The boy followed his orders, and the man continued to stare at the bottom half. "I wish I had me a stove like that. 'Course, I'm not one of the chosen few," he said, sarcastically. "Got to be on relief to get one of them things." He looked up at Millie and grinned, his teeth full of empty spaces.

"It's a nice stove," she said.

He looked around the kitchen and peeped into the living room. He was dressed in soiled overalls and wore an oversized hunting jacket. "Y'all got a lot of nice stuff. The gov'ment give it to you for nothin'?"

"No, we're renting it for the time being."

The helper came back into the house dragging another wooden crate. "Me 'n' my boy, here, are renting a house on the other side of the project. We don't have no nice stuff like this, but what we do have is our'n."

"This will all be ours someday," Millie said. "We just have to pay for it."

The man laughed. "Yep, I reckon you do! I wanted one of these here houses, but the man over there in the office said I could work here for wages, but I couldn't live here."

"Why not?"

"Said I weren't legible, or something like that."

The three of them stood looking at the crated stove. "Are you going to hook it up for me?" Millie asked.

"No, mum. Not our job. We's just delivery men. We'll bring that mattress in, but you'll have to git somebody else to hook up the stove."

After they'd put the mattress on the bedstead, Millie closed the door after them and looked at the boarded-up stove. Len would be starving when he came home. He'd asked for a pan of biscuits. She settled the children in the living room, where a fire in the fireplace was taking the chill off the cold house. Then she retrieved a hammer from a box of tools and set about pulling the boards away from the crated stove. The legs for it were inside the oven, but she found she couldn't lift the stove to fit the legs under it. Not to be outdone, Millie turned the stove over on its back and worked until she had all four legs screwed on. The next big chore was to set the stove right side up again.

By this time, the baby was fretting and Annie was asking to go outside. Millie decided to set the stove project aside and take the children out. Rummaging through Emily's basket, she found tea cakes and a jar of cold tea. She filled the baby's bottle with milk and poured a cup of milk for Annie. "We'll have a picnic," she announced, bundling the children up. Locating the stump of a huge live oak tree, she spread out a quilt and sat Cathleen down on it. Annie crawled up and sat beside her.

Sipping her tea, Millie looked at the small cottage with its striped awnings reflecting the sunlight. Above her, tall pines whispered in the light breeze. Beyond the barn, their horse and colt grazed in a stubbled field. It was like they'd been scooped up by a big bird and put down in a whole new life. She vowed to herself that she would do everything in her power to make Len happy. She'd be the best wife and mother on Penderlea. She was sure she could do it.

CHAPTER 40

Millie had her back to the road when she heard someone call out to her. "May we join you?" She turned around to see a woman with a baby on her hip and two children in tow coming up the unpaved driveway. The woman wore a short brown jacket over a print dress, and looked to be about Millie's age.

"Afternoon. I'm Sula Mullins," the woman said warmly. "You must be Millie." She stretched out her hand. "I declare, y'all are pretty as a picture sitting up here on a stump having a tea party."

Millie laughed. "Thank you, Sula. Dan is your husband?"

"He sure is," Sula said. "And this is Frances, the first baby born on Penderlea." She hefted the baby up and turned her to face Millie.

"Really? Well, it's an honor to meet you, Miss Frances," Millie said, shaking the child's hand. She stooped to look at the other two children. "And who are these pretty little girls?"

"This is Edith, and this is Dorothy," Sula said, touching the heads of each of her children. Both little girls had straight blonde hair, neatly brushed to the side and gathered up in a bow.

"My goodness, how old are you?" Millie asked. Dorothy held up four fingers, Edith held up two. "You're the same age as Annie," she said to Edith.

"I'm Miss Millie and this is Cathleen, and this is Annie. Tell them how old you are, Annie." Annie held up two fingers.

"Look at that baby's red hair. Just a bunch of ringlets," Sula said.

Millie touched the top of her oldest child's head. "Annie's hair is straight as a stick."

Annie clung to Millie's leg and looked up at her. "Mama, 'et's paint us hair red."

Millie blushed. "Everybody makes over Cathleen's red hair."

"I love your hair, Annie," Sula said. "You don't need to paint it red. It's pretty like your mama's."

"Let me get another quilt," Millie said. "Annie, you go show the girls the horse and colt." Millie went inside and brought out another quilt and spread it on the ground. "Please sit down. I'm going to make some yard chairs, but I haven't figured out how or when yet. I've been inside all afternoon trying to set up the stove."

Sula, laughed, knowingly. "I never knew moving into a new house with everything furnished could be so much work, did you?"

"That stove has thrown me for a loop."

"I had to put all the doorknobs on after we moved in," Sula said. "They were just sitting there in a box. I knew it'd be a while before Dan got around to it. Have you noticed how men don't attach the same importance to things that we do?"

"I'm learning about that, too," Millie said, watching the girls climb up on the fence to get closer to the horse. "Annie's never had any playmates," she said, turning back to Sula. "I'm so glad you came over."

"The fresh air feels good, doesn't it?" Sula said. "It's hard to believe it's January."

The two women sat for an hour or more getting acquainted and watching the children play before Sula said she had to get home to start supper. "About the only thing Dan gets upset about is when I don't have his supper ready."

"Len does, too," Millie said, "but I'm afraid he'll just have to be upset tonight. I couldn't get the stove set up by myself. He asked for biscuits, but—"

"Let me help you," Sula said. "I'm strong as an ox."

"Do you think we might do it together?"

"We can give it a try," Sula said.

With a lot of lifting and tugging, the two women righted the stove and slid it back against the wall. "We have to attach it to the flue," Millie said.

"Yeah, I know," Sula said. "I thought the stoves were going to be electric."

Millie laughed. "I did, too." She looked at the remaining parts of the stove still in the crate. "Do you think it will work without those warming ovens on it?"

"Sure, they're really just decoration. But that's the easy part," Sula said. She picked up the hammer and knocked the crate away. Millie picked up one side of the stove back and Sula the other. "It looks like it stands alone, but we have to screw these screws into the stove top, and these onto the back of the stove," she said. "Else, it'll fall over the first time you open one of the doors."

When they had the back of the stove secure, Sula put her hands on her hips and looked at their accomplishment. "Many hands make light work," she said.

"Mama used to say that," Millie said.

"Look, don't you ever try to do something like this without some help. There's too many willing hands among the homesteaders. Me, especially."

Millie hugged her new friend. "I could never have done it by myself," she said. "In fact, I'm not sure how we did it together."

Sula laughed. "Penderlea is like that, Millie. The women work together. Don't tell the menfolk, but the government calls us their 'secret society.'" She picked up Frances and started for the door. "C'mon, girls. Daddy will be home soon. Millie, you better get a fire going and those biscuits started. Don't forget to open the damper," she cautioned.

Millie hugged her new friend again. "You're wonderful, Sula. It's so good to make a new friend here on Penderlea. I haven't had a real girlfriend since Len and I got married."

"You'll have lots of them here. That reminds me. Home Demonstration Club meets next week. I usually take Dan's truck and pick up one or two of the girls. Come and go with us. We have a lot of fun."

"I'll have to ask Len. He's so tired when he gets home at night. I've never left the children with him."

"Well, you tell him Dan does it on Home Demonstration night. It's expected."

CHAPTER 41

L iving in the new house was even better than Millie had imagined. It was perfect for the two children. She hoped they wouldn't have any more—two seemed just right. The baby was sleeping all night now, and Millie's breasts had gone down to their normal size. Once again she could wear the lovely satin nightgown that her mother had given her. Recently, Aunt Lilibeth had sent a box of clothes to Rebecca for distribution among her sisters, and Millie had gotten a brassiere and two slips, both items fitting her perfectly in her postpartum state. Finally, she had a figure, although Len didn't seem to notice.

During cold weather, Millie spent most of her spare time inside, the children settled down on a quilt playing with yarn and empty spools while she sewed. So far, she'd made curtains for the bedrooms and coverlets for their beds. Rebecca had sent the fabric, saying that she never had any time to sew. Actually, Rebecca never *did* sew much, and Millie suspected that some of the gingham and prints were bought especially for Millie's house. Her sister, who still had no children of her own, always included a dress for each of the girls and something simple for Millie, if nothing but a card of bobby pins.

Home Demonstration Club meetings were held every other week. Len said he was happy to stay with the children. As she'd promised, Sula picked Millie up. "Did you tell Len what the program was about tonight?"

Millie pulled the truck door closed and took a deep breath. "I wouldn't dare. He'd probably make me stay home."

"These small houses weren't meant for a passel of young'uns," Sula said. "I think the government wants to make sure we know that."

"They can't tell us how many children to have."

"I guess they can try. When we first got married, Dan said he wanted ten children, but Penderlea has changed all of that. Now, he says we can't afford any more mouths to feed. We were going to stop at two, but then Frances came along. I wouldn't take anything for her though. She's the sweetest little thing—hardly ever cries."

"I wouldn't mind another baby if I knew it would be a little boy," Millie said. "Len would like that."

"You can't stop a man when he wants you-know-what," Sula said, laughing.

Millie laughed too. "I know what you mean, but won't it be embarrassing, talking about it with other women tonight? Becca is always giving me advice, but she's my sister."

"Well, just think about these women as your sisters."

"I don't know if I'll tell Len," Millie said. "He thinks the government is butting into our lives too much anyway."

Sula laughed again. "Honey, he's the one you *need* to talk to."

⌣

In early March, Maggie Lorena wrote that Will was bringing Tate and her to see their new home in Penderlea. Maggie's letters were always an entertainment for Millie.

> *Rations have been mighty slim since you and Len left, barely enough to keep body and soul alive. But don't you worry*

about poor old Mama and Papa, Bud sees to it that we keep from perishing. One of Lizzie's boys brought us a load of chopped wood yesterday, so we're keeping warm by the fire. Mama has been doing a little writing again for the Journal as I'm able. Thank goodness that my mind is not as feeble as my poor old body.

I know the government is taking good care of you over there in Penderlea. We don't have all that here in Colly, but we make do. Just keep Mama in mind if they provide you with any stamps or extra rations that you could set aside for us. These are hard times, but we can all be thankful that you are there in Hugh MacRae's "utopia."

"What in the world is she thinking, Len?"

"Same thing everybody else is thinking. They think Penderlea is some kind of fairy tale. I guess it does sound pretty damn good if you don't have any better than Mama and Papa."

"But, Len, you know they're not *perishing*."

"You don't know," he said, with an edge to his voice.

"No, I don't know, but I can't believe Will would allow such a thing as that. I'll fix up a box of canned goods and some sweet potatoes for them to take back. I've also got a few stamps I could give Cousin Maggie if they're that bad off."

"Mama likes to poor-mouth, and I can't hardly stand it. You know I'd give them the food off my plate if I thought they were hungry."

⌣

Will was driving an old Chrysler sedan that he said he'd traded for a rebuilt tractor. The car was still in good shape. "It'd been wrecked, and the frame has a little twist in it," he said, "but it runs real good."

Len laughed. "I don't doubt that a bit," he said.

Tate opened the car door and stepped out into the sunlight. It took him a few minutes before he could get his legs going and extend his hand to Len. "I declare, son, this is a mighty pretty place. Umm-huh!"

"Thank you, Pa. I thought y'all would never get here."

"Help your mama out, son, she's been 'bout to worry me and Will to death." He stuck his head in the car window. "Wait a minute, Maggie Lorena, Len'll come around to the other side to get you out."

"I thought y'all were just going to stand around out there jawing all day," Maggie said.

"No, ma'am," Len said, hurrying around to open the car door. "I'm so glad to see you, Mama." He took her arm and helped her get her feet on the ground.

"My, my, this is a pretty place," she said. "You need to get some of my yucca plants to put out there by your mailbox. A clump or two of dusty miller would be nice, too."

"Come on in the house. You can tell Millie yourself."

Will and Tate were already in the kitchen hugging Millie and teasing the little girls. It took Annie a minute before she recognized them. "Don't you remember your poor old granddaddy?" Tate asked. "I'm going to cry." Annie ran to him and he took her up in his arms. "That's my girl!"

"What about Uncle Will?" Millie said. "He needs a hug, too."

"Hmmm. Let me see what I've got here," Will said, patting the pockets of his suit coat. "What's this?" he said, slowly pulling out a pack of Mary Jane taffies. "Oh, look, there's two of them!" he said, feigning surprise.

"Will Ryan, don't you be giving those children candy before their dinner." Millie reached out for the candies and put them up on top of the cabinet. "We'll have those after dinner."

Len and his mother stood on the porch looking out at the little farm scene behind the house. "I declare, son, this is heaven."

"It's close, Mama, but if we don't get on inside, Millie's gonna make it hell for us." He laughed and took her elbow and led her inside.

Millie hugged Maggie and pulled a chair out for her at the table. "We've just been waiting for this day. I can't believe you're finally here."

"Well, I can't either," Maggie said. "We've missed y'all so much over there between the rivers. Your papa sends you his love. Says he's coming to Penderlea at Easter. I reckon you didn't want to invite your poor kinfolk at the same time. But that's all right."

Millie was dumbfounded. She'd never imagined that Maggie would feel hard. "I was afraid we'd be too crowded if the weather was cold," she said.

"I suppose it might be. Easter is early this year. I 'spect we'll go to church at Bethlehem. I need to pay my respects to Mama and Papa's graves. Of course, little Yancey is buried there, too," Maggie said, dabbing at her eyes. "Maybe Kate and Nathan will ask us home to dinner."

Millie dropped long strips of pastry into boiling broth and covered the pot with a lid. She never quite knew what to say when Maggie reminisced about the child she'd lost. Losing a child was hard to imagine, now that she had two. Her own mother had lost a baby boy when he was only a year old.

"I declare, these are the prettiest little girls I've ever seen." Maggie reached out to touch Cathleen's curls, but Cathleen drew back. "Hair just like Grandmother's," she said, ignoring the rebuff.

"Annie, could you take Grandmother in and show her where the bathroom is? When you come back, I'll have the deviled eggs ready."

"Land sakes, I don't have to go right now," Maggie said. "Will stopped just outside of Penderlea, and I went behind some bushes." She smiled at her granddaughter. "That's what country folks do, Annie."

"You could show Grandmother your room," Millie said. She was feeling behind, and Len had abandoned her with his mother. "Oh, I do want to see that," Maggie said. She heaved herself up out of the chair and shuffled along after Annie, holding her hand. A new corset had trimmed Maggie's figure down a little, but her increased weight was taking its toll. Her arches had fallen, and she wore mannish shoes to support the added weight on her small feet.

Len showed Tate and Will the rest of the house and where to find the toilet. "You won't find any outhouses in Penderlea," he said. Will came out laughing.

"I thought that thing was going to take me down with it. Do you have to let it out every time you use it?" Will asked.

"Millie says you're supposed to, but I think it's a big waste of water," Len said. He started to laugh. "This one fellow that moved in here said that the hardest thing for him to get used to was the 'conveniences.' I think lots of folks agree with him."

"He was just showing his ignorance," Maggie said. "That's the first thing I want you to put in my house when we get electricity and a pump," she said.

"Have you heard any more about the cooperative?" Len asked.

"They say it will be awhile before they string wire as far as Colly," Tate said. "We've waited this long, I guess we can wait a little longer."

⌐

They sat around the small drop-leaf table in the kitchen while Millie served their plates. The young chicken that she'd stewed was tender, and her pastry was smooth and thick just like her mother's. She'd also made tomato pudding and opened two cans of green beans. "These beans were grown right here on Penderlea and canned in the cannery up there at the community center."

"I hope you've got a can or two to send our way," Maggie said.

"Yes, ma'am, there's a box of things out there on the porch," Len said.

"Now, don't go shorting yourself," Tate said.

By the time the meal was over, Millie was more grateful than ever that they'd been able to get out of the country and come to a farm city like Penderlea. If they hadn't, she might have become another Maggie Lorena, feeling sorry for herself and talking poor-mouth. Eva McBryde had often admonished anyone in her family talking poor-mouth. She thought it was low-class.

Len pushed his chair back from the table. "Say, Will, I don't want you to get dirty and greasy, but remember that old car you sent us the money for when Mama was having all that trouble with her gall bladder?"

"Yeah, I thought you sold it."

"No, it's setting out there behind the barn. I bought a battery for it, but I haven't had time to mess with it."

"Let's have a look at it," Will said. He tinkered with the car and soon had it running. "It's in pretty bad shape," he said. "Needs rings and new spark plugs."

"I've got the truck," Len said. "If you want to take it on back home and work on it, I'd be mighty obliged. One of these days, I thought I'd teach Millie to drive it."

Will laughed. "That ought to finish it off for good."

"Keep it as long as you like. Maybe Pa'll take Mama to church sometime."

Will grinned. "Pa'll be in hog heaven. He's been after me to work on his jalopy."

"I was worried about him before I left," Len said. "How's he been?"

"Pretty good. He don't like for you to make over him much," Will said. "He talks about going to see the boy some time—just me and him—going up there to Oak Ridge."

"Mama would have a fit," Len said.

CHAPTER 42

Millie wrote to all of her brothers and sisters, asking them to come on Easter Sunday to see the new house. Even Belle in Washington, D.C., had not declined. She'd married last spring and her little boy had been born in November, making him only three months younger than Cathleen. *They must get to know each other,* Millie wrote. *Since they are so close in age, they'll probably be like brother and sister.* Belle replied that her husband wanted to come, too. The prospect of meeting her new brother-in-law and her nephew at the same time excited Millie.

Saturday before the family gathering was warm and sunny. When Easter Sunday fell in March as it did this year, one never knew what the weather would be like. Millie decided she'd set up tables outside under the three peach trees she'd planted. They were just over head high.

While the children napped in the afternoon, she'd raked the yard and burned a pile of brush that had collected over the winter months. After she'd picked up all the buckets and tools that Len had left here and there, she set up the sawhorses and boards to make the table. When the children woke from their naps, she kept them happy outside the rest of the afternoon.

She'd just gone inside and put her apron on when Len came home from work that evening. She cringed when he went straight for the bottle he kept stashed under the sink. "Thank God for Saturday night," he said. "I haven't had a drink all week." He poured himself a stiff toddy and tossed it down his throat, sighing heavily.

"You look upset," Millie said. "What's wrong?"

"Where're the girls?"

"Right there in the other room. Why?"

"I sold the colt today. He's coming to get her Monday morning." Len read the look on her face. "You didn't think we'd keep her, did you? Not as tight as money is?"

Millie looked away. "What'll we tell Annie?"

Len poured himself another drink. "Dammit, you can tell her I had to do it," he said, pulling off his heavy brogans. She could see what was coming.

"I'll get your supper ready."

"I'd rather you go out there and feed the animals. I'm worn to a frazzle."

"The girls are hungry."

"Can't you give them a cracker or something?" He pulled his sock off, rubbing his foot. "I'll watch the baby. My poor old feet hurt me so bad."

If Millie hadn't been so tired herself, she would have laughed. Len was sounding just like his mama. She put the baby on the floor near Len and helped Annie with her sweater. "Come on, Annie, you can help Mama." The child was out the door before Millie could finish buttoning her sweater.

Millie took a deep breath and told herself she could do this and get supper on the table, too. She didn't want anything to ruin her plans for Easter Sunday. Services would be in the community center this year, but there was talk of a new church being built soon. Millie thought it would be wonderful to go to a real church again. While Annie threw out corn for the chickens, Millie put a bale of hay in the trough for the horse, humming "Christ the Lord Is Risen Today." She'd been told all her life that she couldn't carry a tune in a bucket with a hole in it. *God doesn't care if you can carry a tune or not,* she thought, laughing at herself.

She heard the baby crying. Len shouted out the back door, "Millie, come here! This young'un has burned her hand!"

Millie ran to the house, imagining the worst. She could hear the baby screaming. She was so careful with the baby, keeping her away from the stove. "Weren't you watching her?" she shouted, as she pushed past him.

"Hell, yes, I was watching her, but she crawled over there before I knew it and tried to stand up. She just reached up and touched the damn thing."

Millie picked up the baby and kissed her reddened palm. "It's okay, honey, Mama will put some butter on it." She quickly dipped a finger into the butter dish and smeared it gently over Cathleen's palm. "There, doesn't that feel better?" Cathleen held her hand up to Millie's mouth. "Oh, you want Mama to put a kiss on it?" Holding the baby on her lap, she cooed and rocked Cathleen until she quieted down.

Annie was leaning against her leg. "I'm hungry, Mama."

"Okay, honey. Mama's going to fix dinner right now."

"How long will it take?" Len asked. "I'm just about perished." He sat down at the small kitchen table to wait for his dinner. "It looks like you could have supper on the table when I get home from work."

"I do the best I can, Len."

"I know you do, honey, but a man needs his supper waiting for him. What have you been doing all day?"

"Well, I made a pound cake for Easter Sunday, and I cleaned up the yard. We've got company coming tomorrow, you know."

He took a swig of his whiskey. "Oh, yes, that's it. Your folks are coming, and all you have on your mind is what you're going to feed them."

"Len, that's not fair. They've never been to Penderlea. I thought you wanted them to come."

"Oh, I do," he said in a sarcastic tone. "I do want them to come and see how poor we are down here in *Reliefville*."

She turned her back to him and stared at the black stove top. *Don't say anything!* A tear ran down her cheek and sizzled on the burner. The baby was on her hip and Annie fidgeted in a chair, but it was too late: Len was on a rant, and nothing would stop him. "I can't get a damn straight answer out of nobody," he said, lighting a cigarette. "Now ol' man Harrell wants me to try raising turkeys. Says it'll look good on my record if I do something besides truck crops. I oughta be growing tobacco. That's what I ought to be doing right now—growing tobacco. But no, the government don't want you to grow something you want to grow—something you can make a little money on."

Earlier in the day, Millie had boiled a hen to make chicken salad for the Easter gathering. Her plan was to take a small portion of it and add pastry for their supper. Instead, she opened a can of pink salmon and placed it in the skillet along with several eggs. When the eggs were nearly scrambled, she added a large spoonful of cold rice from a pot on the stove. She spooned up the eggs onto his plate and added a piece of cold cornbread. "I know you're tired," she said.

"You're damn right I'm tired. Working my ass off and getting nowhere fast." He salted his meal heavily and took a bite. Annie was watching him. "Where's your dinner, shug?" he said sweetly. "Did Mama forget to give you your dinner?"

"It's right here, Annie. Mama didn't forget." Millie set a plate in front of Annie and another at her place. Cathleen was on her lap. Annie placed her palms together and closed her eyes.

"Oh, my goodness," Len said. "Did Daddy forget to say the blessing?" They bowed their heads in unison. "Bless this food to the nourishment of our bodies, and bless the hands that prepared it. In Jesus's name we pray. Amen."

⌣

That evening, as she did every night, she prayed that God would give her strength not to make Len angry. He was a hard-working man, and he loved her and his family. She knew he did.

⌣

The weather changed overnight, and Easter Sunday dawned cold and rainy. Millie woke up with a terrible headache brought on, she was sure, by being out in the wind all day on Saturday. She took a BC powder and went into the kitchen to poke up the fire in the stove. Len's unpleasantness was forgotten. There was no time to mope and think bad things about him. With her headache, it would be all she could do to start dinner and get the girls ready for church. Annie was restless, coughing on and off during the night. She hoped they weren't all coming down with bad colds.

Len was up right behind her. She could hear him in the living room making a small fire in the fireplace. "Bring the girls' clothes in here when you get a chance," he called out to her. "After I shave, I'll help them get dressed while you get breakfast ready."

"I'm not sure I should go, Len," she said. "I think I am coming down with a bad cold."

"Now, Millie, you know you can't miss Easter Sunday church. It wouldn't look right." Len set great store by what other people thought of him, especially any of the government officials. Although Len considered himself a cut above some of the homesteaders because he wasn't a tenant farmer before he came to the project, he realized he had to stay on his toes. Those mortgage payments had to be made, but allowances might be given to a man in good standing with the project administrators.

The small kitchen warmed up fast once the fire was hot enough to boil water for coffee. A large water tank on the side of the stove provided hot water for the kitchen and bathroom. They said that the next houses would have an electric stove, but Millie could hardly wait to tell her sister how she and Sula had installed the quaint little wood stove in her kitchen.

Millie fried bacon and stirred grits into a pot of water. She had a million things to do before they'd leave for church. She wasn't sure she could do them all. "Breakfast is ready," she called to Len.

"Come on in here with Mama," Len said to the girls. He held the swinging door for Annie and Cathleen. Annie crawled into her chair, and Len lifted the baby up into the high chair. "Hurry up now and eat your breakfast so Mama can get ready."

"Len, I don't see how I can go," Millie said. "Everybody will be here for dinner by the time we get back. There's no way I can have it all ready in time."

"I thought you got everything ready yesterday."

"I did as much as I could. I cleaned up the yard and set the tables up. Now it looks as if the weather is going to be too cold to eat outside. We'll have to eat inside." She pulled a handkerchief from her pocket and wiped the baby's nose. "I've got to make the potato salad—"

"Look here, now, you just get yourself ready. That crowd from Wilmington will have to wait."

"I don't think a single soul will miss Cathleen and me at church," Millie said. "You can take Annie."

"Damn you, Millie, I told you we needed to be there for Easter Sunday church. Then you went and invited your folks to come. I've got a reputation to maintain here. If we get kicked off the project because of this, it'll be your fault." He stomped out the back door, then turned and stuck his head back in. "We'll be leaving in thirty minutes. You be ready to go, you hear me?"

She had her back to him, looking at the boiling potatoes. "I'm not going," she said.

He slammed the door shut and stood behind her. She was afraid he was going to hit her. He'd never hit her before. "I said I can't go. I don't feel like it. I need to get dinner ready."

"Damn your soul to hell. I told you I wanted you to go to church. And you tell me you're not going with me? Do I deserve that after all I do for you and this family? I work my goddamned fingers to the bone doing for you so we can have something, and you won't even go to church with me?"

"Len, it's not like that." She walked out of the kitchen and the door swung shut. He hit it with his hand, and it banged against the wall. Millie kept going, closing herself up in the bathroom and latching the door.

"Don't you close this damn door in my face, you bitch." He rattled the doorknob and hit the door with his hand. "Open the damn door before I knock it down." Millie opened the door and pushed past him. He didn't touch her. He never hit her.

Annie followed them into the bedroom. "Mama, Cathleen's tyin' to get down." Millie tried to push past Len, but he blocked her way. "Cathleen might fall," she said, not looking at him. He moved slightly, and she forced her way between him and the wall. His breath was on her neck.

In the kitchen, Millie helped Cathleen down from the high chair. She sat down at the table and held the baby in her lap. In a few minutes, Annie was back in the kitchen wanting help putting her shoes on. "Mama, not go to church wif' Daddy?"

"No, darlin', Mama is going to stay home and cook dinner for Papa and Aunt Rebecca." She buckled the shoes. "You look so pretty in your new dress mama made you. You go with Daddy."

"Don't cry, Mama. Annie wuvs you."

"I love you, too, sweet Annie."

⌒

Why wasn't I ready to go to church? I could've gotten up before light and cooked dinner so I could go to church. A good wife would've done that.

CHAPTER 43

The Wilmington crowd arrived a little before one o'clock, just after Len and Annie had returned from church. Harry and Vera had ridden with Mr. Jones and Rebecca up from Wilmington to Penderlea. Cal would bring his father, Belle, Bentley, and the new baby, driving over from Rob's house where they'd all spent the previous night.

"Honey, it's beautiful," Harry said. "Unless looks are deceiving, I think you and Len have done the right thing." He'd cornered her by his car while Len showed Rebecca, Vera, and Mr. Jones the horse. "Are you happy here?"

"Yes, it's a great place to live," Millie said. "The people are wonderful. People like us who are just trying to get out of the Depression the best way they can."

"Penderlea seems a little better than *just* the best way." He looked about at the small homestead, at the house and barn, the white running fence and the other outbuildings. "Honey, I don't think you can do any better than this."

"All that glitters isn't necessarily gold," she said. "There are a few things yet to be worked out by the government."

"Like what?"

"Well, Len says we still don't know how much the house is going to cost us in the long run. We're already in debt to the government for lots of things. Nothing is free."

"I don't think anybody ever said it would be, did they?"

"No, but they made it sound like we wouldn't need a thing—everything would be taken care of. Really, it's not much different than living anywhere else, except we have lots of friends in the same boat we are. We help each other out."

Harry eased a little closer to her. "Look here, honey. Are you and Len doing all right? I mean, is he good to you?"

"Of course he is, Harry. I wouldn't put up with him if he wasn't." She hugged him. "I'd better get inside and finish up dinner. As soon as Papa and Belle get here, I'll put it on the table."

Rebecca and Vera followed Millie inside. "I see you made up some of that material I sent you," Rebecca said, examining the gingham curtains at the kitchen window.

"Oh, Becca, thank you so much. I even made a dress for Annie out of that piece."

"You're welcome. I thought you'd put it to good use."

Vera rushed into the house, red-faced and perspiring. "Uncle Len put Annie up on the horse, and she loved it. May I have a drink of water?"

"Sure, Vera, it's right there in the pitcher. Help yourself."

Vera poured herself a glass of water and took a deep draft. "I'll be back in a minute. Uncle Len said I could have a turn."

"Wait, who's got the baby?"

"Uncle Harry," Vera called out.

Millie and Rebecca looked at each other and laughed. "Not for long, I'll bet," Rebecca said. She was slicing boiled eggs on top of a bowl of potato salad. "Len's quite a fellow, isn't he?" she said.

"Yes, quite a fellow," Millie said. "He's made lots of friends on Penderlea. Everyone here thinks he's the nicest person they've ever met."

"What about you?"

"Look, the kitchen is so small, I'm just going to leave everything on the stove if that's all right?"

"Sure," Rebecca said, "but I asked, what about you?"

"Nothing's changed, Rebecca. He's a Dr. Jekyll and Mr. Hyde. When he's nice, I really love him."

"Like the little girl with the curl in the middle of her forehead?"

"Exactly," Millie said.

The back door opened again, and this time Vera came in carrying a baby boy. "Look," she cooed. "It's Belle's baby. Isn't he the cutest thing you've ever seen?" She turned him around to face his aunts. "Say hey to Aunt Becca and Aunt Millie, Scotty." The baby took one look at the two unfamiliar women in front of him and began to cry.

"Oh, for goodness sake," Belle said, coming into the kitchen. "Give him to me. He's such a crybaby." She took the baby, put him on her shoulder, and looked around. "This is a cute little kitchen."

"Hey, Belle, I'm glad you like it," Millie said.

"Hey, honey. Hey, Becca. I thought we'd never get here. Cal didn't know the way, and Bentley and I sure didn't. You should've sent us a map."

"He's precious, Belle," Rebecca said. "May I hold him?" Rebecca reached out for the baby and he started to cry again.

"That's what he does every time his daddy reaches out for him," Belle said. "Where is the asshole anyway?" She stuck her head out the door. "Bentley, come in here. Right now!"

A squat, good-looking man with dark hair swung through the door. Wearing a brown leather jacket and khaki-colored pants, he could have passed for one of the project administrators. "Well, hello, ladies," he said nodding to Millie and Rebecca. "I was coming, honey," he said to Belle.

"I need the diaper bag and a bottle for some milk."

"Okay, honey, just hold your horses. I'd like to meet your sisters."

"This is Millie and that's Rebecca," she said, nodding to each of her sisters in turn.

"Well, well, Belle didn't tell me her sisters were beauty queens."

Rebecca giggled. "Aren't you the Sir Galahad!" Bentley bowed and kissed her hand.

"And this is Auntie Millie," he said, taking Millie's hand.

"Hey, Bentley, I'm glad you could come."

"My pleasure," he said, his eyes twinkling.

"Would you go get that diaper bag now, Sir Galahad?" Belle said.

Millie had not seen her frail father in almost three months. When Len escorted him into the house, she stopped everything and went to him. "Papa, I've missed you so much. We've got a good dinner. All your favorite things," Millie said. He glanced around for Belle, but she'd gone into the bedroom to change her baby.

"All my favorite cooks, too, since your mama died," he said. Millie and Rebecca looked at each other, silently agreeing. Belle had never liked to cook.

Dark clouds raced about in the March sky, letting sun sneak through from time to time. They all fixed plates and carried them outside anyway, finding seats wherever they could. Millie lamented not being able to seat everyone at the improvised picnic table, but no one seemed to mind. The last time they'd all been together like this was Thanksgiving before Millie and Len were married. "I asked Emily McAllister to join us," Millie said. "But she was going to see Jeanne up in New York state. She has a friend. He's going with her."

Both of her sisters turned to stare. "*He's* going with her?" Belle asked.

Millie looked like the cat who ate the canary. "Yes, *he*. *He* works for the Resettlement Division. She met him on Penderlea."

"My goodness," Rebecca said. "It's spring, and love is in the air." She picked up her plate and gathered up several more. "Who wants a piece of my coconut cake?"

"We all do," Cal said. "I'll bring it out here."

"There's pound cake, too," Millie said, starting into the house. "I'll get some more plates. Belle, you want to help me?"

"I guess so, I need to check on the baby."

After Cal and Rebecca had taken the cakes out to the picnic table, Millie filled a pitcher with more tea and handed Belle a stack of small plates. "Oh, take this knife, too. I forgot to give it to Becca."

"Did you notice the way she was flirting with Bentley?" Belle said.

"Who?"

"Rebecca, that's who!"

"I don't think she was flirting with him, she was just…"

"Just *flirting* with him," Belle said. "She was all over him like a dirty shirt."

"Really, Belle. I think you're imagining things."

"Oh, I am, huh? Well, let me tell you, if Emily McAllister had used a little *imagination*, she might have figured out that Jeanne was having an affair with Dr. Jon McNamara."

"Emily doesn't blame Jeanne. She said Jeanne was injured—she got carried away by her emotions. Dr. Jon is really the one to blame."

"Yeah, right. Well, you better wise up, little sister. There are women everywhere that can't keep their hands off another woman's man. You'd do well to keep your eye on Len."

After lunch, Len offered to take the crowd for a tour of the Penderlea Homesteads project, but Harry said he needed to get on back to Wilmington with the crowd riding in his car. "Let me ask Bentley and Belle," Cal said. "We can all go. I'm in no hurry to get back. You can drive my car."

"Well, now, I'd say that's mighty generous of you, Cal," Len said, sliding into the driver's side of the Ford.

Belle declined, but the men all climbed into Cal's car and drove over the entire project with Len who pointed out homes of people he knew. "We've got about six hundred people living on the project now," Len said. "I know most of them. They call me the mayor of Penderlea," he said, throwing up his hand to a crowd of boys hanging around the general store.

"You get elected?" Rob asked.

"It's just a figure of speech, Papa," Cal said. "I don't doubt that Len could get elected if he wanted to."

"No, sir," Len said. "There's only one mayor of Penderlea, and that's old man Harrell. He's like a lord around here."

"Where does he live?" Cal asked.

"Over yonder at Willard," Len said. "He's got a big two-story house with columns out front."

"Puts on the big dog, does he?" Bentley asked.

"Oh, he's all right, just not one of us."

CHAPTER 44

Construction work on the "new project," which had been a drawing card for Len Ryan, was slow getting started. Roy Park, who was in charge of the last stages of construction for the original project, had arrived on site the second week in January. Everyone, including Len, had expected construction to start then since the land had already been cleared. But there had been problems. Not only had the weather been unusually cold and wet, the North Carolina Employment Service in Wilmington couldn't fill Park's order for labor. There were many men available in the county—men like Len begging for work—but the problem was that the employment service operated under a restriction requiring that all nonskilled labor come from relief rolls, men already on the dole, as it were.

Finally, at the end of March, the restriction was lifted and work began on the new construction. No one had promised Len that work, but he'd figured that's what Mr. Harrell had in mind when he hired a full-time pump man. Len's work in the last few weeks had been reduced down to fixing broken pipes caused by several days of freezing weather in February. Len was ready to move on now, meet Mr. Parks, and be on the construction schedule. But Mr. Harrell had other ideas about Len Ryan.

"Let them get somebody else to do the new work. I want you to take care of what we've already got here on Penderlea," Harrell said. "These people expect the government to keep their pumps running. Besides, you've got a farm to run yourself. You thought about that?"

"Yes, sir, but I could really use more money coming in," Len said. "Some homesteaders are hiring outsiders to do their farming so they can hire on to the new construction."

"No, sir. That's not the way the system works," Harrell said. "Besides, you've been handpicked by me," he said, jabbing his finger into Len's chest. "Those fellows in Atlanta and Washington are going to be watching you. You're supposed to pay off your note with the crops you grow. We can't have everybody hiring out their farmwork. That's not the resettlement way." Len was stunned. He felt like Mr. Harrell was making this up—talking to hear his head roar. "I've got people coming here all the time checking up on me," he continued, pacing around the office in a strut, gesturing with his pipe. "If I had to say, 'Len's off working on new construction, neglecting his crops,' how'd that look? No, sir, there's no reason why you can't take care of the little bit of work keeping these pumps running on the old project, and making good on your land too."

⌒

"He's tying my hands," Len said, when he told Millie about Mr. Harrell's orders. "I was counting on that work to make our payments. All I'm doing now is fixing broken pipes. Everybody knows it'll be years before a man can make a decent living farming on Penderlea." Len was wound up and Millie knew he had to get it out of his system. "Old Joe Newsome did a fine job on that running fence around the pasture and hog pen, but one of the reasons he couldn't pay his mortgage was because he couldn't grow good truck crops. It'll be years before decent crops can be grown in this here raw soil. Any farmer worth his salt knows that. New ground has to lay fallow for awhile. Sometimes it has to be sweetened with lime and turned over several years in a row. Ray Wilkins, one year back home, had me till under a whole crop of soybeans without harvesting a single pod, just to improve the soil."

⟶

As it had been in the communities from which they'd come, the general store was a gathering place for the men on the project. The only difference was that the Penderlea store was owned and operated by the government. That being the case, most complaint sessions took place out under the trees away from the watchful eyes of Melvin Harrell's informants. Jess, Len, Dan, and Dutch tended to collect together in the same spot every evening. The topic of growing tobacco usually came up. "They don't call tobacco a cash crop for nothing," Dan Mullins said. "Tobacco would grow good here. I don't see why we can't give it a try." Like most of them, he'd come from farms where tobacco had dominated the farming scene.

"If we could've brought our allotments with us, we might've used them on this small acreage," Len said. "As it is, I don't believe you could make much off twenty acres. Thirty, maybe."

"Look, here, Len," Dan said. "I know it could be done, but it'll take a constitutional amendment to get the government to see it that way."

"They just did away with one," Len laughed. "I would've gone completely broke last year if I hadn't of gotten those allotment checks."

"Y'all need to be thinking about growing some flowers," Dutch said. "I've got the prettiest field of irises you ever saw. I'll ship every one of them up north in June."

"Yeah, but will you make anything on them?" Jess Alden asked.

"This is my third year," Dutch said. "Every year it gets a little better."

"That's because you're the only one growing the damn things," Jess retorted. "Everybody in Pender and the three counties that surround us is growing strawberries. They say the price is going to be way down this year." It was a common concern of all of the homesteaders. Since strawberries were perishable, a market had to be determined early on and the berries shipped in a timely manner to arrive in northern cities before they rotted.

The same was true of cucumbers, potatoes, beans, and such, all of which were grown not only on Penderlea, but on the surrounding farms in the area. When the market was flooded, prices stayed down.

In May, director Reginald Ashworth, accompanied by a spokesman from the North Carolina Department of Agriculture, called a meeting of the homesteaders at the community center. The spokesman at the podium announced that Congress had passed the Farm Security Act, an effort on the part of the Roosevelt Administration to provide loans to subsistence farmers like those at Penderlea. "We've already secured loans to form two stock companies under North Carolina law," he said. "The Penderlea Mutual Association will operate the cannery and gristmill—such as that, and the Penderlea Homestead Association will handle finance and construction." He paused when a ripple of murmurs passed through the crowd of homesteaders.

Ashworth joined him at the podium. "It's what you fellows have been asking for. It's the cooperatives you were promised early on." The disgruntled spokesman found a seat. "Look here men, this should come as good news to you," Ashworth said. "The boards of advisors will be made up of homesteaders, with the exception of your project manager and your farm manager. Under the Mutual Association, the general store, filling station, warehouse, gristmill, the hammer mill, feed mill, and sweet potato curing house will all operate as cooperatives." Reginald expected a round of applause, but heard only a few half-hearted claps. "To create even more revenue, anyone over eighteen who is a low-income farmer, on or off Penderlea, can become a member of the Mutual Association for one dollar a share."

"People who don't live here can vote on what we do?" Jess shouted.

"Yes," Reginald replied. "That's the way it works."

"I'm not sure I like that," Len muttered.

Reginald was aware of the dissatisfaction, but he persevered. "No matter how many shares of stock a member owns, he has only one vote as a stockholder."

"I guess old man Harrell gets one too, so he can cancel mine out," Jess said under his breath.

But owning stock in the Mutual Association did bring some satisfaction. Homesteaders now had a voice in how things were run. Although the project management had a position on the board, the officers were homesteaders. Len, Jess, Dan, and Dutch were all elected that evening.

⁓

It was a regular thing for Len to be gone one or two nights a week to attend the meetings of the Mutual Association. Sometimes Millie thought it was just an excuse to get out and chew the rag with the other men. But she understood that, like all of the other homesteaders, dread that they might be evicted was never far from Len's thoughts. A feeling of camaraderie existed among the men. They were all in it for the same reasons. The worst part was the knowledge that if a homesteader was asked to leave, nothing he'd worked for would be his to take with him. When Len came home from a meeting, he'd bend Millie's ear for an hour or more. "Dan said he'd planned to add on to his house after the new baby got to sleeping in a regular bed, but he's not now—not until he knows how much he's paying for his house."

"Sula said they might move to a larger house if one became available."

"That's what I'd do, if it was me," Len said. "I'd be afraid to make any improvements I couldn't get my money back on." He lit a cigarette and walked over to the cabinet where he kept a bottle of whiskey. "I declare, all this makes me so nervous. Dutch said he might never get his money back on the barn he built. I went over there the other day and saw his flowers. They were growing in this beautiful black soil that looked as if he'd sifted every grain of it. I'd give anything if ours looked like that. What if he got kicked off the project? He'd still owe the money and the next fool that came along would have the benefit of that beautiful black gold."

"We didn't get much benefit from Joe, did we?" Millie said.

"We got that fence out there. Nobody else has one like it."

CHAPTER 45

When Emily returned from her trip to Hyde Park, she came with stories of the wonderful furniture factory at Val-Kill where women who had no skill at all had been put to work and were now making furniture and crafts for their own homes.

"We're doing that here, too," Millie told her. "Come outside and see my new chairs. I cut every board myself and nailed them together."

They went out through the screened-in back porch and stepped out into the grassy yard. In the small washhouse, a washing machine rocked on spindly legs, swaying from side to side like a chubby old woman walking down a road. On the clothesline, another load of wash flapped in the April breeze. Emily sat down in one of the Adirondack-style chairs and leaned back. "They're not only pretty, they're comfortable, too," she said. "I'm so proud of you. If I were a little younger, I'd build some for my place."

Millie sat down beside her. "I could help you," she said. "I get a lot of things done while the children are napping."

"No, dear, you have more than enough to do." She looked around at the small home, at Millie's efforts to landscape the exterior. It would be several years before the rosebushes that climbed gracefully up trellises on either side of the porch steps bloomed. Bricks were still scattered along a walk area where she'd worked on the walk to the front door. "Are you happy here on Penderlea, Millie?"

Millie thought for a minute. Emily didn't want to hear her heartaches. She didn't want to know the things she'd discovered about her husband. "Yes, Penderlea is wonderful. We've made such good friends. No one has any money, but there's plenty to do and plenty to eat."

"I'm sure Hugh MacRae would love to hear that. I was with him a few days ago. There's something brewing that I wanted to tell him about before the news gets out to the public. You'll be interested, too."

"What's that?" Millie asked.

"Eleanor Roosevelt is coming to Penderlea."

⁓

That evening at supper, Millie told Len about Mrs. Roosevelt's visit. "Isn't it exciting? I've never seen a president, much less a president's wife."

"I reckon," Len said. He was finishing up his plate and looking for the cane syrup to sop up with a biscuit. "I hope she's not just nosing around like the rest of those government people—coming down here asking questions, wanting to see our houses."

"Emily says she just wants to come and see how well we're doing," Millie said. "She's the one who talked the president into resettlement communities like ours."

"We'll see. I bet she has a bunch of damn reporters with her. They'll be swarming all over the place, taking pictures and trying to find out our business." He wiped his mouth and pushed his chair back. "Jesse told me the other day that one of them field workers stopped at his house and asked Miss Katybelle how much she was spending on clothes for the children. Wanted to know how much underwear costs down here. You'd think we're guinea pigs or something. Don't the government have anything better to do?"

"Penderlea is an experiment, Len. I think they're just interested in how we're making out."

"Like I said, we're a bunch of damn guinea pigs."

"There are a lot people who don't have what we have," Millie said, regretting her sass immediately.

"There you go, taking up for the government again. Won't you agree with me just one damn time?" She tried to think of a reply, something that would smooth his ruffled feathers. But he was on his way into the living room to take his nap and listen to the news. "Keep those young'uns quiet now," he said. "I want to hear the farm report. Jesse said he heard tobacco prices were going to be way up this year." He plopped into a Morris-style chair next to the radio, mumbling under his breath, "and here I am, trying to grow strawberries and not making a damn dime."

⁓

The radio had been a Christmas gift to them from her brother Cal who'd bought it from an appliance store in Wilmington. Cal was always buying things like that. He'd say, "I had one and thought you'd like it, too." Although Cal had never married, he had a longtime girlfriend. They'd been to Penderlea for Sunday afternoon visits, but Millie was sure they'd never get married. She thought you could look at some couples and see right off that they weren't the marrying kind.

Cal's radio and the fact that they had electricity brought a welcome diversion into their new life—entertainment. It would be years before they had electricity in Bladen County. Len became obsessed with the news and farm report over WPTF out of Raleigh. Daily, he planned his work so as to be home at noon when it came on. During the day, Millie listened to music mostly, but on rainy days when she couldn't have the children outside, she'd listen to *Ma Perkins* and *George Burns and Gracie Allen*. She hated the news. There was always something worrisome on it—something she couldn't do a thing about. Len had been listening to the radio in May when a German hydrogen-filled airship, the *Hindenburg*, arrived at Lakehurst, New Jersey, after an Atlantic crossing. It crashed into the docking station, killing everyone aboard. Len called to her to listen. Millie had spent the next few days thinking about the tragedy and reliving the horror of the live broadcast.

As part of their benefit from living on a government project, home-steaders received free copies of the *Wilmington Star*, delivered by the mail carrier to their homes twice a week. Copies of the Sunday *News & Observer*, a statewide newspaper out of Raleigh, were delivered to the project office for anyone to pick up after church. Len enjoyed the comics and spent time with Annie reading them to her while Millie cooked dinner. He loved to act out Lil' Abner and Popeye, making crazy sounds to hear Annie laugh.

⟶

Millie longed for an opportunity to go to Wilmington. Every week, the shows changed and she thought how wonderful it would be to go to a movie again. Rebecca said she had seen Claudette Colbert in *Cleopatra* three times. As she had always done, Millie looked at the department store advertisements for dressmaking ideas. There were patterns offered, too. Not that she had money for fabric, but she loved to figure out how dresses were made. One of these days, she thought she might become a dressmaker, so she tore out the pictures and kept them in her dresser drawer.

While Millie relished the news from Wilmington, Len became obsessed with national and world news. Adolf Hitler, who had come to power in Germany, was rattling his sabers throughout Europe. "He's trying to get rid of all the Jews in Germany," Len said. "Can you beat that?"

"Emily told me that Mr. Alvin Johnson was inviting Jews to settle in Van Eeden. She said some of the men from Penderlea had been hired to do construction work."

"Oh, yeah? That'll mean wells and pumps. Maybe I ought to look into a work grant to go over there. Might be the only way we can make our payments."

"How much do we owe, Len?"

"How in the hell do I know? I can't get a straight answer out of that god-damned project manager. He sure as hell keeps a tight rein on the books. I asked him again the other day why I couldn't grow tobacco. I told him flat out that you couldn't make truck farmers out of tobacco farmers." He said there was some talk about allowing tobacco on Penderlea, now that they're bringing the tobacco allotment program back in. But unless you already had an allotment, you couldn't build a barn. I told him that I already had my allotment from Bladen County, but it would mean I'd have to take out a loan to build a tobacco barn. He said I was overextended already."

"What does that mean?" Millie asked.

"Means I can't borrow any more money until I pay some on my damn note."

Millie tried to think of something reassuring—anything to make him feel better. As a rule he didn't want to hear it, but she tried anyhow. "The strawberries look good," she said.

"That's the only thing Joe Newsome put in the ground here that's going to make my life easier."

"Is anybody going to plant tobacco this year?"

"It's too late. You ought to know that."

"I don't know a lot about tobacco, Len. Papa never grew any. Uncle Angus did. I remember the girls used to talk about him coming home from the tobacco market with pretty dresses for them."

"That's all you're thinking about? Here I am trying to get ahead in this world, and all you're thinking about is pretty dresses for you and the girls. It looks like you could support me sometime instead of suck the life out of me."

They'd been sitting in the small living room listening to the radio. Millie picked up her sewing and put it in a basket on the floor. "I'm going to bed. Don't forget to turn off the lights," she said. After checking on Cathleen and Annie, she slipped into her cotton nightgown and crawled into bed. She'd left the door open so Len could see by the hall light. *If he hit his toe or anything like that, it would be reason for another tirade of some sort. Would he always be like this? Could I change him if I acted differently? What made a man fractious with his wife?* She tried to do everything possible to make him love her. She'd always been told that she was kind and sweet. She didn't have any enemies that she knew of. The thought made her sob out loud, and she put her hand over her mouth. *He was so mean. How could he say all those things that weren't true? One of these days, I'm going to write down everything hateful he's said to me and show it to him. He'd never believe me otherwise.*

CHAPTER 46

Within days after confirmation from the White House, Emily McAllister began coordinating Eleanor Roosevelt's visit to Penderlea Homesteads with local officials. The First Lady would come in by Pullman train on June 11, arriving in Wallace around seven o'clock in the morning. She would be met by Governor Hoey and U.S. Senator Bob Reynolds. Various dignitaries from the surrounding counties would be there also. Schoolchildren, including Boy Scouts, would form an honor guard along the street. The Fort Bragg Military Band would lead the procession of the First Lady and her entourage to the home of Dr. and Mrs. John Robinson, where the Wallace Woman's Club would host a small reception for about fifty persons, including Hugh MacRae. Next, Emily would go with her by car, a new Chrysler sedan provided by a Wilmington dealership, first to the Department of Agriculture's Coastal Plains Test Farm at Willard where Mrs. Roosevelt would be treated to a real North Carolina breakfast.

After the breakfast, Emily, who'd been asked to be the chairwoman of the Penderlea portion of Mrs. Roosevelt's visit, would escort the First Lady and various guests to Penderlea, where homesteaders would entertain the crowd with a historical pageant and a square dance featuring an old-time fiddler. Mrs. Roosevelt would be given a tour of the project and invited to see as many of the homes as time permitted.

Emily said she would coordinate the festivities with a representative from the Resettlement Administration in Washington. "Miss Sissy Varden is due to arrive any day now," Emily told the pageant committee. "She'll help you put on a pageant for Mrs. Roosevelt. The First Lady is big on plays that tell the story of the New Deal. She's been in one herself, playing herself."

They all laughed, and someone commented that playing Mrs. Roosevelt would be a difficult part unless you were hard-favored. "Really, she's not hard-favored," Emily said. "She's warm and kind with a lovely smile. I guarantee you'll love her."

Emily told the pageant committee that they'd only have a few hours to impress the First Lady. "She'll return to Wallace for a luncheon at the Robinson home, address the Strawberry Festival over a national hook-up at two forty-five, then be honored at a tea for three hundred persons given by the Wallace Woman's Club. The grand finale will be a supper in the Robinsons' outdoor living room attended by some two hundred guests before her train departs that evening."

"That wears me out just hearing about it," Sula Mullins said.

When Sissy Varden arrived at the project office driving a small red Ford coupe, word spread quickly among the men that the pageant director was a "real looker." Melvin Harrell was the first to meet her. He took her arm and escorted her into his office. "Miss Varden, we are honored to have you on our humble project." Emily followed along, almost completely ignored by Harrell. "You'll be staying with Mrs. Harrell and me in our home in Willard. We intend to do everything in our power to make you comfortable and happy," he crowed, glowing with excitement.

The attractive twenty-two-year-old woman smiled and thanked him. She was accustomed to these local fellows thinking she was a Washington government official sent to check up on their management. "You are most kind, Mr. Harrell, but I'd like to stay on the project. There'll be a lot of night rehearsals. I really prefer not to drive at night."

Emily interceded. "I'm sorry, Melvin, I made the arrangements," she said. "My daughter, Jeanne, has been asked to come here to help Sissy. They'll stay in the two rooms in the community center that were previously occupied by the National Youth group." Melvin Harrell did not look pleased. She could see that she had crossed him. "I hope that's all right with you?" she said.

"Is it all right with Miss Varden? Those quarters are not very private. I'm not even sure the facilities are working properly. But I'll look into it. In the meantime, I'll take Miss Varden on a tour of our offices. You can run on now, if you like, Emily."

"Could you do that a little later in the day?" Emily asked. "Our Home Demonstration Clubs are hosting a luncheon for Sissy in the cannery at noon. Martha Smith, the regional director for home economists from Raleigh, will be here."

"Oh? No one told me," Harrell said.

Sissy Varden had been watching and listening to the exchange. When she spoke up, there was little doubt that she was an experienced political worker. "After the luncheon, I'd love to come back here. You can show and tell me about the project then, Mr. Harrell. We should be finished by three o'clock, shouldn't we, Mrs. McAllister?"

"Yes, of course. Perhaps Mr. Harrell may even run you over to Willard to see his home and gardens. It's a real showplace."

"Yes, yes, of course," Harrell said. "I'll call my wife. You'll stay for supper, won't you?"

"Yes, if I take my car and can get back before dark."

"Then it's all set," he beamed. "Emily, I suppose you'll need to get on home, too, but you're welcome to come for supper."

She quickly decided to let him off the hook. Miss Varden could fend for herself. "Thank you, but I do need to get back home. Jeanne will arrive tomorrow."

Sissy Varden's arrival and plans for the pageant breathed new life into the Penderlea Homesteads project. Friendly and enthusiastic, she spoke to everyone as she found her way around Penderlea. Her childlike face was saucer-shaped, her brown eyes expressive below thinly arched eyebrows. She had a tiny nose and painted her lips into a pink peek-a-boo mouth like a movie starlet. A mass of brown curls, wound tightly on curlers every night, were left unbrushed to bounce along with her every step.

Although Sissy Varden might be described as cute and sassy, her passion for the theater was obvious. She'd told the pageant committee that, before the Depression, her parents had taken her to Hollywood, thinking she might be a stand-in for Shirley Temple. The dream had been short-lived when she'd gotten the chickenpox and missed her audition. But she'd majored in history in college and gone on to drama school, finding her niche in directing historical plays. Her job within the Resettlement Administration had come about through her friendship with the director, who was now her fiancé.

Jeanne McAllister's arrival on the project the following day brought another stir of interest among the homesteaders, most of whom knew Emily from the warm reception they'd received when they'd come to Penderlea. Few of them knew that she had a daughter. If any were expecting Jeanne to be like her mother, they soon found out differently. Jeanne moved about the project like a debutante. Aloof and haughty, some described her behind Emily's back. But because she was Emily's daughter, Jeanne was accepted. Millie thought she looked wounded, like an animal that had been hurt. Maybe it was the scars, which escaped no one's notice.

Having two sophisticated city girls running around and directing the various rehearsals kept interest at full tilt among the hard-working home-steaders who had formerly passed most of their social time working out problems associated with living on a government project. Now there were rehearsals every night, sets to be built and painted, and a stage to construct. Somehow, it made all the rest easier.

Under Sissy Varden's direction, homesteaders had written the entire script,

calling it *From Settlement to Resettlement: A Panorama of Local Life, 1771–1937.*
The pageant would open against a colonial backdrop. There would be brave
pilgrims who'd come to settle in the vast untamed forests, and Indians
who gave them a hard time. Then the scene would shift to 1937 and show
descendants of the same 1771 pioneers resettling at Penderlea, aided by a
kind and charitable government. There were to be two choruses—the Men
of Penderlea and the Women of Penderlea—to vocalize the action in song.
There would also be a kitchen orchestra concert and a performance of Negro
spirituals by a choir from the nearby community of Newkirk.

⁓

"I tell you, it's going to be more fun than a barrel of monkeys," Len said. "Jeanne
and Sissy really know how to pull things together. Of course, some of us fellows
are a little better at this than others. Like me, for instance. I know how to get up
there with some decent clothes on and sing like I mean it."

They had finished supper, and Len was bathing at the small sink in the
bathroom. "You always look nice, Len." Millie said. "I've got some clean clothes
laid out for you on the bed. Everybody tells me you're the star of the show."

"No, no, I'm not that, but I did have a part in our senior play in Cotton
Cove. I reckon it shows." He lathered his face and scraped a razor over it,
feeling the smoothness with his other hand. "Some of those fellows go up
there to the community building in a pair of dirty old overalls, smelling
like a horse. I declare, you'd think they'd have more pride."

Annie and Cathleen splashed in the tub behind Len while Millie sat on the
commode seat watching them play. "What time will you be home tonight?"
she asked.

"Shouldn't be too late. Jeanne is setting up the kitchen orchestra tonight.
I sure do want to see that." He laughed loudly, and the little girls looked up.
Len waved to them in the mirror. "You'll take care of Mama, won't you, girls?
Daddy's got to be the star of the show." He looked at Millie and laughed
again. "Like I said, we're having the most fun, honey. You ought to be in that
kitchen orchestra."

"Can't hardly do that and watch the girls," Millie said.

Len ignored the comment, splashing Aqua-Velva generously on his cheeks. "Oh, I almost forgot. Jeanne wants you to make her a dress. You know, something like what the ladies on Penderlea wear."

"A dress like I'd wear?"

"Yeah, you know, nothing fancy. She doesn't want to stand out as being different from the other women on the project."

But she is different, Millie thought. *A house dress isn't going to change that.* "I don't know when I'll have time, Len. I promised to help with some costumes."

"Now, don't go saying things like that. You can do it if you want to. I want you to do it. Jeanne's real nice to me. I told her you would."

Millie lifted the girls out of the tub, wrapping them in large towels. They were so cute and sweet with their skin damp and their hair in ringlets. "Tell Daddy good-bye," she said, sending Annie after Len. She sat on the lid of the commode and finished drying the baby on her lap. "What time will you be home?" she called out.

Len stuck his head back in the door. "Don't wait up for me. I'll need my breakfast early tomorrow morning."

"Earlier than usual?"

"Well, no, but I've got to catch a couple of pump service calls before Jeanne and I run over to Nunalee's in Burgaw. Jeanne said Mr. Nunalee told her we could have all the boxes and wooden crates we wanted. We just need to pick them up."

Millie followed Len to the door. "She's going with you?"

"Well, yes. Jeanne's in charge of that," he said.

"What're you going to use them for?"

"Part of the scenery." He bent down to kiss Annie. "I'm telling you, this thing is going to be elaborate, honey." He gave Millie and Cathleen each a peck on the cheek. "Mrs. Roosevelt is going to be so impressed. Jeanne and Sissy know what they're doing. These girls are first-class."

"I wouldn't mind having a few crates to store things out in the barn. Could you get a couple of extra ones for us?"

"I'll ask Jeanne. She's funny about things like that. Said we have to be real careful."

"Aren't they giving them away?"

"Nunalee's is contributing them because Mrs. Roosevelt is coming. They're putting an advertisement in the program and all." He pulled the door closed. "I'll run it by Jeanne," he called out.

Sula Mullins was a frequent visitor in the afternoons after the children's naps. She pulled the baby along Crooked Run Road in a rusty red wagon. The two older girls tagged along behind. Millie enjoyed the quiet time with her friend while the children ran about and played in the yard. "I wanted Len to put up a swing," Millie said, "but these pines are all so tall. I wish we had a big old oak tree like the ones we had at Bandeaux Creek."

"We've got one—just one," Sula said. "But Dan said he wasn't about to climb it. He said he thinks more of his neck than that."

"I'll bet Len would do it if Jeanne McAllister asked him to."

"Oh, Dan thinks Sissy is the cat's meow. He says Jeanne is hard-looking."

"It's her scars," Millie said. "She wants me to make her a house dress."

"Jeanne McAllister wants you to make her a house dress? What in the world for?"

Millie smiled. "So she can look like *us*."

"Humph! That'll be the day. Those girls have *city* written all over them. And what a flirt that Sissy is. She calls all the fellows in the men's chorus 'honey' or 'sweetie,'" Sula said. "I went up there one night with Dan, and she had her hands all over one or the other of them, moving them this way and that on stage. When she gets to the women's chorus, she's a cold fish. I can't say as I like her very much, but I guess we have to take what we can get from the government."

"Sissy's been real nice to me," Millie said. "She told me that Len was so helpful. He's building all this scenery for her in the wood shop after rehearsals. I felt like telling her I could use him at home to chop some firewood." Millie sighed. "I guess after it's all over, we'll be proud of the pageant, but right now, I'd like to have my husband home sometimes."

"They're having the time of their lives," Sula said. "I don't see how it can hurt."

Millie laughed. "I guess we're just a little jealous. The pageant will be over in a few weeks, and those girls will be gone. We'll have our men all to ourselves again. I'm not sure if I'll like that better or not."

⌒

Len had come home all excited from rehearsals one night saying that Sissy and Jeanne had asked him to be one of the settlers called "Harry." "You know, like 'Tom, Dick, and Harry,'" he said, tickled at the sound of it.

Millie laughed. "Who're Tom and Dick?"

"That'd be Seth Miller and Orin Peterson. Remember them from over there in the new project?"

"I think so. Who else is in it?"

"You'll probably recognize most of them. I don't know everybody's name," he said. "Dutch got a good part. He's the leader of the adjusters. That's in the colonial part. He's also got a part in the modern scene. Jesse's in both scenes, too, since he was one of the first homesteaders."

"How about Dan Mullins?"

"I don't know about Dan. He's a little bit shy—didn't want to get up on stage in front of everybody. He's doing scenery, I think. Somebody has to work behind stage."

"You're having fun, aren't you, Len?"

"Hell, yes. It's about damn time I had a little fun instead of sitting around with a bunch of bellyachers. That's what Mr. Harrell calls the Mutual Association."

⌒

As soon as Len left for work the following morning, Millie took the girls outside, leaving the breakfast dishes on the table and the beds unmade. She could hardly wait to get started on smaller Adirondack chairs for the girls.

When Len drove up with Jeanne in the truck, Millie felt like she'd been caught with her britches down. Len leaned out the truck window. "What in the hell are you doing?" he asked, seeing the lumber scattered around the yard.

Millie tried to laugh. "I'm making some little chairs for the girls."

"What in the hell for?"

Millie ignored him to speak to Jeanne, who had followed Len out of the truck. "Hey, how're you, Jeanne?"

"I'm good, Millie. Looks like you're having fun. What are you making?"

"There's a home improvement contest. I'm making some little chairs to go with the big ones. Mrs. Roosevelt will be the judge."

"Looks to me like you're making a mess," Len said. "I need to go inside and use the toilet. Y'all talk about that dress."

"I'd ask you to sit down, Jeanne, but…." She tried to laugh nonchalantly, but only a brief "huh-huh" came out.

"That's all right," Jeanne said. She was wearing white shorts and a halter top. Annie looked up at her. "Hi, Miss Annie," Jeanne said. "Is this your baby sister? She's cute." Annie ran away and climbed up to the second rail on the fence.

"Get down from there, Annie," Millie called out. "She's really into climbing. I'm afraid she'll fall."

"I'll get her," Jeanne said. But when she approached Annie, the child jumped down and ran toward the barn.

"She's all right," Millie said. "Len will be out in a minute. He'll get her."

"I'll bet he's a good daddy," Jeanne said. "He said you'd make me a dress. Really, all I need is sort of a costume. Nothing fancy. Just a dress like you'd wear."

Millie looked down at the faded print dress she was wearing. "Like this?"

Jeanne laughed. "Well, no, not exactly. I was thinking of something like the women on Penderlea wear to Home Demonstration Meetings," she said. "Nothing fancy. I'll probably never wear it again."

"We're probably about the same size," Millie said. "When Len comes out to watch the girls, I'll take you inside and we'll look at my patterns. You'll have to overlook the mess. I wasn't expecting company."

"I brought some material. It's in the truck. I'll get it."

Jeanne went to retrieve the fabric as Len approached Millie. He glared at her. "The house is a goddamn mess," he said under his breath. "You're embarrassing me, woman."

Millie blushed, but she answered him back in the same manner. "That's not fair. You should've told me you were bringing Jeanne here."

⌣⌐

Millie brought out her patterns and set them on the kitchen table after removing the remnants of breakfast. Jeanne unfolded a length of the blue dimity with a daisy print overlay and held it up against her. "How does this look on me?"

"It'll make up nice," Millie said. "But you've got way too much. A dress only takes three or four yards. Maybe not even that much."

"I know, but I thought you could make the girls a little pinafore or something. You can have the one you make for me after the pageant. I know I'll never wear it again. Wouldn't that be cute? Matching dresses for mother and daughters?"

Millie looked down at the box of patterns. "Show me something you like. I can put two together if you want a different top on a certain skirt."

Jeanne looked through the patterns halfheartedly. "I don't care. You pick something. Len said you could make anything." She glanced around the messy kitchen. A greasy skillet and half-covered pots of oatmeal and grits littered the stove. "When do you think you can have it done?"

"I don't know. You might have to come for a fitting. I'll tell Len when I've about got it finished."

Jeanne pushed the pattern box aside and started out the door. "Just don't make anything with a lot of gathers at the waist. I don't want to look fat."

Millie thought she knew just what to make. When Jeanne and Len had gone, she looked through the patterns again and pulled out her least favorite. She didn't intend to wear a dress she'd made for Jeanne McAllister. Ever.

CHAPTER 47

Emily McAllister wasn't sure how she felt about her daughter being on Penderlea. Jeanne was flirtatious toward the men and standoffish to the women. It had not been Emily's idea. Jeanne and Sissy had met during the election campaign. Jeanne said they were always running into each other. "She knew I was from North Carolina," Jeanne said, and she asked me if I'd ever heard of the new resettlement project called Penderlea. "'Have I ever,' I said. 'My mother practically runs it.'"

"You didn't, Jeanne! I'm just a volunteer."

"Yes, I did, Mother. I told Mrs. Roosevelt that, too. That's why she agreed to come. She likes you."

"I think it was because she favors resettlement. Penderlea is about everything she supports."

"I know, but she has her pets. They're strong women like you."

"What about you, Jeanne? Are you one of her pets?"

"Not really," Jeanne said. "She's the queen, I'm a worker bee."

⌒

Sissy Varden was the opposite of Jeanne. Younger and more playful, Sissy was a hit with the rowdy crowd of single men and boys. They teased her and played practical jokes on her. She could get them to do most anything by pitting them against one another. "Who'll be the first one to get those chairs up on the stage?" or "Who's going to get me a big glass of water?" or "who's going to scrub that mud off the stage?" But experience must have taught her to keep some distance between herself and her protégés; she was seldom seen with them except at rehearsals.

⌒

Jeanne and Sissy established a plan at the beginning whereby they would spend their weekends in Onslow County. The first weekend, the two young women had arrived at Emily's after dark in time for a late supper. "Wow, this is way out in the country, isn't it?" Sissy said.

"Yes, it *is* pretty far out," Jeanne said. "But I assure you, you'd rather be here than in the little hick town of Jacksonville." She hugged the old Negro housekeeper whom she'd known all of her life. "That's because we have Nellie here. Nobody can cook like Nellie."

"You didn't always feel that way, Miss Jeanne," Nellie said. "I 'member you was a persnickety young'un."

"Well, I got over it, Nellie. I learned to appreciate you when I went away to school."

Emily rose from the table. "Let's go into the parlor. I have some nice sherry wine if you'd like a nightcap before bed."

"I'd prefer port, Mother. Sissy doesn't imbibe."

"Well, of course, there's port, Jeanne. What can we get for you, Sissy?"

"Really, I'm fine, Mrs. McAllister. If you don't mind, I'd like to go on upstairs and wash my hair and soak a while in the tub."

"Certainly, please do. Nellie has put out extra towels. Enjoy yourself."

"I'll be up shortly," Jeanne said.

Before she sat down, Emily asked if Jeanne might rather go out onto the veranda. "It's cool, but lovely out there. The wisteria is blooming."

They sat in wicker rocking chairs, looking out over moss-draped trees at Catherine Lake. "The lake is getting smaller, isn't it?" Jeanne said.

"I think you're just getting older. Things look so much larger when you're young."

"For heaven's sake, Mother, I'm not *just getting older*. The lake is filling in—getting smaller."

"Yes, I suppose it is."

"Rehearsals are going well. We've assigned all of the parts. Sissy thinks they're all a bunch of hicks, but she's whipping them into shape."

"What do you think?" Emily asked. "Do you think they're all a bunch of hicks?"

"No, not really. Some of the fellas are really nice and sweet. Len Ryan is one."

"Yes, Len is nice. You know his father, Tate Ryan, grew up over near Stump Sound?"

"Yes, I know the story. Maggie taught at the school. Uncle Reece fell in love with her. She jilted him to marry Tate. Then she had an affair with Uncle Reece and…" She was pensive a moment. "You know, I hadn't thought about it. Maybe Len was Uncle Reece's son?"

"Jeanne! What on earth are you talking about? Maggie and Reece didn't…"

"Oh, yes, they did, Mother. Amanda told me. She was there with them in Raleigh."

Emily closed her eyes and rocked back in her chair. The frogs along the lake seemed to scream at her *you're a fool, you've always been a fool*. "I'm a bit chilly," she said. "Are you ready to turn in?"

"You go on," Jeanne said. "I have a good book. I'll read in the parlor for awhile—give Sissy a chance to soak." She rose from her chair and kissed Emily on the cheek. "Good night, Mother."

On Saturday, the girls slept late, arising in time for lunch and looking for something to do. "How about the beach?" Jeanne asked. "North Carolina has the prettiest beaches on the East Coast."

"I'd adore the beach," Sissy said. "Will you come with us, Mrs. McAllister? I've got a rumble seat."

Jeanne laughed out loud. "That would be rich. Mother in a rumble seat."

"I wouldn't mind a bit, but you girls go on. I promised Darcy that I'd come to the store today and help him with the display windows," Emily said. "Be sure and show Sissy Lumina."

"That old fire trap?" Jeanne said. "It should have been torn down years ago."

"Yes, it's a little run-down," Emily said. "But it's a historical structure that I think we should preserve. It escaped the fire several years ago, but it might not the next time."

"I had in mind looking at some property while we're there," Jeanne said. "I miss the beach."

"Really? I never knew you enjoyed it that much," Emily said, stifling a memory of her chance discovery of Jeanne and Jon together at the beach house. She swallowed hard. "But look around. There's lots of building going on where the fire leveled everything."

"I will, Mother. Maybe I'll find a cute little cottage to buy and stay the rest of the summer. It feels good to be back home."

Emily had never understood Jeanne. Owning Wrightsville Beach property was the last thing Emily would have expected of Jeanne. Her daughter had never seemed to enjoy times spent there with Emily and her cousins. She was always running off to boat races with her fast friends—never lolling about in the beautiful cottage, or sunning on the sandy beach. Money was not a problem. Jeanne had her own money since college, and she'd managed it well through a broker in Philadelphia who came through the bank failure smelling like a rose. "Are you thinking about staying in North Carolina?" Emily asked.

"Heavens, no," Jeanne said. "But I think it would be fun to own a beach house again. Agatha and Mandy could come like they used to. We could invite the McBryde girls."

What is it with her? Emily thought. *Maybe she valued her previous life more than I thought. Maybe she feels guilty?* Emily had given up the beach as well as the friends she'd made in Wilmington because of Jeanne. As disjointed as it seemed, Emily recognized Jeanne's desire for a cottage as a sign of remorse—something heretofore unseen in her daughter.

⁓

Jeanne and Sissy returned late on Saturday. "We stopped at Paul's Place for hotdogs on the way home, Mother," Jeanne said. "Tell Nellie we couldn't eat a bite."

"Oh, that's a shame," Emily said. "I'm expecting Reginald at seven. I was hoping you two would join us for supper."

"Really, Mother, he is such an old fuddy-duddy. Please tell him we got too much sun. Sissy has a headache, and I'd really like to finish my book."

"Of course, dear, as you choose. But I won't tell him you called him an old fuddy-duddy. He would be so hurt."

⁓

After dinner, Reginald and Emily sat in the wicker swing on the porch. He slipped his arm around her waist and pulled her to him. "Too bad the girls couldn't join us, but I can't say I mind being alone with you, Emily."

"I was thinking the same thing," she said. "Would you like to walk down by the lake? We have a screened-in gazebo there."

"Well, I'd say that's even better." He took her hand and put it in his arm. "You're mine alone tonight after all, Mrs. McAllister. The gods are good to us." He took the steep steps two at the time and turned to catch her as she descended, taking her into his arms and planting a kiss solidly on her lips.

Emily pulled away and pointed up. "Sissy's room," she whispered.

"Oh my, we don't want to shock her," he said, scooping Emily up and starting down the path.

"Put me down, Reggie," she said, laughing softly. "You'll trip, and we'll both end up in the water."

He set her down gently. In the shadows, he kissed her again, languishing over her soft lips. "We'll skinny-dip," he whispered.

"No," she said, but she went limp in his arms, allowing him to kiss her neck, her throat, her cleavage.

"You are so beautiful. I want all of you," he said.

She wanted him, too, something she thought she'd never feel again. His maleness was hard against her, and she longed to touch him there, to feel his heat. "We'll go away—somewhere," she said. His hands caressed her thighs, slipped closer to the seat of her excitement. She arched back wanting more. He picked her up. The gazebo was only steps away.

⌒

Jeanne and Sissy did not appear until lunch on Sunday. "Darcy, Gardenia, and the children should be here momentarily," Emily said. "They're anxious to see you, Jeanne. To meet Sissy."

Both girls were wearing white shorts, revealing their tanned legs and shapely ankles. "You'll love Darcy," Jeanne said to Sissy. "He's a small-town stuffed shirt, but as brothers go, he's all right."

"Really, Jeanne, must you be so disparaging?" Emily asked. "Calling Reginald a fuddy-duddy; Darcy, a stuffed shirt?"

Jeanne threw back her head and laughed. "Mother, you're becoming much too provincial. You can't see the woods for the trees." She looked out the window. "There's the stuffed shirt right now. Let's go give him a hug, Sissy." Jeanne bounded down the steps and scooped up both her niece and nephew. "Auntie Jeanne is here, and she has presents for you. Go in and look on Grandmother's settee." She reached out for her brother. "God, I've missed you, stuffed shirt that you are."

Gardenia watched the scene disapprovingly. There was no love lost between her and her sister-in-law. "Hello, Deenie," Jeanne said. "I hope you brought some shorts. It's hot as hades today. You're going to burn up in that dress. At least take off your hat and shoes."

"You must be Sissy," Darcy said, extending his hand. "Since my sister has forgotten her manners, I'd like for you to meet my wife, Gardenia."

"See, didn't I tell you he was a stuffed shirt?" Jeanne said.

Emily appeared on the porch with her two grandchildren. "Come on in. The children are hungry, and Nellie says lunch is getting cold."

They all ascended the steps and Darcy and Gardenia hugged and greeted Emily. "Since when is Jeanne allowed to come to the table in shorts, Mother?" Darcy asked.

"Oh, go on with you. Nothing like that seems to matter anymore," Emily said, slipping her arm into his. "Jeanne is Jeanne. I can't tell her what to do."

"You never could, Mother," he said.

At the table, the conversation drifted to Jeanne's interest in beach property. "I know some people there," Darcy said. "I could take you around and introduce you to some real estate agents."

"Too late," Jeanne said. "I think I found the perfect cottage yesterday."

They all turned to look at her. "You did?" Emily asked. "You didn't tell me when you came home."

"Oh, Mother, you were all excited about old fuddy—Mr. Ashford coming. You wouldn't have heard a word I said."

Emily stood up and threw her napkin on the table. "Really, Jeanne, I don't have to stand for this. Reginald Ashworth is not an old fuddy-duddy. You have my word on it." She marched out of the room.

"What's wrong with her?" Darcy asked her.

Jeanne grimaced. "I think Mother's in love with old Mr. Fuddy-Duddy."

CHAPTER 48

Emily stopped in often to see Millie. She adored the little girls, and Millie always had a new project to show her. She studied the miniature Adirondack-style chairs Millie had made, rubbing her hand over the smooth painted finish.

"They're beautiful, Millie. Are you going to enter them in the contest?"

"I think so," Millie said.

Emily clapped her hands. "Wonderful! Why don't you put them out near the road where people can see them? The little chairs nestled into your roadside flower garden would make an eye-catching scene for the judges."

"I never thought of that. It would be sort of like window dressing, wouldn't it?" Millie said. They both laughed. "You always did that so well," Millie said.

"Thank you, dear, but you would probably have thought of it before Mrs. Roosevelt comes," Emily said.

"I'll get Len to help me move them out there when he gets home. There's a barnstormer in Burgaw today. Jeanne asked him to take her there."

"Oh?" Emily looked disturbed.

"It's okay. I didn't mind. They took Annie with them. She was so excited to see an airplane."

"Well, I'll help you," Emily said. "We can do it right now."

Each of them carried a chair to the roadside flower garden. Emily backed her car out onto the road and drove by slowly, first one way, and then the other while Millie rearranged the chairs per her instruction so as to make the best impression. When they were satisfied, Emily pulled her car back into the driveway and parked it. "That's perfect," she said. "The red verbena and blue ragged robins with the white chairs. Perfect!"

Millie hugged her friend. "Thank you so much, Miss Emily. Len would be so proud if we won."

On the drive home, Emily was bothered by something she'd seen at the project office. She'd been in the manager's office working out the details of the pageant program when she'd looked out the window and seen Len's truck pull up. He'd gotten out the driver's side and Jeanne had alighted from the passenger side. While Len started for the office door, Jeanne sauntered off toward the community center. They turned simultaneously, looked at one another—just a quick glance, but Emily was sure she saw both of them smile—a conspiratorial smile—a shared secret smile. She'd wanted to warn Millie, who'd told her that Len was at the cannery every night until late. But how could she? Millie was so vulnerable—so naive.

Len was popular in the community. She'd often seen him draw a crowd outside the project office. They'd stand around egging him on, listening to his tales of wayward bears and other wildlife, of colored folk and stubborn mules, of children lost in the swamp. He loved to talk about his heritage and knew so much about the early settlement of Bladen County. She'd found herself listening and laughing, too. Once he told about an uncle who dug a drainage ditch from Colly swamp to the Black River, only to find that the river flowed into the swamp instead of the other way around.

Len was funny all right—funny and charming. But there was a side to Len that distressed her. She recognized him as a ladies' man. A sharp dresser even in the most casual situations, she could always spot him in his white pants and shirt, a straw-colored Stetson cocked at a rakish angle. Unlike most of the other male homesteaders, he never came into the office in his work clothes. She thought he was bound to get dirty on his pump jobs, but she had never seen him in overalls or soiled work clothes. Instead, he'd step inside her office clean shaven with his contagious smile, bow a little in a courtly fashion, and ask her how things were going. His eyes would twinkle, and she'd wonder if he was flirting with her. Maybe that's all it was, a little flirting. Maybe that's all it was with Jeanne. And Mazie Rivenbark.

A hundred or more homesteaders and their families turned out for the final pageant rehearsal and the fish fry that followed that evening. It was a soft summer night, and the air was filled with the smell of hush puppies and fresh-caught fish. Around the stage, a score of men and women draped and nailed the bunting into swags and tails, while on stage the fiddlers practiced their rounds. A painted backdrop representing a vast wilderness of pine trees had been hammered into place. Millie recognized the art as some of Len's handiwork, and she wished she had a camera.

Sula Mullins beckoned her to a picnic table where she and her children had saved seats for them. "You must have walked. I could have picked you up."

"Oh, it wasn't a bad walk now that I have a wagon for Cathleen," Millie said. "The road graders have been out getting the roads ready. They're nice and smooth."

"Len should've gone back to pick you up."

"He forgot. It's okay. They went to see the barnstormer in Burgaw. He dropped Annie off. I didn't say anything. I needed to put the hem in Jeanne's dress. It took a little longer than I thought."

"As if you didn't have enough to do," Sula said. "She's up there now helping tack up the bunting. I've never seen her in anything but shorts."

"Well, she better wear this dress tomorrow, or I'm going to be mad at her, and Len, too."

"Can't say as I blame you. Seems like a put-down to have you make a dress like us po' folks wear."

"It doesn't matter. I just thought of it as a costume," Millie said. "It's right pretty as *house dresses* go. Want to see it?"

Sula hopped off the bench and peeked into a paper sack that Millie was carrying. "Hold it up for me." Millie shook the dress out for Sula to see. "Oh, a gathered skirt. Gathers make me look fat."

Millie smiled. "That's exactly what Jeanne said. But it's *just* a costume."

⌒⟶

The two women took turns going for hot dogs to feed the children. The babies played on a quilt on the ground while the older children climbed on a swing set. Every now and then Millie caught a glimpse of Len on the stage arranging things. "I haven't seen Len since breakfast this morning," she said. "He's so caught up in the pageant. Won't you be glad when it's over, Sula?"

"In a way," Sula said. "It's real exciting, though, all the attention we're getting. We're part of history, you know."

"I guess," Millie said. "I just wish we could do all that the government expects of us. Seems like Len and I can never catch up. He gets so mad at me if I forget to write something down in the book."

"Oh, you'll catch up, honey," Sula said. "We've been here a year now, and I'm finally getting the hang of it. It's kind of fun, really. Dan says he's asked for a larger house, one of the first ones that was built. It's on Garden Road."

"Oh, no. That means you won't be so close to us." Millie said.

"Nothing is that far away from anything. We can still walk over in the afternoon. The girls like your yard better than ours. When we move, maybe you'll help me plan some flower beds. I love yours."

"I've got lots of things I can share with you," Millie said. She was looking around for Len, but he was nowhere to be seen. "Cousin Maggie gave me some dusty miller and several clumps of yucca. By next spring they'll need dividing."

"That's real nice of you, Millie."

"Here comes Len now," Sula said.

Millie turned to see Len saunter toward them, a big smile on his face. Annie raced to meet him, and he scooped her up and sat her on his shoulders. "Hey, Millie—Miss Sula. Have y'all eaten yet?"

"The children have," Millie said. "We were sort of waiting for you and Dan."

"Oh, don't wait for me, shug. I'm going to be pretty tied up all evening. Did you bring the dress?"

"It's in the bag there. Tell Jeanne I'm sorry we didn't have time for a fitting. It fits me, so I'm sure she can wear it." She smiled sweetly. "Remind her that it's just a costume."

Len peeked into the bag, rolled it up, and put it under his arm. He took Annie down off his shoulders and held her hand. Then he picked up Cathleen. "C'mon, baby, Daddy's going to show his girls what it's like to be up on the big stage with everybody looking at you."

The women watched as Len headed off toward the stage. "He really loves those little girls, doesn't he?" Sula said.

"They love him, too," Millie said.

⌐

Millie had gotten a ride home with Sula and waited up for Len despite what he'd told her. One thing after the other entered her mind. When Len wasn't home by ten o'clock, she began to worry about an accident. She'd smelled whiskey on his breath. Maybe he was lying in a ditch somewhere? It would be better for Len if he was found by his own wife drunk in a ditch than someone who'd tell Mr. Harrell. But she knew in her heart why she was really going out to look for him. She thought he might be with Jeanne.

The night was quite warm, and Millie was wide awake. She tiptoed into the girls' room. They were both sound asleep. A light breeze blew over their tiny forms. How she loved those precious children. Len did too. She knew he did. She put on her garden shoes. They were thick soled and sturdy for walking across the fields toward the community center. By staying off the road, she would not be seen by anyone who might still be out. If Len should pass on the road, she'd duck down out of sight, run back home, and tell him she'd been in the barn—thought something was after the chickens.

The moon was full, a huge ball of light that lit her way along a worn path that had developed on the edges of the fields allowing homesteaders to get from one field to the other without going out on the road. When the road was muddy, as it often was, the path was used much like a sidewalk in the city. A drainage canal was the only obstacle. Any other time, a fear of snakes or other squirming varmints along the ditch bank would have held her back. But she pulled off her shoes and stepped gingerly into the cool water, waded across it, and came up on the other side where she stopped only long enough to put on her shoes. She walked fast, her breath coming out in huffs, more afraid of being caught checking up on Len than anything else. As she neared the community building, she saw trucks parked around under the trees. The smell of fried fish lingered in the air. Loud laughter and fiddle music rang out from up on the stage. Someone was calling the figures. Ducking down, she made her way among the parked trucks, careful not to be seen. When she came up on the back of Len's truck, she gasped. *What if he's in it—passed out, or—?* But she waited and listened for something, she didn't know what. Certain that the coast was clear, she put her foot on the running board and lifted herself up where she could see the stage.

Len's white shirt and pants stood out like a beacon. A tall and handsome figure, he was dancing with a woman in a blue dress. A blue dress with daisies on it. Jeanne laughed as Len spun her around on the dance floor. Len was laughing, too. Four or five other couples, along with the fiddler, were on the stage. They were having so much fun. Then Mazie Rivenbark appeared, tapping Len on the shoulder. Millie stepped off the running board when she heard voices. Someone was coming. She struck out again, more afraid than ever of being seen.

Millie was in her nightclothes, sitting on the settee mending Len's work pants when he came in through the kitchen door. He stuck his head in the living room. "I thought you'd be in bed," he said.

She didn't look up at first. "I wasn't tired. I had some mending. I was listening to the radio." She glanced up. "Did you have fun?"

"Well, it really wasn't supposed to be fun. There was still a lot of work to be done." He opened the refrigerator and poured himself a glass of milk. "Have you got any of those tea cakes left?" he called out.

"They're in a jar in the cabinet," she said. "I thought I heard fiddling."

"You may have. The boys were tuning up and practicing."

Len brought his milk and a handful of cookies into the room with her and leaned against the mantle. "Was anybody dancing?" she asked.

"What're you getting at?" he asked, whipping around to confront her. "Hell, yes, there was some dancing. When there's music, people like to dance."

"Were any of the womenfolk there?"

"Sure there were. Some stayed to help out. Nobody you know."

"I know all of the homesteaders. Who was there I don't know?"

"What in the hell is this, the third degree? I don't have to listen to this. I'm going to bed."

"Did Jeanne like her dress?"

He glared at her, but she knew she'd caught him off guard. "I guess so," he said. "She put it on." He picked up his shoes and started back to the bedroom. When he got into the hall, he turned around and came back, pointing his finger at her. "I don't like you questioning me, woman." He'd meant it as a threat, and she knew it.

CHAPTER 49

M rs. Roosevelt arrived in Wallace on the Atlantic Coast Line Railroad promptly at seven-twenty in the morning. Emily was among the dignitaries waiting to greet the First Lady when she stepped off the train wearing a white linen dress, white shoes, and a white straw hat. Eleanor Roosevelt was accompanied by several women, most of whom Emily had met in New York. As soon as she appeared, the crowd began to chant her name, Eleanor! Eleanor!

Mrs. Roosevelt seemed surprised by her reception and her popularity. She raised her hand and waved, turning from side to side to see all of her fans and to let them see her. "This way, Mrs. Roosevelt," Emily whispered, leading the First Lady toward the governor and other dignitaries who stood in line at the end of the platform. Several cars and highway patrolmen on motorcycles were waiting to escort the procession slowly down Main Street where hundreds of little children were waving small flags. Just as planned, Boy Scouts and the Fort Bragg military band led the parade.

At the Robinson house, Mrs. Roosevelt held a brief press conference to the delight of a few invited local journalists and national correspondents who had traveled with her on the train. One of the things the First Lady was asked was to state her views on resettlement. She nodded and smiled at

Hugh MacRae. "I think it is very necessary to get back to the small, well-cultivated, self-sustaining farms owned by the farmers," she said. "Mr. MacRae was the first to propose that we take unprofitable land out of production. Let's give him a hand." MacRae bowed and thanked her. "Good to see you here, Hugh," she said.

Emily broke into a grin when Mrs. Roosevelt was asked by a female journalist what she thought a woman's place in the world today should be. "It isn't a case of *should be*," Mrs. Roosevelt said. "I don't see how they can help being interested in everything. I know I am."

After the press conference, the First Lady was taken to the Coastal Plains Test Station at Willard where she was entertained at a lavish breakfast featuring North Carolina products, including grape juice, four kinds of berries produced at the farm, chicken, ham, potatoes, and tomatoes from surrounding counties. Cream and milk products from the test farm's dairy were in plentiful supply. Mr. Charles Dearing, the director, asked for permission to name a strawberry after Mrs. Roosevelt. After declaring that a bitter-sweet strawberry, formerly known as Berry #373, would now be known as the *Eleanor Roosevelt* strawberry, the director presented her with a heart-shaped box of strawberries.

After the breakfast, Emily directed drivers to load up their cars again for the short trip to the Penderlea Homesteads project. "I have a fan for you, Mrs. Roosevelt," she said, handing her guest a pleated fan from the Orient that Emily carried in her purse. Mrs. Roosevelt's face was damp with perspiration.

"Thank you, Emily. It is so much hotter here in the South in June," she said. She leaned forward for a better view of a pickup truck in front of them. "What is that man doing?"

Emily laughed. "Oh, that's Mr. Alden, one of the homesteaders. He's spraying the road to keep the dust down."

"Oh, for goodness sakes, that's not necessary. I've been in a little dust before," she said. "Tell him to move on ahead. He's slowing us down, isn't he?"

"No, not really," Emily said. "I think he's helping a lot. With this caravan of cars, the dust would really be bad."

"I just don't want anyone to think they have to pamper me," she said. "I came to see the farms. If dust is a part of it, so be it."

"I'll point out a few of the nice homesteads. This one we're passing now is particularly nice. It belongs to some friends of mine. Millie and Len Ryan. Millie made those chairs herself for their little girls."

"Please stop. I'd like to get a closer look." The First Lady gazed out the car window at Millie's roadside garden with the small chairs nested among the flowers. "They're darling, aren't they? White chairs set in a bed of red, white, and blue flowers. What could be more perfect and patriotic?"

"Millie will be so pleased that you liked them," Emily said. "I'll tell her."

Eleanor Roosevelt smiled. "I'll tell her myself."

⌒

A crowd of six hundred or more had gathered on the grounds of the community center to greet the first lady. Earlier in the morning, every inch of the area under the tall pines had been raked clean and fresh pine straw spread in bare spots and around the shrubbery. But when Mrs. Roosevelt stepped out, all she saw was a sea of happy smiling faces cheering and whistling, eager to welcome their First Lady of the United States. Seating for the dignitaries had been arranged at one end of the long platform stage, which was adjacent to the wide steps of the community center auditorium. The ten steps served as a tier of bleachers upon which the men's and women's choruses stood. A good breeze ruffled the American flag and the North Carolina state flag while the joint choruses sang "The Star Spangled Banner" and "The Old North State."

The pageant opened with the colonial scene depicting early arrivals to the province of North Carolina in 1771. Laughter erupted from the audience time and time again as various homesteaders acted out their parts. Even the governor had a laugh when a portly actor represented the early governor with his equally portly sister. Dan Mullins had been called upon at the last minute to be one of the settlers who had to deal with an unfriendly "adjuster" played by Dutch Van Bruggen. The second scene depicted Penderlea, first as a "shantytown," then turned into a "farm city" by a benevolent government, anxious to create a whole new life for its inhabitants. Len, Dutch, and Jesse had parts in this scene, and they played off each other like minstrel men. Most of the lines were sung by the choruses, first one and then the other, but Sissy and Jeanne stood on the sidelines ready to cue individuals if they forgot their lines, or when they began to ad lib beyond their limits. In the last scene, everyone was on stage to sing the final ditty, accompanied by a group of fiddlers.

Mrs. Roosevelt stood and led a raucous round of applause. Melvin Harrell took the cue to ask the First Lady to square dance while Jesse Alden made the calls. Within minutes, a line of Penderlea men formed to dance with her. The square dance went on for five or ten minutes before Mrs. Roosevelt, out of breath, reached for the microphone. "Please, this is so much fun and you have been wonderful, but I'd like to say a few words before we return to Wallace."

⌒

Len had looked for Millie the whole time he was on stage. She was nowhere to be seen. While Eleanor Roosevelt was talking, he caught Emily's eye. She raised her eyebrows and mouthed, *Where's Millie?* Len glanced to the left and the right. He shrugged his shoulders. Emily had seen him briefly before the pageant began and told him to tell Millie that their roadside garden had been selected for the home improvement award. He'd figured he'd see her when he was on stage. She'd be surprised, and maybe it would get her out of the bad mood she'd been in when he left. The First Lady was going on and on about community life—experimenting in a new way of living—what the country needs—small farms operated by owner-farmers. Len wanted to listen, but his mind would not hold still. *What if something had happened to Millie... to the baby?*

When Mrs. Roosevelt concluded her talk, Emily handed her a piece of paper. "And now for the winner of the best home improvement project. I'm pleased to announce that award goes to Millie and Len Ryan. If they will come forward, please." The crowd applauded while the First Lady watched and waited. Len watched and waited, too, but there was no one moving toward the stage. Everyone looked at Len. He started forward, still expecting Millie to meet him. "Mr. Ryan, congratulations," Mrs. Roosevelt said, handing him an envelope. "I understand that Mrs. Ryan made those lovely chairs in front of your home on Crooked Run Road."

"Yes, ma'am, she sure did," Len said, his face beaming.

"Well, I'm giving you this check for safekeeping. You tell her for me that she did a wonderful job."

"Yes, ma'am, I will. I sure will." Len bowed a little. "Thank you very much." Len accepted the check as the fiddle music started up again. The crowd began to clap and stamp their feet. Len bowed again and asked Mrs. Roosevelt if she'd like to dance.

"Well, one more round won't hurt, but then I must move on," she said, taking his arm.

⁓

After the last dance, Len and several other men escorted Mrs. Roosevelt through the woodworking and crafts shops, showing her furniture and other items that had been made by the homesteaders. Emily pulled Len aside and asked if she might show their home to the First Lady. "You better not," he whispered. "I don't know where Millie is."

"What do you mean? Is anything wrong?"

Len didn't know what to say. He wasn't sure if he should be mad, embarrassed, or worried sick. Millie had been sore with him. "I don't know. I haven't seen her," he said, wondering if Millie might not have come at all? *There'd be hell to pay for that*, he thought.

⁓

"We only have enough time for a few of the houses," Emily told Mrs. Roosevelt. "We'll skip the Ryans since they won the prize if that's alright with you?"

"Of course, dear. Whatever you say."

As they drove past the Ryans' house, the First Lady asked to stop for just a minute. She pulled a small camera out of her large purse. "I must have a photograph. I'll have someone do a painting for Val-Kill."

⌐

Millie saw the car stop. She'd pulled back from the window, stood behind the curtain, and watched Eleanor Roosevelt take a picture of her garden. She smiled to herself. She hadn't missed the First Lady after all. Len and Annie had been gone since just after breakfast. He probably didn't even notice that she wasn't there at the pageant. *Probably didn't care*, she thought. When he finally came home, Len wasn't sheepish like she thought he'd be. She tried to act as if nothing had happened, too, knowing that if she said anything, he would pounce on her as he always did. She swallowed the lump in her throat. "How was it?" she asked.

"You should've been there," he said, without looking at her. "Your chairs won a prize."

"I did? I mean, we did? What is it?"

"It's some money. Fifty dollars. We're going to need it next week."

"Well, that's fine. I'm glad I could help out."

He sat down at the kitchen table. "What's for supper?"

"I'll fix you something. Where's Annie?"

"She's out there playing with the cats. She said they missed her."

⌐

Millie warmed up some leftovers and fixed Len a plate. He hadn't said another word. "What did she look like?" she asked.

"Oh, she's not pretty," Len said. "In fact, that old drunk, Elmo Fartz, told her that. He walked right up to her and said, 'You're not pretty.' Mrs. Roosevelt turned around to him and put on this great big smile and said, 'You're drunk.' Elmo looked up at her and said, 'Well, tomorrow morning when I wake up, I won't be drunk, but you'll still be ugly.'" Len almost fell over laughing.

He was loosening up now, and she was proud of herself. All she had to do was *not* say anything to rile him. But she knew he was exaggerating. She'd heard her brother Harry tell a similar story, attributing it to Winston Churchill. "I could hear the music," she said. "How was the square dance?"

"Oh, it was great. The boys were up there doing the fiddling, and Jesse was doing the calling. Dutch danced with Mrs. Roosevelt. Then I bowed and asked her if she would dance with me."

"You did? What did she say?"

"She just took hold of my arm and I swung her around. You would of thought I was the president himself."

"I heard that Dutch sent a bouquet of iris to the White House last week."

"Oh, he told her he was the one, first thing. I wish I'd of done something like that," Len said. "But I'm sure she'll remember dancing with me."

"You could send her a letter," Millie said. "You know, thank her for coming and all."

"I don't think that's necessary. Jeanne said Mrs. Roosevelt had her own reasons for coming." He glanced off for a second or two, reflecting on his last statement. He did that when he wasn't sure he should have said something. "She didn't come just to see us, you know."

"Did Jeanne say that?"

"Say what?"

"Say that Mrs. Roosevelt didn't come *just* to see us."

"Listen here now," he said, agitated. "I said I didn't *think* she came here just to see us. You act so dumb sometimes. Don't you know anything about politics?" Millie hadn't answered, but busied herself with the kitchen cleanup, her back to him so he couldn't see her tears. *Why was he so hateful to her?* When he finished his supper, he poured himself a drink from his pint. He stood leaning against the doorway, the drink in his hand. "You know you embarrassed me today—not being there. I had to lie, tell folks you were sick. I didn't like that."

She stood very still, her back to him. "I didn't like what you did either."

"What in the hell are you talking about? I didn't do a damn thing to you. You walk around here with your ass on your shoulders most of the time, and you expect me to be all lovey-dovey. You're not even pretty, you know. I have to think of somebody else when we make love—just to go off. You know that? Huh? Answer me, damn you."

She turned on him, her eyes flashing. "That's the meanest, hatefulest thing anybody has ever said to me in my whole life." She threw the dish towel at him and darted out the back door, slamming it hard. She didn't stop until she reached the barn loft where she buried her face in her hands and sobbed. *How had Papa known? How had he known?*

CHAPTER 50

Jeanne and Sissy both took their time about leaving Penderlea. Unbeknownst to most of the homesteaders, a farewell party was being planned by some of the pageant crowd. Len had gotten word of it, and he intended to go. Millie wouldn't go, he knew she wouldn't. He really didn't want her to, so he'd kept it to himself. Jeanne and Sissy had taken a shine to him. They'd be real hurt if he didn't show up. Luke Padgett, the farm manager who'd taken Hank's place, had arranged for a fish fry on the Northeast Cape Fear River at a cabin owned by some Wilmington gentlemen who'd asked to be invited if there would be some unattached women present. Luke had assured him there would be, then asked Len to round up Mazie and some of her friends.

⌒

Millie was relieved to have the pageant behind them. She wanted to get back to a normal routine, but Len was in a foul mood at supper on Monday night. "The new school will be finished in September," she said. "Annie will go to first grade there next year."

"Annie go to school!" the child said excitedly.

"If we're still on Penderlea," Len said.

"What do you mean?" Millie asked.

"I mean I could take this damn pump business anywhere and make it better than I can here on this damn project. You think I like having to keep books on everything we do? I could take what I make on pumps, and we could have something instead of giving it all to the government. I'm just sick and tired of it."

"But we've got this nice little house, a farm that's going to get better when you have time to work it."

"Oh, I see. You think it's my fault that this sour soil won't produce a damn cucumber, much less a hill of corn?"

"I didn't say that." *Keep quiet, Millie,* she told herself. Anything she said would infuriate him. There were so many things she could say, like if he did what the farm manager had told him—plant some cover crops—turn it over a couple of times. "Maybe next year will be better," she said.

Len took a deep breath and sighed. "I guess my heart's just not in it. Nothing really belongs to me. I have no desire to get out there and bust up that dirt when I don't know how long we'll be here."

"Where else would we go?" she said. "Where could we find something as nice as this? We have neighbors—good friends who help us like we help them." Len didn't answer. He just gazed out the small kitchen window. Mad or melancholic, that's the way it went. He lit a cigarette, studied it, twirling the ash tip in a small brass dish. She wondered what he was thinking, but she decided not to push her luck by asking.

⌒

Rebecca's letter arrived the following day.

Vera and I are coming to pick you up on Friday. Belle and the baby are at Papa's and they want us to come for a visit. Tell Len I'm taking you and the girls off his hands for the weekend so he can sleep late.

Len never slept late, and Rebecca probably figured that, but it was her way of saying he wasn't invited to come along.

⌐

Junius Jones's old Packard rattled and knocked up the driveway, sounding badly in need of a tune-up. "While you're down there in the country, you ought to take this old car over to Will and let him do a valve job on it," Len said. "I can't believe Mr. Jones let you drive it up here sounding like that."

"Oh, it always sounds like that," Rebecca said. "He won't allow anybody but him to touch it. He's been a little under the weather."

Len lifted the hood and looked over the idling engine. "Turn it off and let me check the oil. I declare, it don't sound like anybody's raised the hood in a while." He pulled the stick, wiped it with a rag, and read the gauge. "Damn, you wouldn't of made it far without damaging the engine. I've got a couple of quarts in my truck," Len said. "Let me get them."

⌐

Millie put her suitcase in the trunk of the car and started back inside to get the remainder of the girl's things. "You can come and help me, Vera."

"Rebecca was afraid he wouldn't let you go," her younger sister whispered. "She said she knew how much he liked to be waited on."

Millie put her arm around Vera. "Believe it or not, he's been real pleasant about it. I think he's looking forward to some time to himself. Just doing nothing, you know?"

"Papa says an idle mind is the devil's workshop."

Millie smiled. She'd heard Papa say that many times. "And I'm surprised Rebecca could leave Mr. Jones. He looked so old when he was here at Easter. How's he doing, anyhow?"

"I reckon he's okay," Vera said. "He sleeps a lot."

Millie loaded up Vera's arms with satchels and a sack filled with diapers and clothes for the children. "We'd better hurry before Len changes his mind," she laughed.

The girls were already in the car. Len had poured the oil in the engine and slammed the hood shut. "Give daddy a hug," he said, sticking his head into the back of the car.

Millie turned to kiss Len on the cheek. "There's plenty to eat in the icebox," she said. "I made a pound cake for Papa, but I'm leaving some of it for you. I'll be back in time to fix supper on Sunday."

"I won't starve," Len said. "You girls go on. Have some fun together. I've got plenty to do while you're gone."

"Are you sure you don't mind?" Millie asked.

"Don't ask, Millie," Rebecca said. "You said he's liable to change his mind."

⁓

Belle McBryde had never been known for her cooking ability, but she tried. Rebecca, on her best behavior, decided compliments were in order. "This stew is wonderful, Belle. It's got something different from Mama's in it. What is it?"

"Bay leaf."

"Oh, I never thought about that. Did you pick that up from whatshis-name?"

"I didn't pick anything up but a bad time from whatshisname. My landlady always put bay leaf in her stew. Scotty loves it, don't you, darlin'?" Nine-month-old Scotty grinned just before he opened his mouth, allowing the pureed stew to tumble over his toothless gums and down his chin.

"I believe I'll go out on the porch and smoke my pipe," Rob said. "Annie, why don't you come with granddaddy?"

"I'll come, too," Vera said. "Let me know when you're ready to do the dishes."

"Mr. Jones loves my stew," Rebecca cooed. "I would miss him so much if anything ever happened to him," she said, fluttering her hands anxiously. Tears came into her eyes.

"What is it, Becca?" Millie asked. "Is something wrong with Mr. Jones?"

Rebecca pulled a handkerchief from her pocket. "Oh, I'm sorry, y'all. It's just that the doctor says he has some congestion around his heart. There's nothing he can do about it." She sniffed and wiped her eyes.

"That's what you get for marrying an old man," Belle said.

"Humph," Rebecca said, still sniffling. "At least he didn't run around on me."

"All men run around on their wives," Belle said.

Rebecca pushed her chair away from the table and stood up. "That's not true! Mr. Jones would never ... and Len doesn't." She looked at Millie. "Len doesn't, does he?"

Millie was taken by surprise. "No, of course not. I don't think so."

"Oh, listen to that," Belle said. "See, I told you. Millie has her suspicions, don't you, little sister? Don't say I didn't warn you."

"No. No, really. It's just that we have a lot of single girls who work in the project office. And you know Jeanne McAllister and this girl, Sissy, that the Resettlement Administration sent down to help, they're big flirts. They're leaving soon though. Some of the wives didn't like it much—all those rehearsals for the pageant, but I—Len would never. He just likes to flirt. You know him, Belle. He'd never—"

"Never say never, Millie. He zips his pants up or down just like the rest of them. He's good-looking too. Mark my words—"

"Shut up, Belle," Millie said, pushing her chair back so hard that it overturned. "You don't know everything!" She stormed out of the kitchen.

Belle looked at Rebecca, satisfied that she'd touched a nerve. "I'd say our little sister has some problems of her own," she said.

⌒

Millie had left the dishes for her sisters and filled the Jasper tub full of warm water for the children. "Mama's going to take a bath with you in Papa's big ol' tub. Won't that be fun?" she said, climbing in with them. The girls splashed and played while she chastised herself for her outburst. Belle hadn't said anything that wasn't true.

⌒

When she returned home on Sunday afternoon, there was no sign that Len had been there. None of the food she'd prepared for him before she left had been touched. There was no Sunday paper spread out on the floor by Len's chair, and the bed had not been turned back. With a lump in her throat, she unpacked their things, bathed the children, and got them into their pajamas. When Len came in around six o'clock, he was carrying a small white dog in his arms.

"Hey! I'm home, and look what Daddy's got you." He put the trembling puppy on the floor and watched their startled expressions. "Well, come on over here. Come see Trixie. He won't bite you." He scratched behind the puppy's ears. "It's okay, Trixie."

Cathleen sat in her high chair kicking her feet and squealing, "Down, down!" Annie picked up the puppy and hugged the little dog until he wiggled free and jumped down and hid behind the stove.

"How about a hug for Daddy?" Len said.

Annie hugged him while Cathleen continued to squeal with delight, toddling after the puppy, her bare feet making little pats on the linoleum floor. Millie retrieved the puppy from behind the stove and noted a yellowish puddle. "He's really cute, Len," she said, smiling at him.

Len leaned over her to give her a kiss on the cheek. He smelled good. "I thought you'd like a little doggie, too," he said. "He'll be company and kinda guard the place."

"Oh, I do like him. It'll be fun to have a dog. I've never had one." She handed the puppy to Annie. "You'll take good care of your little doggie, won't you? Give Daddy a hug and tell him thank-you."

"Thank you, Daddy."

⌐

The gift of the new puppy had briefly eased her doubts about Len, but not completely. When Millie heard through the grapevine about the fish fry, she was but one of the project wives who were upset. Many of the men had not come home until the wee hours of the morning. Some, not at all. Dan

Mullins was not one of them. "I heard about it Friday afternoon and told him it was alright with me if he wanted to go," Sula Mullins said. "But he didn't. Said he didn't like the idea that the wives weren't invited."

"Did they say that?"

"I don't think so, but none of the wives seemed to know about it. I guess Luke knew we wouldn't approve."

"I'm sure Len went, but he didn't mention it."

Sula looked concerned. It wasn't easy for her to cast a bad light on Len. "That's because he knew you wouldn't like it. If it was me, I'd just not say anything. Maybe he'll tell you about it anyway."

Millie never heard a word about the fish fry from Len, but at the next Home Demonstration Club meeting the word was out. Most of the men who'd participated in the pageant had been at the party, cooking the fish and catering to a crowd of men and women who included Mr. and Mrs. Harrell, Dr. Wolfe and his wife, one or two nurses from the health clinic, a few girls from the project office, and the two pageant directors. But the party had broken up early when Mazie Rivenbark spit on Jeanne McAllister and told her to get on back where she came from. No one knew what started it, but Jeanne had disappeared soon after and the unpleasantness had put a damper on the rest of the evening.

"My husband said it was just a catfight," one of the women said. "When he told Mr. Harrell what happened, he said Mazie was jealous of Jeanne right from the start."

"Why?" Millie asked. "I don't even like Mazie, but she's a lot prettier than Jeanne."

"Humph," the woman said. "I'm sure it had something to do with a man."

⁓

That man had been Len Ryan. No one had noticed Len take off his apron and step into the shadows following the spitting incident. He knew Jeanne would be sitting in his truck waiting for a ride. She'd asked him earlier that evening—not that she knew Mazie would insult her. That had taken her completely by surprise. It started when several of the women waited in line for the outdoor toilet, a wooden shack that stood behind the camp house. Jeanne had walked up to get in line when Mazie threw back her head and said, "Well, look who has to pee." "I thought that's why you rich girls were so full of it, you don't ever go to the toilet." At first, Jeanne looked startled and hurt, but Mazie kept it up. "I'm surprised you're still here with all us 'po' folks, Jeanne."

Jeanne's face turned red, her eyes narrowed, and her breath quickened. "What's your problem, Mazie?"

"You're the one with a problem, Miss Jeanne. You've overstayed your welcome. There's lots of people here who want you gone. One of the wives to be sure."

"What about you, Mazie? Why do you want me gone?"

"Let's just say you've upset the applecart."

"Whose applecart?"

"You know what I'm talking about."

"No, I don't, Mazie. I have no idea what you're talking about." Jeanne turned to walk away, but Mazie followed her.

"Don't you walk away from me like I was some trash," Mazie said, grabbing Jeanne's arm.

"Take your hands off me," Jeanne said, jerking her arm free. When she turned to walk away, Mazie spit on her. Jeanne stopped for a minute, then continued through the crowd that had gathered around them. When she passed Len, she said under her breath, "I'll be in the truck."

⌒

Len had never mentioned the fish fry or told Millie where he'd gotten the puppy. He couldn't. Not without telling her the rest of it. He didn't think he had anything to be ashamed of. Jeanne had asked him if he'd take her to Wrightsville Beach in the truck. She said she needed a ride and wanted him to see the beach house anyway. She'd planned to wait until Emily came to Penderlea on Monday, but under the circumstances, Jeanne said she wanted to get as far away as she could from Penderlea.

They'd stopped by her room at the community center and picked up her things before heading for Wrightsville Beach. On the way, Len asked her what had happened. "Just the kind of thing one might expect from her class," Jeanne said. "It had to do with you, you know."

"What in the hell?"

Jeanne laughed, gave him a dirty look. "Come on, Len. Don't play dumb with me. One of her friends told me she had a thing for you. I thought maybe there were two sides to the story."

Len was dumbfounded. *Do girls really talk about these things?* he wondered. "I don't know where she got that idea. I like to kid around with her, but she don't mean a damn thing to me," he said.

"Let's just drop it then," Jeanne said. "When are you expecting Millie back?"

A twinge of guilt shot through him. What in the hell was he doing making excuses about Mazie Rivenbark to Jeanne McAllister? "Rebecca said she'd have them back before supper on Sunday," he said, excuses bouncing around in his head as the words tumbled out. Searching for a different topic, he said, "How come you didn't want to go home—to Onslow County? Won't Miss Emily be wondering where you're at?"

"Not hardly. She's preoccupied with her own life." Len was taken aback. He'd never heard Miss Emily described as selfish or self-centered. Jeanne must have sensed his reaction. In the dark with only a faint light from the dash, he couldn't see her face. "Let's just say I felt the need to get to my own place. Mother's keeping regular company with Reginald Ashworth. I saw them necking in the gazebo one night," she said. "It was downright funny. My mother, the prim and proper Emily McAllister, necking with an old fuddy-duddy in the gazebo."

Len had asked her if that was the only reason she wanted her own place. "I need my privacy, too," she'd said. "Some of my friends from New York want to come down this summer. The beach will be fun."

"I want to take my girls to the beach when they're a little older," he said. "I love the ocean."

"Good," she said. "It'll be light in a few hours. We can spend the day on the beach, and I'll cook us supper. You can stay tomorrow night, too, if you like."

Len had given her a questioning look. "What?"

"Oh, come on, Len, I won't bite you. Millie doesn't have to know about it. You can still be home before she gets back."

CHAPTER 51

Jeanne's beach cottage was more elaborate than any regular house Len had ever been in. She said a decorator had furnished it as a model home on the new stretch of beachfront cottages on the north end of Wrightsville Beach. The old cottages with the wraparound porches like Emily's were gone now—burned to the ground in the Wrightsville Beach fire two years ago. Where the Oceanic Hotel had been, developers had moved in before the ashes cooled and started building.

Inside the cottage, everything was coordinated. There were coral and green striped cushions on all the chairs on the porch, the colors repeated again in the upholstery on the sofa. Large coral-colored tropical flowers were in the drapes and the carpet on the floor. Len thought all that flowery stuff would drive him crazy.

"There's a drawer full of swimming trunks in here," she said, showing Len into a bedroom that looked out over the tumbling sea. "Get a couple of hours of sleep and put one on. We'll go for a swim before lunch."

"Listen, Jeanne, I'm not going to stay," he said. "I've got some chores to do."

"Oh, sure you are. You're already here, and you may as well enjoy yourself. I told you, I won't bite. I'll wake you in a little while. You better have those trunks on next time I see you." She slipped into another room that also faced the ocean.

When Len woke, the beach cottage was deathly quiet. He peeped through the drapery and was blinded by the bright noonday sun. Reluctantly, he located the swim trunks and put on a pair. Glancing in the mirror at his ruddy complexion above snow-white shoulders, he wished he'd taken his shirt off like the other men when he was working outside. But his skin didn't tan. He'd end up looking like a lobster. In the closet, he found a loose-fitting shirt lined in terry cloth. After slipping it on, he checked himself in the mirror again. *I reckon that'll do*, he said to himself.

"I hear you stirring around in there," Jeanne called out. "Lunch is ready."

"Is it dinner time already?" he said, stepping into the living room.

"No, but it's lunch time up north. My, my," she said, giving him the once-over. "Don't you look nice. I'd have a grand time dressing you up."

"Look here now, Jeanne, I know I'm not a city-slicker like you." He smiled, his entire face lighting up. His smile was one of the things Jeanne had said she really liked about him. She'd also told him he was everything she'd ever wanted in a brother. Len wasn't sure how he felt about that. Jeanne was fifteen years older than him, but she sure set his loins to stirring. The way she looked at him sometimes, he thought the feeling was mutual.

"Come on out on the porch. I've got everything set up out there," she said. "I hope you like Eggs Benedict with crab."

"I guess," Len said, wondering what in the hell she was talking about. That was the trouble with women like her. You didn't know what they were talking about half of the time. He sat down at the small table covered with a white linen cloth. Colorful napkins that matched the stripes in the chair pads were folded neatly beside two plates brimming with sauce-covered poached eggs that looked as if they weren't cooked through. "Looks good," he said.

"Bloody Mary?"

"Who?"

"Would you like a Bloody Mary? It's a drink made with tomato juice and vodka."

"I guess," he said.

Len was sure he'd never tasted anything as good as the eggs and the spicy tomato juice. The closest thing he'd ever had to the sauce that drenched the eggs was Aunt Kate's homemade mayonnaise that he'd once eaten with a spoon until he'd gotten sick. It had not turned him against mayonnaise though, just made him crave it even more. Jeanne had refilled his tomato juice drink twice. "I might have to have a nap after we finish, but I sure am enjoying this, Jeanne."

"That's what it's all about, Len. 'Gather ye rosebuds while ye may.'"

"Mama used to say that all the time." Len thought about it for a minute. "What the hell," he said. "Let's go swimming."

Jeanne was wearing a white bathing suit with a short little skirt and a halter top that tied around the neck. He tried not to look too closely at her as she ran toward the surf, but he wondered how much longer he could resist putting his hands on her. "Last one in is a rotten egg," she called out. He ran faster to catch up with her, his heart racing more from anticipation than from the exertion. Once he hit the water, he was in another world, a childlike world, bobbing up and down in the salty water. He'd loved the ocean the few times Maggie and Tate had ventured there when he was a boy. Once they'd come with a church group to picnic at Carolina Beach. He and Will had played all day in the sand and surf. That night, Maggie had smeared Noxema over both of them, and he'd vowed he'd never get sunburned again.

When they were out in deeper water, Jeanne grabbed his hands, sending a thrill through him. "Let's ride the waves together, it's more fun that way," she said. Len laughed. This was one fun-loving girl—the kind of girl he loved to be with. Jeanne didn't wait for anything or anybody. She did what pleased her. She scared him a little—the way she didn't worry about how things looked or what was right. But that's what made it fun to be around her. Millie was so goddamned timid sometimes. He had to tell her everything. Even how to make love.

"Look, Len!" Jeanne shouted. "Look behind you! Porpoises! Aren't they beautiful?" Len turned to see four or five of the giant fish in succession arch themselves up and out of the water, then plunge into the frothy sea, over and over again. "They're playing—just like us," she said. Suddenly, she swung around and wrapped her legs around him from behind and put her arms around his neck. "Ride me piggyback. You'll be my dolphin."

Shocked by her weight pulling him downward, he struggled to free himself. "Wait, Jeanne, dammit, I can't swim that good."

But Jeanne didn't wait. Her breasts were hot against his naked back, skin to skin. "Sure you can," she said. She let go, floating away from him on her back, her bare breasts like two beacons in the murky water. She looked down. "Ooops! My strap came untied." Flipping over, she retied the strap and started swimming for shore. Len reached for her and caught her by the arm. "I'll race you," she said, pulling away. If the water hadn't been so cold he was sure he would have caught her and something would have happened when they reached the shore. Instead, they fell on the sand, exhausted. "That was fun," she said.

Len was looking up at the clouds. "I'd better put that shirt on. I feel some heat in my shoulders," he said. He didn't tell her where else he felt some heat.

"You won't get burned this late in the day. I'll put some lotion on you after you shower."

The thought of Jeanne, of any woman besides Millie, rubbing him down with lotion set his mind to whirling. What in the hell had he gotten himself into? *There is no telling what will happen if I don't get out of here soon. Another one of those Bloody Marys and I won't give a damn if it does.* "I'll wash off under the house. I saw a shower there," he said.

"Only cold water down there. Just rinse yourself off, and I'll bring you a towel. There's steaming hot water upstairs. It's much nicer." She cut her eyes toward him, smiling impishly. "Then, I'll put that lotion on you."

⌒

There were several bottles of lotions in the bathroom. Now that the shower had helped calm a few things down, his head was clearer. Len knew he should be on his way. He could sure as hell put his own lotion on. He unscrewed the lids off a couple and thought one smelled especially nice. In the medicine cabinet, he found a razor, brush, and shaving soap. *Smooth as a baby's bottom,* he thought, running his hand over his cheek following his shave. *Damn, this is what I call living,* he said to his reflection in the mirror.

Jeanne tapped on the bathroom door. "I've got a whiskey for you, honey. Want it in there?"

Honey? This is getting rich, he thought. "Thanks," he said. He opened the door and saw her in a white terry-cloth robe, a towel wrapped around her head. "I was just coming out," he said.

"Oh, I was just coming in—to put your lotion on," Jeanne said.

Damn, he thought, *she's really making this difficult.* "Already did. Found it right there on that little shelf." He took the whiskey she'd prepared in a tall frost-covered glass. "Looks good. Thanks," he said.

Jeanne led the way to the porch where they sat in two painted rocking chairs that faced the sea. From their right and just behind them, the last rays of sunlight cast long shadows across the porch. Len tried not to think about where he was or what he was doing, but he wondered if it was really wrong to feel this kind of peacefulness? He and Jeanne were just friends, that's all. He'd liked her as a person right from the start—the way she was so sure of herself—always laughing and joking around. *Like himself,* he thought. She really wasn't that pretty with her scarred-up face, but Len looked past that. Mama always said that beauty was only skin deep, and she was right. Jeanne was the most beautiful woman he'd ever known. Most of her beauty was on the inside. He thought this must be what true friendship was like. Of course, he knew he had no business being friends with Jeanne, not without Millie.

"You're awful quiet," Jeanne said. She put her bare feet and painted toes up on the porch rail, and her robe dropped open, revealing long, tanned legs.

"Must be all that swimming," he said, looking down at the drink in his hand. "What kind of whiskey is this? I've never tasted any whiskey this smooth."

"Let's just say it wasn't made locally." She laughed, pulling the towel off her head and shaking out her blonde curls. "Goes down good, doesn't it?"

"I could get used to this," he said, meaning not just the whiskey, but the whole shebang. He took a large swallow, almost draining the glass, and shook his head. "O-o-o-wee, I mean to tell you, that is good!"

"Let me sweeten it a little," she said, reaching for his glass.

"No, no, that stuff's too good. I might never get home."

"Oh, come on, Len. You need something to eat, and I'm going down to that fish shack we passed and get us some shrimp to boil. I'll fix you a drink to sip on while I'm gone."

"Well, alright, if you say so." He reared back in the rocking chair until he could get his long legs up on the railing. His mind was a blur, but he liked the feeling. No worries, no cares. *What the hell? I might as well enjoy it*, he thought.

She'd changed into shorts when she returned with his drink. "I'll only be gone a few minutes. You just relax, and I'll be back in a jiffy."

He'd wanted to protest, knew that he should, but his anticipation of that second glass of fine whiskey held his conscience at bay. He leaned back again and wondered why, when he lived so close by, he'd not been to the beach more often. Maybe he should rent a cottage and bring Millie and the girls. He closed his eyes and just let it all happen.

⌒

Len hardly remembered eating the shrimp. Jeanne had boiled them in a big pot on the stove, drained them in a colander, and dumped them out on newspaper on the kitchen table. She'd peeled a few for him, then told him he was on his own. They sat and ate the shrimp, dipping them into a spicy sauce she'd made with catsup, until he felt he might turn into one. She'd bought beer at the shrimp shack, and the cold, sweet taste of it was perfect with the shrimp. "I've really got to go now," he said.

"Maybe you should stretch out on the sofa for a few minutes," she said. "You're looking kind of bleary eyed."

"Sure, sure thing," he said, lying down on the sofa, tucking his hands under his head. "A little nap is all I need."

⁓

He'd slept until six o'clock in the morning. When he awoke, he was still on the sofa in his clothes. Jeanne was nowhere to be seen. *My God*, he thought, *I'll be a dead man walking if I don't get out of here.* He shook the sleep from his head and tried to remember if anything had happened. He'd sure as hell thought about it. Maybe even dreamed about it. She smelled so sweet, her hair brushing his cheek. Maybe a kiss—on his lips? But he remembered nothing else. Now, she was coming up the steps to the porch. She was talking to someone. He stepped into the bathroom and closed the door.

"Yes sir, Len's going to love you—those precious little girls, too." The screen door slammed shut. "You're so cute, I might even keep you myself." He heard a cabinet open and the sound of running water. Opening the bathroom door a crack, he watched Jeanne spread newspaper out on the floor and put down a bowl of water. "There you are, Mr. Trixie, but don't you piddle on my floor."

Len used the toilet and doused his face and hair with water. When he opened the door, Jeanne was on her knees reading something on the newspaper. He tried to appear nonchalant.

"Look at this," Jeanne said. "Amelia Earhart is in Khartoum. She's just flown over the Sudan. That's about twelve hundred miles of desert and jungle."

"What's that you got there? A puppy?" he asked.

"*Your* puppy," she said, laughing and tossing her blonde hair back.

"My puppy? But—"

"No buts about it. I got it for the little girls."

Len tried to hold it back, but a smile spread across his face as soon as the puppy ran to him and put his paws on Len's leg.

"See, he loves you already. Pick him up."

Len bent and picked up the little white dog. "What's his name?"

"Trixie. I'm not sure if that's a boy's or a girl's name, but the guy at the shrimp shack said that's what he called him."

"You got him at the shrimp shack?"

"Sure did. 'The last of the litter,' Pop said."

"I don't know, Jeanne. Millie might not—she might wonder—"

She stood next to him and kissed him on the cheek. "Millie will love him. Now you'd better get on home before Mother gets here."

Len thought he was going to jump out of his skin. "Miss Emily's coming here?"

"Not until after church. Darcy bought me a car, and he and Mother are going to bring it. They'll ride home together."

"I heard you didn't like to drive since—"

"I don't, but it seems like that's the only way to get around this one-horse town. I'm going to start taking flight lessons at Bluethenthal Field in Wilmington next week. I'll have to get from the beach to the airport every day. I guess I can handle that."

"You're going to fly an airplane?"

"I hope so. I'm going to learn how to anyway. Maybe I'll be the next one to fly around the world. Amelia Earhart says that everybody thinks she's crazy, but when she's up there in the clouds, it's like being in the hand of God."

He looked up in the sky. "I'd like to do that. You know, be up there in the hand of God."

"Would you, Len?" She grabbed him by the shoulders and hugged him. "We could do it together. Fly up into the hands of God," she said, wistfully.

Len backed off a little. "Do you know her? Amelia Earhart?"

"I met her once. She and Eleanor Roosevelt are friends. Mrs. Roosevelt wants Amelia to teach her how to fly."

"I'll bet the president will put the squint nibbles on that."

"Ha! You don't know the First Lady like I do, Len. She does pretty much what she wants to do."

"FDR ought to put his foot down."

Jeanne laughed. "You know, Len, I really like you. You are one of the sweetest, nicest men I've ever known, but you've got a lot to learn about women."

⌒

Len told Millie that he'd stopped alongside the road and bought the puppy from someone for a dollar. "He's pure Eskimo Spitz," Len said. Millie had never questioned him more about it, but in July he'd almost slipped up. Late coming home from work in the evening, he'd gone straight to the barn to feed the livestock. Millie had sent Annie to get him. "Mommy says come quick. The radio man say something."

Millie kept the radio on most of the day, listening to music or the news. Earlier in the day, she'd heard a report that Amelia Earhart's plane had not been heard from in many hours. She'd meant to tell Len when he came home, but as usual, he'd only spoken to her shortly before he'd gone to the barn. "Your supper is getting cold, Len," Millie said. "What were you doing?"

"Maude's got a lame foot. I was putting some salve on it. Annie said something is on the news."

"Amelia Earhart's plane is missing. They haven't heard from her and that guy she's flying with since they left New Guinea."

"Fred Noonan," Len said, turning the radio volume up.

"Who?"

"Fred Noonan, that's the guy she's flying with. Now hush, let me hear this."

The announcer had droned on and on about the missing aviatrix and her copilot. "Lady Lindy and her friend Fred Noonan left Miami in June on the first leg of a journey around the world, making it to New Guinea in twenty-one days. But the couple has not been heard from by a near-by Coast Guard ship since they'd departed for Howland Island, a tiny island in the middle of the Pacific." Len was mesmerized.

"Your supper's getting cold," Millie warned again. "Do you want me to bring it in here?"

"Yes, yes, bring it in here," he said, anxiously. "Keep those young'uns quiet. This is big news."

"I made a sweet potato pie for you. I'll get you a piece after you finish your supper."

Millie put the children to bed and went into the kitchen to clean up. The newscast was over shortly, and Len turned the radio off. "I was afraid something like that was going to happen," he said. "That's all Jeanne could talk about. Lady Lindy was going to fly around the world. She's taking flying lessons right now. Wants to be just like her."

"When did you talk to Jeanne? I thought she was at the beach."

Len ran his fingers through his hair. "Oh, she was. I mean, I guess she is." He yawned, shaking his head. "I think I'll go to bed. It's been a long day."

"I asked, when did you talk to Jeanne?"

"I don't know. When she was here for the pageant, I guess it was. You coming to bed?"

"In a minute," Millie said. "I have some sewing—some finger work I need to do. You go on to bed."

She sat in the living room for a long time, her sewing in her hands, her mind on Len's remarks. Stitches of love, Mama had always called her sewing. "They don't bear inspection," she'd say. Wasn't that the way love was? If you inspected it—looked too closely—you could see the flaws, even in the most intricate stitches. Len's flaws didn't bear inspection. Millie lay her head back on the chair, closed her eyes, and wished she didn't care. But she did.

Life returned to normal on Penderlea a few weeks after Mrs. Roosevelt's visit. Jeanne McAllister and Sissy Varden were forgotten by the time the strawberry season ended. But the project had received a lot of attention from the media before and after the pageant. When controversy developed between county and government officials over plans for the proposed new school, Melvin Harrell had to schedule meetings in the community center to accommodate the crowds of reporters.

Reginald Ashworth kept a car at the Willard train depot to facilitate his trips back and forth to Washington where he spent days on end at the secretary of the interior's office convincing government officials that the greatest deterrent to Penderlea's success was the lack of alternative income. In July, the Farm Security Administration, which would soon replace the Resettlement Administration, announced Penderlea as one of five resettlement projects in the United States to receive funding for a hosiery mill. With a loan of $750,000, the Penderlea Homesteads Association would buy land and build a mill that would be owned entirely by the homesteaders. Reginald Ashworth was ecstatic. He'd fought long and hard for this. Marriage to Emily McAllister would be his reward.

PART FIVE

The Boy

CHAPTER 52

JANUARY 1938—GUILFORD COUNTY, NORTH CAROLINA

From his window on the third floor, Colin Jackson watched the automobile turn into the drive in front of the Administration Building at Oak Ridge Academy. Colonel Dwyer had just left after telling him that a Mr. Cal McBryde was coming up to see him. Mr. McBryde had called from Kernersville to say he was a relative passing through and wanted to see Colin. "He said you might not know him," the colonel said. "But he wanted to meet you since he'd been to school here himself. Just to be certain, I looked him up and, sure enough, he graduated in 1923. Do you know him?"

"No, sir," Colin said. "I didn't know I had any cousins."

The colonel looked at the boy with amusement. "I'd just as soon not know some of mine, how about you?" he laughed, putting the boy at ease.

"Yes, sir," Colin said, thinking of his Aunt Clarice.

"Well, look sharp, now. You might like him," the colonel said.

⌒

Colin Jackson would turn fourteen in March. At least, that's when Hank Hudson decided his birthday would be. "Let's just say it's the middle of the month," Hank had said. Until Hank Hudson had come along, no one knew or cared. His old great aunt Clarice had held him bound in her home like a captive from the time he was three years old. Someone told Hank he'd seen a boy tied to the bedstead when he'd gone to collect some money from a woman who owed him. Hank had asked around until somebody said they thought the boy was kin to the woman, but his mama and daddy were dead. Hank told the sheriff, who got an order from the judge saying she was unfit to have a boy living with her. Hank said he'd take him because he and his wife didn't have any children and wanted one. All this time, Colin had been afraid his Aunt Clarice would come after him. She said she would. She'd yelled out to Hank in the yard that day that she'd find him and snatch him back when no one was looking. She was crazy like that, and Colin had been afraid of her then. He still was.

Miss Emily and Mr. Reggie told him he'd never have to be afraid of his Aunt Clarice again, but he couldn't help it. She'd burned him with her cigarettes and tied him to the bedstead like a hound dog and left him all day long with nothing but a Mason jar of water and a cake of cornbread while she went to work in Harold's Department Store in Burgaw. When she'd come home in the evening, she'd bring him candy and talk all sweet to him. Sometimes she'd cook a big pot of stew and untie his foot and invite him to sit at the table with her. That's when she'd get real prissy and act like he was company. She always had a bottle of whiskey at the table, and she'd pour him a little bit in a tin cup. When he tried to get up to leave the table, she'd grab his arm and jerk him back and say she was going to tie him to the table leg if he didn't mind his manners. She was scrawny as a jaybird, but strong. "You'll sit here like a gentleman until I finish my dinner," she'd say. Once he'd tried to leave the table when he thought she'd fallen asleep sitting up. But she'd reached over with her cigarette and stamped it out on the top of his hand.

Hank had asked Colin why he didn't leave. "Why didn't you run away?"

"I was afraid," Colin said. "I tried to get loose one time, and she came home and found me rummaging in the kitchen." He cringed, the memory almost as frightening as Aunt Clarice had been. "She tied my other foot to the bed and hit me on that one with an iron skillet. She said that would 'learn me,' and she'd break the other one if I tried that again."

"I wish I'd known about you before she hurt you," Hank had said. "I would've beat her to a pulp."

Aunt Clarice had told him that *nobody wanted him.* She said that's why she had to take him. *You're just a little bastard. Your mama was a whore. Don't nobody know who your daddy is. The devil wouldn't have you.* He could still hear her, still see those hate-filled eyes and that wrinkly old face, twisted and mean.

But Hank had told him different. He said Colin had people, who when they found out where he was, they'd *want* him back. *Want* him. That'd made Colin feel real good. The trouble was, Hank had to find them first. He'd thought he was on to it, just before he got killed. That's when Miss Emily and Mr. Reggie came into his life. They'd shushed Colin when he'd asked questions about it. "It's best not to go looking for trouble. You might not like what you find, son," Miss Emily said. She always called him "son." Colin loved that. If she was his real mother, it would make him the happiest boy on earth. Not that he didn't wish for his own mother. Her name was Patty Sue, and she made him call her that instead of "mama." He could see her now, dead as a doornail, her head split wide open. Mr. Tate had come, and he'd taken him home with him. Uncle Will had held him and made toys for him. Then Aunt Clarice had come. That had been the end of the world to Colin.

⌒

"Your daddy went to Oak Ridge," Cal McBryde told him. "You're a McBryde, all right. You may have your mama's yellow hair, but you are your daddy's boy. I can see it in your eyes."

Colin didn't know what to say. He'd been at Oak Ridge for almost a year then. Since Mr. Reggie and Miss Emily had gotten married, he'd begun to think of himself as an Ashworth. They'd told him he could change his name if he liked. He didn't have to be Colin Jackson anymore. He could belong to somebody. Now, this man Cal McBryde had shown up at Oak Ridge and told Colin that his daddy was his cousin and his best friend.

Colin stood at attention as he'd been taught to do in the presence of an older gentleman. He was ramrod straight and tall for his age. His blonde hair, shaved close over his ears, stuck up in a cowlick above thick eyebrows. He looked straight into Cal's eyes when he said, "My daddy's dead, sir."

Tears came into Cal McBryde's eyes. "I know that, son. I know that sure as hell."

"Aunt Clarice said if Davy McBryde was my daddy, he never laid eyes on me until the day he died. He killed my mama that same day," Colin said. There was little emotion in his voice. He'd told himself that same thing many times. He wouldn't let it make him cry anymore.

"I know that, son. Davy told me he didn't mean to. She pulled a gun on him." Again, there were tears in Cal's eyes. "Nobody really knows anything different. Only the two of them were there." He looked away, out the window overlooking the parade ground, trying to find more to say. "Davy wasn't a mean person," Cal said. "But he'd been hurt by all that had happened to him. I think he blamed your mama, but that didn't mean he was out to kill her."

"Was Davy McBryde an outlaw, Mr. Cal?"

"Yes, that's what the law called him. He was on the run. Escaped from the insane asylum up in Raleigh," Cal said, recalling vividly his visits with Davy. "They'd put him in Dix Hill with all those crazy people, but your daddy wasn't crazy."

Colin studied Cal. He wanted to believe him. "How do you know he was my daddy? Did he say so?"

Again, Cal was at a loss for words. How much did Colin know about the birds and the bees? How much did he know about Davy—about Patty Sue? Cal was afraid of saying too much. "I guess no one can know for sure who their daddy is, but if you favor somebody, it's a pretty good sign."

Colin relaxed, sat down on his bed in the dormitory room. Cal sat down on the opposite bed. "How did you come to know about me?" Colin asked. "Who told you I was here?"

"My sister, Millie Ryan. She lives on Penderlea. She's friends with Miss Emily McAllister."

Colin had been leaning on his knees. He bolted upright. "Miss Emily? *My Miss Emily?*" His brown eyes brightened, and he couldn't hold back a smile.

"That's right, Colin. My sister is married to Len Ryan. Do you remember him?"

"Yeah, sure. But I remember Uncle Will and Mr. Tate better. They were my mama's friends."

"Well, Mr. Tate and Will still live in the same place, but Millie and Len live on Penderlea now and they told me they want you to come to see them sometime."

Colin looked down at his hands. "Miss Emily said I shouldn't look back. I should move on, make new friends."

"That so? She seems to think right smart of Len and Millie."

"Miss Emily promised to take me to Penderlea at Thanksgiving. I have lots of friends there."

"I imagine you do, son."

There it was again. "Son." Cal had called him "son," like he was a real member of his family. Colin stood up and smiled. "Would you like to look around the campus?" he said. "We can invite family to eat with us in the cafeteria."

Cal stood and put on his Stetson. "That'd be great, Colin. It's been a long time since I was here. Went four years."

"Did Davy McBryde graduate from Oak Ridge?"

"No, he didn't," Cal said, a chortle escaping unintentionally. "Davy got into a little trouble even back then. He brought a pistol to school."

"My gosh! They'll expel you for that," Colin said.

"That's what happened," Cal said. "I warned him, but he was hardheaded."

"Did you know my mama, too?"

"Met her once or twice. She was a pretty girl."

"Hardheaded, too?"

"Don't know too much about Miss Patty Sue," Cal said. "After they were married, I didn't see much of your daddy."

CHAPTER 53

MARCH 1938

The sight of Emily McAllister's Packard coming up the driveway sent a thrill though Millie. Months had passed since she'd last seen her friend. In the interim, Emily had sent a note announcing her marriage to Reginald Ashworth. Millie ran to meet her. "Miss Emily, I haven't seen you in a coon's age!"

Emily got out of the car and hugged Millie. "You've put on a little weight, haven't you?" she said, pushing Millie away to look at her belly. "Are we expecting?"

"A little," Millie said, blushing and casting her eyes down. "Don't I look awful in this old dress?"

"You look beautiful to me," Emily said. "When are you due?"

"Not until July sometime." She looked away. "I'm not sure exactly when."

"Well, I'm glad it's you and not me," Emily said, laughing. "My life is so busy, I can't imagine how it would be if I had little ones running around." Emily was wearing a lovely blue dress and a matching lightweight spring coat. She removed a small hat that sat just above her forehead and threw it onto the car seat.

"You couldn't look more beautiful to me," Millie said, hugging her again.

"I've been to a luncheon meeting in Burgaw," Emily said. "I couldn't come this close to Penderlea without stopping to see you."

"I'm so glad you did," Millie said. "I made a wedding present for you. I should have mailed it, but I really wanted to give it to you in person."

"That's so dear of you, Millie. I can't wait to see it."

"Please come on in. The girls should be waking up from their naps. They'll be so happy to see you."

"No, you go on in. I've got some things in the car. I'll wait out here in the yard." Emily opened up the car trunk and pulled out two red Murray three-wheelers, one slightly larger than the other. She'd seen them in Darcy's store at Christmas and knew they'd be just right for the little girls. She'd planned to bring them at Christmas, but after a brief honeymoon in early December, she'd come home to find Jeanne there making elaborate plans for a large Christmas gathering with her cousins, Amanda and Agatha. The families had arrived en masse from Savannah and Atlanta almost a week before the big day.

Millie returned carrying Cathleen while Annie ran ahead. "Miss Emmy," the child called, holding out her arms for Emily who stood with her back to the tricycles.

"My goodness, look how you've grown," Emily said.

"I'll be in first grade when school starts," Annie said.

"First grade? I can't believe it!"

Annie held up six fingers. "I'll be this many when school starts." Suddenly, she spied the tricycles. "Look, Mama, tricycles!" Millie put Cathleen down, and she went straight to the smaller tricycle.

"Yes, they're for you and Cathleen," Emily said. "Do you like them?"

"Yes, ma'am!" Annie said, ringing the little bell on the handlebar. Cathleen stood by the toy and smiled at Emily.

"What do you say, Annie?"

"Thank you."

"Ta-tu," Cathleen said, without being prompted.

"We have this for you," Millie said, holding out a small quilt she'd made. "It's just a little lap robe, but it's full of stitches of love," she said.

Emily held up the lap robe with its small squares of pastel prints set in a star pattern. "It's perfectly beautiful! This must have taken you weeks to make."

"A lot of the women in my Home Demonstration Club contributed fabric for it. When I told them I was making it for you, they all wanted to help."

Emily hugged Millie. "Thank you, my dear. I will treasure it always."

They sat outside bathed in the warm spring sun. When the children had settled down with the toys, Emily told Millie about the Christmas gala. "You should see all the little ones. Amanda has two girls, and Agatha has a boy and two girls. My brother Reece would have enjoyed them so much," Emily sighed.

"Jeanne seems to love children, too," Millie said. "She's asked Len and me to bring the girls to the beach this summer."

"That would be wonderful," Emily said. "Maybe I'll rent a large cottage for Amanda and Agatha, and we can all be together at Wrightsville."

Millie looked down at her expanding belly. "I don't know. Dr. Wolfe said the baby ought to be here about the middle of July. I couldn't plan on anything until after that."

"I'll reserve something in late August," Emily said, making a mental note to look into it right away. Beach cottages on Wrightsville Beach were at a premium that time of year. "But speaking of the summer, I wanted to ask a favor of you," Emily said. "Colin is begging to come to Penderlea to see his friends. You know he was here quite a bit when Hank was alive. He feels like he belongs to the project."

"You'll bring him to see us? Wonderful," Millie said. "I'm curious about him. Cal says he has Davy's eyes."

Emily cringed. "I wouldn't know, but Cal told him of the possible connection," she said. "I'd hoped Colin could leave the past behind. There are so many questions that no one can answer."

"There'll be lots more as he gets older," Millie said. "Maybe it will help for Colin to have Cal to turn to. Cal saw Davy in a better light than most folks."

"That's a good thought," Emily said. She scooted to the edge of her chair. "Look, what I wanted to ask you was if Colin could come and stay with you a couple of weeks in June. He's asked to stay with one of his friends on the project, but they're people I don't know very well. I thought about you and Len. Maybe he could help Len with the pumps. You know, earn his keep."

"We could sure use some help," Millie said. "The pump work is mostly repairs now. But I'm sure he could help Len with the farm."

"Yes, that would be good. We could pay you for his board," Emily said. She jumped up excitedly. "It's just for a couple of weeks, but I know he'd be a big help."

Millie laughed. "I don't know, Miss Emily. I'll ask Len, but I'm already wondering where we'll put this baby."

CHAPTER 54

JULY 1938

Colin came in June and stayed most of the summer instead of the two weeks Emily had proposed. Len moved the washing machine to the back porch, and put a small army cot in the washhouse for Colin to sleep on. "That's what Jim Marshall did when his brother-in-law came to live with him," Len said. "It's like a little camp house. The boy will love it."

Colin was remembered on the project as "Hank's boy." Some called him just "the boy." But it didn't matter to Colin. He was at home on Penderlea, and before long, he was like a pied piper drawing other youngsters around him. When Len didn't need him in the fields to chop weeds or pick beans, one of the other homesteaders did. "He's a real hard worker," Len said. "I was afraid we'd have some trouble with him. One thing I don't need right now is trouble with a young'un."

But trouble did come in the form of some damage to the windows in the community center. "They say it's a bunch of boys throwing rocks," Len said. "Somebody said it was that crowd that Colin runs around with."

"Colin's never out at night, Len."

"You don't know that for sure, do you?"

"He goes to bed before we do," Millie said. "He's got that little radio he brought with him. I have to wake him up every morning. The radio is still playing, full of static by then."

"I can tell you don't know much about boys," Len said. "You let me check on him."

That evening, after supper, Millie got the children ready for bed while Len played a game of checkers with Colin at the kitchen table. Len got a big kick out of the way Colin had grown over the summer. He thought it was good for a boy to work up an appetite out in the field, then fill up on good country food. "I believe you've grown five or six inches since you've been here," he said. "Look at them high-water britches you're wearing. Miss Emily's going to have to take you to Mr. Darcy's store for some new clothes before you go back to school."

Colin was studying his next move. "Don't need much in the way of clothes at Oak Ridge," he said, absently. "We have to wear those scratchy old uniforms *all* the time." He quickly made his next move. "Beat you!" he said, in the same breath.

"Yes, you did. You beat me good that time," Len said. "Wore me plumb out."

"Oh, come on, Len," Colin said. "Let's play one more game."

"No, siree. I'm going out there in the other room and listen to Gabriel Heater. There's a lot going on in Europe," Len said. He stretched and yawned. "You go on to bed now. We're up early tomorrow. Corn's come in strong. I want to get it in before we have a storm."

"Yes, sir. I'll see you in the morning."

⟜

"I'll be out on the back porch," Len said when Millie turned off the bedroom lamp.

"I think you're wasting your time," she said. "He's sound asleep by now."

Len smiled to himself, remembering the fun he and Will had after Tate had blown out his lamp. *Mama had eyes that could see in the dark*, he thought. *But Pa was deaf in one ear and couldn't hear out of the other.* The boys had done things like smoke cigarettes. Occasionally, they'd gotten into Tate's jug of scuppernong wine. Mostly, it was just fun being up and outside when everybody else was asleep.

Len slipped out the back door onto the screened-in porch and sat down in a straight chair where he had a direct view of the washhouse. Once or twice he liked to have dozed off, but he didn't have to wait long before he saw Nick Alston sneak across the field and tap on the washhouse door. Colin opened it as he pulled on his shirt and overalls. They whispered and giggled, shushing each other. "You're gonna wake up Len," Colin said. "Let's go."

The moon was out and Len could see them go lickety-split across the field. He picked up the shotgun he held across his lap and went outside to the fence. He fired one time up into the air.

Millie came to the door. "Len!" she called out in a loud whisper.

"What?" he whispered back.

"You didn't—"

"Hell, no, I didn't shoot nobody. Just wanted to scare 'em. Colin will be crawling back in his bed shortly. You can count on that."

Len slipped into bed while Millie stood behind the curtain and watched out the window. "There he is," she said. "He's on the ground, coming back this way."

The next morning at breakfast, Millie dished up large platters of scrambled eggs and grits. Colin ate like it was his last meal. "Did I hear a shotgun go off last night after I went to bed?" she asked Len.

"Yep," Len said. "I thought I heard something after the chickens. Fired a shot, just to scare him off." He turned to Colin, who had his face almost in his plate. "You hear it, boy?"

"No, sir. I must've been sound asleep."

⌒

Len loved to tell the story when the menfolk gathered. "I'm sure going to miss that boy when he goes back to school. He's been right good entertainment this summer."

"You scared the shit out of my boy, too," Jesse Alston said. "He's been good as gold ever since."

Len would miss more than the entertainment Colin brought into his life. He knew he'd miss "the boy." Millie was always asking him if he wanted a boy, and he sure as hell did.

⁓

Millie's third pregnancy had not gone well. She was on her feet most of the day, and her legs and ankles swelled to twice their size. "You need to get some help," Rebecca said. "Your varicose veins are worse than Mama's, and she had thirteen children."

"We can't afford any right now. We're barely able to make ends meet. What little comes in has to go to the bank. I hate to talk poor-mouth, but with that last loan, we're four hundred dollars behind. I don't know how we're going to pay Dr. Wolfe."

"How's the Medical Association working out?"

"We started out paying into it, but Len and I get behind on everything. The clinic is really nice. There are two nurses over there most of the time. They'll treat most anything. Even know how to set a broken arm. Len had to take Colin there with an infected toe. We were afraid he'd get lockjaw."

"He probably had a tetanus vaccine at Oak Ridge. They give them in schools now."

"The project manager says we have to call Dr. Wolfe first to deliver the baby. He charges twice as much as Dr. Johnson in Wallace, but he's the first one on the Medical Association's list."

"Call me, honey. I'll come. Aren't there any midwives around anymore?"

"Not on Penderlea. Not unless the government says so."

⁓

Millie had contractions during the night, but nothing regular. *False labor*, she thought. *It's a little too early.* But as Len started out the door in the morning, she told him about the pains. "I don't want to worry you, but something might be about to happen."

"Well, is it, or isn't it? I can't sit around all day waiting for a baby to come. I promised Mr. Harrell that me and Colin would pull his pump and overhaul his system. He said he was only getting a trickle of water in the evening."

Millie thought it made more sense that the well had gone dry, but she didn't like to argue with Len. "Maybe Colin could stay with me today. He could go get help if I needed it."

"All right, but I was counting on him helping me today." If the truth be told, he thought, he was looking forward to Colin's company. "Alright, if she tells you, son, you run up there to the clinic and get that nurse, you hear?"

"Yes, sir."

"No need to come find me. I'm not much good at delivering babies."

"You want to know though, don't you, Len?" Millie asked.

"Sure, sure, honey. To be sure."

Colin was good with the children, who'd come to love him dearly. He'd crawl around on the floor with them and play like he was an elephant or a vicious tiger. They'd climb over him and pull his hair and his ears. Sometimes Millie couldn't stand the racket, but she was glad to have him there, especially today when she felt that her labor pains could begin for sure at any time.

The pressure on her privates was awful. Millie wondered if chickens felt like this every time they laid an egg. She was stirring a pot of cream corn when her water broke and ran down her legs and onto the floor. "Colin, come quick! Bring a towel!" Colin appeared in the kitchen door and stared at her straddling the puddle. "Well, go on, get a towel. Quick! The baby is starting to come!"

Colin was ashen, looking as if he was paralyzed. "Colin, get me a towel, and then you've got to go get the nurse." He gaped at her, then at the puddle spreading beneath her on the floor. "Colin, you have to go now!" At that,

Colin took off across the field. With his limping gait, he looked as if he was running helter-skelter. *Oh, God*, she thought. *Maybe he's gone crazy!*

Annie appeared in the doorway. "What's the matter, Mama?"

"The baby's coming out, honey. Go get Mama two towels, please. Right now."

Annie went into the living room and called to her two-year-old sister. "Come on, Cathy. We need to go get two towels for the baby. You get one, and I'll get one."

Millie could hear the children's bare feet slapping against the floor as they ran into the bathroom. "They're in the bedroom, Annie. On the bed," she yelled. Avoiding the puddle, Millie laid down on the floor and prepared to have her baby right there on the kitchen linoleum.

Annie appeared with a dish towel. "No, honey, mama needs a big towel. Please go get me a big towel." Annie darted out of the kitchen and ran smack into her little sister sending her sprawling on the floor. When the nurse opened the back door, she saw Millie writhing on the kitchen floor and the little girls crying at the top of their lungs.

"Millie, honey. Let me help you to the bed," the nurse said. "Dr. Wolfe is on the way. We sent for Len, too. "

When Millie got up off the floor, she saw Colin on the back porch. "Thank you, Colin. I'll be alright. You'll look after the girls for me, won't you?"

"Yes, ma'am," Colin said, his eyes full of tears. "I thought you'd wet your pants."

"Take the girls outside, Colin," the nurse said. "Everything's alright now. Just tell the doctor when he gets here to come on in."

Len was there shortly and found Colin on the back stoop. "I heard you ran all the way, son. Thank you for looking out after Miss Millie." Colin stood quickly and put his arms around Len.

"I was so scared," he said, sobbing. "I thought Miss Millie had wet her pants. When I was with *her*, she used to beat me when I—when I—did it."

Millie had prayed for a son, especially since Colin had been with them. She'd seen the bonding between the boy and Len. Not that Len didn't love his little girls, but things had been better with them all summer with Colin there. Len wanted a son of his own. She knew he did. This had been her chance to give him one. She'd wanted to wait another year or so before having a baby, but despite all of her efforts to keep Len off her when it was her time, nothing had stopped him once he got that look in his eye. One of the nurses from the clinic had come to Home Demonstration Club and given out what they called prophylactics. Millie had put them in the dresser drawer and told Len he was supposed to put one on when he felt the urge. "They're not going to want to put it on," the nurse had said. "But you just remind them that they'll have another mouth to feed if they don't." She'd been right. Len had tried it one time and lost his erection. He threw it in the commode and told Millie she could forget about those "damn rubbers."

⌒

Lucy looked like a plucked chicken when she came into the world. The other two girls had been chubby and pink, full of wrinkles and rolls of pudge. But Lucy, although fully developed, was long and lean, weighing only six and a half pounds. "She's a skinny little thing," Dr. Wolfe said. "You'll probably have to supplement your breast milk with a bottle. Get some meat on her before cold weather. She looks like she might be a sickly baby."

"Oh, no," Millie cried. "We lost my little brother when he was a year old. It like to have broken Mama's heart."

The doctor was washing up and packing his bag. "That was way back in the country, Millie. You've got the clinic right here within walking distance." He grinned. "That baby belongs to the government. She won't lack for a thing."

CHAPTER 55

E mily and Reginald Ashworth went all out for the gathering at Wrightsville Beach the last week in August. They rented a large, old, green-shingled cottage on the sound side of the island that would sleep twelve. It was one of only a few cottages that had survived the fire four years ago. Jeanne's newer cottage would accommodate the rest of the crowd on the ocean side. Amanda and Agatha arrived with their husbands and children early in the week. Belle and Scotty arrived midweek. Rebecca would come one day at the time as her work at the hospital permitted. Julius Jones said he preferred to stay at home. Because the baby was only six weeks old, Millie and Len would only spend the last Saturday night.

"Colin will be there, too," Millie told the girls. "You'll have so much fun playing in the sand. We'll build sand castles and catch sand fiddlers."

"What are sand fibbers, Mama?" Annie asked.

"They're these little buglike crabs that run around really fast over the sand." Millie ran her fingers up Annie's arm and made her squeal. "If you try and catch them, they burrow into the sand really, really, fast and disappear."

"Me! Me, Mama!" Cathleen said, holding out her arm to be tickled. Millie picked her up and tickled her tummy. "Those little crabs might go right into your little ol' borey hole. Right there!" she said, poking her finger gently in Cathleen's navel.

Years had passed since Millie had seen Emily's nieces. She'd never met their husbands or children. *So much water over the dam,* Millie thought. Agatha and Amanda had grown up with wealth, and the Depression had likely not changed a thing for them. There'd been no camp houses in their pasts—no resettlement communities. According to Miss Emily, Agatha had married well, just as Amanda had done. They had husbands who were educated—family wealth on both sides. But Millie knew it wouldn't make a bit of difference. Both girls had been so down-to-earth growing up. They couldn't have changed that much. Millie's sisters would be there, just like old times. Jeanne might be the only fly in the ointment.

On Saturday morning, Millie assembled the children's clothes on the sofa in the living room where she had set up the ironing board the night before. Len liked to sleep late on Saturday morning, and she knew she'd need every minute to get their things ready. Little Lucy had been nursed at five that morning and slept peacefully in a small crib next to their bed. Millie prayed that the baby would sleep another hour or so to allow her time to put the hems in matching sun dresses she'd made for the girls.

Rebecca had sent a box of beach wear and toys for the children, including blue and white striped bathing suits, a large inflatable ball, and two tin buckets with matching shovels. Painted on the sides of the buckets were happy children digging in the sand. Rebecca had also included a black bathing suit with a little skirt for Millie. "If I know Len," she wrote in her letter, "he'll have a pair of bathing trunks."

Millie had just gotten the coffee going when Len came into the kitchen wearing his underwear and carrying the baby against his shoulder. "She was in there fretting, and I couldn't sleep," he said, in an accusing tone.

"I'm sorry," Millie said. "I thought she'd sleep on awhile. I guess you want your breakfast."

"I do. I woke up perished. Soon as I finish, I'll go get Dan's car."

Holding the baby on her shoulder, Millie browned four slices of fatback in the skillet. She slipped in three eggs. "Do you want grits?"

"Yes, and a couple of those cold biscuits. I know you didn't make any this morning."

"I'll toast them in the oven," she said, juggling the pans with one hand. "That was real nice of Dan to offer us his car, wasn't it?"

"He owes me a favor or two."

"Will you leave the truck for him to drive?"

"I will, but if old man Harrell finds out about it, it'll be hell to pay."

"Will we get in trouble?"

"Damn if I know what he'll do about it. All he's got on his mind right now is that damn hosiery mill. A bunch of big shots from up in Pennsylvania have been down here all week talking about it. Reggie Ashworth was here, too. Harrell doesn't like Ashworth. I think Reggie steals his thunder."

"He'll be at the beach, you know."

"I know he will. I need to ask him a thing or two."

"When are they going to start building the mill?" Millie asked.

"They've got the land cleared. Supposed to start any day now. Colvet Lee and that Malpass fellow have been selected to go up there to Lansdale and learn how to operate all this machinery. It's real complicated, they say. Colvet said he'd be gone four or five months."

Millie opened her dress to nurse the baby while Len watched her out of the corner of his eye. "Sula said Dan told her that the association voted not to let anybody but Penderlea homesteaders work there," she said. "Dan said everybody in the world was going to want to come here and work in the mill."

"We'll all own stock in it," Len said. "Of course, that don't mean we'll have the last word. Harrell thinks he's the government's god. You better believe he's a stockholder. He put his damn dollar in the association pot just like he was one of us. That new farm manager did, too."

"What time do you want to leave for the beach?" Millie asked, deliberately changing the subject.

"What time can you be ready, is more like it," he said, giving her a sharp look.

"I'll do my best," Millie said, but she knew better than to give him a time. He'd hold her to it and be mad as a hornet when she wasn't ready. He was already agitated, and she hoped the beach trip would take his mind off some of his worries.

⌒

It was after two o'clock when they pulled into Jeanne's cottage on Wrightsville Beach. Millie had gotten further and further behind as the morning had worn on. She'd fried chicken and made potato salad while Len had gotten the car from the Mullinses and loaded roasting ears and butterbeans in boxes to take to the beach. She'd put a pound cake in the oven at eleven o'clock and it had not been done until almost twelve-thirty. While it cooled, she'd fixed Len and the girls a plate and gone to the back of the house to get herself and the baby ready. "I declare, it looks like you could be ready to go," Len said. He'd followed her back to the bathroom and was in her way every time she turned around. She'd felt like screaming.

"Watch the girls for me, honey," she said. "I'll put their things on the back porch so you can load the car." But he'd continued to harass her every five minutes or so. When she finally got the rest of her things together and was starting to the car, she thought of the dog. "Who's going to feed Trixie? She might run off."

"We're going to take Trixie with us. Jeanne wants to—she said to bring him." He stopped when Millie's jaw dropped. "She said she loves dogs. She wants to see him."

⌒

On drive to the beach, Millie's heart was in her throat. *When did he talk to Jeanne? All of the conversation about the beach plans had taken place between Millie and Emily,* she thought. *It doesn't matter,* Millie reminded herself. But her doubts resurfaced when Len drove straight to Jeanne's beach cottage as if he'd been there before.

⌣⌐

"Hey, y'all," Jeanne called out from the porch balcony on the street side of the cottage. "Wait a minute, and I'll get Colin to come help with your things."

Colin plunged down the steps two at a time. He'd left them reluctantly two weeks earlier, making them promise he could come for a few days at Thanksgiving. He'd been such a help to Millie, and she'd hated to see him go. "Miss Millie, Mr. Len! You brought Trixie! I'm so glad y'all are here. I've got a bunch of things to show Annie and Cathleen." He hugged Millie and shook Len's hand before running off with the girls and Trixie following along behind him. "Don't let them get near the water," Millie called out.

Jeanne was wearing a white bathing suit that showed off a deep tan. With her long blonde hair waved over her eye, she looked like a movie star. The suit Rebecca had sent Millie was a black stretchy wool with boy legs and a narrow belt to be worn around the waist. Millie had tried it on that morning and wished for something a bit more glamorous, while reminding herself that she couldn't look a gift horse in the mouth.

"Let me see that baby," Jeanne said. When she reached out for Lucy, Millie smelled her rich exotic perfume, a trademark scent she remembered from the pageant. She was sure she'd smelled the fragrance a time or two on Len's clothes "She's so tiny," Jeanne said, cradling the baby in her arms. A glint of tears appeared in her eyes when she looked up at Millie. "You must just love her to death."

"I do," Millie said. "She's like a little china doll. No trouble at all." She made a mental note to keep reminding herself that she had something Jeanne didn't have—three beautiful little girls.

"Well, I just may hold her the whole time you're here." Jeanne said, glancing at Len. "You did good, big boy. She's beautiful, just like the other two."

Len grinned from ear to ear. He looked so young and handsome, his ruddy-tan complexion a stark contrast to his white sport shirt. *Eyes on, hands off!* Millie thought.

Jeanne, carrying baby Lucy, led them up the steps and into the cottage, completely taken with the treasure she held in her arms. "Auntie Jeanne just loves you to pieces," she cooed softly. *If Len Ryan had thought he'd be the star of the show,* Millie thought, *he was completely mistaken.*

⌒

Emily said that Jeanne had insisted that the Ryans stay with her in the new cottage. Colin had asked to stay there, too. Jeanne said they'd have their meals, except for breakfast, at the big house on the sound. But Millie thought she would have been happier where Emily and her nieces were. As it turned out, Jeanne was the perfect hostess, doting over the children as if they belonged to her. She put Millie and Len in a room with the baby, and put Annie and Cathleen in her own room in a three-quarter bed next to her double bed. The room seemed more crowded than it should have been, and Millie suspected that Jeanne had bought the bed especially for the children. "You'll keep Auntie Jeanne company, won't you, girls? I get *so* lonely at night."

CHAPTER 56

The air was festive at Emily's house on the sound that evening. Reginald, dressed in an old-fashioned striped blazer and white trousers, presided over the evening as if he had been the patriarch of the family all of his life. Enjoying the repeal of Prohibition, he had tubs of beer iced down on the porch, and a separate refrigerator in the kitchen held dozens of bottles of wine. Emily organized the food preparation while the girls set up tables on the large wraparound porch.

"Doesn't this house remind you of Aunt Emily's beach house when we were growing up?" Agatha asked, to no one in particular.

"You can say that again," Amanda said. "Only there are a few more children around."

They all took turns holding Lucy so Millie could help in the kitchen. "We've heard who the best cooks are," Amanda's husband Tom said. "Let me have that child. I know a thing or two about babies." Millie was uneasy at first, having the baby out of her sight, but it seemed like such a big happy family. Before the evening was over, she knew she would feel as safe and comfortable as she might have felt in Rebecca's or Belle's home. Belle and Jeanne had taken up perches on the porch rail where they entertained the men in the family, including Len, who seemed to be swilling a bottle of beer every time she looked at him.

"Pass these shrimp around," Millie said to Belle. Under her breath, she added, "Make sure Len gets something on his stomach."

Belle took the bowl of shrimp and another of red sauce. "Bring some napkins, Millie," she called out as Millie retreated to the kitchen

"Stop ordering your sister around," Jeanne said. "She's been working the whole time she's been here. She peeled every one of those shrimp."

"Millie's not happy if she's not in the kitchen," Belle said. "Look at Len. Doesn't he look well fed?"

Jeanne ran her eyes over Len. "I'll say he does. I might have to take him for a midnight swim."

Belle was right up in Jeanne's face. "You'd better think twice about that, honey," she said. "You might have me coming after you!"

⌒

Reginald Ashworth cornered Len early in the evening. "When we get that hosiery mill at Penderlea, you homesteaders will be set for life. Every member of a family could be employed there, if need be," he said, putting his arm around Len's shoulders. "Another source of income in a family will allow you to work your farm and pay off your debt to the government."

"Yes, sir, I'm sure it will be a good thing for some of the homesteaders," Len said. "I don't believe I'll be working in the mill, but some of the fellows with sons who need work will find it mighty nice."

Reggie looked at him askance. "You had you a boy this summer, didn't you?"

"Yes, sir. Colin's a good boy."

"Might be nice to have a boy come live with you permanently."

Len was taken aback. "I don't think Miss Emily would allow that."

Reggie took a long swig of his bourbon and water. "You never know," he said, watching Emily approach them with a drink in her hand.

"Reggie, honey, we need to open a couple more bottles of wine. Would you mind?"

Reginald bowed, sweeping his hand to his heart. "Your wish is my command, m'lady," he said.

Emily led Len out onto the wide porch that overlooked the Intercoastal Waterway. The fishy smell of the marsh at low tide drifted in over the water. "I want to thank you for looking out for Colin this summer," she said. "The boy needs some guidance. You've been like a father to him."

"He's a good boy," Len said. "Colin is always welcome at our house."

Emily looked out over the sound. When she turned back, there were tears in her eyes. "I'm afraid that Reggie was not cut out to be a father. He does not always respond to a boy's needs. After what Colin has been through, I don't want anything else to hurt him."

"Me neither," Len said. "I've been wanting to take him over to Bladen County. Papa and Will want to see him in the worst way. But there's Mama, and she—"

"Don't, Len. Let it be. Someday, he'll go on his own."

After supper, Millie found Rebecca in the bathroom crying. "What in the world, Becca? Why are you crying?"

"I was just thinking that Mr. Jones *is* an old fuddy-duddy. I begged him to come, but he said *no*, there'd be too many people. I *love* these people. They're like my family," she sobbed.

Millie hugged her sister. "It's alright, Becca. You should just go on and have a drink or two and forget him this evening. He's where he wants to be, and you're where you want to be." She patted Rebecca on the back.

"He's just so *old!*" Rebecca sobbed.

The children chased each other all over the house, up and down the stairs, through the halls, in and out of the large rooms, their little feet thumping and pattering over the wooden floors. No one seemed to mind, least of all Emily. "Let them have fun," she said when Millie expressed her concern. "They'll remember this the rest of their lives. So will I."

When Millie woke the next morning, Len was not in the bed beside her. During the night, when she'd gotten up to nurse the baby, she'd found him sleeping on the porch in a lounge chair. She'd tried to wake him, but he'd shooed her away and said it was cooler on the porch. She wrapped herself in a terry robe Jeanne had put out for her, and bundled the baby in a light blanket. Jeanne's door was ajar, so she peeked in to see her sleeping children snug on the bed. Jeanne's bed was neatly made, but she was nowhere to be seen. Millie wandered out to the porch, looked up and down the vacant beach before assigning herself to an oversized wicker rocking chair stuffed with pillows. *They've gone for a walk,* she thought. Jeanne had said she loved to walk on the beach early in the morning.

The children slept until seven-thirty. Millie sat quietly on the porch watching the vast ocean tumble and toss as the tide moved in. She was thankful for the quiet time, although in the back of her mind the thought that Len was enjoying a long stroll on the beach with Jeanne McAllister poked holes in her composure. *Where are they? Have they gone swimming—maybe drowned?* She stood with the sleeping baby and peered up and down the beach. There were more people strolling now. Should she go down and ask if they'd seen a man and woman? *Foolish*—that's what they'd think.

The girls began to stir—little squeals of laughter as they bounced about on the soft bed. Annie appeared first. "I'm hungry, Mama. Where's Daddy?"

"I think Daddy's out walking with Auntie Jeanne," she said, not wanting her irritation to come through. "Let's go into the kitchen, and Mama will fix you some breakfast." Lucy was sound asleep in her arms. She put the baby on the bed and went to the refrigerator to see what she could pull together for breakfast. That's when she saw the note scribbled in Len's hand.

> *Gone up in the plane with Jeanne. Watch for us over the ocean.*
> *We're going to touch the hand of God! Be back in time for lunch.*
> *Love, Len.*

Whether from shock or irritation, Millie felt a wave of heat run through her. The thought of Len being in an airplane terrified her, but she was mad that he'd gone off on a lark with Jeanne and left her and the girls. The children couldn't take another full day of sun on the beach. They'd planned to ride the beach car down Lumina Avenue before lunch, leave early in the afternoon, and stop by Greenfield Park to ride the merry-go-round. What if something happened to him? She put her fingers up to her temples to make the thoughts go away.

"What's the matter, Mama?" Annie asked. "Does your head hurt?"

"No, honey. I'm okay. Do you want some scrambled eggs with grits and butter?"

"No, Auntie Jeanne said we would have muffins when she comes back from flying the airplane this morning. Did Daddy go with her?" Millie looked up and out the door. The sound of an airplane was unmistakable. They all three ran to the door. "Look, Mama, barnstormer!" Annie squealed. "It's Daddy and Miss Jeanne."

"Yes, I think it is," Millie said. "Let's go down on the beach where they can see us." She picked up Cathleen and followed Annie. If she hadn't been so excited, she would have remembered to be frightened. Jeanne was waving. Len sat right behind her, gripping the back of her seat. Anger welled up inside Millie. They were having so much fun. She thought of turning her back on them, going back into the house as if she didn't care. But she couldn't take her eyes off the plane, whose engine had begun to sputter when Jeanne had made a sudden loop to bring the plane back in front of the cottage. Several strollers had stopped to watch the small show. Someone shouted that the plane might be in trouble. Suddenly the plane tilted skyward, the engine straining—just as quickly, it nosedived into the ocean and vanished.

Millie screamed and ran toward the surf. The onlookers watched, trans-fixed. Not a sound was heard above the roar of the waves. "Do something!" Millie shouted, wading into the water, her eyes fixed on the spot where the plane had gone into the ocean. "Somebody, do something!"

"I'll go get the Coast Guard," a man said.

Suddenly, Colin, rubbing his sleepy eyes, was beside Millie and the girls. She grabbed hold of his arm. "Oh, Colin. I'm so scared. Jeanne and Len—the plane—it went down in the water."

"What?" Colin said, staring across the waves. "She said she'd take me." He stopped short. "Len's with her?" he asked in disbelief. Colin plunged into the surf.

"No, Colin, you can't! Stay here!" Millie shouted. "Colin, come back!"

"Look! Look!" a bystander said. "A man has floated up. He's trying to swim. The boy sees him. Somebody get a doctor."

Millie, holding Cathleen in her arms and Annie by the hand, waited in the surf as Colin pulled Len through the breakers. She was all to pieces and the children were crying. Several men in the crowd rushed to meet them. Len was white as a sheet and barely able to speak when they pulled him up on the shore. "Get a blanket!" someone shouted. Colin ran to the house and retrieved the brightly colored striped spread from Jeanne's bed. They wrapped Len in it, and Millie held his head in her lap while Colin embraced the children.

"Where's Jeanne?" Len asked dully.

"The Coast Guard is coming, honey. Don't try and talk."

Someone ran to the house where Emily and the rest of the family were staying. It seemed only minutes before Emily and Reginald joined the crowd on the beach. Agatha and Amanda soon followed. A policeman had arrived on the scene. "Mrs. McAllister, the Coast Guard is on its way. They'll do everything they can."

Len said he thought the plane hit the ocean floor and broke apart. He never saw Jeanne before he bolted to the surface. The next day, a diving boat came and a diver hooked a winch to what remained of the fuselage. Jeanne was not in it. Pieces of the wreckage washed ashore for days, but Jeanne's body was not found until four days later, miles from the crash site.

CHAPTER 57

Reginald had called Mr. Harrell to tell him about the accident. On the way home, Len told Millie that he'd been asleep in the lounge chair on the porch when Jeanne woke him and told him she was going to Wilmington. "She'd wanted to get some muffins for breakfast," he said. "She said she'd promised to take Colin with her, but he was sound asleep. I said, 'I reckon he is, it's only six o'clock in the morning!'"

"Colin was real disappointed," Millie said.

"Well, I guess he's damn glad now," Len said. "He might've been killed. I almost was."

"Don't get upset. It's alright," she said.

"No, I want you to know what happened. You're mad about it."

Millie turned to look out the window. "No, I'm still scared. Like you said. You might've been killed."

"Just listen, dammit," he said. "Jeanne said she couldn't wake Colin up—why didn't I go with her? I said, 'What? Drive all the way to Wilmington to get some store-bought muffins? Millie will make us a pan of biscuits.' She told me *no*, this was a little vacation for you, besides she wanted to surprise the girls. Next thing I knew, we were in her car going to the airport."

"You didn't get any muffins?" Millie asked, her suspicion getting the best of her.

"Hell, yes, we did," Len said. "We got muffins at the airport restaurant where the flyers get breakfast and all. I tried to tell her that you'd be mad as hell, but she said you'd get over it when Annie and Cathy looked up and saw us in the airplane."

"It didn't matter to her that I'd be mad?"

Len's face turned scarlet. He shook his finger at her. "Don't you say a word about that. All Jeanne was thinking about was the girls. She said she couldn't wait to see the looks on their little faces when they saw their daddy in an airplane."

Millie had seen the looks on their "little faces." It was sheer terror as they watched the plane dive into the ocean. She knew she'd never forget it. She was sure the children wouldn't either.

The Ryans were returning home only a day later than planned. Len had been taken first to Babies Hospital on Wrightsville Beach, then to James Walker Hospital where Rebecca had gone with the ambulance. Except for a sore shoulder and a cut on his forehead Len seemed fine, but the doctor wanted him to stay overnight to be certain. Millie and the children had stayed with Rebecca and Mr. Jones. Millie said she couldn't bear to go back to the beach. Agatha, or Mandy, she never knew which, had packed up their things in Dan's car and brought them to her.

⌒

Emily refused to leave Jeanne's beach cottage as long as Jeanne was missing. "Jeanne's left before," she said. "She always shows up again when least expected." But when Jeanne's body was picked up by a shrimp trawler, Emily collapsed. Darcy was the one who'd arranged for an elaborate funeral at the small church in Jacksonville, the only church Jeanne had ever attended. In the four-day interval while Jeanne was missing, word had gotten to most of her friends. Many attended the funeral, others sent huge floral tributes by refrigerated train cars.

Sally Forester, a representative from the First Lady's office, called to say she'd attend, and she'd like to say a few words on behalf of Mrs. Roosevelt. Miss Forester arrived an hour before the service and parked her Chrysler automobile under the large oaks that shaded the adjoining cemetery. Darcy watched from the window while one of the church deacons directed her to the parsonage. "She's driving one of those big cars like Mrs. Roosevelt drives," he said. "Got the top down and all."

Emily did not get up from the sofa where she sat with her husband. "Jeanne rode with the First Lady once. She said Mrs. Roosevelt loved to drive fast, too."

"I'll go and meet her," Darcy said. "Shall I bring her in to see you, Mother?"

"Of course, son, she's come all this way."

Darcy greeted Sally Forester at the door, bowing slightly in his genteel southern manner. Women from up north were always taken back by his southern hospitality, but it was as natural to him as walking across a room. "Thank you for coming, Miss Forester."

The diplomat laid a gloved hand in his. Despite the heat, she was wearing a dark linen suit and a crisp white blouse. Darcy wondered if she might be in the navy. Everything about her was sharp and creased, including the skin on her deeply tanned face. "You must be Jeanne's brother," she said. "I see some resemblance."

"Yes, Jeanne and I favored, but that's about the only similarity we shared."

Sally raised her eyebrows. "Oh?" The edges of her mouth curled slightly. "Mrs. Roosevelt sends her condolences," she said, presenting him with a picture of a small classical statue of Aphrodite. "She is so sorry for your loss."

"What's this?" Darcy asked.

"A statue to be delivered to your mother's home in a few days," she said. "The First Lady has asked that you place it in her garden."

"It's beautiful," Darcy said. "But please come with me. You can present it to Mother yourself. She's waiting in the pastor's study to meet you."

"Yes, of course, if she's up to it. I don't want to intrude." Darcy led Mrs. Forester through the dimly lit parsonage that smelled of musty furniture and lemon oil. She was an attractive, sporty-looking woman with sensible shoes and a no-nonsense stride. "Mrs. Roosevelt considered driving down herself," she said, "but the president is expecting her in Warm Springs in a few days and she was unable to get away."

Darcy stopped in the hallway. "Did you know Jeanne personally, Miss. Forester?"

"Yes, Jeanne was one of the girls. She was always the first one of us to volunteer."

"Really?" He opened the study door. Emily and Reginald Ashworth sat on a small settee engaged in conversation with the pastor who sat opposite them. "Mother, Mrs. Forester is here."

Emily rose to meet her, followed by her husband and the pastor, who excused themselves. "You are so kind to come," Emily said.

"Mrs. Roosevelt would have it no other way, Mrs. Ashworth. She sends her deepest sympathy," Mrs. Forester said with a slight curtsy. "I'd like to add my own condolences and those of all of Jeanne's friends in Hyde Park. We agree that your daughter was one of the loveliest, most unselfish women we've ever met. You should be very proud of her."

"Yes, yes, I am," Emily said, dropping to a chair.

"And she was very proud of you, telling us how beautiful you were—how accomplished. Do you have any idea how often ER is asked to go here and there for this and that?" she asked, throwing her hand up.

"Well, yes, I'm sure—but we—I never expected her to come to Jeanne's funeral."

"Oh, no, I didn't mean that. Of course not. But you must know that ER came to Penderlea because Jeanne convinced her that something wonderful was going on here and her mother was a part of it."

Emily stared at her folded hands in her lap. "We were estranged for awhile."

Sally stood, ready to excuse herself. "Yes, Jeanne told us. She was a very honest person," she said. "I'd like to say a few words at the funeral about her work with us, if I may, but I wanted to tell you personally, in case there was any doubt in your mind, that Jeanne came back to North Carolina to make things right with you." She reached for Emily's hand. "Penderlea—the pageant—was a way to become involved in your life again. The beach house was, too."

Emily rose to meet her, took Sally's hand, and pulled the woman into an embrace. "You are so kind to tell me that. I'd hoped it was so," she said.

After the tragedy, Len was a different person. When Millie took Lucy in for her checkup, Dr. Wolfe asked about her husband. "I'm sure he won't forget the experience for a long time," the doctor said.

"He's real quiet," Millie said. She was about to cry. "He doesn't play with the children much anymore."

Dr. Wolfe put his arm around her. "Give him a little time, Millie. When he gets back into farming, it'll take his mind off it."

But Len never really got back into farming that fall. First, he went off with his Uncle Nathan for two weeks, leaving Millie and the children to fend for themselves. When he came home, he had some cash that he put into their account, giving Millie twenty dollars for running money. Then he went with his uncle again and was gone almost a month. Each week, Millie received a letter with five or six dollars in it. He said he missed her and his girls.

CHAPTER 58

OCTOBER 1938

With his new wife, the former Emily Evans McAllister, at his side, Reginald Ashworth had become not only a political force on Capitol Hill, his name was on every social list for the season's most highly sought-out parties. Of course, Emily loved being a part of the social scene, but she was even more thrilled with what Reginald had been able to accomplish for the Penderlea project.

"We've been asked to dinner at the White House on November twenty-fifth," Reginald said when they returned to Onslow County in late October.

"Isn't that Thanksgiving weekend?" Emily asked. "Colin will be home."

"Yes, of course, we'll take him with us," Reginald said. They sat out on the veranda where tree frogs on Catherine Lake were producing a shrill cacophony lamenting the end of warm weather. "He's turned out to be quite a nice-looking little fellow since he's been at Oak Ridge. He can wear his uniform to the White House."

"Oh, dear, he may not want to go," Emily said. "He's looking forward to seeing his friends on Penderlea. He promised Millie and Len that he'd spend a night with them."

"No, dear, this is too important. Colin's history, the fact that his guardian was the first farm manager at Penderlea—that he lost his very life there—will attract a lot of attention to our little homestead project."

"I don't know…. I promised him, Reggie. I don't want to disappoint him."

"Trust me, dear. I have plans for Colin that include his friends at Penderlea. I've already talked to Len Ryan about it."

"You've talked to Len?"

"Yes, Len is quite the proponent for the new mill. I've enlisted his help."

"But Millie said he hasn't been able to get over the plane crash, over Jeanne's—"

"Yes, I know, dear. I thought this would help, and it has already. With his mechanical abilities, Len's a natural to work in the mill. We're going to send him up there to Lansdale, Pennsylvania, for training. He'll teach others. Like I said, he's a natural. You'll see," Reggie said, excited at the premise.

"He can't go and leave Millie and the children," Emily said. "They say these men will need to be gone several months."

"We'll get Millie some help. She'll be fine. This will put the Ryans on their feet for good. Len's all for it."

What is going on? Emily thought, stunned by Reggie's announcement. "How do you figure Colin will have a part in this?"

Reginald jumped up from his chair. "Ah, yes, Colin. By the time Oak Ridge is out for the summer, Len will be back home at work in the mill. Colin will live with them and help out with the farm. The sixteen-year-olds will get all the mill jobs the first year, but the following summer Colin—"

Emily was up and on her feet, too. "Wait! I'm not sure I want Colin to ever work in the mill," she said. "We've talked about a trip to Philadelphia in the summer. I have no objection to him helping Len part of the summer, but Colin has other opportunities available to him."

"A mill manager is nothing to sneeze at, Emily," he said. "He can work his way up and be the boss in a few years."

"I have college in mind for Colin," Emily said. "How could you not have known this?"

"I'm not convinced that Colin is college material," Reggie said. "After all, we're unsure of his heritage. We know that his mother was the worst sort, and his father was a cold-blooded murderer." He took a deep breath. "There is such a thing as eugenics, my dear."

"Reggie, really! We do not know that Colin is Davy McBryde's son. And, *if* he is, the McBrydes do not believe that he intended to kill Patty Sue. There *is* a difference."

"Be that as it may, my dear, you mustn't put too much hope into the boy's future. Let's give him lots of opportunity, but I'm not going to waste money on sending him to college."

Emily stared at him, enraged. *Waste whose money?* she thought. "Please don't mention this to Colin," she said.

"Right-o," he said. "There's plenty of time for discussion. I'm sure you'll agree with me after you've thought about it a bit."

Never, she thought, wondering why she had chosen to remarry. It was not the first time she'd pondered the situation. She had acquired quite a bit of wealth, and she liked to spend her monies without having to ask permission. She did not intend for a marriage contract to alter that.

CHAPTER 59

JANUARY 1939

Len left for Lansdale, Pennsylvania, with four other homesteaders. His expenses were to be paid by the Penderlea Manufacturing Company, and he would receive a salary of twelve dollars per week for the next three months. "Hot damn," he said, when they pulled out of Wallace at seven-thirty at night. "Don't nobody wake me up till we get to Lansdale. I want to be ready to raise some hell." The other fellows laughed.

"Colvet Lee said it was a one-horse town," one of his traveling companions said. "We'll be staying in a boardinghouse instead of some big hotel."

"I don't care," Len said. "I need a breather, and this ought to do it."

But the days were long and hard, and Len found out that the hosiery mill was a far cry from the kind of work he had always done. Closed up in a huge mill, the only daylight he saw came in through dingy windows. It was dark when he got off work, still dark when he went to the mill in the morning. If he'd wanted to go out on the town, there was no place to go. It was a mill town, and mill towns shut down at night while those working the next shift fed raw silk to the hungry looms. The incessant racket of the machines was deafening, reverberating all night in Len's head when he closed his eyes to try and sleep.

In Pennsylvania, Len had never been so cold in his whole life. Not even in Boston. Winter in Lansdale was harsh, the ground still covered in deep snow by late March when the four men left for home. As they neared the North Carolina–Virginia border, he saw the first signs of spring in the apple orchards—a faint glow that comes over trees when the sap starts to run. Pastures on the large horse farms hinted at green just beneath the dry grassy stubble. Len was so homesick he could die. The breather that he'd thought he so badly needed had turned into a nightmare. He'd had one head cold after the other working the looms that threw out a fine dust of lint. He lost weight. He missed Millie and his girls. He longed for home, the home he and Millie had built together. Why had he gone to Lansdale, Pennsylvania? He was a farmer—a good farmer. He hadn't been able to make it farming on Penderlea for all the same reasons some other of the men there weren't making it. If Harrell had let him do the pump work on the new project, he wouldn't be in this fix. He was just be damned if he was going to spend the rest of his days or nights in a dingy hosiery mill.

If Len thought that his days in Pennsylvania were long and lonely, they had been pleasant compared to Millie's. Nothing had seemed right to her. Tears soaked her pillow every night. When she heard the strains of "I'll Never Smile Again" on the radio, she was sure the song had been written just for her. Unable to keep up the quiet time needed to nurse a baby, Millie had put Lucy on a bottle. The other girls needed her, too, wanted her attention, cried for their daddy. With Len away, she couldn't keep up with the farm, the repairs, the constant demand of the animals. *So much for a whole new way of life,* she thought.

"You should never have agreed to this," Rebecca said. "Len should be here. You can't live alone—raise three children by yourself."

"I don't have much choice," Millie said. "Please don't worry about me. Len will be home soon. The money's been good. Look, I ordered new shoes for Lucy. She's standing now. Dr. Wolfe said she needed hard soles on her shoes."

"How's her breathing?" Rebecca asked, inclining her head close to the child's chest. "Asthma is hard to treat. They don't know what causes it."

"I'm up with her sometimes at night. We walk out on the back porch. The cold air quiets her right down."

"The other girls, are they doing okay?"

"Annie and Cathleen are fine. Just fine. They miss their daddy, but they are fine," Millie said.

Rebecca was pensive, concerned about the children. "When he comes home and goes to work in the mill, what will you do then?"

"Len says he's not going to work in the mill full-time. He intends to farm." Millie lowered her eyes. "In his letter last week, he said if it doesn't work out, we might go back to Bladen County—live with Cousin Maggie and Mr. Tate until he can build us a house. He said he misses having his land—knowing that it's his. He says he hates the way the government is always on his back."

"My God, Millie. Don't let Len take you back there. No electricity, no running water. You can't go back. Think about the children."

"Papa is there. I miss him. He needs me," Millie said.

"Belle is with Papa. You don't have to go back for Papa. He wouldn't want that, honey."

"I know," Millie said. There were tears in her eyes. "I want Len to be happy. He hated the mill in Pennsylvania. He doesn't think he's going to like coming back to Penderlea either."

Rebecca sidled closer to her on the sofa. "Look, honey, there's a war coming. Everybody says so. Adolf Hitler wants to be rid of all the Jews in Germany. Some of them are coming to Wilmington. The paper says that a rich Jewish man has bought that old farm colony called Van Eeden from Mr. MacRae. He's going to set them up with ten-acre farms and a Guernsey cow. Van Eeden's not five miles from here. Maybe that will mean some pump work for Len."

"I don't know what he'll do, Becca. Right now, Len feels like a failure."

"Make him stay, honey," Rebecca said. "Anything would be better than going back to Bladen County. You'd end up waiting on the Ryans, living from hand to mouth. Nobody over there has any money."

After Rebecca had gone back to Wilmington, Millie looked around at the simple cottage. It was far better than anything the Ryans had. The government furniture, some of it made right there on Penderlea, was sturdy, with durable cushions in a pretty dark green fabric. Millie had oiled the wooden frames and the tables every week, polishing them until they gleamed. She'd made curtains to cover the bottom half of the double windows from a bright flowered fabric that Rebecca had given her. There were pillows to match in the corners of the sofa. The girls had beds covered in bright quilts, pretty curtains on their windows. They had good mattresses on all the beds, not the corn-husk-and-feather combination back home. If they left Penderlea, they'd have to leave everything behind—along with their hopes for a better life.

CHAPTER 60

W alking up the driveway to the house on Crooked Run Road, Len felt like he'd been gone a year instead of three months. Mr. Harrell had met the men at the bus station in Wallace, brought them back to Penderlea, and dropped them off at their homes. Everything looked different, unfamiliar, like it belonged to someone else. But when he saw the girls at the window waving to him, Len picked up his pace. Millie met him at the door. "Welcome home, Daddy," she said.

"Hey, Mama," he said, kissing her on the cheek and giving her a little hug. "Mmmhmm, Daddy sure is glad to be home." Annie and Cathleen were right behind her. "Well, lookie-here how Daddy's girls have grown." He squatted down to hug them, one in each arm. "How about a big ol' hug for the papa bear," he said, nuzzling them with his scruffy beard. They squealed and pulled away, running to hop up on the sofa.

"Daddy's a bear," Annie said, squirming deeper into the cushions.

Cathleen backed away. "No, bear, Daddy!" she said.

"Daddy's not a bear," Millie said, trying to ward off trouble. "But I bet Daddy's hungry as a bear. When did you last eat, Len?"

He hung his coat and hat on a hook near the door. "We stopped in Raleigh, and I got something in the bus station. That was five or six hours ago. I'm about perished."

"How does fried chicken sound? I made rice and gravy. There's biscuits, too."

"Oh, honey, it sounds too good to be true. I might not even wait for the blessing," he laughed.

"Well, it's ready. The baby is asleep. If it's alright with you, I'm not going to wake her. You can give her a hug in the morning."

They sat down for supper in the small kitchen, the girls giggling and showing off for him. "Straighten up now," Millie said. "Daddy's going to think you forgot your manners while he was gone." She was so happy, she was about to cry. Nothing was going to spoil it.

"Daddy's just so glad to be home," Len said, sopping up gravy with a biscuit. "I brought all my girls a little present. If you're finished, Annie, go get my satchel and bring it to Daddy."

Annie hopped down out of her chair and ran into the living room. "She can't carry that heavy bag, Len," Millie said.

"Yes, I can," Annie said, dragging the satchel across the floor. "May I open it, Daddy?" Annie asked.

"You sure can. What I brought you is right on top."

Annie struggled with the catch on the satchel. Cathleen ran to help. "I've got it," the older child said, pushing Cathleen away. "Daddy said for me to do it."

"Alright, now," Millie said. "No fussing. Daddy might go back to Pennsylvania."

"Not in a million years," Len said. He opened his suitcase and retrieved a box of chocolate-covered cherries for Millie and a small brown paper sack of penny candies for the children. Annie dumped the contents of the bag onto the table. There were tiny wax bottles filled with orange liquid, packets of Mary Janes and Tootsie Rolls. Len smiled at Millie, his eyes glistening. "It's not much, but it comes with a lot of love," he said.

Len had dozed in the chair in the living room while Millie put the children to bed and cleaned up the kitchen. She stood in the doorway drying her hands on a dish towel. "I know you're tired. Would you like to go on to bed or sit in here and talk?" she asked.

"What I'd like is a drink of whiskey, but I'm too tired to go out and find some," Len said. "I reckon we might as well go on to bed."

She'd expected he'd want a drink, just as she'd expected him to want the other. They undressed in the half-light cast by the bathroom light from the hall. Len peeked at the baby, who turned and looked at him when he touched her. He patted her bottom. "Nice baby, go back to sleep now." Lucy did so without another sound. He chuckled under his breath. "Better to let a sleeping dog lie," he whispered.

Millie reached into a drawer and pulled out a small package. "Dr. Wolfe's nurse said for you to use this."

"What'n the hell?" He took the package and threw it across the room. "I've been gone from my wife for three months and this is the reception I get? The damn government telling me to use a damn rubber?"

"Len, you'll wake the baby. Please don't. The nurse just said it was a good idea."

"I don't give a damn what she said, or what the government says anymore." He picked up a pack of cigarettes and stomped out of the room. "I'm sick of Penderlea. I'm sick and tired of all of it."

Millie knew then that it was just a matter of time before they'd leave. But the next morning, he told her that he'd give it another year, but it would be on his terms.

⁓

Reginald Ashworth was furious when Len told him that he did not want to work in the mill. "You must, Len. We've spent money training you. You have an obligation to the corporation."

"I earned my pay in Lansdale," he said. "I won't give it back."

"That's not the point," Reggie said. "We need men of your caliber to teach the others. Now that the mill is in operation, we have to keep it running. You'll set a bad example."

"Alright, I'll work the afternoon shift, but not until I get my cucumbers and potatoes planted," Len said. "The farm manager has talked us into raising turkeys. He's bringing the poults the end of the week. Millie says she can do most of it, but I've got to build a pen and a shelter."

"Your wife has enough to do, raising three children," Reggie said. "You ought to work full-time at the mill and earn enough to make your payments. I've asked Colin to help you this summer."

"Look here, now, Mr. Government Man. I don't like you or nobody telling me what to do. Colin's just another mouth to feed." It wasn't true. Len loved Colin. He'd found him to be a willing helper, a good boy—all the things he wanted in a son.

Reginald Ashworth backed away, afraid of the look in Len's eyes. "You misunderstand, Len. I'm just trying to help. Colin is practically kin to you, so Emily tells me. I thought you might want to help bring him up."

"What in the hell are you talking about?" Len shouted. "Miss Emily said she wanted to raise that boy. I know her. She wouldn't have it any other way." He looked hard at Reginald Ashworth. "You wouldn't be trying to get rid of him, would you?"

CHAPTER 61

The summer of 1939 passed quickly with Len at work afternoons and evenings at the mill. Millie had picked up many of the chores at home that Len had always done. Colin McBryde had come and stayed with them only three weeks before Emily McAllister took him on a monthlong tour of New York and Philadelphia that ended at Split Rock Lodge in the Pocono Mountains of Pennsylvania. They were talking about colleges now. When he left, Millie had felt as close to Colin as to one of her brothers. He'd taken her aside one day and said he wanted to ask her a "personal question."

"Of course, Colin," she'd said, afraid of what it might be.

"Do you think Cal or anybody in the family would mind if I use my daddy's name? I'd like to call myself Colin McBryde. That's who I am, isn't it?" Millie had hugged him and told him that she knew that Cal—that everybody in the McBryde family—would be proud to call him a McBryde.

⌒

Working only part time at the mill, Len had moderate success with truck crops that summer. The cucumbers and potatoes had done better than he'd expected. The soil was conditioned now, enriched by manure and the plowing under of crop after crop of beans and peas. He wasn't happy with the farm manager's insistence that he raise turkeys. Turkeys weren't like chickens. You couldn't just let them pick at bugs in the grass. Len had to haul wood shavings from the wood shop for their litter, and they required a special mash. If it hadn't been for Millie and the girls, he'd have told the farm manager to take them and shove them up his ass. "I don't even like chickens running around in the yard," he told Millie. But she'd insisted they give it a try. "You don't know a damn thing about raising turkeys," he said.

"We had a Home Demonstration Club program about it, Len. I know a little something," Millie said.

"Did they tell you how bad they stink and that they're mean as the devil? They'll peck the eyes out of the young'uns if they get in the pen." He'd finally given in.

Millie loved taking care of the turkeys. The little poults were awkward until they feathered out. Then, they were downright ugly with their fleshy bronze-colored leaders hanging askew over narrow little heads. But the girls loved them and thought of them as pets. Annie was a big help hauling water, and Cathleen threw corn the best that she could from her tiny hand. Millie dreaded the day the full-grown turkeys would be hauled away squawking in wooden crates.

The turkey project was but one of the things Millie did to try and keep Len on Penderlea. Whenever he got discouraged and talked of going back to Bladen County, she took on another chore. Even when he was home, she still slopped the hogs and fed the horse and mule so Len could sleep a little later. Len had planted the garden, but she kept the weeds down and picked the vegetables. She canned everything they didn't eat. When the work order for the pump service ran out, Mr. Harrell told Len that he'd need to go full-time at the mill. "Some of the women are working there," Millie said. "Annie will be in school. I could get a girl to stay with the other children, work the day shift in the mill part-time—be here to cook supper and put them to bed."

"You mean you'd work in the mill instead of me?" Len said. "That's crazy, woman. I might not like it, but I've been trained to work there. And I can make more money at it."

"Yes, but you'd be happier working the farm, wouldn't you? Maybe you could pick up a little of that pump work over at Van Eeden."

"I've got more options than working over there with those immigrants," Len said. "I've got my own land in Bladen County. Will said Mama and Papa are praying I'll come back. They want to give us the house. Mama says they'd move down to the old place. Nobody has lived there since Aunt Mag died."

Millie was astounded. "You've been talking to Will about this?"

"Hell, yes," Len said. "We're going to have to do something. I've been beating my damn head up against a brick wall. We're deeper in debt than we've ever been. I told you Penderlea wasn't right for us, but you wanted to come."

"Len, that's not fair," she said. He stared at her for a minute, then turned on his heel and walked out. Millie followed him out into the yard, begging him. "Len, please, we've made a life here. We have this little house—our barn—our friends. We've made some payments. Nobody has said they're going to kick us out like they did those other folks. We just have to keep trying. If we give up, we'll lose everything we've worked for, just like they did."

Len ignored her, acted as if she didn't have a brain in her head. But the next day, he came home from the mill and said he'd quit. If she was of a mind, she could try it for awhile, but if it didn't work out, he wasn't making any promises.

⌒

On September 1, the same day that Annie Ryan started the first grade in the new school at Penderlea, news of a war in Europe was all the talk. Germany had invaded Poland. France had declared war on Germany. President Roosevelt was standing fast that the United States would remain neutral, but the U.S. economy was booming with orders for arms to supply the allies in Europe. In nearby Wilmington, the shipyards were hiring men and women right and left. Some came from Penderlea. The little Dexdale Mill at Penderlea Homesteads soon switched over from making hosiery to parachutes, but not before Millie was issued an engraved metal Social Security card proclaiming her as a potential recipient of the new government program by which she and her employer would contribute each month to a fund providing income in her old age.

Opportunities for mechanical work outside of the project lured Len away for weeks at a time. Millie Ryan's hope for a better life was constantly clouded by Len's dissatisfaction with Penderlea. The small house that she had loved and made into a home felt hollow and empty without him there. When Emily McAllister came to call one Sunday afternoon, Millie was in deep despair.

"Millie, honey, I've caught you at a bad time," Emily said.

"No, no, Miss Emily. I'm so glad you've come. Len just left, and the girls and I were feeling a little lonely. You're what the doctor ordered," Millie said, trying to hold back her tears. Lucy, still just a babe in arms, was wanting down on the floor where Annie and Cathleen were playing with their dolls. The older girls ran to greet Emily who, as always, was dressed to the hilt in a beautiful suit with a matching hat.

"Aunt Emmie, we're so glad you've come to see us," Annie said.

"Daddy's gone to work," Cathleen said. "He's gonna be gone a long time."

Emily looked at Millie. "What's wrong?"

Tears rolled down Millie's cheeks. "He said he didn't know when he'd be back."

"Oh, Len wouldn't leave like that, Millie. He'll be back soon." She looked about the room scattered with toys. "Won't he?"

"Sure," Millie said. "He just gets mad and stomps off. I think he's over in Bladen County." She pulled Emily into the kitchen. "Let me fix you a glass of tea. You girls play in the living room while Miss Emily and Mama talk."

She chipped some ice from a block in the ice box and poured glasses of tea for both of them. "What brings you to Penderlea?"

Emily seated herself at the small table and watched while Millie fixed the tea. "I came to tell you something. You must never say I told you, but I want you to know. Promise you won't tell Len who told you this."

Millie stared at her friend, wondering what Emily was about to tell her. "I promise," she said.

"Reggie told me about a man from Raleigh who came looking for Len. He was going to offer him a job in Raleigh working for a big supply company that was starting a pump department. They'd heard about Len and wanted him to come to work for them. They were offering a house as part of the pay. It was good pay, too, Reggie said."

"Did Mr. Ashworth tell Len about it? Len didn't say anything—"

Emily looked down at her hands in her lap. "No, honey, Reggie didn't want Len to know about it. He said Len had an obligation here at Penderlea. He's not going to tell him."

When they drove away in the crowded cab of a used truck that Len had purchased from his brother Will, the little white dog followed them a mile or more down the road before turning back. The girls cried, but Len assured them that the Mullinses had promised to care for Trixie. He said they might come back for him in a month or so, once they were settled in Raleigh and had a place to keep him. But they never did.

It is a matter of historical record that as a result of delinquencies on loan payments, one-sixth of the families on the Penderlea Homesteads Project left voluntarily in 1939. My family was among them. In 1942 the Farm Security Administration reduced the number of farm units on Penderlea from 192 to 109 larger units, selling off more than 50 of the small cottages. In 1945 the government liquidated the remainder of its holdings through a public auction.

According to Ann S. Cottle in her book *The Roots of Penderlea: A Memory of a New Deal Homestead Community*, a brave band of homesteaders stayed on and worked out an arrangement with the government in 1943 whereby homesteaders could finally purchase their farms through a deed-mortgage arrangement. Today, Penderlea is a viable community, home to many who value rural living, including the children and grandchildren of those hearty homesteaders who were among the chosen few. Aspects of the farm city that Hugh MacRae envisioned are still visible. The horseshoe plan with its complex of community buildings and school remains central to the project.

Recently, a Penderlea Homesteads Museum was established as a gathering place for events and as a repository for historical materials from this early resettlement project. The museum is located at 284 Garden Road in the Grey and Sula Murphy home, one of the first ten houses completed on the project. Their daughter, Frances, was the first child born on Penderlea in May 1936. My favorite memories of Penderlea are the summers I visited with the Grey Murphy family and indulged in all the privileges of the younger set, including working in tobacco and attending the Potts Memorial Church's youth fellowship.

Penderlea Homesteads Inc. ultimately failed as the farm city envisioned by Hugh MacRae and later the government, but it did achieve its goal of giving many young farmers a chance for a better life. My parents' reasons for leaving were unclear to me until I did the research for this novel. Why would they leave utopia? I found my answers, but once again, I must remind you, as I have in the first two novels in this collection, that this book is a work of fiction. If I have used my own life as a model for a historical reflection on what many North Carolinians experienced in the early part of the twentieth century, then I have only done what all writers must do. If I have taken certain liberties with names, including those that may or may not call to mind members of my own family, then I have used a device all writers use to capture your imagination and propel the story along. As for known historical figures like Eleanor Roosevelt and Hugh MacRae, I have used actual accounts of their involvement with the Penderlea Homesteads project. To create such larger-than-life characters would be far beyond my ability as an author.

For their encouragement and help in bringing this story to print, I want to thank my husband Dick for pointing out the good and the bad in my manuscript; to my dear mother Mildred Smith Rawls, who passed away August 8, 2007, for her inspirational courage as a woman; and my sister Katie Anne McKendry for her unending support. Others who have contributed significantly to the preparation of my manuscript are Barbara Brannon, Frances Murphy Love, Betty Sue Murphy Klavins, Ann Southerland Cottle, Susan Taylor Block, and Patricia Johnson. If you are interested in learning more about the Penderlea Homesteads Project, I refer you to Ann Cottle's book mentioned above, or to the Penderlea Homesteads Museum Web site at *www.penderleahomesteadmuseum.org*.

C.R.B.

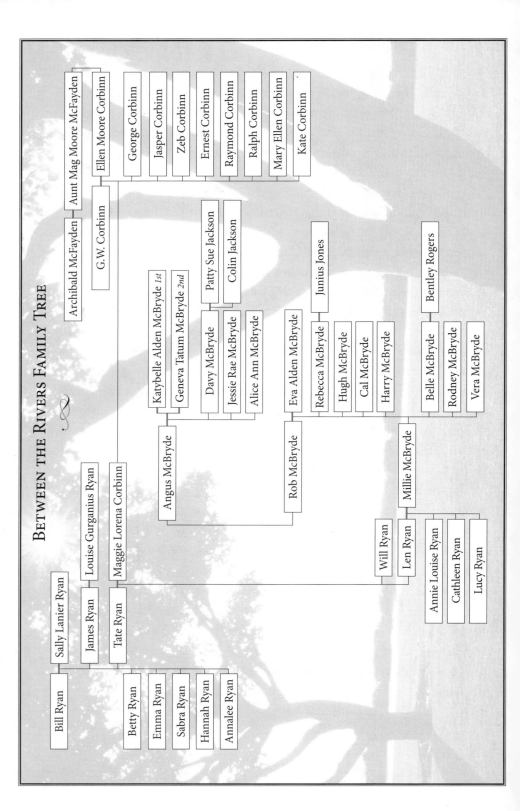

BETWEEN THE RIVERS FAMILY TREE

Evans Family Tree

Evans Family Tree

- Silas Evans
- Maude Padgett Evans
  - Burton Evans
  - Malcolm Evans
    - Jean Evans
    - Reece Evans
      - Christine Aubusson
      - Amanda Evans
      - Agatha Evans
    - Emily Evans McAllister
      - Duncan McAllister
        - Darcey McAllister
        - Jeanne McAllister
        - Gardenia Croom McAllister
          - Alison McAllister
          - David McAllister